FUNERAL GAMES

ALSO BY JAY ALLAN

FAR STARS

CRIMSON WORLDS

PORTAL WARS

PENDRAGON CHRONICLES

FUNERAL GAMES

FAR STARS BOOK THREE

JAY ALLAN

HARPER Voyager
An Imprint of HarperCollins Publishers

FUNERAL GAMES. Copyright © 2016 by Jay Allan Books. All rights reserved. Printed in the United States of America. No part of this book may be used or reproduced in any manner whatsoever without written permission except in the case of brief quotations embodied in critical articles and reviews. For information address HarperCollins Publishers, 195 Broadway, New York, NY 10007.

HarperCollins books may be purchased for educational, business, or sales promotional use. For information please e-mail the Special Markets Department at SPsales@harpercollins.com.

FIRST EDITION

Harper Voyager and design is a trademark of HarperCollins Publishers L.L.C.

Designed by Shannon Nicole Plunkett

Library of Congress Cataloging-in-Publication Data has been applied for.

ISBN 978-0-06-238893-3

16 17 18 19 20 OV/RRD 10 9 8 7 6 5 4 3 2 1

FUNERAL GAMES

CHAPTER 1

KERGEN VOS SAT SILENTLY, STARING OUT OVER THE GRANDEUR OF the main hall, a magnificent space of polished marble, giant columns, and a vaulted ceiling soaring fifty meters above the mosaic floor. The walls were covered with faded frescoes, the work of an artist long dead and forgotten. The monstrous structure projected an image of imperial power and majesty that had long been a fraud in the Far Stars, a façade with no real strength behind it.

And that's why he was here.

Vos had come to this fringe of human habitation to change all that, to finally bring the wild planets of the Far Stars under the iron control of the emperor. He was determined to gain the victory that had eluded his predecessors, to become the man who brought this last cluster of independent worlds in all of mankind's dominions to heel.

The existence of this defiant frontier was an affront to the imperial dignity—and a symbol that men could resist the dominion of empire. Vos knew it was a false symbol, though—that nothing could stand before the might of the empire—and he intended to prove that on the bodies of his enemies.

The hall was silent, but it had been filled just a few moments before, the throngs of petitioners craving his favor jockeying for attention alongside petty courtiers basking in the reflected glow of the emperor's chosen representative. Those of real rank could obtain private access to the governor, meetings at which things could be actually be accomplished. But the grand levees were for the commoners and the low-ranking merchant classes. The huge assemblies were a pointless affair, largely for show. Nothing would be done in response to most of the appeals of those in attendance but the illusion of access, of justice, had its uses.

Vos cared little for the rabble that had just left the hall, but despite his coldness and efficiency, a part of him long buried couldn't help but sympathize, at least a little. Once upon a time, he hadn't been that different from them. The lower classes clung to their hope still. They flocked to the capitol to present their cases, to seek redress when the local nobles seized their farms and meager possessions, casting them out into the streets. What they didn't understand was, the noble who had stolen from them had already paid for direct access—and thus had the governor's stamp of approval on their actions. The poor, the untitled—there was no justice for them. Not in the empire.

Not in any nation that ever existed, Vos thought.

No, what the peasants didn't understand was how the system worked . . . or how, long ago, Vos had worked his way through it.

How he had hacked and clawed—in some places, literally—to be sitting where he now was. That, like the nobles, he had bought his way to preeminence, albeit with cunning and blood, rather than money and influence. And that's why he could only sympathize so much.

Because weakness—begging in public, like these miscreants—accomplishes nothing. I took what I needed and created my own justice.

He leaned back against the cold hardness of the governor's chair. He was still wearing his ceremonial robes, the formal uniform of his office. The position of imperial sector governor carried with it a considerable amount of pomp and ceremony, an aspect of the job Vos had always hated. He understood the use of spectacle in the implementation of power, but he always felt foolish when duty demanded he go forth clad in the full regalia. Such theatrics might be understandable in the empire proper, where the iron rule was complete, and therefore ceremony was crucial. Out here, though . . .

The hat was the worst of all, unwieldy and uncomfortable—a ludicrous, bejeweled bit of foppery that was so heavy his neck ached for hours after wearing it. Now, though, he was free to pull it from his head and cast it aside. He twisted around, trying to work out the kinks.

The images of imperial power were fictions because the governor controlled only six worlds from his headquarters on Galvanus Prime, a tiny foothold in a frontier full of pirates, mercenaries, and rogue adventurers. The insignificant cluster of imperial planets was a mockery, a symbol more of the empire's impotence in the Far Stars than its great power, and it chafed Kergen Vos to no end. *I don't need costumes*, he thought angrily. *I need weapons! Ships! Men!*

And, for the first time since he arrived on Galvanus Prime,

he was starting to get just that. His plans were almost in motion, and by the time he was finished, he would ensure the imperial flag was planted on every world in the Far Stars—and the unruly Rim-worlders who occupied those planets would know their place, finally bowing down to their rightful master.

Vos sighed softly and shifted his weight, trying vainly to get comfortable in the massive chair. He knew it was futile. Three years in this detestable place, and he'd never managed to find a position that lessened the discomfort of that infernal seat. But the powers that be had centuries before decided that magnificence was more important than comfort. The bejeweled golden chair of the governor was hard and uncomfortable, but it was worth a planet's ransom, and like so much else, it spoke silently of the wealth and majesty of the empire.

The session had been a long one—indeed, it had gone on all day, and Vos was exhausted. Now, at last, he was alone with his thoughts. The levee had been more than the whining and complaints of the lower classes. He had heard many reports, too, filtered the truth from the blatant exaggerations and propaganda, and he had given his commands. His minions had been briefed and dispatched. The routine business of administering the small cluster of imperial worlds was done. But there was no time for sleep, for now Vos had to attend to business he viewed as far more important.

Soon it would be time to launch the final phase of his plan to gain dominance over the sector. Soon the black-and-gold flag of imperial authority would fly unfettered in the breeze of every planet in the Far Stars. And soon he would return to the empire in triumph, and the way would be opened for him to ascend to even further heights of power and influence.

How far I have traveled to have arrived here, in this most unlikely of places . . .

As it had with the peasants moments before, his mind drifted back, the years peeling away like the pages of an old-style book. Before he was governor. Before he was an agent of the empire. To the filth-infested streets of Belleger and a penniless orphan eating from piles of garbage and surviving on what he could steal.

Belleger was a cursed world. It had committed the most grievous of sins—it had rebelled against the empire. For a brief, defiant few months, the flags of revolt flew over its cities, and the leaders of the insurgency gave speeches and led throngs of cheering citizens through the streets in the stirring spectacle of one massive rally after another. They pulled down statues of the emperors, murdered the imperial legate, and burned his palace. Belleger was free of tyranny, they declared defiantly.

But the glory had proven to be short-lived. The imperial battleships soon arrived, and the legions landed, bringing with them death and destruction unimagined. The rebellion died in fire, its leaders executed, the streets cleared with massacre after massacre. The pitiless imperial soldiers fell on the civilians with a savagery so terrible, its memory was seared into the very souls of those who survived. It was as if the gates of hell itself had opened, and every nightmare contained within had burst forward, to feed on the very life of a world and its people.

Belleger was in ruins. Its industry had died in the fires along with half its citizens. Those who remained, crawling through the rubble, struggled to survive amid the chaos, fighting over scraps of food and killing each other for an imperial copper. Even when the troops stopped their massacres, the dying continued, with disease, starvation, and violence in the streets taking a steady toll.

Vos had been a penniless boy then, weak, scared, cast out into the streets when the imperial soldiers slaughtered his family. His parents had been tailors, well regarded locally and moderately prosperous. The young Kergen had expected nothing grander than to follow in the family trade. But any hope of that ended the day he stood in the wreckage of his family home, staring at the burned bodies of his parents. Then the terrified boy stumbled out into the streets, seeking survival any way he could.

There were others like him, the lost children. They were like animals, acting on instinct. Feral. They gathered together, their fear driving them into a huddled mass. But weakness added to weakness did not equal strength, and in time, all of them died.

All save Kergen Vos, who learned to survive.

He'd watched his companions as they fell. The boys quickly, from the elements and disease, but also in violent altercations, battles over food or a dry place to stay . . . or doomed attempts to establish dominance over the group. The girls went more slowly, too often amid scenes of unspeakable debauchery and brutality. Some few survived for a time, as slaves mostly, in the brothels that served the imperial garrison.

Not Vos, though. No, not only did he survive, he *prospered*.

He curried favor with the imperial troops, sold out his companions, stole from them what little of value they'd managed to find. He murdered them in the dark to silence their tongues, to prevent anyone from learning what he had done. He turned them in to the imperial garrisons, accusing them of whatever offenses he could invent. In postinvasion Belleger, as in most of the empire, accusation was largely tantamount to guilt, as least for the poor and those without influence and allies.

He collected coin for leading the imperial enforcers to the prettiest of the young girls—and a few of the boys as well—to feed the appetites of the soldiers. And the imperial agents further paid him for his assistance—a few coins of no consequence, but a fortune in that time and place—and to spy on his fellow citizens and report anything suspicious.

It was the latter—the agents—who truly captured his imagination. The soldiers were omnipresent, patrolling the streets, milling about the garrison. They were all-powerful to the helpless and oppressed citizens, but Vos realized immediately they themselves were minions, servants, subject to constant discipline and draconian punishment if they failed in their duties. Apart from a few pleasures designed to sustain morale, they were only marginally better off than the broken, desperate citizens of Belleger.

But the agents were something else. They were rarer than the soldiers, more discreet. They were smart, educated. They wielded considerable power, and they possessed seemingly endless coin, one of the main tools of their trade. Money and information—*that* was power. Vos had been captivated from the start, mesmerized by the cosmopolitan swagger of the operatives.

Even as he scraped in the garbage for food, he began to imagine a future for himself, one far beyond the daily routine of a tailor. He scrambled to get the attention of the agents, gathering information everywhere he could, selling it—sometimes even giving it—to the operatives. Relentlessly, he worked his way closer, became useful to them. Then one day, after he'd alerted the agents to a particularly dangerous group of surviving rebels, he was approached by one of them, impressed by the young boy's ability to consistently produce information.

Thus began his rise, from the depths of despair and poverty to . . .

To where? he thought, pulled from his memories for a moment. *How high do I dare to imagine myself? What reward, what positions of power and honor, what wealth, might the emperor shower on the man who brings the Far Stars to heel? The man who crushed this affront to imperial honor?*

The man who had done terrible things, committed unspeakable acts of cruelty as he ascended the ranks of imperial intelligence.

For there had been no rewards for gentleness, no place for squeamish morality in the imperial service. Vos had struggled at first, especially on Belleger, where he had betrayed his former companions, climbing over their broken bodies to secure his own escape from the destitution and squalor. But he'd quickly learned to deal with such feelings. He hadn't created the universe, nor was he responsible for the fact that mankind lived under the iron boot of imperial rule. His choice had been a simple one: live—and die—in the filth and deprivation of the streets, or find another way, place himself above the sheep who stampeded to their doom and carve out a better place, build his own power and prosperity.

He chose himself, whatever the cost to those around him.

It wasn't that he'd lost all ability to feel. There had been guilt and self-doubt, of course—arising in the dark nights, when he was alone—but those moments had mostly been long ago. Yes, Vos was still occasionally troubled by the things he did, the decisions he made. But he had made his choices in life, and for the most part, he had made his peace with them.

He stood up slowly, twisting his torso, stretching to loosen his aching muscles. He'd been seven hours in the infernal chair, and his body was rebelling. He put his arms over his head, stretching his aching muscles. It was time to do his real work. Time to plot the final conquest of the Far Stars.

"Augustin Lucerne is a brilliant man, a military genius of almost unmatched skill. And he has built a cadre of enormously capable officers around him." Mak Wilhelm sat across from Vos, poking at the food on his plate with only marginal interest. He'd just arrived, back from nearly six months of constant travel through the Far Stars, and he was only on Galvanus Prime for a few days. Then he was heading to Vanderon, to finally put matters with the Far Stars Bank to rest.

"Even if your effort to . . . remove him . . . is successful," he continued, "do we have any reason to expect his successor will be less formidable? His generals are highly skilled."

"Indeed, Mak, they are extremely capable soldiers . . . though none of them are a match for their commander's abilities. But Lucerne presents a danger far beyond his tactical skill. He is incorruptible. He has a vision, and a dedication to see it realized no matter what. He is charismatic, an inspirational leader. One of his generals could lead the army, almost certainly. But none of his officers can hold something like the Far Stars Confederation together, not for the long term. Without Lucerne, his diplomacy will crumble. The Primes will squabble with one another, and they will begin to fear and envy Celtiborian power." He paused and smiled.

"Even his soldiers will begin to fight among themselves. They are loyal to Lucerne, out of respect, admiration, fear. Because they have served him for decades and walked with him through fire. But there is no one among their ranks all the others will accept, no clear successor save Astra. And for all her impressive abilities, she is not truly a soldier. She cannot take power alone—she must have one of the senior generals stand with her, someone with military credentials to back her claim to the succession."

"A marriage, perhaps?"

"That would be a logical move. But the others will attempt to prevent a rival from taking such a step. They will fight each other over Astra, knowing the one who wins her hand has the clearest road to claiming Lucerne's power. And some, at least, will go to extreme measures to prevent any of their rivals from attaining such a dominant position.

"You can take the killer off the battlefield, but he's still a killer."

Vos stared at his longtime ally, holding a forkful of Lusanian fangfish. "If Lucerne dies, it is likely his forces will fracture, that civil war and a struggle between his key subordinates will result. And as it continues, it will accelerate. As the confederation crumbles into ruin, even those who had banded together out of respect for their departed leader will find themselves at odds. It may not be immediate, but it will happen. Human nature will begin to assert itself.

"Augustin Lucerne's magnificent army, the product of three decades of war and struggle, will destroy itself."

Vos reached out and took his goblet in his hand, drinking deeply. "And we will help them move in this direction, Mak. We will aid in creating and expanding those fissures, ensuring no one among them succeeds in filling his master's shoes."

"You plan to intervene in their conflicts." Wilhelm had picked up his fork while Vos was speaking, but he put it down again. "No . . . it's more than that." He thought for a moment. "You are going to provide support to one or more of the claimants."

"Very good, Mak." Vos was chewing as he spoke. Unlike that

of his subordinate, Vos's normally sparse appetite was, for once, excellent. "In most situations, I would choose a single man to back, the most capable among those susceptible to corruption. But we do not want a victor here. We want chaos, a descent into entropy. And that is best served by supporting multiple claimants." He turned and stared at Wilhelm. "And once you complete your work on Vanderon, we will be able to provide much of that aid in a clandestine fashion, utilizing the good and unquestioned offices of the Far Stars Bank."

"An extraordinary plan, Excellency." Wilhelm's tone was sincere, but there was a hint of concern there too.

Sensing his subordinate's hesitation, Vos said, "Out with it."

"It's just . . . how can you be sure Lucerne's soldiers will react as you anticipate? After all, they must be aware of our machinations by now—the senior leadership, at least. They will suspect our involvement in Lucerne's death. Perhaps they will band together, look toward us with vengeance in their hearts?"

Vos smiled. "Indeed, Mak, they will react just as you say. At first, at least. But they have one weakness. They are soldiers and, most of them at least, honorable men. They understand intellectually the ways of the spy, the workings of espionage and manipulation. But they do not *live* them, breathe them as do we. To them, honor is a distinction, and usually I would agree. But they are still men, like any others. They harbor ambitions, they nurse grievances. Honor, in those moments then, is self-serving, and easily manipulated.

"And let us remember, not even Lucerne's grand army can boast universal honor. Many of his people came into his service as the vanquished officers of defeated warlords, absorbed into the ranks of their conquerors. Lucerne has an extraordinary ability to turn old enemies into devoted allies, but men are men, and they rarely forget old injuries. The marshal's extraordinary charisma is the glue that holds his remarkable army together. When he is gone, those bonds will begin to fail—they must."

"Why, though? How can you be so certain?"

"Because men are what they are. Most are followers, the rest will seek power at all costs."

"But Lucerne . . ."

"Lucerne is an extraordinary man, a very rare breed. His generals are highly skilled, and loyal to him. But they are *not* him. They do not have that same inner strength that makes the marshal incorruptible."

"So even his most loyal followers will become mad for power when he is gone?"

"No, Mak, nothing so stark and simple. Many will sincerely attempt to follow through with Lucerne's work . . . and they will challenge those who grasp quickly for power. Yet what will they do if they prevail in the early conflicts, when they have the control Lucerne does now? How many men do you think would surrender such power once it was theirs?"

Wilhelm nodded. "It appears your plans address all possibilities. Save, perhaps, one. What if the assassination of Lucerne fails? We have been unable to kill Blackhawk after more than two years of effort. How can you be so sure we can arrange Lucerne's death?"

This, in fact, had been the problem that had vexed Kergen Vos since he'd come to the Far Stars. "Indeed, Marshal Lucerne is a difficult target, a man constantly surrounded by a cadre of extremely capable and fanatically loyal warriors. And our efforts with Blackhawk have been disappointing. We must look to where we went wrong, Mak, at how our efforts failed. We relied on the adventurers and mercenaries of the Far Stars, and their greed.

But Blackhawk is the best of them all, and that is why he is still alive. None of those we set against him are his equals, and those who tried to kill him were outmatched and destroyed.

"We tried to kill Blackhawk with inferior resources. We will not make that mistake with Marshal Lucerne."

He paused and smiled. "To that end, I have obtained some imperial assistance, Mak. The emperor is quite satisfied with our progress and pleased at last to see real action in the Far Stars. He has dispatched a . . . *specialist* . . . to aid us with the good marshal." Vos pressed the small comm button on the table. "Please come in, Lord Rachen."

The door on the far wall opened slowly, and a man walked into the room. He was tall and slim, clad from head to toe in black robes. A hood hung down over his face, obscuring even the slightest view of him. Vos watched his second in command, gauging his reaction, and Wilhelm didn't disappoint. The general clearly knew Rachen immediately for what he was, and a shiver ran visibly through his body. Vos was not surprised. Wilhelm was a soldier and a spy, accustomed to danger and death. But there were some things all men feared. Some terrors that defied courage, cutting into even the bravest with icy pangs of dread.

Vos understood—he understood because he felt the cold fear himself.

The operatives of the Exequtorum Mortis were the emperor's personal assassins, the deadliest killers humanity had ever known. To the billions of commoners in the empire, they were a legend, a shadowy myth to scare children. But the Exequtorum did not exist to control the peasants, nor the merchant classes and professionals—the emperor had his fleet and his legions for that. The members of this dark brotherhood of death existed for one purpose—to instill the emperor's terror in men of power—his nobles, and the generals and admirals who commanded his military.

And highly ranked spies like Wilhelm and Vos.

They were above all others, exempt from any law or authority anywhere in the empire. No fate inspired more dread in the powerful functionaries of the empire than being placed on the Exequtorum's proscription list.

The terrible guild of imperial assassins had existed as long as the empire itself, longer even, for the early imperial histories tell vaguely of how the organization had allied with the first emperor and slain all his rivals. In fact, the rumor was that they had never failed an assassination attempt, and while it was probably apocryphal, it clearly had a ring of truth no man wanted to risk.

It was said, too, that the order's grandmaster was a thousand years old, an undead monstrosity who served the emperor with unwavering loyalty in exchange for immortality. Vos knew that was nonsense, a bizarre myth that endured because it served the imperial purposes.

It didn't change the fact that even for a man of Vos's power, the black-clad figure standing there was like a cold nightmare out of the darkness.

"Thank you, Lord Rachen. Once again, I offer you my gratitude for coming so far to aid us in our struggle." Vos's tone was one of respect, almost subordination.

The shadowy figure nodded silently.

"Lord Rachen, with your agreement, I would like to begin your mission immediately. You have at your disposal all information and resources we possess."

The man simply bowed his head again in affirmation of Vos's request. Then he turned and walked out the way he had come, having said not a word.

"Perhaps we will be able to remove Marshal Lucerne after all." Wilhelm's voice was animated, hopeful. "I hadn't reckoned with the Exequtorum. Indeed, the emperor must be *quite* pleased with progress to dispatch one of his personal assassins to our cause."

"Yes, Mak. Now, we will see how Marshal Lucerne's vaunted soldiers deal with one of the most capable killers in the galaxy." He paused, and a wide smile crept onto his lips. "And the emperor's largesse does not end there, my friend. For when Lord Rachen has rid us of Marshal Lucerne, he will remain in the Far Stars with us and complete another mission." He stared across the table, and his smile broadened.

"He will also kill Arkarin Blackhawk."

CHAPTER 2

AUGUSTIN LUCERNE SAT AT HIS DESK STARING AT THE GLOWING screen of his workstation. There was a plate off to the side, his dinner, picked at and stone-cold. His steward had brought the meal unbidden and come back three times, offering to get something else or to reheat the plate. Lucerne appreciated the concern, but finally he'd sent the aide away with orders not to return until morning. He'd snacked on the gourmet food as he worked, but he'd eaten no more than a quarter of it.

He knew he needed to eat more, if only to keep his physician off his back. He'd been down two kilos at his last exam, and he'd endured an endless series of lectures on taking care of himself. But there was simply too much work to do. And he just wasn't hungry. The workload was vast, and he had too much to think about. Lucerne didn't have the luxury of cutting back. He needed to stay on top of everything.

When he made mistakes, people died.

He'd come close to making a tragic error with Antilles. Even now, months later, it still shook him to his core. If it hadn't been for Blackhawk—and Danellan Lancaster's surprising, eleventh-hour courage—his ships would have destroyed the Antillean fleet. His soldiers would have landed on the planet, and a costly war would have raged for months, the result of which would have been catastrophic. For while Lucerne was confident his people would have won, he could only guess how many of them would have been lost. Hundreds of thousands, certainly. Perhaps millions. And along with the body count, the economic powerhouse of Antilles—vital to the prospects of Lucerne's plans—would have been a ruin, its magnificent factories reduced to smoking rubble, its awesome industrial production no longer available to build the nascent economies of the less developed worlds joining the confederation.

You need to have better data before you act. And you need to be more careful with your decisions. You let your temper get the better of you, you old fool, and you came a hairsbreadth from throwing away thirty years of sweat and blood.

The marshal closed his eyes tightly and opened them again, trying to clear his vision. The screen was blurry in front of him, his eyes so tired they could barely focus. It was long after midnight, but he was nowhere near done. Soon he would dispatch the second wave, and his soldiers would travel to another twenty worlds, sweeping tyrants and petty dictators from their positions of power.

He wished he was bringing true freedom to the people of those worlds, but he knew in his heart he was as absolute a ruler as any of those his armies fought. He was uncomfortable with the apparent hypocrisy of his actions, but he also understood that he was different. He would command with an iron fist only to defend the worlds of the Far Stars from the empire. Once the sector was united—and strong enough to defend itself—he would yield his power and retire to private life. He knew few people would believe that, but in his heart he was sure it was true.

He would walk away when he could. Gratefully.

Lucerne had never understood the drive of those who struggled to acquire power for its own sake. He hated the constant responsibility, and nothing made him as uncomfortable as the ceaseless accolades, the endless worship of those around him.

If only they all knew how badly I wanted to step down, how truly exhausted to the bone I am. But I can't. Not until I am finished.

Because what will follow when I am gone? Who will hold the confederation together, lead its fleets and armies if the empire attacks one day? Astra? How can I do that to her? Lay that terrible responsibility at her feet?

He knew his daughter was as capable as he was, but he still felt guilty about the responsibilities he knew would one day fall on her shoulders. He'd told himself she was not obligated to follow in his shoes, but he knew it was a lie. Augustin was a creature of duty, completely unable to walk away from the people and the responsibilities, and despite Astra's seemingly wild and uncontrollable spirit, she was no more able than he was to abandon this dream. He didn't think she shared his full passion for it, but he also knew she wouldn't let it die . . . out of love for him, if not dedication to the ideals he espoused.

Again, though, the thought crushed him. This was a prison, but one of his own choosing. For Astra, though, the choice was made *for* her, and not just by him. Lucerne had hoped for a time that Blackhawk would agree to succeed him and to shepherd the Far Stars Confederation alongside Astra. His daughter clearly loved the rogue adventurer, and he was just as sure Blackhawk returned the feelings. He'd tried to convince his friend more than once, but he understood the resistance he'd always met.

For many years he had been the only person who knew the truth about Blackhawk, about how he had broken his conditioning and fled from a life as a brutal imperial general, a monster responsible for killing millions. Yet it was obvious he couldn't truly understand what the imperial scientists had done to Blackhawk, the unfathomable effect of the decades of mental and emotional conditioning that had stripped him of his sense of self and made him the perfect tool of imperial aggression. How much of that was still inside Blackhawk, fighting to regain control?

So when Blackhawk said no, Lucerne had to respect it.

That is why I do this. It is why I sacrificed so much, the life I might have had—quiet, full of joy, and not one filled with death and the endless call of duty. But everywhere men breathe the air, the iron rule of the empire controls all. Everywhere save here, in the Far Stars. This tiny flicker of freedom has been kept alive not by the courage of men, nor by their steadfastness, but by a natural phenomenon. The Void has saved the Far Stars from domination, held back the imperial battleships that surely would have brought the shackles of empire to all who dwell here. But we must take responsibility—and ensure with our own strength and resolve that no one is ever to take that liberty from us.

I have willingly sacrificed myself to this quest. But I would spare Astra this fate.

It was a pipe dream, though, no doubt the result of his tired mind. He knew even as he sat there that the quest he had begun would claim her, that she had no more chance than he had to escape the call of duty. And for the first time in thirty years of death and war, he truly regretted the path he had chosen.

Rafaelus DeMark stood on the small balcony of his headquarters, staring out over the crowd in the piazza below. It was a stunning space, a sea of multicolored cobblestones surrounding an immense fountain. Nordlingen was famous in the Far Stars for its architecture, but now the scars of war were upon its magnificent buildings and monuments.

DeMark's eyes caught the detachments of soldiers he'd positioned all around the square. He had roving patrols, snipers deployed on the buildings, and a whole battalion in reserve, ready to respond to any unrest. The war on Nordlingen had ended when Blackhawk liberated the planet's captive king, and the grateful monarch had ordered his armies to stand down. But peace hadn't lasted long, and his soldiers had been dealing with random violence and terrorist attacks since the formal hostilities had ceased.

DeMark had expected to be off Nordlingen by now, back on Celtiboria and ready to carry out the next mission for Marshal Lucerne. King Gustav had signed the peace accord and the Confederation Treaty, and he'd enthusiastically announced his commitment to a new future for his world. The king was popular, and the news that he'd been abducted and held hostage by his renegade prime minister enraged the populace. Indeed, they had turned out today because of that seething anger, and they were gathered to witness the execution of Loren Davanos.

DeMark had been against the execution. Not the idea of it, just the timing. He agreed Davanos deserved death. Indeed, the bastard was responsible for the resistance that had caused his troops to suffer thousands of casualties, and the native Nordlingeners even more at the hands of his enraged soldiers. But he thought the public spectacle was dangerous and ill-timed. Something was wrong on Nordlingen. DeMark had expected things to calm down immediately after the fighting ended. The king was restored to his throne, and he was allied with the Celtiborians. All soldiers had been granted amnesty, by both their king and Marshal Lucerne. By all accounts, Nordlingen should be quiet, pacified.

But it wasn't. The incidents had begun shortly after the surrender. Bombings, shootings, various acts of terrorism not uncommon in the wake of war. But instead of lessening, the problems escalated.

Once more, fear spread among the people.

DeMark had responded by tightening controls, imposing curfews, and threatening martial law. The king backed him up on his decrees, but the tightened security was increasing the resentment of the Celtiborians. The king had declared them allies, brothers in the confederation, but more and more of the people came to view them as occupiers, as foreigners who exerted an unclean influence on their monarch.

I'm a soldier, not a policeman, DeMark thought, looking out over the hundred thousand gathered below. *I do not know how to win this kind of war.*

It didn't help that the situation didn't make sense to him. None of it. His people had been extremely careful to avoid incidents with the population. Where did this resistance come from? How could he root out those behind it—and do it without oppressing the people and feeding the opposition through his own actions?

"General DeMark, sir . . ."

DeMark turned to face his aide. Emile Varne had served him with great skill and dedication, and the Celtiborian general had come to rely heavily upon the orderly.

Varne stood at attention, his brand-new major's insignia freshly polished and dazzling on his collar. "King Gustav wishes to know if you are ready for him to proceed."

DeMark nodded, suppressing a sigh as he did. "Yes, Major." *The sooner this is over, and all these people disperse back to their homes, the happier I will be.*

"Very well, sir. I will advise the king that you give your permission to begin."

DeMark winced at his aide's choice of words. "Just tell him I am ready whenever he wishes to proceed." His people were veterans, the terror of the battlefield, but they were not diplomats. DeMark had gone to great pains to forge a working relationship with the Nordlingener monarch, but he knew no king liked to ask for permission for anything.

"Yes, sir." Varne snapped a perfect salute and turned on his heels, marching swiftly away.

DeMark sighed. He found being a diplomat no easier than his soldiers did being babysitters and police, and he was exhausted at trying to stamp out the insurgency with gloves on his hands. He knew sterner measures would be counterproductive, that Marshal Lucerne wanted willing allies and not battered and bloody slaves. But he had to do *something*.

He looked back across the crowds, as if another glance would expose any enemies to him. The truth was, DeMark expected trouble. He'd had to allow Gustav to continue with the execution, but he knew the spectacle gave the leaders of the underground movement a perfect opportunity. Whatever happened, if his men ended up firing on Nordlingeners today, it would only further inflame emotions. He'd tried to convince Gustav to wait until things were calmer, but the normally mild-mannered king had been insistent on executing his treasonous minister as soon as possible. DeMark understood the king's outrage, but that didn't change the fact that something felt very off.

Eich Morgus glanced out the window, staring down at the large platform in the forum below. It was a rough wood structure, hastily erected to serve as a scaffold for the execution of Loren Davanos.

Davanos stood spread-eagled in the center, his arms and legs chained to two metal pillars. Adjacent to the pillars stood a large generator, ready to administer a lethal dose of electricity to the condemned traitor. If Morgus had been a different sort of man, he might have felt something like guilt. It was because of his actions that Davanos was in his current position. Morgus had been sent to Nordlingen by Kergen Vos, and he had been the architect of Davanos's treachery. He had supplied the weapons and funding for the prime minister to launch his secret coup—and to resist the Celtiborian invasion.

But Morgus was who he was, and guilt was not part of his makeup.

The fool did this to himself. All he had to do was keep the king from being rescued, and yet he couldn't even protect a fortified position from a small group of raiders.

Now the king was free, Davanos was captured, and half a dozen imperial operatives had been killed—including Morgus's visiting superior, Vagran Calgarus.

Calgarus had been found dead after the raiding force withdrew with the king. Somehow his head had been cut off, and that gave Morgus pause. Calgarus had been one of the best the imperial service had to offer, and the idea that someone out there was capable of utterly defeating him was disturbing to say the least.

What's done is done. Calgarus was a loss, but it doesn't change the mission. The collapse of the war on Nordlingen was a setback, but it was far from the end of the matter. Morgus's mandate was to disrupt the Celtiborian efforts to consolidate the planet into their confederation, and formal warfare was only one of many ways to achieve that goal. Morgus and his team had been the force behind an increasingly active campaign of terrorism and clandestine resistance.

And that campaign was about to ramp up enormously.

Davanos may be lost to us, but he still has one more use. His execution would be the signal for a series of attacks throughout Nordlingen, taking Morgus's covert war to an entirely new level. The Celtiborian commander had proven to be extremely intelligent and patient, but sooner or later he would have no choice but to launch reprisals and expand martial law. And the population would come to resent the occupiers. Resistance would grow . . . and slowly turn to hatred. Morgus wasn't foolish enough to think he could drive the Celtiborians off Nordlingen, but he would keep them busy, pick away at their strength, and tie large forces down on the planet—soldiers Marshal Lucerne would not have available to deploy elsewhere.

Morgus smiled. The same thing was happening on a dozen other worlds: imperial agents dispersing coin, spreading propaganda, sowing discord. It had been Governor Vos's plan from the start. He'd never expected any of the targeted worlds to actually defeat the Celtiborian invaders, just to inflict as many casualties as possible and then occupy the remaining forces with one act of resistance after another. Most of the revolutionaries were paid criminals and mercenaries, not true believers.

But as the Celtiborians necessarily cracked down, Morgus knew more genuine resistance would develop in response.

Augustin Lucerne's Far Stars Confederation would struggle to control the worlds it absorbed, and his magnificent army would slowly bleed to death of a thousand cuts.

And only *then* would Governor Vos strike.

Morgus heard the sounds of the crowd outside growing louder. He refocused on the scaffold, watching as the last of the speeches ended.

It was time.

"There have been at least twenty attacks, General. All over the planet." Major Varne's uniform was disheveled and coated with dust, one sleeve was shredded, and a rough blood-soaked bandage covered most of his arm. He'd been down in the piazza when the bombs there had detonated. Over three hundred had been killed and almost a thousand wounded. DeMark suspected Varne hadn't included himself in the number of injured any more than he'd gone to the infirmary before reporting to headquarters.

The general was struggling to maintain his calm, but inside his rage was reaching a dangerous level. Thousands were dead planetwide, including several hundred of his soldiers. He ached to strike back, to send his people out to avenge their lost brothers and sisters. Unfortunately, he had no idea who was behind the attacks.

He'd been worried about unrest after the execution, but he hadn't imagined anything like the wave of attacks that began almost the instant Davanos was electrocuted. It wasn't more than a few minutes later the other reports began coming in: a freight monorail two hundred kilometers from the capital blown up by a carefully placed mine; government buildings in the second- and third-largest cities vaporized by massive explosions; over two dozen sniper incidents planetwide. All occurred within a window of less than one hour.

It had been nothing less than a coordinated planetwide operation.

Whoever was behind this campaign—and there was no longer any doubt in DeMark's mind that's exactly what he was facing, an organized campaign—knew exactly what they were doing.

And DeMark knew the only way to end the violence was to crush it root and branch, using whatever overwhelming power was necessary—and accepting any level of collateral damage. But such a response carried its own risks. If his forces cracked down, they would feed the resentment of the locals, adding to the dissent and throwing fuel on the fire of rebellion. But if they failed to defeat the terrorists, the locals' hatred would grow with every incident—and every dead civilian the Celtiborian soldiers failed to protect would become a rallying cry for the resistance.

More important, Marshal Lucerne's orders were clear. The confederation, however it was coming into existence, was not to become a totalitarian regime, brutalizing the citizens of its worlds. DeMark had agreed completely when he'd first been dispatched to Nordlingen. But he'd seen too many of his soldiers in body bags since the fighting had supposedly ended, and his idealism was rapidly fading.

And it was being replaced by something ugly.

He felt the anger coursing through him, and he tried to hold it back, keep it in its place. As a man, he was entitled to his rage, but as an army commander and military governor, he had to make rational decisions, unaffected by emotions. Still, intellectually he realized he had few viable choices. Waiting it out, hoping the violence would die down, had proven to be a failed strategy, leading only to the latest massive wave of attacks. Now, he would face the inevitable blowback, the rage of the Nordlingeners at the thousands of murdered civilians. They weren't dead by his hands or his orders, but they had died on his watch. And he knew the people would blame him and his army. He had to do something else. Now.

The general shook his head and stared down at the floor. He knew he was about to do just what his unseen enemy wanted, that he was playing into their hands. He felt like a fool, a puppet dancing on some unseen master's string, but had no other choices. He wasn't going to allow someone to keep killing his soldiers—and if too many more civilians were targeted, he'd have widespread uprisings to deal with on top of the orchestrated terrorism.

DeMark turned around and stared at Varne, pausing an instant before speaking. "I am declaring full martial law, Major. Effective immediately. All civilians are restricted to their homes when they are not at work or engaged in necessary activities. All public entertainments are canceled. All broadcast facilities will be supervised by designated Celtiborian censors. All Nordlingeners, save duly appointed army and police units, are banned from possessing any weapons or explosives. Any individuals caught with proscribed materials will be imprisoned indefinitely. All those apprehended participating in terrorist activity will be summarily executed."

"Yes, sir," Varne snapped. It was clear the aide agreed completely with his commander's decision.

DeMark sighed. *Yes, Emile, I know it feels good to do something. But do you realize deep down, as I do, that this will only escalate things?*

We are doing just what our enemy wants.

CHAPTER 3

MAK WILHELM SAT QUIETLY IN THE ANTECHAMBER, WAITING TO see Chairman Vargus. He'd been there over an hour, and he had to suppress his amusement at the petty power game the chairman was playing. Vargus had been in the bank's upper management for thirty years, and he'd held the top position for the last fifteen. Wilhelm realized the banker hadn't come that far without a degree of skill and ruthlessness, but men like Vargus rarely possessed those traits without considerable ego accompanying them.

Wilhelm knew Vargus was perfectly aware he was Governor Vos's top deputy, and that he was here representing the largest single depositor at the bank. Still, the old financier couldn't resist attempting to assert his authority. *Enjoy it, you damned fool, for the precious little time you will still have it.* When the meeting about to take place was done, Vargus might still remain in his chairman's seat, but he would be a puppet, doing the bidding of his new master. *And that will cut at him like a blade in his gut . . .*

"General Wilhelm . . . Chairman Vargus will see you now, sir." Vargus's assistant was young, and very beautiful. *Is the old fool sleeping with her? Or does he just want his business associates to think he is?*

"Thank you." Wilhelm stood up and straightened his uniform. The dress reds were uncomfortable as hell, but there was an undeniable intimidation factor that came from standing in a room in the full regalia of an imperial general. The scarlet coat and spotless white breeches were symbols of the unimaginable might of the empire—instantly recognizable, even in the Far Stars. Wilhelm thought it might be overkill—he had all the real power he needed to control Damian Vargus. But in the end, he'd decided there was no harm in a little added strength.

He followed the aide down the long hallway. Wilhelm was a serious man, totally focused on his duties—a soldier, a spy, a killer. He didn't let nonsense interfere with his clear-mindedness, not while he was on the job. But still, he couldn't help but notice how tight her skirt was.

She stopped and opened the heavy walnut doors, the portal to the inner sanctum of one of the sector's most powerful men, the chairman of the Far Stars Bank. One of the most powerful men for another ten minutes, at least. Then just another tool, hard at work for Governor Vos. Or a vacant chair and a body that would never be found.

Either way.

"General Wilhelm, I am pleased to see you." Vargus rose slowly from behind his enormous desk, moving around and extending his hand to the visitor. He was clad in a dark gray business suit with a barely visible pinstripe, the height of current Vanderon style. And any of Wilhelm's thoughts that Vargus was sleeping with his secretary instantly vanished.

God, he's gone to fat.

Vargus hadn't been all that slender when Wilhelm had first met him three years before, but the chairman was considerably heavier now, and he looked older too, more than Wilhelm had expected just a few years later.

"And you, Chairman Vargus." He reached out and took the banker's hand, suppressing his reaction at the sweaty clamminess of Vargus's palms. Wilhelm was a fastidious man, a bit of a neat freak, but he'd experienced worse things in a lifetime of imperial service than an old man's sweat on his hand. "I trust things are going well for the bank?"

Vargus gestured to one of the guest chairs in front of the desk. "Please, General, have a seat." He stood, watching Wilhelm sit, and then walked back around his desk, dropping his bulk into his plush leather chair. It was clearly an expensive piece of furniture, well built and exquisitely crafted, but it still creaked loudly as it absorbed the impact. "Yes, certainly," he said, addressing Wilhelm's question. "Our profits are up 11 percent for the first half of the year. And your own . . . ah . . . special accounts have a cumulative return of 19 percent since inception. Considering the economic . . . instability in many areas of the sector, that performance is quite strong."

Vargus smiled. Wilhelm suspected it was a friendly, if insincere, gesture, but there was a creepiness to it nevertheless. *What was the return before you stole as much as you could?*

"That is good news, Chairman. I am certain the governor will be pleased. But that is not why I am here." He hesitated, allowing Vargus's tension level to rise a bit.

"Yes, General? Is there something else the bank can do for Governor Vos?"

Wilhelm held back a smile. *Impatience,* he thought. *He is worried. He should be worried. But I will offer him a lifeline. The only question is: Will he be smart enough to take it?*

"Yes, Chairman, there is. Or, I should say, there may be." He stared right into the confused banker's eyes. "You see, as of three days ago, the governor controls 50.16 percent of the voting stock in the Far Stars Bank." Wilhelm paused, allowing his words to sink in. It had been a difficult road securing control, one that had taken every moment of his time for the past six months—and a truly enormous deployment of imperial financial resources. But Wilhelm had seen it done, leaving behind a sordid trail of threats, deals, and bodies.

Vargus stared blankly for a few seconds. "I'm afraid you must be mistaken, General." His tone was halting, nervous. "I would know if so much stock had changed hands recently."

"Come now, Chairman. Must we doubt each other? Do you think I came here with empty bluffs, charades you would see through in a heartbeat? No, I think not. What I have told you is true. Our accumulation has been executed with great care and subtlety. In many cases, we have purchased the right to vote shares without actually buying the stock itself. In others, we have taken control of the entities that own the stock, specifically to avoid any direct transfers of Far Stars Bank shares. It was an enormously expensive process and quite difficult to execute in secrecy, especially on such a short time frame. I assure you, though, that we now effectively own controlling interest in the bank."

Vargus sat at his desk, white as a sheet. He stared back a long time before any words came. "Assuming this is all true, General Wilhelm, may I inquire about the governor's intentions?"

Very good, Vargus. Wilhelm knew the banker was seething with rage, that every impulse in his body was pushing him to hurl back threats, to declare his defiance in no uncertain terms. But Vargus was controlling himself, hiding the anger and fear—and seeking to obtain more information. *Perhaps he will be useful, after all.*

"Well, Chairman, that is largely up to you." His tone was cold. "You may oppose us, seek to fight our control. You will lose that battle in the end, but I have no doubt you could delay us for a period of time." *Assuming we let you live that long.*

He paused, still staring intently at Vargus. "It would be futile, though. For starters, you would be ousted from your position—and no doubt you would face significant punitive actions once we are able to ascertain the specifics of your activities as chairman. No doubt, a thorough review will uncover a variety of undertakings not properly sanctioned by the board." There hadn't been a Far Stars Bank chairman in three centuries who hadn't stolen all he could get his hands on, and Wilhelm knew Vargus was no exception. Indeed, he had a fairly complete file detailing the current chairman's above-average rapaciousness.

Vargus stared across the desk, clearly trying to maintain a calm demeanor as he faced the imperial agent. "And if I do not fight the governor's control? If I agree to cooperate? What then?"

"Then you would prove you are a wise man, Vargus." Wilhelm nodded slowly. "In that case, the governor would be pleased for you to retain your position—and all your privileges and perquisites. Including your unsanctioned, shall we say, participations in certain investments. Governor Vos believes his loyal allies deserve to be compensated."

Wilhelm sat bolt upright in his chair, the posture a leftover from his days of active military service. It made him appear tall and imposing, though he and Vargus were the same height.

"The governor would expect you to run the bank as you see fit," Wilhelm continued, "as you have done so effectively for years now." A pause, then: "Of course, he will from time to time request that you take specific actions that are necessary for his own plans. And in such cases, I am afraid the governor's word will transcend any other considerations."

The chairman swallowed, betraying the fear he was trying vainly to keep in check. "Of course, General." Vargus's tone was complex, a mix of his fear and acquiescence. "I will serve at the pleasure of the governor." He hesitated then added, "As soon as I see proof of his controlling interest, that is."

"I will show you proof as an act of good faith. But know this: the only thing that concerns you is that I'm telling you Governor Vos is now in control. Anything besides that is just detail. I'm sure you're feeling a sensation in your gut right now—that's the knife we already have in you . . . it just hasn't been twisted yet. So in the future, do not unduly test my patience."

Wilhelm let his words sink in. He was tired of the man's bluster and the sooner the damned foul understood the reality he faced, the better."

"I understand, General. Let's proceed."

"Very good, Chairman. The governor will be extremely pleased." Wilhelm reached down to the small pouch hanging from his belt. He pulled out a small data chip and set it on the desk.

Vargus glanced down at the chip. "And what, may I ask, is on that chip, General?"

"It contains a list of loans, Chairman, the sum total of the bank's business relationship with Lancaster Interests."

"The bank is involved in hundreds of ventures with the Lancasters."

"Over a thousand, in fact," Wilhelm replied. "One thousand, two hundred and eleven as of yesterday. Total value in excess of twelve billion imperial crowns in allowable credit, with approximately eight billion of that drawn down and outstanding."

Vargus shifted nervously in his seat. "Your information is impressive, General."

"Thank you, Chairman." His voice was deadpan, disinterested. The last thing Mak Wilhelm craved was praise from Damian Vargus. He held up the chip again. "It all stops. Now."

Vargus had a confused look on his face. "What stops?"

"All business with the Lancasters, Chairman. All credit lines are to be frozen immediately. All outstanding balances are to be called due. You will notify Lancaster Interests of this tomorrow via bonded courier. You will also prepare to institute legal proceedings on the various worlds to take control of bank-funded Lancaster projects in their jurisdictions." He paused. "Unless Danellan Lancaster is somehow able to produce eight billion imperial crowns to repay his loans."

Vargus stared back, a look of pure shock on his face. Finally, he stammered, "But . . . General . . . that is not pos—"

"I'm afraid the governor will be extremely displeased if his first request is rebuffed."

"But the bank has a centuries-long relationship with Lancaster Interests!"

"Yes, Chairman, and that has lulled Danellan Lancaster into a false sense of security. He has placed his company in a perilous position, complacent in the belief that the bank's financing would always be available. The stoppage of funding alone will cause enormous damage to Lancaster businesses sectorwide. But the subsequent foreclosure actions will push the company over the edge."

"But the collapse of Lancaster Interests would have enormous economic repercussions throughout the Far Stars." Vargus's voice was tinged with panic.

"Indeed. No doubt many worlds will experience severe depressions. Nevertheless, the governor is adamant about this. Are you reconsidering your cooperation already, Chairman? I am scheduled to depart in several hours for Galvanus Prime to brief the governor. He will be very disappointed if I cannot assure him this has been handled as he requested."

"No, General," Vargus said, slumping miserably. "I am not reconsidering."

"Excellent." Wilhelm shifted his weight, as if he was about to get up. But he stopped and turned back to look at Vargus. "Lord Villeroi will remain on Vanderon to oversee the governor's interests, so if there are any problems, you may discuss them with him." Wilhelm paused, noting the reaction on Vargus's face. Sebastien de Villeroi was an unsettling presence wherever he went, a perfect choice to keep a potential enemy—or a friend of indeterminate reliability—on his toes.

And if Vargus knew what a psychopath Villeroi truly was, he'd ruin that expensive suit.

"That is of course the governor's prerogative, though I can assure you, it is not necessary."

"It is indeed his prerogative, and one he intends to exercise. Lord Villeroi will remain, Chairman. The governor is more . . . comfortable with him here." Wilhelm paused for a few seconds. "He is a man of many skills. His last mission before his time here was on Kalishar."

Vargus stared across the desk, his face a mask of confusion and tension. "Kalishar?"

"Yes, Chairman. He served as our intermediary to the ka'al . . . the previous ka'al. His position here will follow much the same function as it did on Kalishar."

Wilhelm let that sink in and watched Vargus squirming in his seat. Beads of sweat were forming along his hairline, and one had already begun to slide down the side of his face. The imperial general suppressed a smile. Villeroi tended to have that effect on people, but Wilhelm wanted to be perfectly clear.

"His availability arose from the fact that his previous assignment unfortunately came to a tragic end. I'm afraid the ka'al proved to be less than reliable. He took advantage of the governor's trust, accepting mountains of imperial coin, but he failed to come through on his promises. All very sordid business, but Lord Villeroi has a very diverse set of skills, and he was able to address the matter with the appropriate action."

Vargus didn't respond. He just stared back at Wilhelm, trying to maintain his composure. He was, of course, well aware that the previous ka'al had met a gruesome end. Wilhelm briefly considered providing details—it had taken the ka'al over two days to die, and it was almost impossible to describe the personal pleasure Villeroi had derived from the entire episode. But he decided it wasn't necessary. Scaring Vargus enough to prevent treachery was one thing.

Turning the man into a useless wreck was counterproductive.

"Well, Chairman, I am afraid I have pressing commitments," Wilhelm said, rising slowly from his chair, "and you have considerable work to do to prepare for tomorrow's actions."

Vargus leaped out of his chair, racing around the desk to offer his hand to Wilhelm. "Indeed, General. Please inform the governor that he may rely completely on me."

"He will be most pleased to hear that, Chairman." Wilhelm shook Vargus's hand and nodded briefly before turning to walk toward the door.

Though I rather think Lord Villeroi will find it disappointing . . .

CHAPTER 4

BLACKHAWK CLIMBED THE LADDER FROM THE LOWER LEVEL AND stepped out onto the bridge of *Wolf's Claw*. The past four months had been the longest period of time he'd been away from his ship since he'd acquired her ten years earlier.

It's good being back.

Danellan Lancaster had offered to repair the badly damaged *Claw* in his own shipyards, paying for all the work himself. It had been an unexpected show of gratitude and magnanimity from a man Blackhawk was, against all odds, beginning to respect. He had nurtured some serious doubts about the Antillean magnate, but Lancaster had been true to his word about everything. He'd seen to Antilles's admission into the Far Stars Confederation, forcing the resolution through the Senate with all the pressure the planet's premier family could bring to bear. He'd kept every promise he had made to Marshal Lucerne, and now he'd delivered the *Claw* a month ahead of schedule.

And what a job his people had done on Blackhawk's ship.

The bridge was almost blinding, a visual feast of gleaming metal and bright new walls and floors. Everything had been replaced—the workstations, the seats, the floor. Blackhawk had a pretty good idea the *Claw* had been in service since before he was born, but now the old girl looked like she'd just rolled off the assembly line. Blackhawk's ship had always held a surprise or two—top-of-the-line weapons systems and a hyperdrive no one would expect to find on a battered old free trader to name a few. But now *every* system on the ship was leading edge. He'd put her toe to toe against a world-class imperial spy ship now.

He suspected it was all Lancaster's way of saying thank you. Blackhawk had saved the industrialist's life more than once. He'd extricated him from his imperial entanglement, rescued him from Augustin Lucerne's titanic wrath, even pulled him through after he'd been gravely wounded when the *Claw*'s crew had been attacked in a botched assassination attempt.

There was probably a bit of selfishness at play too, Blackhawk suspected, or at least familial concern. Danellan's relationship with his son had improved, but the magnate had to realize that when Blackhawk's people lifted off, Lucas would be with them, at his place in the pilot's chair as always. Every upgrade to the *Claw* increased the chance his son would return again to Antilles, and it was no surprise a man as wealthy as Lancaster had spared no expense.

Blackhawk sighed sadly. He'd been glad to help Danellan Lancaster find his inner courage, but the last thing Blackhawk had done for the magnate had been the costliest of them all—at least to the *Claw*'s tightly knit family. Tarq Bjergen had been a valued member of the crew, a friend who had given Blackhawk absolute loyalty through one desperate struggle after another. But now he was dead. He'd died on the *Claw*'s sick bay table while Doc worked ten meters away—to save Danellan Lancaster.

Because Blackhawk had told Doc to save Lancaster over Tarq.

There hadn't been any choice. That's what Blackhawk told himself, what he had continued to tell himself. If Lancaster had died, there would have been no chance to stop Marshal Lucerne from attacking Antilles. Millions would have been killed, and the confederation would have been destroyed, the Far Stars lying almost naked before the rapaciousness of Governor Vos and the empire.

Instead, only Tarq was dead, a tragedy for his friends and comrades, but by any reasonable measure, a fair trade for the millions on Antilles.

It was all true, but it didn't bring his friend back. Doc had told him Tarq would have died anyway, that his wounds had just been too severe. Blackhawk knew that might be true, but he also suspected Doc might be full of shit, telling him what he needed to hear. Tarq had been one of the strongest, most powerful human beings Blackhawk had ever seen. It was impossible for the *Claw*'s captain to accept that the giant's awesome constitution couldn't have pulled him through if he'd gotten the care he needed soon enough.

Worse, Blackhawk tried to imagine what might have gone through the huge man's mind as he lay there, his life slipping away. Was he conscious enough to understand? Were his last thoughts of Blackhawk's betrayal, of death approaching because the man he had followed with unshakable devotion—the man he had fought beside countless times—had abandoned him?

It was one thing to make a command decision, to choose to save millions over a single man, and quite another to live with yourself afterward. Arkarin Blackhawk had killed his friend, a man who had followed him everywhere he had led for years, with no regard whatever for the danger. And he knew he would carry the pain with him the rest of his days. *Along with all the other guilt I bear.*

The crew had surprised him, hearing his admissions about his past and granting him absolution without question. Astra had been right. They didn't care what he had been twenty-five years before. They accepted him for what he was, and he felt a gratitude to them he knew he could never express. The past didn't really matter. The present, though . . .

In the end, Tarq's death had done more to drive a wedge between Blackhawk and his crew than his heartfelt confession of the atrocities he'd committed as an imperial general so long ago.

Tarq had been theirs, and for the first time any of the crew could recall, Blackhawk had chosen an outsider over one of their number. They understood the situation, and even Tarq's brother, Tarnan, had agreed Blackhawk hadn't had a choice. And they all pledged their continuing loyalty. But the fact remained—the dynamic of the *Claw* was no longer the same. Accepting something intellectually was one thing, but his crew were human beings, not computers, and their emotions defied total control.

No one behaved differently or showed any signs of discontent, but he could still feel it. They had been like a family before. Blackhawk had been the unquestioned commander, but there had been a special closeness among them all. Now, there was a more formal feeling. He was their captain and they were his crew. It was something no one else could have seen, something barely perceptible to an outsider. But it was real. Blackhawk knew it was real.

And it hurt.

"She looks great, doesn't she?" Ace's voice came from below, and Blackhawk turned to see his informal second in command climbing the ladder onto the bridge. He was his usual self, cocky as hell and radiating confidence.

"She does indeed. I hardly recognize her." Blackhawk watched Ace hop off the ladder onto the spotless surface of the bridge's new metal floor. It was good to see him so active. He'd had a long and difficult recovery from the wounds he'd suffered on Castilla, but now he was back. Almost, at least. Blackhawk could feel the extra distance between them, just as he could with the others. He suspected Ace tried to rationalize away whatever he was feeling, but it was there despite his efforts.

Decisions have consequences, you old fool. You should know that better than anyone. And having no choice doesn't get you off the hook for being responsible for what you have done. He wondered if time would heal this invisible wound, and he decided he just didn't know.

"So, now that the *Claw* is ready, where are we going?" Ace walked across the deck, flopping down into his new chair.

Blackhawk walked over to the command seat, but he stood behind it instead of sitting, his hands gripping the soft leather of the backrest. "Castilla, I guess," he said softly. "Aragona has been back there for months now, and against all odds, he's managed to survive and regain his position. I don't want to give him too much of a free run. And we need to make sure everything is going smoothly. The bank isn't going to wait forever before sending someone else after him. He still owes them a lot of money."

Ace took a deep breath, but he didn't say anything immediately. Blackhawk knew his friend couldn't be too anxious to return to Castilla. They'd been a few seconds from getting away from that world when Ace took the two shots that had almost finished him. He'd been four months recovering, and now he was being asked to go right back.

"You really trust that piece of shit, Ark?"

Blackhawk noticed an edge to Ace's voice when he mentioned Aragona. The Castillan gangster/politician was far from the most unsavory character the crew of the *Claw* had dealt with. Though, of course, he was the only one who'd had his hands all over Katarina during the op . . .

Blackhawk had noticed Ace and the *Claw*'s resident cold-blooded assassin acting strangely toward each other. He was pretty sure it hadn't gone past a bit of carefully controlled flirtation, but if it had—or if it did in the future—he only wished them both the best. They seemed like an odd pairing to him, but they were certainly both capable of taking care of themselves. And they were two of the people he cared most about in all the galaxy.

At least someone in the Far Stars might be happy.

"Trust him?" Blackhawk replied. "By Chrono, no. But he's got the Far Stars Bank on his ass already, and he spoke directly to Marshal Lucerne, who promised to send a Celtiborian expeditionary force after him if he betrayed us." Blackhawk's voice deepened. "And I promised I'd kill him myself if he pulled something. I don't think he has the guts to betray both the marshal and me." His voice held a touch of menace, something he knew was in part a vestige of his distant past. He controlled his conditioning, but it was always there, like a voice in his head, urging him, pushing him. And neither the new Blackhawk, nor the imperial monster imprisoned inside him, suffered traitors.

There are more than a few who'd call you traitor, he thought to himself. *Starting with the voices from deep within . . .*

"I guess we'll see." Ace's tone left little doubt he'd be willing to put a bullet in Aragona's forehead if the Castillan pulled anything. He looked like he was about to say something else when the comm unit crackled to life.

"*Wolf's Claw,* this is Lucas. *Wolf's Claw,* this is Lucas. Is anyone on board?" The voice on the comm was tense. Something was wrong.

Blackhawk and Ace spun around together, turning toward their comm units. "Lucas, Ark here. What is it?"

Lucas had been visiting with his family, none of whom he had seen for nearly five years before he had walked into his father's office five months earlier.

Lucas had gone only out of necessity, to save millions of Antilleans, and he hadn't intended to turn the trip to his home world into a family reunion. But Blackhawk had urged him to go, to at least visit his mother. The trip hadn't exactly mended fences—Lucas and his family saw things very differently, and they always would—but his relationship with his mother and father had definitely improved. Danellan Lancaster's willingness to do what was necessary to work with Marshal Lucerne had been a big help, and Lucas had begun to see his father as a human being, something he hadn't done for a long time.

"It's the Far Stars Bank, Skipper. They've called Lancaster's loans. *All of them.* Everywhere. My father is in the office trying to find out what is going on."

Blackhawk was silent for a moment. Lancaster Interests wasn't a normal company. It was a vast conglomerate with tentacles that spread throughout the Far Stars. There was no reason for the bank to provoke a conflict with the Lancasters, none except . . .

Blackhawk knew immediately. Vos. There was no other answer. Somehow, the imperial governor had managed to influence the bank. He had tried to manipulate Danellan Lancaster by intimidation, then later by a race to acquire a controlling interest in the company, a contest the Lancasters had ultimately won with the help of Marshal Lucerne. Things had gotten a bit rough, and a few share purchases had been negotiated under the guns of the Celtiborian fleet, but the combined Antillean-Celtiborian cartel had ultimately managed to acquire just over 51 percent of Lancaster's stock.

But as Blackhawk learned more about Kergen Vos, he had come to realize that the governor was not one to accept defeat. If he couldn't control Lancaster Interests, he would destroy it. And the only entity in the sector with the power to threaten such a vast enterprise was the Far Stars Bank.

Was he able to gain control of the bank?

Blackhawk felt his breath grow short as he thought about it. The Far Stars Bank was sewn into the lifeblood of almost every world of the sector. If Kergen Vos controlled the bank, he wielded enormous economic power, enough to dominate—or destroy—almost anything in the Far Stars.

"Get down to Lancaster Tower, Lucas." Blackhawk flashed a glance to Ace who had been staring back with a look of surprise on his face. "Ace and I are on the way."

"I just don't know what to do." Danellan Lancaster sat at his enormous desk, the magnificent view behind him presenting a vista stretching from Charonea's Old City to the New, and then to the rolling hills beyond. The other massive buildings of the New City rose into the sky all around, like proud monuments to Antillean wealth and prosperity, but Lancaster Tower reached higher than any, the symbol of the greatest company in the Far Stars. But that enormous empire was a troubled one, under attack and in grave danger of destruction.

"The situation is dire." Silas Grosvenor had been the financial wizard behind many of Danellan Lancaster's successful projects, but the numbers man had the same bleak expression as his master. "We'll have to shut down operations everywhere. The fallout will be disastrous."

"Are we that dependent on credit, Father?" It was the first time Blackhawk had heard Lucas address his father as such. He doubted the two had resolved all their differences, or that they ever would, but at least they'd found a way to exist civilly together. That was a start, and if it was as far as they got, it was enormously preferable to what had been before.

"No, not normally," Danellan said. "But we drained our capital to buy back stock to fight off the governor's takeover attempt. And we overextended ourselves in conjunction with Marshal Lucerne's expansion plans. Our liquidity is very poor right now. Given time, we could sell off some properties and free up cash, but none of us saw this coming. I doubt we can move quickly enough to make a difference." He paused for a few seconds. "Worse, what capital reserves we do have are mostly on deposit at the Far Stars Bank. No doubt they will freeze those accounts and set them off against the balances due. Vanderon law essentially allows the bank to do whatever it wants. We will be fortunate to keep the company running for a week under these conditions."

The implications were staggering. The governor clearly had the full financial backing of the emperor, which meant his monetary resources were virtually limitless, as least by Far Stars standards.

Blackhawk frowned. *I should have seen this coming. I'm a damned idiot. It never even occurred to me that Vos could gain control of the Far Stars Bank. I hate to say it, but I have to give this man due respect.*

"Do what you can to raise capital on Antilles, at least to get you through the next few weeks." Blackhawk hesitated, looking at Danellan and trying to gauge his reaction. "I know you'll have to take a hit for that money, but I suggest you agree to whatever terms you must. Speak to your friends in the Antillean government, and see what they will do for you. You have a lot of influence, and more than one politician who owes his position to the Lancasters."

Danellan nodded. "I am sure we can get some government assistance, but it's not going to be enough to avoid widespread shutdowns of operations." He looked up at Blackhawk. "We're talking about millions of jobs, Arkarin, on dozens of planets. And they're all going to disappear without warning. Factories will stop producing, mines will shut down. It will be a death spiral, as the products working through the Lancaster ecosystem slow to a crawl. Revenues will dry up, leading to another round of cuts." He put his head in his hands and took a deep breath before looking back up. "We can buy time, that's all. But there is no way we can survive long term without that funding."

"How can the bank move against our properties on so many worlds? We must have binding loan agreements. They are in breach of contract, aren't they? Can't we fight them?" The anger was clear in Lucas's voice. He didn't really care about his family legacy, but this was something he understood—an enemy making a hostile move. And five years on the *Claw* had taught him how to handle a situation like that. How to fight.

"Yes, of course, Lucas," Danellan replied. "But it is not so simple as all that. The Far Stars is a corrupt place. Indeed, I suspect everywhere men live is. The courts and magistrates and local monarchs who adjudicate disputes like this will act in their own interests, not according to any impartiality or concept of fairness."

"But keeping those factories and mines and other businesses running is in the local interest." Lucas shifted his gaze back and forth between Blackhawk and his father. "There will be massive disruptions if they shut down. People will suffer."

"Yes, Lucas," Blackhawk said before Danellan could answer, "but the people who will suffer are not the ones in control. The leaders will not go hungry if the economy collapses, and they will seek to profit from the disruption. Long term, you are right, they need those assets working . . . but they don't need them operating under Lancaster ownership. If I was in the governor's shoes—and we can all assume Governor Vos is behind this by whatever means he is exerting control on the bank—I would make sure it was worthwhile for the locals to see things my way. They will direct the anger of the unemployed and the starving toward Lancaster, and in the end they will reopen the facilities after they have awarded themselves ownership. Judges and lords who stand to buy such assets for half their actual value will be poor guardians of justice."

"Besides," Danellan said, "even if we could find honest magistrates and officials, such actions take time . . . time we simply don't have."

Blackhawk turned toward the elder Lancaster. "We must stop underestimating this governor and what he is capable of doing. Danellan, you must do all you can to keep Lancaster Interests afloat. Abandon any operations on worlds where you are unsure of your control over the local authorities. Those are as good as lost—at least until confederation military can be dispatched to assume control. Even where you feel you have friends in power, be cautious. Vos's agents may have gotten there first, and old allies may have been turned, lured away with bribes or threats."

"I will," Danellan answered, showing more courage than Blackhawk had expected. "Governor Vos is a formidable enemy," he continued, "but I doubt he has been able to completely erase centuries of Lancaster influence."

Blackhawk nodded. "I will send word to Marshal Lucerne and request that he provide any aid he can. Celtiboria is not as wealthy a planet as Antilles, but its resources are still considerable. And if you have any specific assets you feel are especially important, he may be able to send troops to intervene and prevent the locals from turning them over to the bank." Sending military in to intimidate local authorities wasn't something he suspected Lucerne would feel very good about—but that didn't mean he wouldn't do it.

Lucas was looking at Blackhawk with resolve. Against all odds, it appeared the *Claw*'s pilot was feeling a wave of family pride. "Thank you, Skipper. Lancaster will not stand by and allow this to happen."

"No, Lucas, none of us will. But now, I want you to get back to the *Claw* right away. Find Sam and do a complete check on the ship's new systems, and get her ready to launch."

The pilot nodded. "Will do. Where are we going, Skip?"

"Vanderon," Blackhawk said, darkness in his tone.

"We're going to find out just what is going on with the Far Stars Bank . . . and we're going to put a stop to it now."

CHAPTER 5

RACHEN WALKED SLOWLY THROUGH THE ALMOST DESERTED streets of the Celtiborian capital. It was early, not quite dawn, and a dim glow was barely illuminating his way. The city was quiet, most of its population still asleep. He'd passed a couple of patrols, but neither had stopped him. That wasn't surprising. He looked completely unthreatening, like a man of letters seeking wisdom.

He had shed his black hooded robe for a gray one, of far coarser material, the attire of a Taralian monk. Taralia was a barren world, an inhospitable place of little value, swept by brutal sandstorms, baked during its long, relentless summers and blasted by frigid winds through its dark and dreary winters. It was a poor world, with little to offer, save the monks of its many and varied orders, who toiled endlessly to preserve and maintain the Great Histories, the records of human habitation in the Far Stars.

The imperial assassin was posing as a brother of the Chronoastrian brotherhood, a guild dedicated to the cult of Chrono, the legendary explorer who had first crossed the Void and discovered the Far Stars. There were many histories about the origins of human habitation in the sector, but they were contradictory and none were complete. Many details had been lost to the ravages of time, but most major accounts agreed that Celtiboria had been the location of the first settlement.

Celtiborian archaeologists had searched for centuries for the site of Chrono's semimythical lost colony, but all they had uncovered were a few artifacts, and the sparse remains of an ancient city that might—or might not—have been the legendary home of the first humans in the Far Stars. But despite the lack of certainty—and even active allegations that the findings dated to centuries after Chrono's fabled arrival—it had long been a custom for Taralian brothers to make a pilgrimage to Celtiboria, to walk among the ancient and haunted ruins. Taralian lore had long held that the pure of mind could commune with the past, and that they would come away with greater knowledge and understanding—and return home able to add new insight to the sacred texts.

Rachen knew little of Chrono or the first settlers, nor did he care.

He slipped down a small side street, little more than an alley, working his way deeper into the complex maze of passageways that wound behind the buildings of Celtiboria's capital city. The metropolis was old, and its crumbling structures had been built upon the ruins of an even more ancient city. It had been called Alban in the days of the Senate's rule centuries before. But it had endured multiple name changes as one warlord after another gained temporary hegemony and occupied it with a mind toward empire. And for three hundred years, none of Celtiboria's militaristic lords could achieve lasting dominance. Not until Lucerne and his armies crushed the last of their enemies and restored planetary unity.

Lucerne had begun efforts to bring the faded jewel of Celtiboria back to its ancient luster, and there was construction activity everywhere. The city was once again the capital of a united planet, and the massive palace dominating its center was alive with the activities not only of a whole world, but of a new and growing interstellar confederation. Alban was coming out of its dark age and stepping into a future where it would be the center of the entire Far Stars sector.

But it wasn't there yet. Much of the expected grandeur lay ahead, and Alban was still mostly an old city, the scars left by its former occupants ever present. Lucerne had vowed the city would regain—and indeed surpass—its former glories, yet that was a vow for the future, and Rachen now prowled through crime-ridden, trash-strewn backstreets. The assassin was bound for the catacombs that lay beneath the crumbling buildings of the oldest parts of the city, a shadowy underworld filled with criminals, lost souls, and anyone else seeking to disappear.

He shed his monk's robe, discarding it in a mound of rotting garbage. It was more conspicuous in these back alleys. He was one of the Lost now, the homeless, destitute castoffs who still prowled the forgotten parts of Alban. There were thousands of such vagabonds, the detritus of a society that had torn itself apart through three centuries of combat between its warring lords. Deserters from the armies, those who had succumbed to alcohol or drugs, displaced farmers, and survivors with no prospects and no one to aid them—they all called this hellish netherworld home.

Rachen made his way through the garbage—human and otherwise—looking to any onlooker as though he belonged there. He'd scavenged tattered rags from a corpse he'd passed, and he moved on, ignoring the stench, the filth, the foul odors of rotting garbage and human excrement.

A normal man, unaccustomed to such destitution, would be revolted by the sights and smells of the Hidden City, but the assassins of the Exequtorum were trained to ignore all pain, all discomfort. Rachen and his brethren would walk through fire and swim across a river of shit, dragging their broken limbs behind them all the while, but they would let nothing interfere with their mission.

So here in Alban, even as his senses were filled with scenes of human misery and unending filth, Rachen's only thought was this:

They serve their purpose.

Because the city's blight was providing the cover he needed to move closer to his target.

Rachen was on his way to kill Augustin Lucerne.

The flickering light from the fireplace reflected off the cut glass of the decanter. The bottle had been full three hours earlier, but now the line of amber liquid had dropped at least two-thirds of the way down.

The room was silent, save for the crackling of the logs in the hearth. The Celtiborian black oak was ideal for use in a fireplace. The hardwood burned slowly, and the two heavy chunks now ablaze would last almost until morning. The scent of the burning logs was rustic, and it filled the room with a scent that spoke of home, of the low river valleys and surrounding woodlands where the campaign to unite Celtiboria had begun so long ago.

It was deep into the night, though the room's sole occupant had lost all track of time. Nor did he notice the fragrance of the fire, the smells of his youth. He was lost, wallowing in a stew of brandy and regret, and nothing else existed for him right now.

Augustin Lucerne sat in a plush leather chair near the fire, his body slouched low, a half-full glass sitting on a small table to his right. He was disheveled, his uniform jacket tossed carelessly aside, the rest of the outfit rumpled and half unbuttoned. His face was downcast and unshaven. His eyes stared intently at something in his hand, a small frame of pure silver.

"Happy Birthday, Eliane my love," he said, his voice slurred. His eyes were fixed on the likeness in the frame, that of a strikingly beautiful woman. The image looking back at him was young, perhaps midtwenties, and her expression was one of joy, of looking forward to a life that still lay largely ahead.

"Alas, sweet Eliane, it was not to be." Lucerne's face was drawn, his eyes watery and sad. He had loved his wife, more than anyone knew. More than anyone could imagine, considering how often he'd left her alone while he went off on campaign. Young Eliane had died just a year after the image in his hand had been taken, leaving a devastated Augustin to raise their only child, a precocious little girl with golden blond hair, the nearly perfect likeness of her mother.

"I did love you, Eliane . . . always. I still do. With all my heart. Did you know? Did you believe it? Or did you die feeling as unloved as you were alone?"

Lucerne had always treated his wife tenderly, and he'd seen to her every want and need. But he had ignored her too, cast her into a life of loneliness he hadn't entirely understood, not then. He was just beginning his quest to unify Celtiboria, and the call of war took him from hearth and home, leaving his young bride alone in the coldness of his grim stronghold.

Marriage to a warlord like Lucerne meant a life of loneliness, but it was only in the years after her death that he began to realize what a hell he had created for her. Eliane had been a happy girl, outgoing and warm. An extrovert who loved people, and who withered away in the protected fastness of her husband's cold fortress, far from her family and the friends of her youth.

Theirs had been an arranged marriage, a calculated bit of political maneuvering by the young and ambitious warlord. Eliane had brought with her the inheritance of her father's lands, almost doubling the strength of Lucerne's nascent forces—and providing the rich grain-producing plains he needed to feed his soldiers. He had contracted to marry the young Eliane Fortier sight unseen, but when he finally saw her in the flesh, with sparkling blue eyes and a wild mane of blond hair—and her smile, he had never seen a smile like hers—the young soldier had fallen in love immediately.

Lucerne—the warrior, the unstoppable force who had crushed the famous warlords of Celtiboria, who had drawn the other Prime worlds into confederation, who had sent his soldiers to twenty planets to impose his will upon millions—shed a tear for his long-departed wife. He felt it moving slowly down his cheek, and he ran his fingers across the image, as if doing so allowed him to somehow touch his lost love.

"Did you love me, Eliane? Is it possible that somehow, through the loneliness and the torment I caused you, your love for me survived?"

He was sure she had loved him . . . once at least. He'd been a dashing warrior who had achieved unprecedented success at an early age. Eliane had been as taken with the handsome young general as he with her, and their first months together had been happy ones. Lucerne was sure of that, and he had held on to those memories ever since, the half year of happiness he had given her instead of the lifetime he'd promised.

It was months short of their first anniversary when war beckoned again. Lucerne kissed his wife as he left to go to the front, promising her he would return as soon as he could. He saw her perhaps fifteen times over the next five years, for no more than three months in total. War had demanded the rest of him, and he gave it what it craved. It had paid him back—in glory, in power—but his victories had come at a cost beyond the death and destruction of the battlefield, and the renowned conqueror had sacrificed the life he might have had to the demands of the gods of war. He had chosen victory over home and family, conquest over love. He had thrown away the happiness he knew could have been his. And Eliane's.

Augustin reached to the side, grabbing the glass and bringing it tentatively to his lips. His hand was shaking, and he spilled a few drops on himself before draining it. He set it back on the table at an angle, and it fell over and crashed to the floor, shattering. He didn't notice. His eyes were still fixated on the image, his mind lost in time.

He had done this on Eliane's birthday every year since she had died, and he swore he would commemorate the day without fail as long as he lived. It was a tribute to his lost love, but also a reminder, a bit of self-flagellation for his failings. For while she was alive, he had never once been there on her birthday. Always battle had called, the field taking him, his soldiers, the lure of conquest. He sent her treasures as gifts, artworks ripped from fallen fortresses, mountains of gold and jewels wrested from those he had defeated. But never once had he sat beside her on this day, held her hand, and wished her happy birthday from his own lips. And now, despite the fact that she was so long gone, he allowed nothing to interfere, as if he was petitioning her soul for forgiveness, showing through his steadfastness the true sorrow he felt. That he would always feel.

She had died of a fever, in an epidemic that swept through the low Riverlands area around Augustin's ancestral fortress. He had been a thousand kilometers away, fighting at Plactae, the first of the Sisters, his five greatest victories, battles of annihilation so complete they had made him a living legend. He had received word of her illness during the height of the struggle, when he couldn't leave his soldiers without endangering his army. When the battle was past the crisis, he immediately turned command over to his generals, and he boarded a gunship and flew home—only to find he was too late.

His beloved wife was dead.

He had missed the chance to talk to her, to tell her one last time he loved her, to hold her hand and bring her what comfort he might have in her final hours. He hadn't been there, and he knew she had died sad and with only a young girl who was kept from her, for fear that Astra would become sick, too. Swearing his regret to her body, Lucerne had clenched his fists and shouted into the empty air, but it was all in vain. It was too late. For all the power he possessed, for the awesome military might at his disposal, he was helpless. She was gone, and there was nothing he could do.

"If only you could know, my sweet Eliane, what a burden life has become. I live for duty now, and nothing more. Save Astra. And now I fear my quest will destroy her as it did you. I love our Astra more than anything in the universe, but . . . my affection is poison." He was speaking to himself, his tone thick with misery and self-recrimination.

Once more, the marshal found himself debating Astra's fate, knowing he had set her along a course that would lead her to be as alone as he was . . . as Eliane had been. Given over to the dark god Duty, never to make a choice of her own.

The thought roiled in him, physically jerking him from his chair as he made his way to the lavatory. His stomach unknotted, the expensive brandy flushed from his system along with his tears.

Kneeling on the cool tile floor, a new thought washed over him. And while it did not make him feel any better, it was the beginning of something close to atonement.

"No," he said simply, his voice heavy with determination. "I will not sacrifice my daughter . . . as I did you. As I did myself.

Lucerne stumbled from the bathroom, uncertain, almost as if he'd forgotten the way. But his new thoughts had taken hold. Yes, he knew what he had to do,

"I will free her, Eliane. I promise you. I will free her from the chains her birth placed upon her. I cannot save you, my love, for you have been lost to me for a lifetime now. But I will save our daughter, our beautiful Astra." He paused as he reached the chair, his hand moving to the table, feeling about vainly for the glass that was no longer there.

It would be his penance. He would free his daughter, release her from chains his own achievements had placed on her.

"I will save her, Eliane. I promise."

Rachen walked through the crumbling sewers, ignoring the stench and following the path he knew led to the palace. He had studied the maps of Alban, every file he'd been able to find. He'd scoured the archives on Galvanus Prime, and he'd hacked into every database on Celtiboria as well. Even the ancient hand-drawn schematics hanging in frames in the museum had been useful.

He remembered it all, every detail. Like all operatives of the Exequtorum, Rachen possessed remarkable abilities, including artificial eidetic memories. The surgical implants in Rachen's brain allowed him to remember everything he saw, everything he heard. He had processed every aspect of each map, and he'd compared them to create his own highly accurate mental image. True, it was a composite, a best guess of the actual layout of the underground city beneath Alban. Yet his analysis told him his conclusions had a 94 percent chance of being accurate.

He turned right at a small intersection, and he could feel the grade begin to rise as expected. He took a few steps, and then he caught a hint of movement in his peripheral vision. His hand dropped to his side by reflex, grabbing the hilt of his blade and swinging it around in a blindingly quick motion.

The Celtiborian cave rat fell to the ground, its thick body neatly cleaved in two. Its halves splashed in the five-centimeter-deep water running down the center of the archaic sewer. The fifty-kilo rats occasionally scored a delicacy when one of the Lost wandered too far underground, but this specimen had been unfortunate in its choice of prey.

Rachen returned the weapon to its place and continued on his path. Fifty meters ahead he found what he had been seeking. There was a hatch in the ceiling, long sealed shut. The assassin's eyes darted from side to side, quickly assessing the situation. There was a ladder—or, more accurately, the remains of a ladder—on the ground beneath the portal. It had been made of some type of wood, and it had rotted away to almost nothing.

Moving to the side, Rachen stared up at the round doorway above. It was heavy stone, set in about ten centimeters from the surrounding casement. Whatever mechanism had opened it, he was sure it had long since deteriorated to uselessness. Even if the door had been at ground level, he doubted his own enhanced muscles could have budged it. He hated to make noise, to risk alerting any guards that might be nearby above, but there was no choice.

He pulled back his sleeve, baring his arm, pale and completely hairless. He extended it upward, toward the seam at one edge of the door itself. He closed his eyes for an instant, sending a thought through the artificial neural response systems implanted in his body. A small nozzle extended from inside his arm, piercing the skin, slowly, painfully.

The Exequtorum was an organization shrouded in myth and legend. It had long encouraged the talk of supernatural powers and inexplicable abilities. But the assassins in its storied ranks possessed no magic, no demonic powers, only the application of technology—and a thousand-year PR campaign.

The plasma bolt was the weapon that had most added to the image of the assassins of the Exequtorum as supernatural warriors. It looked like some godlike power, a man hurling bolts of lightning at his enemies. But it was no less pure science than a hyperdrive or a laser. Indeed, the device that made it work was painful to implant—and equally so to utilize—but it was not enormously complex. Still, it all contributed to the show, to the unnatural terror Rachen and his brethren inspired in the emperor's enemies.

Rachen stared quietly for a few seconds, adjusting his aim as he prepared to activate the weapon. Usually he would save the limited charge for a more appropriate use, a desperate situation, or at least a public one, where it could create fear and panic among his enemies. But he had to get through that stone hatch, and he had no other way. He hadn't dared to bring a gun or explosives with him. If he'd been searched on the street with those, he'd have had to kill the police. And that would have set off a citywide alert, increasing security everywhere and making his task even more difficult.

He prepared himself for the pain as he finalized his aim— right for the seam between the ceiling and the hatch. He directed a thought to the mechanism inside him, and a bolt of energy blasted out from the nozzle on his arm. It was a blue-white arc of plasma, and it slammed into the stone hatch, blasting a gap between the portal and the casement.

Rachen stared up at the gaping hole, waiting for the molten edges of the rock to cool. His arm hurt as it always did after firing the deadly weapon, and his hand was red and burned from the discharge. But he'd gotten the job done, and pain was only a state of being. Just as he could control the plasma with his mind, he controlled the pain.

The plasma blaster was a one-shot weapon, at least for this mission. The mechanism charged itself from his metabolism and from the kinetic energy of his movements, and it drew the hydrogen it needed from his own cells. But that was an inefficient way to charge so high powered a device, and it took days to store up enough energy and hydrogen for another shot.

But one blast had been sufficient. The hole wasn't huge, but it was big enough. And even though it wasn't really cooled yet, time was wasting, and enough of the heat had dissipated. He flexed his knees, and he thrust himself upward, his enhanced muscles propelling him high enough to get his hands through the opening and grab on. It was still hot enough to hurt his bare hands, but he ignored it and pulled himself up and into the passageway above. If his maps were correct, he was in the subbasement of the palace, just a few levels below Marshal Lucerne's quarters.

CHAPTER 6

THE FLEET MOVED PAST PARNASSUS'S SINGLE MOON, COMING from the direction of the planet's outer system, like silent death approaching the peaceful world. The ships were mostly transports, an assortment of craft of varying quality. The mass of troop transports was escorted by a small phalanx of warships, frigates mostly, with a squadron of three cruisers in the lead. The armada was a pale shadow of the vast fleets of gargantuan battleships that imposed the imperial will in the empire proper. But, beyond the Void, along this wild frontier of human habitation in space, it was a force to be reckoned with.

Certainly, Parnassus's tiny navy was no match for the invaders. Still, they made an attempt to face the hopeless battle bravely, making their stand at the edge of the system's asteroid belt. The two dozen small patrol ships engaged the enemy in a courageous fight, weaving in and out among the bigger ships, hoping to wreak havoc with their maneuverability.

They failed, overwhelmed by an enemy with a hundred times their firepower.

Three of the imperial frigates lagged behind the main fleet, damaged in varying degrees in the short but vicious battle. But the Parnassans were dead, all of them. Half a dozen ships had attempted to surrender at the end, but the imperials ignored their frantic communications and continued firing until nothing was left of them but floating debris and plasma. It was a demonstration, a symbol of the merciless fury those who resisted the empire could expect.

Now, a squadron of frigates accelerated to the front of the formation as it approached the planet, loosing a storm of torpedoes toward the floating orbital platforms. The Parnassan defenses were minimal, hopelessly outgunned and outclassed. They launched a salvo of their own at the invaders, but their small, slow-moving projectiles were easily intercepted by the defensive arrays of the imperial ships, and not a single shot got through.

The immobile platforms employed their own defensive armaments against the incoming torpedoes, but the imperial volley was too strong, the torpedoes too fast and too many.

The platforms were blown to atoms.

"Enemy orbital defenses neutralized, General." The admiral stood uncomfortably on the command bridge next to his chair, which was currently occupied by the illustrious General Draco Tragonis, Count of Helos, Baron of Saraman . . . and too many other titles to easily name. He was a man who outranked every imperial in the Far Stars save Governor Vos himself.

"Thank you, Admiral Gamara," he said in his usual haughty tone. "All ships are to enter high orbit. Prepare to commence surface bombardment."

"Yes, General," replied the admiral. His tone was respectful and obedient—anything else would have been extremely dangerous around a man like Tragonis. But there was something else in his response too, a resentment, well hidden but still noticeable—at least to someone less arrogant than Lord Tragonis.

The imperial count and general stared straight ahead, his eyes fixed on the large screen displaying the blue-and-white planet below. Draco Tragonis was a true man of the empire, utterly merciless, focused almost solely on obtaining power and then implementing that to gain even more. He had no pity for those in his way, neither enemies nor innocents unfortunate enough to stand between him and his goal. And right now those innocents were the forty million people of Parnassus.

"And, Admiral . . . Parnassus has no vital industry, nothing important that can't be easily rebuilt—so the sooner they understand how things have changed, the better. Hold nothing back. Target everything of strategic value without regard for collateral damage."

"As you command, General."

Tragonis leaned back in his commandeered chair. Rank was everything in the empire, and his noble titles placed him significantly above the admiral. He didn't have any animosity toward his fleet commander, nor had he gotten any particular pleasure from evicting him from his chair. It was just the way things worked in the empire. He had struggled for a lifetime to attain his rank, and he greedily demanded the perquisites of that status.

Gamara was no different. He could have displaced a lesser officer from his seat, taking one of the workstations for his own.

Indeed, there were two empty stations on the command bridge he could have utilized. But the admiral clearly preferred to stand adjacent to Tragonis in the center of the control center rather than accept a lowly workstation.

An imperial battleship would have worked better as a flagship. The great behemoths provided suitable accommodations for both fleet commanders and highly ranked nobles. But the Far Stars Fleet didn't have any of the massive battlewagons, and Tragonis and Gamara had to coexist on the far smaller cruiser-flagship.

"Ready to commence bombardment now, General. All major cities in the eastern hemisphere have been targeted."

Imperial battleships were equipped with mass drivers, the state of the art in nonnuclear ground bombardment systems. The heavy magnetic catapults launched projectiles at hyper-velocities, inflicting enormous damage on ground targets. Tragonis's Far Stars fleet lacked the awesome weapons of a real imperial battle fleet, but his cruisers and frigates still possessed more than enough firepower to soften up a defenseless world like Parnassus.

"Begin bombardment, Admiral." Tragonis knew he had just given an order that would result in millions of deaths on the ground, but his voice was calm, as if he had ordered a routine repair or a diagnostic check. An observer might have marveled at the general's iron discipline in holding in his emotions but, in truth, Tragonis didn't have any emotions regarding this attack. He felt no compassion at all for the people his ships were about to slaughter. The citizens of the empire—and Tragonis considered the Far Stars to be a part of the empire in rebellion—existed solely to serve their masters.

Tragonis knew he and Kergen Vos were different in their

outlooks. Vos had given himself wholly to the empire, committed horrific acts in its name, sacrificed thousands in his rise to power—but it was discipline that kept his own feelings of guilt in check. From the moment he'd begun his rise from the ruins of his home world, Kergen Vos had accepted the reality of the universe, and he'd done what he had to do to advance and prosper. But Tragonis knew his friend still held on to some shreds of his humanity, however deeply suppressed they might be. The tailor's son still lived on inside Kergen Vos, however imprisoned he was by the bars built by twenty years of ruthless service to empire.

What pointless nonsense. Humanity is a construct, like religion. It preys on the weak-minded, compels them to ignore their interests. The natural state of man is to be master or slave, and my choice is clear. There is little to be gained by judging oneself when the nature of mankind is preordained.

Draco Tragonis at his core was as unemotional as a human being could be, a pure sociopath. He considered Kergen Vos a friend, or at least as close to one as a man like him could have. But he also knew his loyalty was conditional. Vos was brilliant, and attaching himself to the governor's victory in the Far Stars would serve Tragonis's own career well. But he knew if Kergen Vos was ever in his way, he wouldn't let anything like friendship interfere with what had to be done. In the end, all men are alone, and they must act accordingly.

"Scanners report all eastern hemisphere targets destroyed, General. Collateral damage is considerable. There are fires in most of the major cities." The admiral was repeating the words of the tactical officer seated at the scanner display. Tragonis had heard the reports at the same time, but he let Gamara repeat them anyway. There was considerable performance art to maintaining dominance over subordinates who were highly ranked in their own right.

"Western hemisphere targets entering field of fire in four minutes, sir."

"Very well, Admiral. Carry on with your orders." Tragonis moved his hand to the control panel on the armrest of the chair. He pressed one of the direct comm buttons. He might have continued his little show with Gamara, commanding him to order the ground troops to prepare for landing. But the admiral wasn't technically in that line of command and, besides, the legions waiting to drop were Tragonis's creation. He'd spent months in the searing hell of Kalishar's desert watching as the soldiers of his single legion turned the scum of the Far Stars into an army. And now, that army was about to launch its first campaign. No, he wasn't going to let anyone else issue the order.

Even a sociopath could feel pride in his creation.

"General Fuering, prepare your landing force. The invasion will begin in twenty minutes."

The dropships moved swiftly through the dawn sky, wave after wave of the sleek craft gliding swiftly toward the surface. The Third Far Stars Legion wasn't on the official rolls of the imperial military, but Fuering would have put them against any line unit on the other side of the Void.

A rookie unit, at least.

The recruits had been difficult, cutthroats and petty criminals mostly, resistant at first to the discipline required of imperial soldiers. Fuering suppressed a smile. The brutal training regimen had broken most of them fairly quickly. And the ones who had resisted, who had proven to be unbreakable—well, they had died in training, and their bodies became a feast for the carrion creatures of the deep Kalishari desert.

Fuering had been a combat leader, his Eighty-Second Legion a line unit. The new legions, the soldiers now assaulting Parnassus, were the first he'd ever trained. He'd had a difficult time, at first, and the initial trainee class had suffered an extremely high fatality rate. But he'd quickly learned to work with the less than desirable raw material available in the Far Stars. The last class had only lost 15 percent of its number in training, graduating an impressive 85 percent, a major improvement over the 34 percent of the first class to survive.

"First wave landing in three minutes." The announcement was automated, and the sound had a tinny quality, a poor imitation of a human voice.

Fuering wasn't in the lead wave, of course. Indeed, it was rare enough for an imperial commander to land at all until the LZs were totally secure. But Fuering knew this new Far Stars Army offered him an unprecedented opportunity to advance his career. Already he was the titular commander of eighty legions, though most of those existed only on paper—and in the form of thousands—and to be clear, *thousands of thousands*—of sweating recruits on Kalishar. Still, it was a massive jump from his previous status as the leader of a single unit. His army wasn't official, not yet at least. But he had no doubt the force that conquered the Far Stars would be greatly rewarded—and given full line status within the imperial military. And Hailus Fuering would be an army commander, fresh from a glorious victory and showered with titles and land grants.

The imperial general was tense. He had trained his soldiers well, he was sure of that. But this would be their first true test. Parnassus wasn't the strongest planet in the Far Stars, not by any measure. But it was still a baptism of fire for his soldiers to face a real enemy, one who would be defending their homes and families, and Fuering intended to be there, on the ground, directing the battle closely.

He had special detachments of his old Eighty-Second Legion deployed among the new units. Those who hadn't been turned into officer and noncom cadres for the new legions were formed into kill squads, heavily armed units operating under a single order—to fire upon any of the new imperial soldiers who disobeyed orders or fled from the enemy. Fuering would tolerate neither cowardice nor disobedience in his army, and the sooner that was clear to the soldiers in the field, the better.

He sat still, held in place along the bench by a heavy metal brace. A landing under enemy fire could be a rough experience, and the imperial dropships were designed for planetary insertions far more difficult than the unopposed invasion of Parnassus. *It will be a damned different experience when we finally hit Celtiboria.* The capital of the confederation was the most populous in the Far Stars, and the best defended as well. Marshal Lucerne's home world wasn't going to be an easy conquest, not by any measure, and Fuering knew he had to turn his trained recruits into a true veteran army before that day came.

He felt the dropship swerve hard to port, positioning itself for the final approach to landing zone Beta. He was watching on the monitor, and he could see his first waves had already landed, establishing the three LZs for the first stage of the operation. Beta and Gamma were completely quiet, and the forces there were forming a defensive perimeter, preparing the site for the waves of dropships still coming in.

LZ Alpha was a bit closer to Heliopolis, the planet's capital, and the local forces were providing some resistance. The imperial advance guard on the ground was in a fierce firefight. The invaders were temporarily outnumbered, but their weapons and training were superior to that of the natives. And they had waves of reinforcements landing every six minutes.

"Colonel Karetes, LZ Alpha is under attack. You are to mount a flanking move around the enemy forces, trapping them between your own troops and the Alpha units." Feuring rattled off the orders calmly. He knew Alpha would hold out, and if he could get a large force behind the enemy and cut off their retreat, he could turn the Parnassans' initiative into a trap. They'd almost certainly committed their best units to trying to pinch out LZ Alpha, and if Feuring could bag them all early, the rest of the op would be little more than mopping up.

"Yes, General." Karetes was the commander of LZ Gamma, which was less than twenty kilometers from Alpha.

Feuring glanced at the display. Less than a minute until landing. He leaned back and took a deep breath. Then he closed his eyes.

So it begins here, he thought. *The conquest of the Far Stars.* He knew Governor Vos had managed to obtain varying degrees of control over worlds of the sector using bribery and deceit. But this was the first naked conquest, the beginning of a campaign that would continue until every world in the sector had surrendered and yielded to imperial authority.

The fifty thousand soldiers landing on Parnassus were but a tithe of the legions Feuring and Tragonis had already trained and equipped. There were half a million men on Kalishar, ready to go into action. And another million were in various stages of preparation. Soon, the great campaign would be fully under way, and the imperial flag would fly above the subjugated remains of a hundred worlds—and every planet where men lived would pay homage to the one true emperor, the master of all humanity.

"Run, quickly. To the tunnels!" Atacles stood in the middle of the street, waving his arms wildly. The firestorm was raging all around, winds whipping wildly down the streets as the flames sucked in more and more oxygen to sustain their rampage of destruction. Heliopolis, the ancient and holy Parnassan capital, was dying, and with it a millennium of independence.

Thousands were dead already, burned in the fires, crushed under the collapsed buildings. They were all Atacles's people, and each one who died took a part of the patriarch's soul with them. He knew he had failed them. Doom had come from the skies, from the depths of space, an enemy so terrible it almost defied the imaginations of the peaceful Parnassans.

Atacles realized even the scattered reports had been incoherent, incomplete. There was defeat and destruction everywhere, and what little false hope had flickered briefly in his mind was gone. He'd sent his warriors, few that they were, to the southern approaches, to attempt to strike the invaders as they landed, before they could organize and reinforce their spearheads. The closest landing point was in the great plain just beyond the city, and that was where the meager Parnassan army had launched its desperate attack.

Atacles longed to be on the field of battle, to die in arms, but he knew that couldn't be. His prescribed place was here, leading the rest of his people, doing whatever he could to keep them alive. And he knew it would fall to him to undertake the most hateful task of all.

To surrender his world—and beg their conquerors to have mercy for the defeated.

He knew that moment would come, when he would kneel down before the enemy, sacrifice what little remained of the quiet dignity he had possessed all his long life. His warriors had no chance. They would fight with all the strength they had, but they would die nonetheless. Any victory they won would serve to gain only a few moments for the surviving civilians to escape their dying cities. Then the enemy would overwhelm them and resume the relentless advance.

He respected his warriors, and he silently saluted their courage. He also envied them in a strange way, for their deaths would be quick, and they would come soon. They would have honor, and they would meet their ends weapons in hand, fighting to the last.

The situation seemed grim, but where there was a future, any future, there was always hope. If any Parnassans survived, even in bondage, it kept alive the promise of a better future.

At least that's what he told himself.

The imperial soldiers moved through the tunnels, firing at the terrified masses of civilians. The Parnassans had fled to the labyrinth of sewers and passages beneath the capital, but their flight was to no avail. The imperial forces had crushed the Parnassan army, hunting down and massacring every soldier who had borne arms . . . and many who had thrown theirs down. Then they swarmed into the cities—and then to the underground world where the people had gone seeking a final refuge.

Major Gav Korren stood in a small alcove, watching as his soldiers raced past, pushing deeper into the tunnels, rooting out the last of the holdouts. The city above was largely in ruins, half its buildings destroyed in the firestorm that was only now dying down. The imperial soldiers had gunned down hundreds of civilians, shooting any who didn't surrender immediately. They had captured thousands more, penning them in make-shift camps just outside the ruins of their city.

He could hear gunfire up ahead, no doubt his soldiers taking out some last pocket of resistance. Or just getting carried away and blasting a few civilians who looked at them funny. It didn't matter to Korren. Imperial conquest was never gentle, but then neither was the empire's rule.

Korren had seen it all as a junior lieutenant in the Eighty-Second Legion. Revolt in the empire was crushed with merciless brutality, and rebels were punished severely, not the least by the soldiers sent to restore imperial control. Korren had experienced a full-scale sack twice: on Eudoria as a corporal and on Junkara as a freshly promoted junior officer. He'd enjoyed it more as a noncom. Officers were expected to exercise a bit more decorum than the enlisted personnel. That didn't mean he hadn't partic-ipated fully in the sack of Junkara, but it paled next to his mem-ories of the unrestrained orgy of debauchery and destruction he'd experienced as a junior noncom on Eudoria.

A long time, and long way, from this shithole.

He heard more sounds from down the tunnel, and he stepped out of the alcove and pushed his way forward. The pas-sage widened into a large underground chamber. At least three dozen Parnassan civilians were standing around, hands in the air under the leveled rifles of a squad of Korren's troops.

He walked up and took a look around, his eyes settling on the sergeant in command. "More prisoners," the noncom reported without being prodded. "And some kind of leader, sir." The sergeant looked to the side, at a tall, older man standing near the wall, guarded by two privates. "He says he is the patriarch, whatever that is."

Korren turned and walked toward the prisoner. He didn't expect his sergeants to understand the hierarchy of Parnassus. Their job was to follow orders, not to think. But Korren was a battalion commander, and he had thoroughly studied the mission briefs. The patriarchs were quasi-religious hereditary leaders. They weren't part of the normal government, at least not for most purposes, but they held exalted positions, and they could overrule most of the regular governmental bodies in a crisis. And if this was *the* patriarch of Heliopolis, he was a valuable prisoner indeed.

"What is your name, Patriarch?" he asked gruffly.

"I am Atacles, son of Misticles. I am the senior patriarch of Heliopolis." The man was injured, and his spirit was clearly broken. But still, there was a hint of pride left in his voice.

"Well, Atacles, son of Misticles, I am Major Korren, and you are my prisoner. Your world is lost, but if you cooperate, you may yet be able to save some of your people."

The battered old man stood silently for a few seconds, and Korren could see the last shreds of strength slip away. "I will cooperate, Major."

Korren nodded then he turned toward the senior noncom. "Sergeant, see that this man is taken to General Fuering's headquarters at once. It is essential that the general see him as soon as possible."

Fuering sat inside his command post, scanning the latest reports. The makeshift HQ had been a house of worship for the defeated citizens of Parnassus, but that purpose was now extraneous. The survivors of the invasion—just over half of the former population—were citizens of the empire now, and they had no further use for any gods beyond he who sat on the imperial throne. Still, the imperial commander was impressed with the structure and amused that it had survived the fires. *Perhaps,* he thought, *I shouldn't so quickly discount the locals' religion.* The cathedral was in the center of the worst-hit area, and for a kilometer in either direction, it was the only building still standing.

The conquest was almost complete. The Parnassan army had been destroyed, its scattered survivors hunted down and summarily executed. Every civilian who had resisted in any way had been put to death—often in graphic, public displays—and the terrified survivors had been imprisoned in the makeshift camps established around the burned-out cities.

Those who had survived would endure the inevitable sack that would follow the conquest. Fuering's soldiers were residents of the Far Stars, but they had been trained in the imperial ways. And central to the dogma of the empire's soldiery was the privilege of the victors over the conquered. The defeated would pay the price for their resistance, for their weakness, and the imperial warriors would run wild in a hideous display of murder, theft, and rape.

Fuering disapproved, at least on a practical level. He had no pity for those who would be killed and brutalized. But the seven days of unbridled license he would give his soldiers would cause more damage that would have to be repaired, and it would delay the work of turning the conquered planet into a productive part of the empire. It would spread disorder through his forces, something that offended his sensibilities. But the spectacle was a necessary one, a crucial part of the morale that sustained the imperial legions—and a lesson in obedience the people of Parnassus would not soon forget. Grandparents half a century hence would recount the stories of the terrible sack to their grandchildren . . . though perhaps they wouldn't speak of the fact that most of those grandchildren would have the bloodlines of imperial soldiers. He looked up from his reports. There was something going on outside the makeshift office. He stood up and walked to the door, sliding it open and stepping out into the anteroom.

A dozen soldiers stood around a cluster of prisoners. Most of the Parnassans looked like they had been beaten or abused in various ways. Fuering's eyes, though, dismissed them all except one, immediately locking onto a tall man standing close to the center of the group. His arm was clearly broken, and he held it up against his chest. There was semidried blood all around his mouth and nose, and a deep cut just over his left eye. But there was a dignity about him Fuering noticed at once, a bearing that identified him unmistakingly as the leader of the group.

"This is Atacles, General," the officer commanding the guard detachment said crisply. "He is the patriarch of Heliopolis . . . and the highest surviving official on Parnassus. He is here to offer the planet's surrender."

Fuering stared at the Parnassan with frigid eyes. "Speak, Parnassan. What have you come to say?" His words were cold, hard.

"I have come to negotiate the surrender of Parnassus, General."

Fuering held his stare. "Negotiate?" A caustic laugh slipped through his lips. "There will be no negotiation, Patriarch. The planet is already ours, as you can see. But I will allow you to acknowledge our complete control at once. I will also allow you to throw yourself on my mercy, and if I'm sufficiently convinced, I might accept. No matter what, you *will* announce to all Parnassans that the planet affirms imperial rule.

"If you do not, my soldiers will kill all your people . . . and leave this planet a silent graveyard."

Atacles stared back for an instant, but it was clear he was a broken man. "Very well, General . . ."

"Kneel when you address me, Parnassan," the imperial said coldly.

Atacles hesitated for an instant, but then he dropped prostrate before the general. "I agree to your terms."

Fuering stood for a few seconds, basking in the moment. He had been a mere legion commander when his force had been assigned to accompany Lord Tragonis to the Far Stars. Now he was an army commander accepting the surrender of an entire world. He liked the feeling, the power. He could feel the rush of it, the satisfaction, and it made him lust for more. He longed to crush more enemies, conquer more worlds, to stare down on the broken enemies brought before him . . .

"Very well. You will go with this man." Fuering gestured to an officer standing along the edge of the room. "He will take you to one of the surviving planetary broadcast centers, where you will direct your people to cease all resistance and to obey any commands given to them by imperial personnel."

Atacles rose slowly, standing before Fuering. His resistance was gone, his dignity destroyed. He would do whatever his new masters ordered.

"Yes, General," he said miserably. He turned and walked toward the officer. He winced in pain as a pair of soldiers took hold and shackled him.

Fuering watched as the old man was led slowly from his presence. He turned to face another officer standing next to him. "See that his message is broadcast planetwide, Major."

"Yes, General," the officer replied. He nodded and began to move toward the door.

"And, Major?"

The officer stopped abruptly and turned back toward Fuering. "Sir?"

"When you have finished with the broadcasts, the prisoner is to be summarily executed. Standard procedure."

"Sir!" the officer snapped smartly, turning back and marching from the room.

Fuering stood silent and still for a few minutes. The old man didn't seem dangerous, but imperial policy was clear. No one who took up arms against the empire, nor anyone who commanded such personnel, was to be spared. The sooner the people understood their new reality, the easier things would be. For all concerned.

And watching their patriarch die slowly, impaled just outside the largest of the camps, was certainly a clear message.

CHAPTER 7

RACHEN CREPT DOWN THE CORRIDOR, SLOWLY, QUIETLY. HE KNEW there were cameras everywhere, but that didn't concern him. The plasma blaster wasn't the only device surgically implanted in his body. The other wasn't a weapon, but it had proved to be a far more useful tool.

The distortion generator created the illusion of invisibility to anyone without the experience and training to notice the telltale imperfections. As far as any guards watching on surveillance systems were concerned, Rachen was a phantom, a ghost.

He walked quietly, his steps so light, even the guards posted along the hallway couldn't hear him coming. Rachen knew the soldiers were Celtiborian regulars, veterans of many brutal

campaigns, but he approached the first two completely undetected. He snuck behind one, slipping his arm around the
man's neck and twisting his grip hard, breaking the man's neck
and dropping him to the ground. By the time the second soldier reacted, Rachen was in the air, delivering a roundhouse
kick to the Celtiborian's temple, killing him instantly.

The assassin pulled them both aside, slipping into a small
room to one side of the hall. He searched them, grabbing a
keycard, a survival knife, and a pistol before slipping back into
the corridor.

He moved swiftly onward until he reached a heavy reinforced door. He slipped the keycard into the lock, and the hatch
slipped open. He crept inside and scanned the room quickly.

Two soldiers were on duty, sitting at adjacent workstations.
They both turned when the door opened, and they stared with
confused expressions.

"What the hell?" one of them said, blinking hard as he
looked straight at Rachen, seeing nothing but the false image
created by the distortion generator.

The other stood up and started walking toward the door. "I
have no idea. Maybe the lock is broken or some—" He stopped
suddenly as a large survival knife plunged into his chest.

His companion lunged forward, reaching for the alarm, but
Rachen was too fast. He grabbed the man's arm, pulling back
hard. There was a sickening snap and then the soldier cried
out in pain. His outburst was brief, however, as Rachen put his
hand over the soldier's mouth and pulled the knife from the
first soldier and across the other's throat, cutting deeply.

The Exequtori dropped the dead soldier and moved to sit in
his chair. His fingers raced across the keypad, pulling up the
security system override. His hand slipped down to his side, to

a small pocket sewn into his overalls. He pulled out a tiny data chip, and he slipped it into the port on the workstation.

Leaping out of the seat, Rachen ran back toward the door and out into the hallway. He directed a thought at the generator, cutting the distortion effect. The device had a severely limited charge, and Rachen wanted to save what he had left for his confrontation with Lucerne. He might catch the legendary marshal asleep or unaware, but he had to be ready for a fight. He was a skilled assassin, and his Exequtorum training told him never to underestimate a foe.

He moved a bit more slowly now, carefully, but he kept up a constant pace. He had to avoid detection, but he also knew his time was extremely limited. The virus he'd introduced to the Celtiborian security network should disable the cameras. To anyone watching in the control room, it would appear there was a hardware failure. In the absence of any hostile activity anywhere else, Rachen doubted they would panic. But they would send someone to inspect the system, and when they failed to report, all hell would break loose. He had to get to Lucerne. Now.

His hand dropped to his side, to the pocket where he'd kept the data chip. One more item was in there, a tiny weapon, a cross between a throwing knife and a dart. He took it slowly in his fingers, removing it carefully from its place.

It's time. He concentrated on the map of the palace he'd memorized, locating himself on the schematic. If his intel was correct, it was just around the next corner.

He'll have guards outside his door, Rachen thought. *At least two, maybe more.* He activated the distortion generator again and gripped the knife hard. *Okay, take them out and then through the door without delay. You've only got a couple minutes of charge left for the generator.* He wasn't worried about getting out. Once he killed Lucerne he could easily disappear, slipping into the ventilation ducts or somewhere else it would be difficult for the guards to find him.

Now is the risk, he thought.

Right outside Lucerne's quarters . . .

Augustin Lucerne had stumbled back to his chair, but he found he couldn't stay there any longer. He climbed slowly up again . . . only to slip to the floor when he tried to rise. He felt a pain . . . his knee, something sharp. The glass, he remembered. He had dropped his glass, and now was kneeling on a shard.

He took a deep breath and rose slowly to his feet, reaching out, steadying himself on the arm of his chair. The room was spinning, and he almost lost his footing, but he managed to regain his equilibrium. At least enough.

You're a drunk old fool, Lucerne. He stood a moment, steadying himself. Eliane's birthday had always been difficult, but it had gotten worse over the years. Time softened pain, perhaps, but regret only grew sharper with the passage of time. His life was one of obligation now, and little of the man he had once been was left. He had truly wanted to unite Celtiboria when he was younger, to build a legacy that would live on after he was gone. But now he existed only to complete that mission, to ensure that he left the Far Stars able to protect itself, to preserve the last independence in all man's dominions. His wants no longer mattered. There was no desire left, no satisfaction. Only duty.

He staggered over toward his desk. He knew he should just go back to the chair, to close his eyes and sleep off the brandy. Tomorrow would be another day. The cold demands of duty would take him again. He would shut away the sorrow once more, push it back into the depths of his mind. Thoughts of

Eliane . . . and more children, fantasies of years of hearth and home that might have been—it was an indulgence he allowed himself only rarely. The ice cold marshal would return in the morning, and the heartbroken husband, the sorrowful man missing his long-dead wife, would be back in his cage.

But there was something he had to accomplish tonight, with the vow still fresh.

Astra.

I have to do something about Astra. I cannot leave this burden to her. She is my daughter, but she does not have to succeed me. She has long believed that to be her obligation . . . and I have as well. But it is too much a price to pay. I will give my life to the confederation, but not Astra's. One of my officers can succeed me, a soldier who has stood by my side through the endless years of war. I did not get here alone . . .

He picked up a stylus and he began scrawling across the surface of the large tablet sitting on the desk. He stared at his hand, seeing double, and he slowed down, trying to concentrate. But his writing was still difficult, messy. He felt a wave of frustration, and he threw the stylus down hard at the desk, watching as it skittered off the edge and fell to the floor.

"Activate," he growled to his personal AI.

Activated, Marshal Lucerne. Awaiting instructions.

"Take dictation." His voice was soft, his words slurred and unclear, but the AI had a sophisticated speech recognition interface, and it understood his commands without difficulty.

Ready, Marshal.

He took a deep breath. His stomach was beginning to lurch . . . again. Augustin Lucerne could hold his liquor, but he'd had a lot to drink over the past few hours. A lot.

"Confederation succession plan," he said, speaking toward the nearest microphone. "I, Marshal Lucerne, hereby establish my final orders in the event of my death with regard to the succession to my offices and positions—as head of state of Celtiboria and president of the Far Stars Confederation and commander of its armed forces."

He paused, taking a deep breath, trying to fight off the nausea he could feel building.

"In the event that Arkarin Blackhawk outlives me, I hereby command that he be offered all my positions in their entirety." *Perhaps Ark will gain control over his conditioning before I die. It may be unlikely, but he is the best choice to follow me, to see my work completed. And there is always hope, however fragile and unlikely.*

"If he is willing to accept this charge, I hereby designate him as my successor, and I charge all personnel—military and civilian—to give him their complete loyalty as they would me."

He sighed loudly. That was the easy part. He knew Blackhawk was the most capable to succeed him, but he also realized his friend probably couldn't accept the role. He needed a real heir. But who?

"In the event that Blackhawk is unwilling or unable to accept this position, it is my wish that my generals meet and swear loyalty to my designated successor."

Many of them are worthy, he thought. Thirty years of war had produced an officer corps of tremendous quality. Augustin Lucerne realized he had been blessed with capable followers. *But only one can command . . . and he must be the best, the smartest, the most capable, one the others will follow, as they have me . . .*

DeMark. Rafaelus DeMark.

It was the name that kept resurfacing in his foggy brain, again and again. He wasn't the highest ranked, nor the longest serving of his generals, but he was the best. And he was a man of considerable self-control, one with the best chance to maintain focus, to resist the moral decay absolute power so often carried with it. *Yes,* the marshal thought again. *If Blackhawk cannot succeed me, it must be DeMark . . .*

"My officers are dedicated and capable," he dictated as clearly as he could manage, "and I have been beyond fortunate in the caliber of men and women who have rallied to my banner over the years. But only one can take my place, only one can lead the confederation into the secure future it must create for all the people of the Far Stars."

He sucked in another deep breath, savoring the cool air for a moment, grateful for the clearing effect it had on his fuzzy mind. Anything was helpful now, even if it was minuscule.

"Therefore, while all my officers and soldiers have my thanks and my eternal gratitude, my responsibilities and power must pass on to the person most able to continue our work without pause.

"It is essential that I leave my offices—and my sacred mission—to the man most capable to carry on in my absence . . . to the strongest . . ." *And DeMark is the strongest. The more I consider it, the surer I am.*

Suddenly, the lights went out, and Lucerne heard the door to his chambers slide open. He spun around, trying to restrain a flash of anger. "I said I was not to be disturbed."

"I am sorry for that, Marshal Lucerne, however I am afraid there was no other option."

The voice was unsettling, cold and totally without emotion. There was no anger to it, no obvious menace. But Lucerne felt a chill throughout his body nevertheless. It didn't make sense in the protected fastness of the palace, but a feeling of dread took him.

A wave of adrenaline swept through his body, and somehow he suddenly knew he was fighting for his life. He was still drunk, but his mind forced its way to clarity, and his soldier's reflexes took over.

"Guards!" he yelled, diving behind the chair as he did. He leaped quickly, strongly, but it was too late. He felt the impact as his body sailed across the room. It was soft, only a touch of pain. Like an insect bite.

Lucerne hit the ground hard. He was behind the chair, but something had hit him, and his hands felt over his body, searching vainly for the wound. His movement was slow, difficult. His muscles felt sluggish, heavy.

"I am sorry, Marshal, but your AI is deactivated, and your security system disabled. Your guards in the immediate vicinity have been terminated. They were not my primary target, but unfortunately, it was a necessary component of my mission."

The voice was moving closer. Lucerne tried to crawl toward the far side of the chair. *I've got to get my gun,* he thought, remembering the small pistol he kept in the wooden chest next to his chair. But his limbs were growing heavier, and he couldn't push himself forward. *Some kind of paralysis dart,* he thought.

His mind was racing, even as his body was failing him. He fell to the ground, managing to roll over on his back before he became completely immobile.

He knew then he was going to die. The concept of surrender had been anathema to him his entire life, but he had always been a realist as well. He was paralyzed, his security disabled, his guards killed. It was the end. After thirty years of war, of countless battles and a dozen combat wounds, Augustin Lucerne realized he was about to die—in his own quarters, deep in the palace at the center of his capital.

The marshal could hear footsteps approaching, but he couldn't see anything. The room was dark, save for the flickering light from the fire. *How?* he wondered. *How did this assassin penetrate all my security?*

He focused, concentrated on trying to move his arms or legs, but his every attempt was futile. He felt a wave of panic, but it only lasted a moment. Lucerne was a man of almost infinite resolve, but in recent years the exhaustion had been growing on him. Even as he struggled to find a way to survive, other thoughts passed through his mind.

Perhaps death is an escape.

"There is nothing to be gained by struggling, Marshal Lucerne. The dart contained a concentrated form of the venom of the Mycenean jackalfish. Indeed, paralysis is merely the first symptom of the neurotoxin. Death is inevitable—and there is no known antivenom." There was still no anger in the voice, no taunting. The assassin spoke to him in unemotional terms, as if he was discussing a business transaction.

Lucerne stared in the direction of the voice, but he still saw nothing. Almost nothing. For an instant, he thought he caught a strange shimmer in the air.

"Why?" Lucerne croaked, finding it more difficult to speak as the muscles in his throat began to stiffen.

"That is both a simple question and a complex one, Marshal. Fortunately, for me, it is quite straightforward. My master commanded your death, and I merely obeyed. As to why those orders were issued, I can only speculate. And I prefer not to traffic in rumor and ill-supported declarations. No doubt, you are aware that your success has created enemies."

"Sebastiani?" Lucerne's voice was weak, fading. *This must be a Sebastiani assassin. No one else could have gotten through my people.*

"No, Marshal, I'm afraid not. Though I understand the Sebastiani are quite capable . . . by Far Stars standards, at least. But the order I serve is far older."

"You are not from the Far Stars?" Lucerne's legs felt cold, and each breath was becoming increasingly difficult.

"No, Marshal, certainly not."

There was a dim flash of light, and suddenly, the emptiness in front of Lucerne was gone, replaced by a tall man wearing a tight black jumpsuit. His dark hair was tied behind his head in a long braid.

"You should be honored, Marshal Lucerne. It is a rare few who are targeted for assassination by the Exequtorum."

Lucerne gasped for breath. "The Exequtorum? But that is a myth, a legend to scare children."

"No, Marshal. As you can see, the Exequtorum is quite real. Indeed, we are one of the most ancient institutions of the empire."

Lucerne turned his head and stared up at the man standing over him. *Am I losing my mind? He was not there a few seconds ago . . .*

"I can see you are confused by my distortion generator, Marshal. It is indeed a rare item, the very leading edge of imperial technology. I doubt there is anything of its like in the Far Stars."

One, perhaps, Lucerne thought hazily.

"You are already dead, Marshal," Rachen continued. "As I said, the jackalfish venom is invariably fatal, and there is no antidote. Even if we were in the imperial capital on Optimus Prime, there would be no treatment that could save you. Yet, still, you have one last choice I will offer you, one final decision to make."

Lucerne lay still, concentrating on forcing air into his tortured lungs. His extremities were cold, numb—he couldn't move at all. The fear was gone, and only a vague sense of sadness remained. Thoughts of leaving Astra behind, images of what her future might be. *I didn't have time to finish my final orders,* he thought miserably. *What will happen to her?*

He was listening to his assassin, hearing the words on one level, while in his head his mind drifted. He saw an image in his thoughts, gauzy, distant. Eliane, young, happy, as she was when he'd first seen her so long ago in the marble halls of her father's stronghold. Was she beckoning to him? He couldn't tell. Was she there waiting for him, longing for him to join her? Or was he simply seeing what he wanted to see, the last hallucinations of a dying man?

"The venom paralyzes quickly. But death is far slower, and by all accounts, there is tremendous pain before the end." The assassin paused for a few seconds. "Your death was inevitable from the instant I received the warrant for your termination. Yet, you are a man of action, of honor by all accounts. I will leave you alone to face whatever torment awaits during the death struggle . . . or I will finish you now, quickly and with minimal pain."

Lucerne's mind was wandering aimlessly. His assassin's words were mixed with other thoughts, memories of long ago, images of Astra. As a child—and as he imagined her older, her face showing the strain, the sadness of a life of sacrifice and duty. *No, please,* he thought. *Astra, do not follow me, do not make the choices I have made.* And floating there, at the edge of his waning consciousness, was Eliane.

"Leave . . . me . . ." he whispered, his mind focusing briefly on his assassin's words. His tortured voice was barely audible. He knew the visions in his mind were false, his memories of

Eliane, the images of Astra standing in his place. They were the last spasms of his dying mind. But he wanted to hold on to them, real or not. He would endure any agony for a few more moments with them.

He had left Eliane before, but now he would stay with her, as long as he could if she would have him. No pain could compel him to sacrifice a second.

He could hear the distant sounds of the assassin. "As you wish, Marshal Lucerne. Farewell."

There was nothing else. No words, no footsteps . . . but somehow he knew he was alone.

No, not alone.

Eliane is here.

CHAPTER 8

"LEAVING HYPERSPACE IN THIRTY SECONDS." LUCAS'S VOICE was crisp, clear. The *Claw* had made the run from Antilles to Vanderon in a single jump, and as far as anyone could verify, they'd done it in record time. Part of that was the extraordinary skill of its pilot. Lucas Lancaster had few peers at the helm of a spaceship.

But it was more than just piloting skill. Danellan Lancaster's improvements had turned *Wolf's Claw* into an unprecedented machine. Her hyperdrive, her reactor—even the reinforced structural supports that held her together during high g-force maneuvers—had been improved and replaced.

The *Claw* was now the fastest thing in the Far Stars.

Blackhawk sat back in his command chair. It was brand-new

and upholstered by the finest craftsmen on Antilles. Blackhawk appreciated the effort and expense Danellan Lancaster had lavished on his beloved ship, but truth be told, he missed his old chair. It was hard to replace a companion of ten years of action and adventure, even with the buttery softness of the finest Antillean leather.

He felt the usual feeling as the ship transited from the alien realm of hyperspace to the normality of man's dimension. Then the relief. He was a hardened space traveler, but he knew no one ever got truly used to traveling through an alien universe at thousands of times the speed of light—regardless of the bluster one tended to hear in spacers' bars. Blackhawk's symptoms tended to be light, but everyone became uncomfortable after a long trip through hyperspace. Sleep was difficult in the alternate dimension, and even when you did manage to drift off, the dreams were generally wild and very disturbing. And a single jump between Antilles and Vanderon was a hell of a stretch.

"Ace, send our greetings to Vanderon Control, and request permission to enter the inner system and land."

"On it, Cap." Unlike Blackhawk, Ace seemed to be enjoying the comfort of his own new chair. It was substantially plusher than the one it had replaced. Blackhawk tended to have a weakness for older things, even when newer and better replacements were available. But he knew Ace Graythorn was always ready to discard the outdated when something new came along. That applied to almost everything—seats, equipment, weapons . . . women.

Though that last part was in question now. Ace had generally defined a long-term relationship as anything that lasted until morning, but now Blackhawk wondered if that was changing.

He still wasn't sure more than a flirtation was at work between Ace and Katarina, but if there was, he was certain it would be a radical departure from any relationship Ace had ever had. Then again, Katarina Venturi was like no other woman the *Claw*'s exec had pursued. Indeed, she was like no other woman Blackhawk had ever known.

The matchup didn't compute for him at first, but then he'd thought about it a bit more—and suddenly it made sense in a bizarre sort of way. He found himself hoping the two managed to come together, though he wasn't sure he really believed they could manage something lasting. Still, they deserved a chance.

"And, Lucas, I want you ready to throw up the field and put us through some evasive maneuvers on my command. Just in case things go to shit." *Again. Something is going on with the bank. I need to find out how bad it is. And if they attack us, then we'll know.*

"It's ready to go, Skip," replied Lucas.

"We're getting a reply, Cap." Ace turned toward Blackhawk. "We are authorized to approach Vanderon." A pause. "They welcome us back."

Blackhawk's instincts tingled. Nothing about Aragona? He had been dodging the bank for months on the results of his previous mission. He'd used the *Claw* being laid up as an excuse for not continuing with his mission, but when Lucerne's people delivered the Castillan lord back to his home world, it had to raise eyebrows at the bank.

It was one thing for Aragona to disappear. For all the extraordinary talents of Blackhawk and his crew, abducting a well-defended target was a risky proposition. The possibility that the Castillan had been accidentally killed, his body lost among the others, was entirely plausible. But for him to appear again, and with some kind of unseen support that allowed him to reclaim his position in a matter of days? It made Blackhawk's earlier reports seem implausible to say the least.

In ten years of working for the bank, Blackhawk and his people had never failed in a mission, and certainly not so comically and completely as it appeared they had in the Aragona incident. He'd expected a communiqué from someone higher up, at least an inquiry. But standard approach and landing instructions?

Something is very, very wrong . . .

"Ace, I want scanners on full." He turned toward the helm. "And Lucas, be on the lookout for any place they could be planning an ambush. Don't take us too close to any of the planets or moons. I want you paranoid. Any dust clouds, comets . . . anything they could use to hide a fleet of ships. Keep your eyes open."

"Scanners at maximum power," Ace replied. "And I have the AI analyzing all incoming data for anything we miss."

Lucas punched hard at the keyboard of his workstation. "Plotting a course, Skip. I can keep us away from anything that would block our scanners, but once we get closer in there's no way to avoid concentrations of patrol vessels. You know how heavily they defend the approaches to Vanderon."

Blackhawk just nodded.

We'll cross that bridge when we come to it, I guess. Same with when we're on the ground . . .

We're walking into a trap. I know it. But what else can we do? We need to know what is going on with the bank. And I don't know any other way to find out.

We'll have to depend on the field to get us out of trouble. If the shit hits it, we'll just disappear—and Lucas will get us out of here. Then we'll know Kergen Vos controls the Far Stars Bank.

And that we're all seriously fucked.

"It is confirmed. *Wolf's Claw* has entered the system and requested permission to approach Vanderon." Vargus sounded nervous. He was still the chairman of the Far Stars Bank, and despite being subject to the whims of his new master, he was still one of the most powerful men in the sector.

But Arkarin Blackhawk made him nervous.

There was something about the rogue adventurer, something deeper he'd never been able to fully understand. He'd wondered about it before, but only academically. It had never seemed truly important. He and Blackhawk had always been on the same side. The bank had long been one of the biggest clients of the crew of *Wolf's Claw.* But now, Vargus suspected, that was about to change. And despite the fact that Vanderon was one of the strongest-held planets in the Far Stars, he found himself uncomfortable as the *Claw* drew closer.

"Grant them permission to approach and land." Sebastien Alois de Villeroi sat across from Vargus, just enough of a scowl on his face to make the banker nervous. He reached down to the table at his side, and he picked up the cut crystal glass that had been sitting there, taking a delicate sip of the pale green liquid. The Argosse was a highly alcoholic— and mildly hallucinogenic—spirit that Villeroi imported at enormous expense, all the way across the Void from his home world of Aquillar.

"This is fortune we could not have expected," the imperial continued, setting down his glass. "We have gone to such efforts to destroy Blackhawk, and now he delivers himself to us." He turned toward Vargus, and his voice deepened. "Issue a coded order to the bank's patrol ships. As soon as *Wolf's Claw* clears the orbit of the fourth planet, they are to attack at once."

Villeroi took a deep breath. "And let us take no chances with such wily prey. Commit every vessel . . . and once engaged, all ships are to continue to attack until *Wolf's Claw* is blown to atoms, regardless of their own losses."

Vargus just nodded, and he activated his comm unit to give the necessary orders. He detested the imperial agent. He found Villeroi's mere presence to be unsettling, but there was nothing to be done. He hadn't been able to come up with a way to expel the imperial when he'd just been the representative of his largest depositor. Now that Vos controlled the bank outright, he realized he was truly stuck with the psychopath.

"The orders have been issued," he said nervously. "*Wolf's Claw* will be ambushed as soon as it passes the orbit of the fourth planet of the system. The patrol fleet has been ordered to concentrate as much as possible without raising undue suspicion."

"Excellent." Villeroi leaned back and took another drink of the Argosse. The spirit was banned on many worlds, including Vanderon, largely because of its hallucinogenic effects, but the imperial agent had never allowed the mandates of local ministers to influence his actions, even in the heart of the empire. He certainly wasn't going to make an exception for the provincials in the Far Stars. He took his orders from Governor Vos, and from the emperor, of course, but as far as he was concerned, everyone else could eat shit.

The governor had ordered him here to keep an eye on Vargus, and to make sure the bank did as he bade. Killing Blackhawk and his whole godforsaken crew of troublemakers would be a bonus, one he was sure would earn him the governor's gratitude . . . and the rewards that would surely follow.

You stuck it out too far this time, Blackhawk. Now you die.

"Shira, better get down to the turret just in case. If things go bad, we're going to engage the field and make a run for it, but we may still have some fighting to do." He paused. He needed Ace on the bridge . . . and Tarq had been his usual backup for the turrets. The giant had been a surprisingly good shot, an especially bizarre fact since his twin brother couldn't hit a planet the ship was sitting on. But Tarq was gone, sacrificed to the needs of the moment by the commander he'd worshipped. Blackhawk knew that bit of self-flagellation was an oversimplification, but he didn't care. He still blamed himself entirely.

"Ask Katarina to man the other turret," he said, his voice grim.

"Yes, sir," Shira replied simply, softly. Her tone said everything.

"We're approaching a concentration of Vanderoni vessels, Skipper. Just beyond the orbit of the fourth planet. I can change course, but it will be a highly suspicious maneuver." There was a lingering sadness to Lucas's voice. Blackhawk knew the entire crew was thinking about Tarq. But there was something else too. A hint of concern?

"Worried, Lucas? You think there is something wrong?"

"No, Skip. I guess I'm just cautious." Blackhawk could see Lucas was staring at the scanners intently.

Blackhawk looked down at his own screen. There were a lot of ships nearby, that was true. More than normal, certainly. But it was nothing terribly out of the ordinary. Still, he didn't like it. And the fact that Lucas didn't either confirmed his suspicions.

He sat quietly for a moment, watching the image of his

ship on the scanning display, moving steadily toward what he strongly suspected was a trap. *Pull away now,* he thought. *Make a run for it.*

No. You have to see this through. If the empire has gained control of the Far Stars Bank, you have to know for sure. The marshal has to know. As soon as possible.

"Stay on course, Lucas." He flipped the comm channel. "Sam, we may be heading into trouble. I need you on top of all that new hardware. We may be running the field and the engines full out at the same time."

"That shouldn't be a problem, Captain. Everything is running perfectly, and I'm watching all of it. I'll make sure you've got the power you need."

"Thanks, Sam." Blackhawk closed the channel, and he sat quietly for a few seconds. Sam was like a daughter to Blackhawk, but the *Claw*'s engineer had always had a prickly demeanor when talking about her engines and equipment. That was gone now, replaced by a straightforward earnestness. Blackhawk knew Sam felt Tarq's loss as keenly as anyone, but he could feel her sympathy toward him too every time they spoke. Of everyone on the *Claw,* she seemed to appreciate most just how deeply Blackhawk himself had been hurt by the decision he'd made, how heavily he bore the guilt for Tarq's death.

He appreciated the thought, and it only made him love her more, but all she managed to do was remind him how things had changed. He found himself longing for her old snarkiness. For anything that made things feel the way they had before.

"Passing the orbit of planet four now, Skip." Lucas's voice was tense. The pilot's tone all but said that the Far Stars Bank had already declared itself as the enemy. But Blackhawk had to *know.* Was this some kind of business dispute, something Danellan Lancaster had provoked somehow? The magnate had been incredibly helpful over the previous few months, but Blackhawk didn't put it past him to get into some kind of dispute with Chairman Vargus. Indeed, he hoped that was the case, because the alternative was terrifying. If Kergen Vos truly controlled Vargus and the bank, the imperial boot was on the neck of the entire Far Stars economy. And Blackhawk had no idea how to counter that.

"Picking up energy readings from the bank vessels, Cap." Ace's voice was sharp, crisp—just as it always was when a fight beckoned.

"Lucas . . ."

"I'm ready, Skip. As soon as you give the word." The pilot was hunched over his board, waiting for the order to engage the field and begin evasive maneuvers.

"They're launching missiles, Captain." Ace's head snapped toward Blackhawk's chair. "Definitely an attack."

"All right, Lucas . . ."

"Captain," Ace interrupted, "I'm picking up ships emerging from hyperspace. Multiple contacts."

Blackhawk sat bolt upright in his command chair. *Who the hell is this?* Did the bank fleet have ships in reserve in hyperspace? No, there was no way they could have timed their emergence.

But then who?

"Captain, we're picking up a communication from the arriving fleet."

"Put it on the speakers, Ace."

The *Claw*'s old speakers had been worn, and they'd rattled and distorted the sounds they broadcast, but the new system was perfect, and every word coming in was crystal clear.

" . . . repeat, this is fleet captain Jeran Nortel aboard the Celtiborian cruiser *Warrington*. The vessel *Wolf's Claw* is under my protection. No attack is to be made, and all ordnance already launched is to self-destruct at once. In the name of the Far Stars Confederation, I warn that any ships taking offensive action against *Wolf's Claw* will be attacked and destroyed."

"Still no response, Captain. Repeating your message on all channels."

"Thank you, Lieutenant." Nortel sat grimly in his chair staring straight ahead. Firing at the ships of the Far Stars Bank was a daunting prospect, but Nortel was fully prepared to do it. His problem wasn't his willingness to escalate. It was the fact that his ships were still out of range, and *Wolf's Claw* was right in the middle of a trap. He'd already decided he'd avenge Blackhawk and his people if the bank fleet destroyed the *Claw*. But that wasn't why he was here. He had come to save Blackhawk and his people, and he was far from sure he'd arrived in time to manage that. *Unless I can intimidate these bank spacers.*

"Put me on the fleet comm, wide broadcast and unencrypted."

"Yes, sir." Lieutenant Harcourt sounded crisp and ready for action. Nortel was pretty sure the newly minted lieutenant had never been in a situation this tense, and the young officer's performance was reinforcing his belief that he'd done the right thing in pushing the former ensign's promotion through.

"Attention all Celtiborian vessels. Any ships firing on *Wolf's Claw* are to be marked and engaged as soon as we enter weapons range. And ships involved in any attacks on *Wolf's Claw* are to be destroyed. No quarter will be offered. We came here to find the *Claw*, not to fight. But if the bank's fleet wants a battle, by Chrono, we will give them one. All ships, arm weapons and proceed at flank speed."

Nortel stared over at Harcourt and made a slashing motion

across his neck. *Well, that probably exceeded my authorization, but it's the only thing I can think of to try and back them off. And if they call my bluff, I'll be the man who starts a war between the Far Stars Bank and the Far Stars Confederation. But desperate times . . .*

"Captain, *Wolf's Claw* is gone!"

Nortel felt his stomach clench. "Destroyed?"

"No, sir. Not as far as I can tell. She just disappeared. One second she was there, and the next she was gone."

"Could they have jumped into hyperspace?"

"Negative, sir," Harcourt replied. "We're not picking up any signs of entry." A jump into hyperspace left an extremely identifiable radiation trail.

Nortel sighed hard. "Get us there, Lieutenant. Now. I want every watt we can squeeze out of the reactor going to the engines."

"Yes, sir."

Nortel stared at the display. *Where the hell did you go, Blackhawk?*

"Bring us around, Lucas. Get us behind." Blackhawk's eyes concentrated on his display—on the three enemy ships that had fired. The battle trance had taken him, and he was focused on destroying his enemies. His initial plan had been to make a run for it, to get out of range of the attacking vessels so the *Claw* could jump back to hyperspace. The instant the patrol ships had fired, he had the answer he'd come for: the empire controlled the Far Stars Bank. He had to get that news back to Marshal Lucerne. But then the Celtiborian ships appeared, and the tactical situation changed in an instant.

"Coming around to their blind spots in ninety seconds, Skip." Lucas flipped a switch and activated the shipwide comm. "Everybody hunker down, we're going to have about a minute of high-g maneuvers."

Blackhawk felt the force of the *Claw*'s thrust pushing him back hard, and he appreciated the new chair much more. The heavy padding and shock absorption were far superior to that of his worn old seat. He could see on the display that the *Claw* was blasting at almost nine g's, and that would have had him fighting for consciousness on the nonrefurbished *Claw*. He knew Lancaster had upgraded the force dampeners too, but this was the first time he was experiencing the results. And they were damned impressive. He guessed the crew could survive at least fifteen g's now, and he shuddered to think what a pilot like Lucas could manage with that kind of thrust—assuming Sam could keep the engines running at that sustained output. Which he bet she could, at least for a while.

"All right, Shira, Kat . . . we're coming around." He hesitated. Operating the engines at full with the field on had been a nonstarter before, but his ship had had two rounds of massive upgrades in as many years, and her new reactor put out more than twice the energy the old one had. But charging the lasers as well was still beyond the *Claw*'s abilities.

"As soon as Lucas cuts the engines, charge your guns." He paused, feeling an urge to de-escalate, to hold back rather than attack the ships of the Far Stars Bank. But the time for restraint was past. They had fired on him, and now it was time for them to discover what happened when people fucked with the *Claw* and its crew.

"As soon as you have a full charge . . . fire."

"Captain, I can't explain it, but I'm picking up laser fire." There was confusion in Harcourt's voice, and surprise.

"The bank vessels? What are they shooting at?"

"No, sir. Not the bank vessels. Something is shooting at

them. One of them just blew, sir. And another is almost gutted. Whoever is shooting at them, they are accurate as hell."

Wolf's Claw. But how?

It didn't matter—there was a fight going on, and they were in it. "The fleet will engage the bank vessels as soon as we enter range." Nortel stared straight ahead, his face a mask of rage. He was taking a lot of responsibility on himself, but things were already going to hell—and his anger was driving him now. All his people felt the same thing. He didn't know how the bank figured into everything that had happened, but Blackhawk was an ally. And that was all he needed to know.

"Entering range now, sir."

Nortel didn't move. His eyes were fixed on the forward display.

"All ships . . . fire."

"Prepare to drop the field, Lucas. We need to make contact with the Celtiborian flagship." Blackhawk's throat was dry, his voice hoarse.

"Ready, Skip."

The battle had been raging for almost an hour. That hadn't been constant fighting—combat in space involved a lot of acceleration and deceleration, punctuated by short bursts of fire.

As he normally did when in a fight, Blackhawk felt the strange combination of free will and partially controlled conditioning driving him. But what he saw from the Celtiborians . . .

They had fallen upon the bank's fleet in a wild frenzy. Their warships hadn't hesitated, hadn't communicated beyond their initial, ignored ultimatum. Blackhawk had never seen Lucerne's people so bloodthirsty. They had lost three of their own vessels as they relentlessly pursued the remnants of the bank's forces, but they hadn't let up a bit, and now they were chasing the last survivors, and closing on Vanderon itself.

"Drop the field now."

Lucas's hands moved over his workstation. "Done, Skip."

Blackhawk activated his comm unit. "Attention, Celtiborian vessel *Warrington*. This is Arkarin Blackhawk in *Wolf's Claw*."

"Captain Blackhawk, this is fleet captain Nortel." The voice came through the speakers, and the instant he heard it, Blackhawk knew something was terribly wrong. "Please switch to your most secure channel. I have something highly sensitive to report to you."

Blackhawk looked over at Ace and nodded. "Double encryption activated, Captain." Ace's voice was deadpan, no sign of his usual cockiness. Whatever the Celtiborian captain had to say, no one on the *Claw* expected it to be good news.

"We're on a secure channel, Captain Nortel. Please proceed."

There was a long pause, as if the Celtiborian officer was having trouble saying what he had come to say. Finally he spoke, his voice soft, grim.

"It's Marshal Lucerne, Captain Blackhawk." Another pause, one that made Blackhawk's stomach twist into a knot. "He was assassinated, sir.

"He's dead."

CHAPTER 9

BLACKHAWK STOOD ALONE IN THE GREAT ROTUNDA OF THE PAL-
ace. The room was an extraordinary display of Celtiborian
power and majesty. It had been restored to the magnificence
of centuries before, when Celtiboria had last been a united
planet, and the entire place shone, from the polished marble
of the floor and walls to the great clerestory windows circling
the dome. Great shafts of white morning light reached down to
the floor, illuminating the patterns of carefully cut and placed
bits of black and white stone.

And, of course, its majesty was overshadowed by the pall of
Marshal Lucerne's death.

There were crowds outside the colossal double doors, great
pulsating throngs. Thousands. No, hundreds of thousands.

The soldiers and civilians of Celtiboria had gathered together for a last look at the man who had united them all, who had dared to dream of a greater future for them and their children. They were somber, silent, come together to share their pain and loss. They waited to pay their final respects, gathered outside the bolted doors, while one friend bade a solitary farewell to another.

The *Claw* had landed that morning . . . and Blackhawk had come right here. No, not right here. He'd made one other stop first. He'd found Astra in her quarters. She'd been locked in there for days, refusing to see anyone except Lys. Her foster sister had been as devastated as she was by her father's death, and the two had sat together for long hours.

Astra had answered the buzz at her door with a shout that she wanted to be left alone, but when she heard Blackhawk's voice on the intercom, she opened it immediately. "Oh, Ark . . ." she'd said, her words mixed with tears. Then she'd just stepped forward, and he'd taken her into his arms. They didn't speak again for a long while. He just stood there, holding her tight. There was nothing to say, no words that could ease her pain . . . or his.

He'd stayed with her a long while—and he would go back soon to check on her again. But he needed to be by himself for a while—a last few moments with his old comrade.

"Oh, my old friend," Blackhawk said sadly, "we have been in so many fights, walked so many battlefields. We always ignored the threats against us, didn't we? We knew that danger was our trade, that death stalked us always. Yet it never seemed real. We mourned those who died around us . . . died for us, but *we* always seemed to survive.

"Until now."

It still doesn't seem real, Blackhawk thought sadly. As he stared at the great clear coffin holding the perfectly preserved body of Marshal Augustin Lucerne, he reached out and put his hand on the smooth surface of the plastic material. *You were the first who accepted me, who helped me when I was running from the monster I had been. The creature they had made me into. Without you I would have been lost twenty years ago. All I have become, the two decades I have held back the vicious creature inside me . . . none of it would have happened without your friendship and support. All I am today, I owe to you.*

"Thank you, Augustin, my friend. Thank you for all you have done, for being the man you were. The human race produces few men of your quality, and I fear it will be a long time before it sees your like again. Your strength served others, and though you accumulated more power than anyone in the Far Stars, always you remained true to your ideals. You won victory after victory, and through all your conquests, you were never corrupted. I wonder if you ever truly appreciated how rare that is, how special it made you."

Blackhawk stood quietly for a few moments, his mind drifting back over the years he'd known Lucerne. Finally, he sighed softly and said, "They told me you designated me as your heir." He paused, sucking in a deep breath. The grief inside him was overwhelming, and he struggled to contain it. Lucerne was dead, but Blackhawk still felt as though he was letting his friend down, and he had to force the words out.

"I cannot accept, my friend, and I know you understand why. If I took your place, I fear I would destroy all that you have done. No, worse. I would begin with the desire to continue in your footsteps, but the power would destroy me. I do not have that inner strength that made you who you were. I would end up a tyrant. The voices are all still there, Augustin, the compulsions, no matter how much I try to banish them. Were I to accept the rule of the confederation, the danger would be too great, and I fear I could not resist in the end. I know, you probably never heard me say it. But I *am* scared. I would embrace my role as your successor, but before all was done, I would fall from the path, and such darkness would I wreak, it would be better that you had never been born. For Celtiboria, for the Far Stars . . . for Astra . . . I must say no."

Blackhawk turned and looked up at the ornate ceiling fifty meters above. "No," he repeated, "I will not risk destroying your legacy." He paused, struggling to maintain his composure. "All you worked for, sacrificed for . . . it deserves a more reliable steward than me."

He looked through the clear plastic at Lucerne's face, serene now, perhaps for the first time Blackhawk could recall. "But I will watch, my friend. I will not allow anyone to challenge Astra, or to put her in danger." His voice was hardening, grief giving way momentarily to anger and determination. "I will kill anyone who threatens her, Augustin. Whatever happens, however she moves forward, I will be there in the shadows watching, protecting her. No one will harm her while I still live, my old friend. If it takes my own life to save her, then so be it. I give you my word on that."

He put his hand on the coffin, his fingers pressing lightly against the smooth cool surface. "You were the best man I ever knew, Augustin Lucerne, and it has been my honor to have called you friend."

Blackhawk pushed back vainly against the grief. Lucerne had been that rarest of creatures, a man true to his ideals. For him to die at the hands of an assassin was an injustice of epic proportions.

"Rest, my friend. Set down all your burdens. Leave them to us, to your friends and loyal allies who mourn your loss and who stand together, ready to carry on your dream."

Katarina Venturi walked slowly down the hallway. Soldiers patrolled everywhere, but they ignored her. Astra Lucerne had granted her unlimited access to the palace.

She was searching for signs, clues—anything to give her insight into who had killed Marshal Lucerne. The Celtiborian authorities had already investigated the area, but Venturi brought a different perspective to the task: the keen senses of a Sebastiani assassin.

How would I have gained access to the marshal's quarters?

It was a daunting prospect, even to an adept of the famed Sebastiani guild. Katarina's victims had been a different sort than Lucerne, a venal cast of characters made vulnerable by their own vices and immorality. She had often used seduction to gain access, but she doubted such tactics would have worked with Lucerne. The marshal had no doubt had his mistresses, but he didn't seem the type to be easily manipulated by a pretty face.

She'd reviewed the files on the murdered guards. Whoever had killed Lucerne had taken out eleven of them, too. Most of those had been killed in hand-to-hand combat or with their own weapons. Indeed, from everything she had seen, the assassin had been unarmed save for the tiny dart he'd used on Lucerne.

Anybody who could kill eleven armed Celtiborian veterans without a weapon was a dangerous adversary indeed. The assassin had managed to disable the automated security system, probably with some kind of customized virus, but Katarina couldn't figure out how he had managed to sneak up on so many guards.

Why didn't the soldiers see him coming and respond?

She continued down the corridor, toward the assassin's entry point. He had come in through the ancient tunnels beneath the city. As tight as Lucerne's security had been, that had been a weak spot, one she suspected she too would have employed.

It was heavily guarded now.

Walking down the stairs to the subbasement, Katarina followed the killer's path in reverse. He had apparently blown a small hole through the sealed portal blocking the palace from the labyrinth below the city, and she wanted to see it. She didn't know if it would tell her anything, but she was damned sure going to take a look.

She worked her way through the bowels of the underground maze until she reached her destination. The hole was small, and fairly regular—no ragged edges. It didn't look like the work of any explosive. A laser? No, this assassin traveled light, and a laser big enough to cut through this stone would have been a hundred-kilo behemoth.

She crouched down, inspecting the edges of the hole. *Something melted this rock. This looks like the work of some kind of plasma torch or weapon.*

Katarina stared for another few moments, thinking. Why would an assassin who could smuggle in a heavy laser or plasma gun face all the guards without a weapon? It didn't make any sense. Anyone who could have brought something like that could have packed a pistol at least.

Suddenly, she felt a cold feeling in her gut, almost a sense of dread. Katarina Venturi was as cool as they came, a stone-cold assassin and a woman of enormous intelligence. But now she felt an urge to run back up to the palace, to flee from this place.

The Exequtorum, she thought, trying unsuccessfully to hold back a shiver as she did. She knew of the Exequtorum, at least as a legend. The Sebastiani guild produced the most capable assassins in the Far Stars, but the oldest lore told of another group of killers, one far more ancient. The histories spoke of the emperor's private brotherhood of assassins, and of the amazing abilities that had been attributed to them over the centuries.

There had been an image in the Sebastiani School, a detailed mosaic of a member of the Exequtorum firing bolts of lightning from his fingertips. She had always considered the image to be apocryphal, a myth and nothing more. But now she began to wonder.

What are we facing here? Could the emperor's assassins be in the Far Stars?

She felt another shiver. Then she stood up and headed back toward the palace, her mind lost in thought.

"There is nothing to be gained by delay, so I will come right to the point." The man was smartly dressed, his impeccable blue business suit almost advertising his status of a man of wealth and power. "Marshal Lucerne's achievements have had a remarkable impact throughout the Far Stars, and his untimely death creates a dangerous vacuum. Many of us involved in the commerce of the sector wish to ensure a timely succession by a man who has priorities that align with ours. For all his brilliant success, the late marshal was somewhat of a dreamer, always pursuing unrealistic goals. It is time now for strong leadership to pursue more reasonable initiatives."

Carteria the Younger sat quietly. He'd taken the meeting with this businessman, but he was nervous about it. After his father's death, the warlord had signed a peace accord and served Lucerne loyally, more or less, but now everything had changed. Someone would step into the marshal's shoes. He hadn't considered making a play for power himself, not until now. But Blackhawk had declared he would not accept the marshal's position, and Lucerne's wishes in that eventuality were far from clear. The Final Orders, found on his AI, were incomplete, lacking a successor's name and referring vaguely to "the strongest." Carteria knew that phrase was being taken out of context. The last thing Lucerne would have willingly done was left behind a call to civil war, challenging his generals to fight among themselves, destroying all he had built in the process. Yet that seemed precisely where they were all heading.

Unless Astra Lucerne could sustain a bid to follow in her father's shoes.

"I appreciate your taking the time to meet with me, Mr. Houser. However, I would submit that many of the marshal's followers will rally to Astra Lucerne's banner, regardless of the fact that the revised Final Orders do not designate her as his heir. Challenging her would be very difficult . . . and dangerous."

Houser nodded slowly. "Indeed, you are correct, Lord Carteria. Such a move would have to be carefully planned and well funded. Which is why I have come to offer you the full backing of the Far Stars Bank. We are prepared to provide you with unlimited credit . . . to arm and equip your forces, and to assist you in, shall we say, persuading others to join your coalition." The banker paused for a few seconds, allowing all he had said to sink in.

The full and unconditional support of the bank . . .

It was an unprecedented offer. Indeed, for the thousand years of its existence, the bank had never before openly supported any claimant without limits.

"Your offer is extremely tempting, but as I said before, I am reluctant to challenge Astra. She is a very capable woman, and extremely intelligent. And even those who question her lack of direct military experience are fond of her. They would rally to oppose any attack made against her."

"But you misunderstand one aspect of the proposed plan, General. I am not suggesting that you challenge Astra Lucerne."

"Then what are you suggesting?"

"I am proposing that you wed her and rule as the marshal's legitimate heir. After, how shall I put this . . . dealing with any potential rival claimants."

Carteria sat silently for a few seconds . . . then burst into laughter. "That is a pleasant idea, Mr. Houser. A union with Astra Lucerne would solidify any general's claim to succeed the marshal. And she is an extremely beautiful woman. Unfortunately, she detests me. She was against the marshal's decree recognizing my position in return for surrendering my father's forces, and I fear her opinion of me has not changed. Any kind of alliance is highly unlikely, much less a marriage, even one based more on politics than affection."

"You misunderstand me again, General Carteria. I am not proposing you *court* Astra Lucerne. The marshal's daughter is an accomplished woman by all accounts, but as you noted, she is not a soldier. She cannot hope to hold the confederation's armed forces together and direct the campaigns necessary to realize her father's dream. She must ally herself with one of the generals, an experienced soldier who can lead the army and effectively command the respect of the ranks."

"I agree with your logic, Mr. Houser, but I am the last person Astra would select, even if she did seek an ally or a spouse. She would choose any one of the other top generals over me."

"You are assuming she is given a choice. I am not proposing half measures, General. Your forces are all located on Celtiboria. Many of the marshal's oldest and most loyal units are scattered throughout the Far Stars, engaged in combat operations or garrisoning worlds newly admitted to the confederation. No doubt this is because the marshal did not trust you and your soldiers to the extent he did others, but his untimely death has turned the tables, leaving you with the largest available force currently located near the capital. Many of the other commanders are here alone, with only token guards, their armies light-years away. The time for a move is now. Such an opportunity will not present itself again."

"You are suggesting a coup?" Carteria was surprised . . . but interested as well.

"I am suggesting that you reclaim your destiny, your birthright."

And that was the crux of it. Carteria's family had been one of the most powerful on Celtiboria. Before the Lucernes changed everything.

Houser pressed on. "Take the fruit hanging at your grasp, before one of the others does. Rally your soldiers, use our funds to bribe key personnel. Then strike, eliminate your rivals while they are defenseless. And take Astra as yours—by force if necessary. Wed her in the rotunda in a ceremony broadcast throughout the Far Stars Confederation. Once she has given you a few heirs you may do as you wish. Keep her as a plaything . . . or dispose of her. By then your position will be secure. You will rule the Far Stars. And you will have avenged your father."

Carteria just nodded. It was incredibly tempting. But it wasn't the morals that really concerned him at the moment . . . it was fear. Even with the bank's unprecedented aid, any grab for power would be a gamble. And failure would mean death.

"You paint an attractive picture, Mr. Houser, but I fear the reality is far more complex. For one, what about Arkarin Blackhawk? He is a formidable man. He may have refused to succeed the marshal, but if I make a move against the others, will he just stand idly by? And if I seize Astra, force her to marry me . . ." The affection between Blackhawk and Astra Lucerne was a poorly kept secret. The adventurer had refused to rule at her side, but no one doubted he would come after anyone who threatened her. And Arkarin Blackhawk's enemies had a way of ending up dead.

"Don't worry about Blackhawk, Lord Carteria. I can assure you he will not be a factor." There was a malevolence in Houser's voice that had not been there before. "If Marshal Lucerne could be eliminated, so can Arkarin Blackhawk. And when he is dead, along with your rivals among Lucerne's other generals, the road shall lie open before you."

Carteria returned his visitor's gaze as understanding slowly crept into his mind. "Are you certain about Blackhawk?"

Houser smiled broadly. "Oh yes. I am certain. Captain Blackhawk's life is now measured in mere hours. He shall have the honor of dying by the same hand as his friend, the marshal.

"By this time tomorrow, Arkarin Blackhawk will be dead."

He turned his head and stared at Carteria. "Will you be ready to follow your destiny?"

Rachen sat quietly on the floor of the small room he had rented. He was deep in meditation, as was his wont after completing a mission. Its purpose was to reinforce the discipline that made him so effective: to endure pain, boredom, and fear. These skills allowed Rachen to do the impossible: penetrate an invincible fortress, kill one of the most heavily protected men in the Far Stars, and slip back out . . . all unseen.

So now he was centering himself, refocusing, regaining his mental sharpness. Like his brothers, Rachen spent most of his time honing these skills and maintaining his conditioning. Usually he'd have a long period of time in which to do this, since the Exequtorum were called upon only to eliminate the emperor's most dangerous and highly placed enemies. It was rare for them to have more than one mission in a year, and typically many months elapsed between assignments. But Rachen had been dispatched to the Far Stars not to target one man, but to kill two.

Arkarin Blackhawk was a shadowy figure, a difficult man to track across the vast space of the Far Stars, but Rachen had a plan.

It is easier to draw prey to you than to go on the hunt. There had been no doubt in his mind the death of Marshal Lucerne would bring Blackhawk back to Celtiboria. And so it had. Now it was time. Time for Arkarin Blackhawk to follow his friend in death.

Rachen needed different tactics this time. He had exploited the unknown weaknesses of the palace security, but now every corridor was guarded by combat veterans, and heavily armed patrols scoured every centimeter of the massive complex—including the ancient passages and utility tunnels below. And his plasma weapon and distortion generator would take weeks to recharge. No, he couldn't get in again the way he had. He needed something different.

Something simpler.

The assassin was clad in normal Celtiborian clothes. He would blend in with the mourners, with the hordes of Lucerne's subjects gathering in front of the palace, walking slowly past his coffin. Blackhawk had been seen more than once among the crowds honoring Lucerne. And that was where Rachen would strike.

He would never get a normal weapon past the heavy security, but he didn't need a gun or a knife. He would work himself close enough to attack, to take Blackhawk down with a poisoned dart just like the one that had killed Lucerne. Then his part in the drama of the Far Stars would be done. The assassination was his only part of the operation. The brothers of the Exequtorum did not involve themselves in the machinations of the empire's intelligence agents or its military. Still, he knew his attack on Blackhawk would be the signal for a much larger initiative. As soon as he struck, Carteria's coup would begin, and troops would be in motion throughout the city.

There would be chaos—and Rachen would simply vanish into the crowd.

"Marshal Lucerne's last orders are clear. In the event that Captain Blackhawk declines to accept the succession, his position should go 'to the strongest.'"

Carteria doesn't have any friends in this room. Rafaelus DeMark's thoughts were dark. He didn't trust Carteria, and he'd cringed years before when Lucerne had spared him and commissioned him into the general staff.

Most of those gathered together were Lucerne's longtime subordinates, and they mistrusted the son of the most savage warlord Celtiboria had ever known. Carteria the Younger had surrendered to Lucerne after the death of his father, saving the thousands who would have surely died if the two factions had fought to the finish. Lucerne had agreed to include the vanquished lord and his soldiers in the new Celtiborian army, but he'd never been able to get his officers to fully accept Carteria. It had been years now, and most of those present knew the former warlord had become bitter and resentful.

"Please, Carteria, we all know that is not what the marshal meant," Arias Callisto said. "He did not finish dictating his Final Orders, but the last thing Augustin Lucerne would have wanted was his generals fighting each other over the succession. Surely, he was referring to the commander he considered the strongest and, for whatever reason, he never finished his dictation. Perhaps he was still thinking, considering which of us to designate." General Callisto's tone was angry, condescending. Of all the generals, he detested Carteria the most, and the feeling was reciprocated with equal intensity. Their mutual hatred was a poorly kept secret throughout the army.

Callisto had declared more than once he'd have refused the warlord's conditional surrender and continued the fight until Carteria's faction had been wiped from the face of Celtiboria. Indeed, he and Carteria had almost fought a duel, stopped only by Marshal Lucerne's absolute orders against such sorry a spectacle as two of his generals fighting each other.

"Who, General Callisto?" Carteria spat. "You? That would be convenient, wouldn't it? And if Marshal Lucerne had intended to nominate a specific successor, why not Astra? We have long assumed she would succeed her father. Can you explain why his Final Orders make no mention of her? Perhaps because he realized that only the most capable man here could see his dream fulfilled."

Callisto's eyes flashed with rage, and DeMark put his hand on his friend's arm. "Both of our esteemed colleagues speak truth," he said. "We cannot know what Marshal Lucerne intended, though we can deduce several things. Astra is clearly her father's rightful successor, and I cannot imagine the marshal intended anything else."

He paused and looked around the table. A dozen generals were gathered, the cream of the Celtiborian command staff. Most of them had rushed back home when they'd gotten word of the marshal's death. They had come alone, or nearly so, leaving armies behind on worlds throughout the sector, entrusted to subordinates while the future of Celtiboria and the Far Stars Confederation was decided.

DeMark was quite aware Callisto was a hothead, as likely to call out Carteria as discuss matters rationally with him. Although DeMark didn't like the former warlord any more than his friend did, he was a more controlled man. And he knew Carteria was in a strong position. DeMark's soldiers were still on Nordlingen, and Callisto's mostly on Rykara. That was true of most of the others he trusted as well—their soldiers were deployed across the Far Stars. Augustin Lucerne had sent his most trustworthy generals, and his best troops, to the target worlds, to serve as viceroys and military governors. As the confederation expanded, more and more of the best Celtiboria troops had been sent off-planet, leaving behind mostly reserve units and less reliable formations.

That strategy had left Celtiboria itself vulnerable. Perhaps not while Lucerne was alive. Even Carteria's soldiers would have refused to defy the marshal himself. But now that he was dead, the situation was far more fluid—and dangerous, ripe for a power struggle.

DeMark looked around the table, trying to gauge the reactions of the officers present. If Carteria was planning to make a bid for power, he wanted to be ready. And he needed to know who he could trust. Callisto, certainly, but who else?

I need more time.

"We must adjourn soon to attend the marshal's funeral. I therefore propose that we resume this discussion tomorrow, and that we devote the rest of this day to a celebration of Augustin Lucerne's life."

Callisto nodded. "Indeed, Rafaelus. Today is for the marshal."

Most of the men around the table nodded, but Carteria just leaned back and smiled . . . and DeMark's blood ran cold. Even as he tried to stand up and stop Carteria, the younger general's hand slipped under the table, reaching for something. DeMark saw it, but too late to interfere. Carteria held a small controller in his hand . . . and DeMark watched helplessly as his thumb calmly depressed the single button.

A second later, the doors on both sides of the room slid open and his soldiers poured in.

By Chrono . . .

Blackhawk wandered around the edge of the massive room, looking out over the flood of humanity filing past the coffin of his comrade. Once more he couldn't help but think of all Lucerne had accomplished.

You led with such strength and determination, my friend, yet you inspired such love and devotion from those you ruled over. You made their lives better, even as you fought your wars to build a more secure future. I wonder if you ever realized how extraordinary a feat you achieved, even if you didn't live to see it completed. There have been few like you in history, Augustin.

He moved slowly, deep in thought. He knew he shouldn't be

out wandering alone among the crowds, but he felt he owed this to Lucerne. To see—and feel—the adoration of these people for a man he respected so greatly.

The captain looked over the mass of humanity, at the somber movement of the mourners. There were faces wet with tears and expressions of desperate grief as they shuffled past his coffin. Augustin Lucerne had always worried that he was nothing but a tyrant, but the grief rising from the crowd told a different story. For three hundred years, these people and their ancestors had lived under the warlords. Their towns and villages had been destroyed in petty wars between feuding lords. Their fathers and brothers had been press-ganged into the armies. They had eked out survival while the vast production of their farms and workshops had been confiscated to support the pointless wars and lavish lifestyles of the nobles who ruled over them.

Lucerne had fought his entire life to free them from such random brutality. He had worried he was no better than those he replaced, but Blackhawk—and these people gathered now to bid him a tearful farewell—knew better. His armies had the same ceaseless hunger for manpower as those of his enemies. But Lucerne's wounded soldiers received the best care he could provide, while the armies of the warlords provided minimal care. Lucerne discharged his disabled veterans with pensions large enough to support their families; his foes cast aside their crippled soldiers to beg in the streets or starve with their helpless families.

The marshal had brought little but more war to a planet that had seen nothing but for three centuries. But he provided something else as well, something that had been long absent from Celtiboria.

The dream of peace.

Blackhawk had long respected his friend, but now his cynical nature was pushed aside for a brief moment, and he looked out on the sea of people who truly mourned their lost leader. He stood silently and watched them move slowly past Lucerne's coffin, tearful faces full or mourning . . . and a shadow of fear, too—concern over what would happen next.

Suddenly, he felt something, a chill, and his eyes caught motion in the crowd, something that didn't feel right. Then . . .

"Ark, run." It was a scream so loud and forceful it ripped across the massive room like a blast of thunder. It was Katarina, and she was racing toward him, pistols in both hands.

Blackhawk's reflexes reacted at once, and he leaped to the side, even as he focused on the threat. It was a man. He looked like the others, the mourners who were just beginning to turn into a terrified mob. But there was a difference. His eyes. They were cold. And focused like lasers on Blackhawk.

Even as he lurched aside, Blackhawk saw the motion. The man had something. A weapon? His arm moved quickly, almost blindingly—a throwing motion. Something was coming right for his chest.

Blackhawk's midsection twisted, trying to avoid the projectile, or to absorb the hit someplace less critical. His powerful muscles jerked his falling body hard . . . but not hard enough.

He felt the impact on his side. It was lighter than he'd expected, less painful, more like an insect sting than a bullet or a knife. He hit the ground in a perfect combat roll and pulled himself up, drawing his own pistol as he did.

His eyes focused on his attacker . . . but the man was gone. He blinked and looked again, but there was nothing. How? How could he have moved so quickly?

Then he felt strange—stiff, heavy—and he fell to his knees. He struggled to move, to hold his shooting arm up, and a second later he dropped to the floor.

"Ace, help Ark!" Katarina's voice, firm, commanding. Blackhawk turned his head toward the sound, and his eyes caught a glimpse of her dashing into the crowd. He'd never seen—felt—such pure feral determination. The Sebastiani assassin was in control of her now, chasing after his attacker. He almost pitied the man.

Almost.

"Ark, are you okay?" It was Ace, leaning over him. "Are you hit? I don't see any blood."

He tried to turn toward his first officer, but he couldn't. "I'm all ri—" But he wasn't. His throat was tight, his chest heavy. Something was wrong. Something was very wrong.

"Ark?" It was Ace, but it sounded like he was far away.

"Ark!" Softer, more distant, yet more insistent, too.

Then nothing.

CHAPTER 10

"THERE ARE SOLDIERS EVERYWHERE. THEY'RE FIGHTING ONE another. It looks like some kind of coup attempt is under way." Shira was running back toward Blackhawk and the others as she spoke.

"It doesn't matter, Shira," Ace snapped back. "We have to get Ark to the hospital now." Ace was holding the stricken captain by the shoulders, and Sarge had his feet. "It's his only chance."

"No," Shira yelled, her head snapping around and scanning the crowd as she did. "We'll never get through. And we have no idea who those soldiers are supporting. It's no fucking coincidence that some assassin takes a run at Ark just as the city descends into chaos. That hospital may be controlled by enemies. Or we could get be attacked by a mob in the street. We could be taking Ark into a death trap."

She stared hard into Ace's eyes. "We have to get him to the *Claw*. Doc can deal with this." She didn't sound too confident about the last part . . . and Ace looked even more doubtful. Blackhawk was white as a sheet and completely paralyzed. He was still breathing, but barely. From what Ace had heard of Lucerne's assassination, it sounded disturbingly similar.

"Okay, Shira." Ace turned toward the giant standing behind him. "Grab the captain, Tarn." Ace handed Blackhawk off to Tarnan, and he slapped at the comm unit on his collar. "Lucas, I need you to get the *Claw* off the ground. The city is going to hell in a hurry, and the captain is hurt. We need to get him on board. Now!"

"Where are you?" Lucas responded, the tension in his voice clear even through the comm unit.

"At the palace. There's a garden out behind. It's more than big enough to set down the *Claw*."

"On the way, Ace. Be there in a flash."

Ace stood up and looked around. The crowd had gone wild. Most of them had stampeded when the shooting started, and several dozen were hurt, trampled by the boots of their neighbors.

There were sounds of shooting, some close, more off in the distance. He could see what looked like a squad running down the street. While he was watching, one of them dropped to the ground. The others stopped and opened up on a building, trying to target the sniper who'd picked off their comrade.

Ace could smell buildings burning, and he could see columns of smoke rising over the city. "Let's go. Behind the palace.

We need to hook up with Lucas and the *Claw*. There's a fucking civil war erupting right in front of us."

Tarnan and Sarge carried Blackhawk. The big man could have managed it easily by himself, but Sarge didn't look like he had any intention of stepping aside, and no one suggested he should. Shira followed behind, staring carefully around and covering the group. She'd reached for her rifles half a dozen times, but they weren't there. The *Claw*'s crew had Astra's authorization to carry weapons in the otherwise highly secure rotunda, but Blackhawk had discouraged it. He felt it was disrespectful to Lucerne. Only Katarina had ignored his suggestion, having slipped a pair of pistols discreetly under her shirt.

"Ace," Shira yelled, "move it! What the hell are you waiting for?"

Ace stood still, staring off into the crowd, in the direction Katarina had run. She'd just taken off into the mob; she hadn't even looked back. But he'd caught a glance of her face as she bolted. He'd seen that expression before. She was on the hunt, chasing after the assassin who had attacked Blackhawk.

He knew she could take care of herself, but still, he wanted to go after her. He felt his legs tense, and he almost ran in her direction. But he realized he had no real chance to track her down. Ace could hold his own in a fight, and he could pull a scam with the best of them, but trying to track one assassin who was chasing another was out of his skill set.

Besides, with Blackhawk out of action, he had to take command. Things were bad, and it looked like they were only going to get worse. He couldn't run off half cocked chasing Katarina. Not now.

Take care of yourself . . . please.

"Ace!" Shira again, her voice farther away this time.

He sighed hard and took one last look. Then he turned and chased the others toward the LZ. The shit had just hit the fan.

Again.

Blackhawk was lost, floating in emptiness. There was no pain, no fear. He had no conception of time passing, only a vague awareness. He remembered being in the rotunda . . . then the shout. Katarina. Yelling to him. A warning.

He had reacted, instinctively, without thought. But he was too late. He'd been hit, the pain. No, not really pain, just a pinprick. He wasn't hurt, at least not that he could feel. What he felt was . . . strange. There wasn't a better word for it. Fatigue, heaviness. His muscles stiffening. Falling to the ground. Unable to move. People everywhere screaming, running. Then someone leaning over him. Ace. Sounds, gunfire, crowds screaming, Ace's voice, speaking to him. It was all distant, fading away, almost unreal.

> **You were struck by a weapon that introduced a toxin into your system. The effects you feel are that of the poison.**

He knew that voice. The AI, Hans, the entity in his head. The nickname was a shortened version Blackhawk used to identify his internal AI system, HANDAIS—an acronym for "heuristic algorithmic nanotech dynamic artificial intelligence system."

Poison? Weapon. Yes, of course . . . the man in the crowd. Katarina's warning.

> **Affirmative. The unidentified man was an assassin attempting to kill you, probability 96.5 percent, +/- 2.2 percent. The weapon was a small dart, likely easily concealed, which would explain how your**

assailant was able to get it past Celtiborian security undetected. Analysis of your bodily functions suggests a potent neurotoxin.

I am paralyzed? Unconscious?

The agent has induced a state of near-total paralysis on your motor functions. Your respiration and heart rates are extremely low. My analysis of the substance is, of course, limited to that possible using your own body's systems. I would not characterize your current condition as unconscious, though I do not believe you are able to communicate externally. I postulate that your own enhanced immune system has induced a comalike state to sustain life and divert remaining bodily energy to combating the effects of the alien substance.

What kind of poison? Blackhawk was struggling to remain coherent, but he could feel himself slipping away despite his efforts.

I am unable to identify the specific source of the toxin. My analysis suggests a compound with a 100 percent fatality rate in normal humans. However, I cannot effectively compute the survival prospects for a specimen with your own special abilities. Even now, your system is working at an efficiency level far above human norms.

Will I survive?

Unknown at present.

A pause, very uncharacteristic for the AI in Blackhawk's brain.

**I am sorry, but I do not have sufficient information,
either on the chemical itself or the details of your
peculiar genetics and the enhanced capabilities of
your bodily systems.**

Blackhawk's last hold on consciousness was fading. *The thing almost sounds apologetic,* he thought as his mind slipped into darkness. *I must really be fucked.*

The sounds of gunfire echoed off the walls as men dove for cover and fought with whatever weapons they had. There were screams—of surprise, anger, pain. It was like a nightmare unfolding around them all, but the blood and death were real, not the phantoms of a dream.

Moments before, the room had housed a summit meeting, a gathering of Marshal Lucerne's top commanders, met to discuss the future of the Far Stars Confederation. Now, it was a chaos, the first battle for the future of the confederation.

There was blood everywhere—on the floor, the table, the walls. The soldiers had burst into the room, assault rifles drawn, but they hadn't fired immediately. Carteria had intended to take his colleagues hostage, at least initially. He saw no downside to keeping them alive, and one or two might yet prove to be useful or corruptible. They could always be executed later if they proved to be of no value. But the men around this table were not the type to yield easily, especially not to treachery.

Arias Callisto had been the first to act. He drew his pistol in a blinding motion, ignoring the guards and aiming his shot down the table toward Carteria. His adversary acted just in time, diving to the side as Callisto's bullets slammed into the chair where his head had been an instant before.

Then all hell broke loose.

The guards opened fire, even as the other generals reached for their sidearms. DeMark leaped to his feet and pushed with all his strength, overturning the metal table and diving behind it for cover.

He held his pistol over the edge of the table, firing in the direction of the renegade guards. The soldiers were more heavily armed, but they were in the open, and now DeMark and his comrades had some cover. Callisto dropped down next to him, bleeding from half a dozen wounds, but still active, gun in hand and a look of disbelieving rage on his face.

It looked like half the generals were down already, but five or six were still active, taking temporary cover behind the table. The guards were on the other side, against the wall, firing full.

"Push forward," DeMark screamed. "The table. Push!" He threw himself into the underside of it, and his colleagues followed his lead. It was heavy, but six men pushed with every bit of strength their adrenaline-charged muscles could manage. It was slow at first, but eventually the table flew forward, slamming the line of soldiers hard against the wall. Men fell, and assault rifles tumbled to the ground.

"Now," DeMark shouted. "Follow me!" He took advantage of the brief lull, and he ran to the door behind the small line of officers. He punched the controls, his fingers moving quickly, entering the override codes to open the lock. He heard the renewed sounds of gunfire, as a few of Carteria's guards recovered from their shock and began to fire again. Then the hatch slid open.

"Now! Everybody through." He waved his arm, watching as two of his colleagues dove through the portal. The rest lay behind the table, silent and unmoving. All save Callisto, who was on his knees gasping for breath, but firing steadily too.

"Arias, now." He reached out and grabbed the back of Callisto's jacket, pulling hard and practically dragging his friend through the open door. He shoved Callisto completely through and he turned toward the access plate on the other side, entering the code again, locking the door behind. The hatch slammed shut hard, but not before DeMark felt a burning sensation on his thigh. He looked down to see the blood soaking through his pants leg. He was pretty sure it was a flesh wound, which he could live with.

It still hurts like hell.

The other two officers were standing, looking to DeMark for direction. "Go, both of you! Try to find loyal units and occupy the key facilities in the city." They both nodded and ran down the corridor.

DeMark leaned down over Callisto, staring into his stricken comrade's eyes. "C'mon, Arias. We have to get out of here."

"No," Callisto said, struggling to get his words out over the gurgling sounds. There was blood on his lips now, more with each sound he forced out. "I'm done, Rafe." He held up his pistol, wincing in pain as he reached behind him and pulled his last clip free. "Just prop me up here, and I'll hold them off as long as I can." He slammed the cartridge in place.

"No way, Arias. I'm not leaving you."

"You have to," Callisto said, his voice a barely audible whisper. "You're the only one left who can stop him. You have to find some loyal troops . . . you have to destroy him . . ."

DeMark's eyes were moist as he stared at his friend and comrade in arms of twenty years. He wanted to argue, but he'd trained at the feet of Marshal Lucerne, and he knew duty came before all. Arias Callisto was going to die, no matter what he did. But he could give that death meaning, allow his friend to perish in arms, buying time for DeMark to escape to rally the troops and destroy the traitor.

"It has been a privilege to serve with you, Arias Callisto."

"And you, Rafaelus," Callisto managed to croak softly. "I would have served you . . . like I served him."

DeMark could hear the enemy firing at the door, trying to disable the lock and force it open. He had used the override codes, something he'd bet Lucerne had not entrusted to Carteria. But that would only buy Blackhawk moments, maybe seconds. He pulled Callisto back, propping him against the wall facing the battered door. Then he took one last look at his friend, and he ran down the corridor.

"The Celtiborians are scrambling ships from the spaceport." It was Lucas's voice on the comm, loud and heavy with tension. "I've got to get us off the ground, fast. We don't know who is in control down here. If those are enemies, they'll blow us to bits if we let them get close enough."

"All right, Lucas, get us somewhere safe." Blackhawk trusted Ace to take care of the *Claw* and its small family when he wasn't able to do it himself. He would do what he knew Blackhawk would want. But he wasn't happy about it.

Katarina is out there somewhere . . .

Ace was standing off to the side of the *Claw*'s single hospital station. He was staring at the back of Doc's head as the *Claw*'s medic worked feverishly on Blackhawk. The captain was deep in a coma, and his vital signs were so low the sick bay monitors could barely detect them. But he was still alive.

Ace's thoughts were frantic, worrying about Ark one instant—

*C'mon, Ark. You'll pull through this. You've got to—*and then . . . *Where the hell are you, Kat?*

He knew the answer, of course: she was after Blackhawk's attacker. And Ace suspected something else.

She was after the assassin who had murdered Marshal Lucerne.

A man dangerous enough to get to two of the most protected, capable warriors in all the Far Stars.

And she was all alone.

Dammit, Ark—pull through. Then you can decide what the fuck we're supposed to do.

"Hang on, everybody," Lucas shouted through the shipwide comm system. "We're lifting off in thirty seconds. If you're not strapped in by then, make sure you're hanging on to something."

"Doc?" Ace asked tentatively.

"I can't leave him now, Ace," Doc answered. He was bent over Blackhawk, working feverishly. Ace could see the sweat pouring over his face and gangly hanks of brown and gray hair hanging down his back, half soaked through. "I don't even know what's keeping him alive. By everything I understand, he should be dead."

Ace felt a rush of anger, but it quickly subsided. He knew Doc didn't mean anything by the comment, but the thought of Blackhawk dying, killed in a room full of thousands of people, with most his crew just a few meters away—it was too much to imagine.

"Just do what you can, Doc. The captain's tough. He'll pull through." *Keep their morale up, that's what Ark would want you to do.*

Of course, it would be easier if I believed my own bullshit.

He looked over Doc's shoulder. Blackhawk was completely still, his skin pale and waxy looking. It didn't look like he was breathing at all, but the monitors showed minimal respiration.

"I hope so," Doc answered grimly. "But if he does, it will

be more him than me." He turned back toward Ace. "I've analyzed the toxin every way I can think of, and the results keep coming back the same. I don't know where it came from, but there is no known treatment. No antidote, no antivenom." He paused and sighed softly. "If he pulls through, it's going to be his extraordinary constitution that does it. There's nothing I can do except keep him hydrated and pump some nutrients into him."

Ace just nodded and watched as Doc turned back to his patient. The crew had all seen Blackhawk do amazing things, pull through situations that had seemed hopeless. Perhaps he could do it again.

He has to.

Ace tried to be hopeful, but he couldn't escape the thought that Blackhawk was facing his greatest challenge. And there was no backup or support that would matter. This fight would take place inside the great warrior. Blackhawk would live or die now, and there wasn't a damned thing any of his people could do about it except watch . . . and wait.

"General Callisto is dead. So are Barstan and Arbela." Rafaelus DeMark was standing in the intersection, shouting to a small cluster of officers, his voice straining to penetrate the cacophony of battle all around. There had been fighting all day, in the streets, house to house.

DeMark had rallied all the troops he could. He'd managed to hook up with a few companies he'd commanded years before, during the final campaigns of the unification, but most of the soldiers who'd served with him were light-years away, struggling to keep Nordlingen under control in the face of its growing rebellion. It hadn't been a good time for him to leave that troubled world, but when word came that Marshal Lucerne had been murdered, he answered the summons and went home . . . to bury his friend and to sit down with the other senior commanders to take care of the succession.

The marshal's daughter had long been expected to succeed her father, though there had always been some minor grumbling. The army loved Astra Lucerne, and many an old sweat had a story to tell of the marshal's daughter bringing him a flask of water in the hospital or reading mail to him as he lay torn apart and sewn back together in a convalescent bed. Even those who hadn't had such experiences knew someone who had, and almost to a man the gruff warriors of Celtiboria had adopted their commander's only child.

But Astra, for all her ability and toughness, had never been a soldier, and in the shadows there had always been questions, doubts that she could completely fill her great father's shoes. Celtiborian women had the equivalent legal status of men, but in the provincial areas, from whence many of Lucerne's veterans had come, war was still considered the business of men.

And for all the unity Lucerne had created, there was no doubt in DeMark's mind: *we're still at war.*

Nevertheless, despite the confusing directives in Lucerne's Final Orders, Astra's wishes would carry great weight with the army. But DeMark knew she would need an effective partnership with a well-known general to secure her hold on her father's offices. That made her incredibly valuable—and extremely vulnerable as well.

If Carteria was making a true play for power—and it seemed certain he was—he would need Astra. He lacked the credibility of one of the longer-serving commanders, and much of the army detested him. But if he was able to force Astra to cooperate with him, he could overcome those disadvantages.

Force Astra. It seemed like an unreal prospect. DeMark had known her since she was a mischievous child, sitting quietly and watching with intelligent eyes as her father and his officers discussed strategies. He knew her too well to think she'd cave in to coercion, and certainly not from the likes of Carteria, whom she despised with a barely controlled passion.

She hated the bastard even more than Callisto had.

That only made DeMark more nervous. Astra was strong and defiant—and that could get her killed. Carteria would want her cooperation, but more important, he would never allow her to ally with a rival.

"I don't know how Carteria managed to gather so much support, but his forces are strong." DeMark stood in the center of his officers, a filthy and blood-soaked rag tied around the wound on his leg. His face was caked with grime and dried sweat. He had a makeshift belt strapped over his torn and dirty uniform, with two pistols and a dozen spare clips. He wouldn't be waging this battle from a plush command post—not that there was anything plush about Nordlingen. But there he was directing from the rear.

This fight required every available man.

"We may have to pull back out of the city. But we can't leave without Astra." He pointed back toward the palace. "Hain, I need you to take your men back there. Astra must be trapped somewhere, and we've got to get her out."

Major Hain Bolton had a rump battalion under his command, about four hundred veteran troops. At just over two meters tall, he towered over the command group. Bolton was a soldier's soldier, a man who had risen from the ranks through fifteen years of service in Marshal Lucerne's wars. As with everyone else in DeMark's small group, his loyalty was without question.

"Yes, sir." Bolton acknowledged DeMark's command, but he didn't salute. They were pretty sure their forces still controlled this section of the city, but it didn't make sense to take chances when any of the surrounding buildings could house a sniper.

Bolton turned to go, but he paused briefly and looked back at DeMark. "We'll find her, sir."

DeMark just nodded. He appreciated Bolton's earnestness, but he had a sinking feeling he was too late. Carteria's strength had taken him by surprise, and his enemy controlled the entire area around the palace. If Astra had managed to sneak out, Bolton's people might find her and get her back safely. If not, he'd just sent four hundred veterans on a hopeless mission, one likely to claim them all. But he couldn't just do nothing. He had to find Astra.

Everything hinged on her.

"Good luck, Major," he managed to add. He watched the officer jog off toward his soldiers for a few seconds, then he turned back toward the others. He was scared to death for Astra, but he had a war to fight—and it required everything from him that he had to give. It was starting to look like a lost cause.

But I haven't lost a battle yet . . .

CHAPTER 11

KERGEN VOS SAT AT HIS DESK, READING THROUGH THE REPORTS coming in from across the Far Stars. His plans were moving along, his tentacles spreading from one end of the sector to the other. Things were finally coming together. Nearly three years after he'd first arrived on this wild and defiant frontier, he felt as though final victory was at last within his grasp.

The army Lord Tragonis was building for him was taking shape, with new legions marching off the training fields and into action each month. Parnassus had been the first world to fall, but not the last. Novara, Amallah, Raettia—the black-and-gold banner flew over all of them.

The stream of incoming data was almost entirely positive. Word of planets surrendering, of armies fresh from the Kalishari depots moving out to conquer new worlds, of economic chaos spreading across the sector.

But there was one report that, despite its brevity, stood out above the others, one he had read half a dozen times.

Rachen's report had been succinct and to the point. *Mission one completed*, it read simply. Then just, *Marshal Lucerne terminated*. Six words, two phrases. But the impact was incalculable. Augustin Lucerne had been the greatest hurdle to Vos's plans, an enormously capable man and a constant threat. Now he was gone. For all his hundreds of thousands of soldiers, his brilliant mind, his fleets of spaceships, it had taken a single man to destroy him. Vos had heard the legends of the Exequtorum before, but he'd mostly discounted them as baseless propaganda. No longer. The work of his agents, the influence of his bribery and blackmail, the thousands of soldiers pouring forth from Kalishar every month—all of it combined had done less to further victory than Rachen's single deed.

Better still, his death left uncertainty in its wake, just as Vos had hoped. It was a perfect opportunity, and he'd already set the gears in motion to exploit it to the fullest.

He stared at the screen, reading Rachen's communiqué again. It was extraordinary news, and he knew he should be joyous, excited. But he wasn't. At least it wasn't what he'd expected it to be.

Kergen Vos had focused on his career as an imperial spy. He'd killed people—and ordered others killed. He'd betrayed those who'd trusted him, bought and sold human beings like they were playing pieces in some massive game. But when he thought of Augustin Lucerne—murdered in his quarters, lying hours on the ground before he was found—it felt somehow wrong to him. On some level, where the tailor's son still survived deep inside the man who'd become an imperial killer, there was grief for Augustin Lucerne. And respect.

I long ago chose my path, he thought. *And that choice means abandoning old ways, leaving behind admiration for selfless men like Lucerne. He was a fool,* he tried to tell himself. *He could have ruled like a king, like the emperor himself, but he never seized it. He just let it go, stood by while the opportunity slipped away.*

Vos wanted to ridicule Lucerne, to laugh at his foolish failure to make himself a king. But he couldn't. Part of him respected the Celtiborian soldier . . . and somewhere, deep inside, he envied him.

"You were a strong man, Augustin Lucerne. Had our lives taken different paths, had I come from your background and not the streets of a broken world drowning in misery and death, perhaps we would have been brothers in arms."

Vos was confused by his feelings, unsettled not just by their contradictory nature, but by the fact he was having them at all. He was a disciplined man, one who rarely let emotions and other weakness interfere with his plans. But there was something about Lucerne that made it hard for him to celebrate the man's death, especially at the hands of an assassin. Augustin Lucerne had deserved a hero's death, storming the last position in the last battle his armies fought—not lying poisoned on the carpeted floor of his bedroom.

Vos's ambitions had saved him. He had tasted destitution. He'd gone to sleep hungry, shivering as he lay on piles of garbage, trying to ignore the aching pit in his stomach. He'd seen his mother and father murdered by imperial soldiers, the shop his grandparents had built torched, completely destroyed.

He'd hated himself at first when he turned on the other lost children, sneaking around, listening for secrets to curry favor with the soldiers. He'd cried himself to sleep the first time he'd reported one of his companions. He'd stood silent, sick to his stomach, watching as the soldiers came and dragged the boy away. He'd tried to tell himself the prisoner was only a kid, that the soldiers would simply imprison him. But in his heart he understood—and he realized he might just as well have pulled the trigger himself.

Vos had become accustomed to the kinds of creatures who dominated the imperial service. Most of them had been born and bred to it, raised to take their place in the emperor's massive machine of oppression. They knew nothing else but cruelty and the ruthless pursuit of power.

Vos had emulated them, sought to remake himself in their images. He'd seen how the others fared, the meek dying in the streets, stripped of everything they had—and the rebellious, those who fought back, slaughtered at the hands of the imperial invaders. He had attained success he couldn't have imagined, gathered to himself power that would have shocked his youthful mind. *Why then do I feel this strange feeling, this guilt?*

He stared again at the report of Lucerne's death, fighting back the thoughts haunting him from deep within. *You were a better man than I, Augustin Lucerne. But would you have been what you were had you lived my life? You were a man of duty, of unselfish devotion to your ideals. But you grew up privileged, your father one of Celtiboria's minor warlords. You were raised in a stronghold, you ate your fill, slept each night in your own bed.*

You inherited lands and wealth . . . and over a thousand loyal fighting men. You never crawled out into the street, the stench of your parents' deaths thick in your nostrils. You never begged for food, fought for it. You didn't see the savages of an imperial sack, watch your people murdered and abused in an orgy of destruction. How would you have fared, I wonder, if you had been there with me, faced the choices I did? Would you have been so honorable, so incorruptible? Would you have died in the streets, true to your ideals, defiant to the end? Or would you have chosen survival, as I did?

No—I think you would have died, trying to save others or something equally honorable . . . and stupid. And that's why you are dead now.

You were an admirable man in many ways, but you were weak, too weak to face reality. You were loved by millions, and they mourn you now, but would their affection have endured had you lived? Or would they have blamed you for all their own misfortunes, for their own failed dreams? For your inability to live up to the unattainable standards your legend created? Would they have demanded ever more from you, sacrifice after endless sacrifice, until you had no more to give . . . and then despise you for your exhaustion?

Maybe I do not exult in your death, Marshal Lucerne, but I do not weep over it, either. For soon my flag will rise upon every capital, and I will sit in absolute control of the Far Stars.

Not bad for a homeless boy scouring the garbage for crusts of bread.

"Are you okay, Kergen?" Mak Wilhelm was a man of formal demeanor, and he almost always referred to the governor by his title. But the two had served together for years, and each was the closest thing the other had to a friend. And Wilhelm had a feeling Vos needed a familiar voice.

"Yes, Mak. I am fine." He paused then added, "I have been indulging a bit of foolish emotionalism, but I have put that back in its place."

Wilhelm just nodded. He understood what Vos was feeling. Service to an entity like the empire carried a cost, one he too had faced more than once. There were soulless creatures, monsters like Tragonis or Villeroi, who served without doubt, without conscience. But most men had to make their own peace with dealing out so much death and misery. The empire was a fact, and for many, serving it was the only way to escape destitution. Wilhelm was sometimes disturbed, not so much by the things he had done but by how easy it had been for him to do them.

"Shall we get to work, Mak? There is always time for pointless self-recrimination later." Vos looked across the table at his friend, and the two shared a momentary exchange of glances. For a few seconds, they were men like any other, friends sitting quietly together. And then Vos looked away, and they became servants of empire once more, pointless guilt and pity again banished to the deep recesses of their minds.

"Definitely, Governor. You are, of course, aware that Lord Rachen successfully assassinated Marshal Lucerne." He paused an instant and glanced at Vos. The governor's cold expression was back, doubts suppressed and the imperial enforcer back firmly in control. "This, obviously, is an extraordinary step forward for our plans. At worst, the Celtiborians are disorganized, giving us an opportunity to consolidate our recent conquests and invade other worlds without interference."

"And at best," Vos interjected, "it gives us an opportunity to intervene in the succession, to make a play for control of Celtiboria . . . or at least the destruction of its armed forces in civil war."

"Agent Houser is already in place, Governor, in cover as a representative of the Far Stars Bank. If everything has gone well, he has already approached General Carteria. Indeed, the power struggle on Celtiboria may already be under way. And of course, Chairman Vargus will endorse anything Houser promises, putting the full strength of the bank behind whatever endeavors we require."

"Excellent, Mak. I wish we had a more reliable tool than

Carteria, but unfortunately, Marshal Lucerne had an extraordinary type of charisma. We've been able to bribe some junior commanders, but not one of his senior officers appears to be corruptible. Save, of course, General Carteria."

"Nevertheless, with the proper amount of support, I believe Carteria will serve our purposes. "

"We shall see, Mak. I just hope he proves more reliable than allies such as the previous ka'al." There was distaste in Vos's tone. Wilhelm knew Vos had disliked the ka'al from the start, but he'd convinced himself to give the client monarch another chance. The result had been a debacle—the total failure to recapture Astra Lucerne and the destruction of more than half the Kalishari fleet.

"This situation is different, Governor. We have more direct control, more agents on the scene. Carteria is a puppet, a tool to serve our ends, nothing more."

"Perhaps. Though I would never underestimate the potential for fools to ruin even the best-designed plans." He paused, looking down at a small tablet on the table in front of him. "We will just have to wait and see how things progress. Meanwhile, let us review other matters. Including the original six planets of the imperial demesne, we now control twelve worlds openly, and another three through clandestine means."

"Yes, Governor," Wilhelm replied. "And invasion operations are under way on four additional planets, all fringe worlds. Of course, except for Galvanus Prime and the other initial imperial holdings, they are all fringe worlds. The six Primes remain independent still, along with all the midtier planets. Unless, that is, General Carteria is successful on Celtiboria."

"Everything appears to be going according to plan. And

with the demise of Marshal Lucerne and the subsequent confusion over his succession, we have little concern about confederation efforts to liberate any of the planets we have taken, at least for some time. Indeed, I have already sent orders to accelerate our attacks. Regardless of the eventual resolution of things on Celtiboria, we have an unprecedented opportunity to seize as much of the sector as we can right now."

"I agree, Governor. However, I will note we are quite constrained by transport capacity. As you know, our naval assets are still quite limited, even with the ships Lord Tragonis brought with him."

"That is true, Mak, but I have some good news on that front. We have finally managed to obtain a degree of control over the shipping guilds. We were able to finalize things while you were dealing with our friend Chairman Vargus. It was fairly messy, I'm afraid, and not without the shedding of blood, but there are now guildmasters friendly to us in charge of both the Starfire and Red Banner guilds. Your success in securing control of the bank was extraordinarily helpful. You'd be amazed how cooperative shipping magnates become when you offer them cheap and unlimited credit to fund the expansion of their fleets. And also show them the cost of refusal . . ."

Wilhelm nodded, an impressed look on his face. "I haven't read the reports yet, but thinking of some of the personalities involved, I have a good guess at where the blood came from."

"And you'd be right. But once the troublemakers were eliminated, things moved quite smoothly indeed. It's amazing how much a little blood can lubricate the gears of progress. That and a pile of coin." Vos smiled. "We will not be idle while events play out on Celtiboria."

Wilhelm sat back, feeling a sense of satisfaction push back

his earlier doubts. Progress was rarely free, and blood was usually spilled before anything truly worthwhile was accomplished. *But we are actually on the verge of success,* he thought. *We just need to make sure we keep this plan in motion.*

"Perhaps I should go to Celtiboria, Governor. Keep an eye on things."

Vos looked back at Wilhelm, shaking his head slowly. "No, Mak. No doubt you would be of enormous value there, but I have a different assignment for you, one that requires a man of unquestioned ability."

Mak felt a wave of curiosity. "What would you have me do?"

"Our new troops, Mak. They have had nothing but success, but they have fought only primitive armies, the militias and feudal levies of backward worlds of the frontier."

"That is true, Governor. Then again, our plan was always to secure the weaker worlds first."

"Very true, Mak. But we come closer to the final struggle, and we must be certain of what the new legions can achieve. We must know how they perform in battle against a strong enemy."

Mak was sitting quietly, wondering where Vos was going. He was as close to the governor as anyone but knew he was a man who liked to play things close to the vest at times. Vos didn't fail to surprise him.

"Nordlingen, Mak. I want to invade Nordlingen."

Wilhelm continued to sit still, trying to understand why. Finally he said, "But it holds no real value. And puts us deep into confederation space with hostile planets surrounding us."

"Yes. But there is a large Celtiborian expeditionary force garrisoning the planet, and that presents an opportunity. Our operatives have been extremely successful at creating disruption, and the Celtiborians have had their hands full dealing with terrorism and rebellion. If we can take Nordlingen, we not only take out a significant Celtiborian force, but also prove our troops *can* defeat such an army."

"The risks, though . . ."

"Are negligible in the grand scheme of things. If we win, yes, we'll be adrift in enemy space. But with all the discord, who will have the time to retaliate before we can secure the surrounding systems? And if we lose, it's of no great concern, because we're pumping out replacements in the Kalishari desert faster than the Celtiborians can recruit their own reinforcements. No, I'm convinced sending our troops to Nordlingen is the only logical move."

"So . . . what? You want me to organize the forces?"

"No, Mak. That is already done. Indeed, they are en route as we speak."

Wilhelm stared back, a confused look on his face.

"I want you to go there, Mak. I want you to take command of our soldiers and *lead* them for the first time against a force of Celtiborian veterans." Vos paused, noting the uncomfortable look on Wilhelm's face. "Yes, Mak, I know you haven't led ground forces in quite some time. But you are a gifted general . . . and a man I trust. I need you on Nordlingen. It is not possible to overstate the importance of the coming battle there. If we can defeat the Celtiborians on Nordlingen, we can do it anywhere."

He smiled broadly. "And if we can do that, the Far Stars are as good as ours . . ."

CHAPTER 12

"ACE, I NEED YOU UP HERE. NOW!" LUCAS'S VOICE WAS FRAZ-zled, almost frantic. The pilot had given them quite a ride, but he'd gotten them off the ground and into orbit in record time.

"On the way, Lucas." Ace stood still, staring at Blackhawk lying on the sick bay cot. Doc was next to him, red eyes fixed on the monitors. The captain was still alive, technically at least. He was in a deep coma, and Doc still had no idea why.

"Anything I can do, Doc?" Ace was still hesitating.

"No, Ace. There's nothing any of us can do but wait. His con-stitution is like solid hypersteel. If he lives, that's what's going to save him."

Ace just nodded. There was nothing to say. He turned and hurried over to the ladder, climbing up to the bridge.

"About time," Lucas snapped as Ace stepped the rest of the way up. "We've got trouble all over."

Ace was about to respond, but Lucas added, "How is the skipper?"

"Not good, Lucas. Doc says there's nothing to do but wait." Ace paused a few seconds then continued, "So what's the deal up here? It's not going to help the captain if we get the *Claw* blown to hell."

"Exactly. We've got Celtiborian ships firing at each other, Ace. All around the system. And it sounds like there's fighting on the orbital platform too." He turned and looked at Ace. "I don't know what to do . . . and I guess you're in command."

Ace walked toward Blackhawk's chair, pausing with his hands on the backrest. He looked down at the empty seat for a few seconds, but then he turned and walked over to his own station. He wasn't ready to sit in Blackhawk's place. *The captain will be back soon enough, and his chair will be waiting for him.* Ace wasn't sure he really believed that, but he needed to at least pretend.

"It doesn't look like we're going to be able to get back down to the surface any time soon." Katarina flashed through Ace's mind. *She'll be okay,* he thought. *This is what she does. She can blend in, disappear.* He was trying to put her out of his thoughts, to focus on what he knew he had to do, but it was difficult. She was one of the most capable people he knew, but that only went so far.

Especially considering the most capable person he knew was now down on the lower deck fighting for his life.

"Definitely not, Ace. Everything's going to shit around here."

Ace sat down hard in his chair and sighed. He didn't know what to do. *Chrono, we need Ark now.*

"Ships emerging from hyperspace, Ace! Looks like a big fleet. Transports and a phalanx of warships up front."

He jerked up. "Any ID?"

"Negative. There's still a lot of interference from the transition." Lucas snapped his head around. "Space around here is getting crowded, Ace. We better get the hell out of here until we can get an idea what is going on."

Ace sat stone still, his mind down on the surface, wondering once more where Katarina was. Even if they risked putting the *Claw* down again, there was no way they could find her. She'd have cast aside her comm unit and anything else that might be traceable. That decided it.

He had to take care of the rest of the crew, and do what he could for Blackhawk.

Ace took a deep breath, taking one last look at the semicircular image of Celtiboria on the display, and he turned toward Lucas.

"Let's get the hyperdrive warmed up and get in position for a jump."

"Got it, Ace." Lucas's hands moved over his controls. "Destination?"

Ace didn't know. Where? Where do we go?

"Antilles," he finally said. "Get us to Antilles as quickly as possible."

"Let's go, Lys. If we can make it to the tunnels, we have a chance to get out of here." Astra Lucerne was leaning against the hatch, her ear pressed against the cool metal. "It sounds quiet outside. This might be our best chance."

She glanced back at her friend, her eyes catching Lys's quick nod. "All right, let's go." Astra pressed her thumb against the security lock. She knew she was broadcasting her location, but she couldn't think of anything else to do. The palace was on total security lockdown, which meant all doors were locked and could only be opened with newly issued codes. But Astra had her father's old black-level overrides, and so far they had all still worked. Whoever had launched the coup, they were going to have to wipe the main computers clean and reload them from the ground up to shut down the back doors Lucerne had put in his security system.

The hatch slid open, and Astra whipped her head around, looking quickly in both directions. Then she slipped out into the corridor and turned left. She'd only been to the tunnels once, but she remembered exactly where the closest entrance was located.

She had a small pistol in her hand and a knife tucked in her belt. Astra Lucerne had no intention of being captured alive. She'd either get out, or she'd die fighting. *They're going to want me alive,* she thought. *But I'll be damned if I'm going to back whatever treacherous piece of shit is behind this.*

Astra moved swiftly, and she could hear Lys running just behind her. She was trying to be as quiet as possible, but speed was more important. She was sure the enemy would be looking for her, and she had no time to try to disable the security systems. *They're probably watching us right now,* she thought . . . *so move your ass, Lucerne.*

She slowed down as they came to an intersection. The entrance to the tunnels was right around the corner. Just a few more meters . . .

And then her heart sank.

A quick glance back at Lys confirmed they had both heard it. Sounds around the corner. Guards, most likely. Between them and their way out.

She instinctively checked her pistol, confirming she had a full cartridge ready, and she looked back at Lys. "Ready?"

Her foster sister nodded grimly, her hands gripped around an assault rifle she'd pulled off a dead soldier. "Ready," she whispered.

Astra nodded and leaped out across the open corridor, firing as she sailed through the air to the other side. She'd taken the soldiers by surprise, and she was already across before they reacted. She was pretty sure she'd gotten one—but there were at least ten of them.

She glanced across at Lys. The two exchanged quick nods, and they crept around each corner, firing down the hall, raking the guards. They'd hit three or four before Astra realized there was no return fire. *They're not shooting at us. Of course . . . they want me alive.* But something didn't quite make sense.

They won't just sit there and let us gun them down forever . . .

She heard a clanging sound. Then another. Her eyes darted to the ground. Stun grenades. "Lys," she screamed as she dove to the side, away from the new threat. She'd just launched herself when the first one went off.

The noise was almost deafening, and she felt it jarring her bones. She was slammed by something painful, disorienting— like a heavy electrical shock, and then she hit the floor hard. She tried to move, but her body wouldn't respond.

Then the second grenade went off, and everything went black.

"We'll hold here until midnight. We have to give Bolton and his men time to find Astra. Then we'll pull everyone out of the city and head north to Riverlands. Home. We should be able to gather more loyal troops in that country—and the marshal settled thousands of retired veterans on farms and ranches up there. When they find out what is happening, they will flock back to the colors. And then we'll march back here and deal with that madman." DeMark's voice dripped venom. He ached to kill Carteria, to avenge the thousands of deaths his treason had already caused. The general would have given his life for one shot at the bastard, but with Callisto and the other generals dead, the responsibility for the opposition fell squarely on his shoulders. He didn't have time for petty vendettas or hopeless acts of vengeance. He couldn't let all Lucerne worked for fall to dust, to allow a savage like Carteria to rule in the marshal's place.

"Yes, sir. We're outnumbered, but we've got good positions. We should be fine . . ."

As long as they don't cut off our retreat. DeMark knew what his comrade was thinking, even if he hadn't said it.

Brigadier Marius Trevannes sat next to DeMark. The crumbling building had been some kind of commercial space, an office building or a school. Whatever it had been, the fighting had taken a toll. The power was out, and the ground was covered with a layer of crumbled stone and shattered bricks. A temporary light strip hung from the ceiling with a portable generator providing power, but that was it.

DeMark and Trevannes sat on concrete blocks around a makeshift table thrown together from the remains of the building's furniture. It wasn't a plush command post, certainly, but right now it was the nerve center of the Celtiborian loyalist forces. Most of Augustin Lucerne's loyal generals were dead now, and his magnificent army was spread throughout half of the Far Stars. DeMark was hopeful he could gather enough loyal units to defeat Carteria, but it would take time. The troops were scattered around the planet in disorder, their communications and command systems shattered, while the usurper's forces were concentrated and ready for action.

"Our supply situation is shit, too." DeMark was exhausted, and every centimeter of his body ached. "We pull out at midnight whether Bolton is back or not." *I'm sorry, Augustin. But we can't stay any longer. The troops will be running out of ammunition by then. We've got to get to the reserve depots back in Riverlands . . . even if that means leaving Astra behind.*

DeMark swore to himself he would do what was necessary, sacrifice anyone—himself included—to prevent Carteria from seizing control of Celtiboria and the confederation. He'd found it easy to put himself on the list of expendables, but far more difficult to contemplate leaving Astra behind. He was trying to stay focused, to keep emotions out of his decision making, but he kept seeing visions of that little girl, sitting quietly and watching her father's officers work late into the nights.

Trevannes nodded. "I'll make sure the orders go out. Hold at all costs until midnight. Then execute a phased pullback."

"Not too phased, Marius. Time is something we are short on. We wait until midnight for Bolton, but then we haul ass out of here. Understood?"

"Understood, sir." Trevannes shifted in his makeshift chair. "With your permission, General, I think I'll head up to the Market District and check on the positions."

DeMark nodded. "Go ahead, Marius. I'll give you half the reserve. If things get too bad, you can move them forward." The reserves weren't much to speak of, just a few companies, mostly replacements who'd been due to ship out to Nordlingen to join his forces there. But the Market District had seen the heaviest fighting, and an enemy breakthrough there would compromise the entire position.

Marius nodded again and slipped through the door and out into the street, leaving DeMark alone with his thoughts—and the three bodyguards his officers had insisted he take with him everywhere he went.

Astra opened her eyes slowly. She was disoriented. She was lying on her side. She tried to bring her hand to her face, but she couldn't. She tried again, but it wouldn't budge. Then she began to remember. The soldiers, the stun grenade.

Her arms were pulled behind her and shackled together. She felt something, hands grabbing her, pulling her up. She scrambled to her feet, looking around. There were soldiers, at least a dozen. Two of them held her arms, and they pushed her forward, down the corridor.

"Let's go, Lady Lucerne," one of them said, clearly trying to be polite despite the firm insistence in his tone.

Lys. Astra turned her head around, looking for her friend. She was lying on the floor, half a meter from where she'd been firing a moment before. She was just regaining consciousness, and she seemed confused and unaware as two of the soldiers jerked her up to her feet.

"Careful with her, you gorilla," she hissed. "And unshackle me. Now. You are Celtiborian soldiers. Obey my commands."

"I'm sorry, Lady Lucerne, but you are being interned for your own protection. There is a rebellion in progress, a naked power grab orchestrated by General Rafaelus DeMark. We are to escort you to a place of relative safety."

"General DeMark? Nonsense. There isn't a more loyal man in all the Far Stars. I order you to release me."

"I am sorry, Lady Lucerne, but my orders do not allow me to comply with your request at present."

"Orders? Whose orders? No one's orders supersede mine!" Astra's clarity had returned, and with it her rage.

"General Carteria is acting as regent, my lady, until your father's Final Orders can be adjudicated." The guard had clearly been told to handle her carefully, but just as clearly he was losing his patience.

"General Carteria can eat shit, soldier. Unshackle me now or I will see you and all your men impaled in the courtyard outside the palace." Astra's rage was consuming her, momentarily overwhelming the cool judgment that normally ruled her actions.

"Please, Lady Lucerne. You are coming with us. Must I have you picked up and carried?"

Astra lunged forward, twisting her body and shaking free of the guards at her side. She took a step forward before one of the soldiers managed to grab hold of her chains and pulled her back. She stumbled and fell to the ground.

"Pick her up," she heard the commander say.

She'd fallen hard on her arm, and it throbbed with pain. She didn't think it was broken, but it hurt like hell. She felt hands on her again, pulling, trying to drag her up. She swung herself to the side, kicking at the legs of one of the soldiers.

Then she saw Lys at the edge of her field of vision, throwing herself at one of the guards holding her. She hit him hard in the knee with her foot, and he collapsed to the ground next to Astra.

"Enough!" the commander shouted. He waved his arm, and one of the soldiers brought his rifle butt down on Lys's shoulder.

Astra could hear the sickening sound as the heavy plastic

of the rifle's stock slammed into her friend's shoulder. Lys dropped hard, and she lay on the floor unmoving.

The commander turned toward the soldier standing over Lys. "Lady Lucerne, if you refuse another of my commands, your friend will be shot."

The soldier standing over Lys snapped his rifle around, pointing it down toward the unconscious woman. He looked at the commanding officer, waiting for the word to fire.

"Lady Lucerne?"

Astra stared at her friend—the woman she'd grown up with, closer to her than any sister, and she felt the moisture building up in her eyes. She struggled to hold back the tears—she wouldn't give these traitors the satisfaction of seeing her cry. She glared at the enemy commander with a look of withering hatred, but she nodded her head slowly. "I will come with you. Leave her alone."

The commander nodded. "Very well, Lady Lucerne." He looked at the soldiers standing next to Lys. "Bring her." He turned back toward Astra, and he gestured toward the hallway.

Astra fought back the urge to resist, fearing that defiance would cost Lys her life, and knowing it wouldn't accomplish a thing. She shuffled slowly forward, feeling a wave of defeat and despair pour over her.

She had taken two steps when the door at the end of the hall blasted open. Soldiers came pouring through, carrying rifles with laser aiming systems.

"Lady Lucerne, get down. Now!" The voice came from down the hall, from the cluster of soldiers now running toward her. They looked just like her captives—the same uniforms, equipment, insignia.

But Astra knew immediately. They weren't the same at all.

And even before she dropped to the ground, she heard the sounds of fire—then saw the enemy commander fall back, his head exploding in a spray of red mist.

"Thirty-two frigates inbound, Admiral. They are adopting an attack formation and accelerating toward Celtiboria."

Desaix sat in his command chair listening to the reports. They just kept getting worse. He had no idea what was happening. Communications with fleet command was down, and a few hours ago, a dozen of his ships had mutinied and positioned themselves to block any vessels approaching Celtiboria.

Desaix responded immediately, moving his forces to intercept the rebels. But he'd hesitated in attacking, holding back to make a last attempt at negotiation before he ordered his loyal units to open fire. In theory, he detested mutiny, and he believed there was only one punishment for its practitioners. But in reality he found the situation far more complex. Those were his ships, and he had no idea if there were loyal officers and crew on board, struggling to regain control or held captive in the brigs.

They responded to his communications with missiles.

If anything, he was relieved when he finally issued the order to fire. He was the commander of the Celtiborian fleet, and he'd be damned if he was going to let a bunch of mutineers get away with their treachery.

The battle had turned into a running firefight throughout the inner system. The loyalists had outnumbered the mutineers almost two to one, and they were just now beginning to gain the upper hand.

Only to have their success greeted by a newly arrived fleet.

The ships were still unidentified, and that concerned him

since they outgunned his forces by a large margin. Worse, his ships were strung out chasing the mutineers. There wasn't time to adopt a strong formation to meet the new threat. The fleet would be on them before they were formed up, and the new battle would be a slaughter.

Desaix hated the idea of running, but his ships were doomed if they stayed. The Celtiborian naval units were scattered all over the Far Stars, escorting troop transports and supply ships, and patrolling systems where confederation ground forces were conducting operations. If he escaped now, he could rally those forces and return at the head of a fleet strong enough to face the invaders.

"All ships are to prepare to jump . . ." He paused. He'd made the decision to pull out, but he hadn't considered a destination. *Antilles? They're supposed to be our allies. Maybe I can rally their support.* He sighed. *No, I need to deal with our own ships first. Whoever is attacking Celtiboria might go after our detached forces too, defeating them all in detail. Or, worse, suborning them as they did these dozen vessels.*

"Destination Rykara," he said suddenly. Antilles might be the smart play—the Antilleans could field a lot more strength than any of his individual fleet detachments. But his first obligation was to his own people. *That's what Marshal Lucerne would do,* he thought, nodding his head slowly. "Fastest possible course."

"Yes, sir. Projected jump in eleven minutes, thirty seconds."

"Very well." There was no point in risking any of his ships while the jump drives warmed up. They might pick off a mutineer or two, but he had no idea what they were facing overall—and he had a bad feeling things were a lot worse than he knew.

"All units, break contact with enemy. Evasive maneuvers until jump sequence initiation."

"Yes, Admiral."

Desaix felt like shit, like he was tucking his tail between his legs and running. *That's exactly what you are doing. But now's your time to prove you learned something from the marshal. Time to put your people—and your duty—first, ahead of your own pride and anger.*

You can count on me, Augustin.

"Lady Lucerne, thank Chrono we found you." Bolton stood in front of Astra. He was at full attention, giving the marshal's daughter—and possible heir—the respect she deserved. But he was a wreck, wounded in the side and clearly in pain. His uniform was torn in half a dozen places, and he was filthy, covered in dirt and dried blood.

"I am extremely grateful, Major. Your people are a sight for sore eyes." Astra's voice was full of emotion. She'd made damned sure not to show any fear in front of the rebel soldiers, but now the relief flooded through her body. They were far from out of trouble, but the situation had certainly improved.

The firefight had been a brief one. Two of Bolton's men had been killed, but they'd wiped out the mutineers. It had passed briefly through Astra's mind that they should take a prisoner for questioning, but she'd remained silent. She wanted these men who'd tried to abduct her—who'd hurt Lys—to die. And she wasn't about to interfere in the fight and get more of her rescuers killed.

"What is going on, Major?" she asked.

"It is a coup attempt, Lady Lucerne. General Carteria assassinated most of your father's high command. The soldiers who abducted you were loyal to Carteria. His forces control the palace and much of the city."

She stared back with shock on her face. "Who is opposing him?"

"General DeMark is in command of the loyalist forces."

I knew he wasn't responsible for this.

"He sent me to find you." He paused uncomfortably. "We were barely able to penetrate their lines and get to the palace. I'm afraid we're going to have a significant fight to get out of here."

"No worries, Major." She reached down and pulled an assault rifle from one of the dead mutineers. "If we have to fight, we'll fight," she said as she jerked hard and pulled the ammunition belt off the enemy corpse.

"Lady Luc—"

"Noted, Major. And rejected." Astra turned and looked at the nervous soldier. "You were going to tell me to stay back, weren't you?"

Bolton nodded. It seemed for a few seconds like he was going to argue, but in the end he just stood there, looking even more uncomfortable.

Astra turned and looked around at the small group. Her eyes fixed on Lys. "Are you okay?" Two privates were holding her friend up. Lys was awake, but she was groggy, and her legs were weak.

"I'll be okay, Astra," she answered softly.

"Are you ready, Lady Lucerne?" Bolton asked. The normally gruff major was tentative, struggling to control his brusque battlefield persona around the marshal's daughter. Needlessly, of course. There was very little Astra Lucerne had not seen of the battlefield. Or of gruff soldiers.

She almost smiled at his attempt.

"Yes, Major. Let's go. I suspect we don't have much time."

Or any time at all.

General Carteria—he hadn't yet dared to begin calling himself marshal—stood at the edge of the spaceport. He was surrounded by guards, an elite unit of veterans who had been with his father before following the younger Carteria into Lucerne's service after the surrender.

Things were going well, but there was still scattered fighting around the palace and the surrounding districts of the city. Most of Lucerne's generals were dead, killed in the initial ambush or hunted down before they could escape the palace. Only DeMark had gotten away . . . but that's what was problematic. The veteran commander had done a tremendous job of rallying the loyalist units around the capital.

Which could ruin everything.

The element of surprise—and the enormous funding provided by his secret allies—should have given Carteria a decisive advantage, at least in the short term. But if DeMark managed to withdraw his forces in good order, he would be able to rally more units from outside the capital. Carteria had only managed to position troops loyal to him near the city, and his bribes had been targeted in the capital district. Things would equalize quickly, and even tip in DeMark's favor, if he was able to escape. DeMark was a gifted soldier and loved by the rank and file, a fact that was all too obvious in the vicious resistance of his outnumbered soldiers. Carteria's superior forces hadn't been able to break their lines.

That was about to change, however.

A cluster of men was approaching from the just-landed ship. One of them wore civilian dress, a conservative business suit. Even from thirty meters away, Carteria could tell it was enormously expensive.

The other men wore military uniforms, but they were nondescript, devoid of any kind of national insignia. The brown-coated soldiers followed the civilian, stopping about two meters behind when the group reached Carteria's position.

"Mr. Bartholomew, welcome to Celtiboria. Mr. Houser spoke very highly of you." Carteria extended his hand. His mysterious ally from the Far Stars Bank had told him to expect a relief fleet with aid for his fledgling cause.

"Thank you, General," the new arrival said as he clasped Carteria's hand. "It is a pleasure to be here. I am impressed with your progress at securing control of the capital city." There was an insincerity in his voice a man more perceptive than Carteria would have picked up. Indeed, the man who would succeed Augustin Lucerne had been oblivious to the talk around him, the grumbling about his failure to destroy DeMark's holdouts, questions about why he hadn't been closer to the front, directing the troops himself. It had only been one day, but even the soldiers who'd backed him—or the ones he'd bought—had begun to see the difference between his leadership and that of the deceased marshal . . . and DeMark.

"I'm afraid we are still facing some resistance, Mr. Bartholomew. I have dispatched troops to deal with the situation, but it has proven to be more . . . ah . . . time consuming than I had expected."

"Please, General, call me Lucius. I am aware of your . . . problem. And I believe I can be of assistance." He turned and pointed back toward his ship. A small column of uniformed men was marching out of the main hold. "I have brought you reinforcements. Indeed, as soon as the rest of my ships land, you will have three fully equipped legions at your disposal, with more on the way."

"Mr . . . Lucius, that is most unexpected." There was an edge to Carteria's voice. He needed the support. If he didn't crush DeMark soon, his problems would escalate rapidly. But his agreement with the mysterious Mr. Houser had called only for financial support, not foreign soldiers landing on Celtiboria. Where had these forces come from?

"Do you not need the aid to destroy General DeMark?"

Carteria's face tightened. "I wouldn't characterize it as need . . ."

"No," Bartholomew said diplomatically, "of course not. However, we seek the same goal, and surely time is not our ally. It is . . . inconvenient . . . that General DeMark escaped from the attack at the summit meeting, and we would like to ensure that you have all the power you may require at your fingertips. It would be most unfortunate if DeMark is able to materially interfere, would it not? And the forces we brought you are prepared to go into the field at once to support your own soldiers."

Carteria was still suspicious, but his new ally was correct. Rafaelus DeMark was a dangerous man. "It would be troublesome if DeMark was able to escape and flee to Lucerne's ancestral homeland. He would likely find much support there. And if your forces are truly combat ready . . ."

"Indeed, General. In fact, there are four hundred fully armed soldiers on my vessel alone. As you can see, they are disembarking in full combat gear. They can be on the way to the battle lines in a matter of minutes."

"What do you and your associates expect of me?" Carteria had been holding back, but now he blurted it right out. "You are providing enormous support. What will you want in return?"

"Just an ally, General Carteria. A man who shares our vision—that the Far Stars should be ruled by men of power and ability. Marshal Lucerne was admirable in many ways, but he was an idealist. He longed to see resources allocated among the populations rather than controlled by those who would see to their wise use."

Carteria nodded. The answer made sense to him. He had never subscribed to Lucerne's republican ideals, and he'd often suspected the marshal's own beliefs were far more theoretical than actual. The great man had often discussed freedom and liberty, but he'd never actually implemented much of either.

Still, something about these mysterious allies troubled him. He sighed. It didn't matter. He'd bet everything on a bid for power. If he lost his fight, he shuddered to think of what DeMark would do to him. And he was far from sure he could win on his own.

"Your aid is greatly appreciated, Lucius. Let us see to the disposition of your troops . . . and the landing of the rest of your ships."

"Those are my orders, Captain. You will obey them at once." Bolton's voice was firm, despite the fact that he was struggling for breath. He was holding a wadded piece of cloth against the wound on his chest with one hand, gripping his pistol firmly in the other. "You will take Lady Lucerne and Lady Dracon to General DeMark. I and the rest of the wounded will stay here and hold off the enemy. We will never escape anyway, and if we hold you back, you will also be killed or captured."

There were sounds of battle in the distance, coming from the loyalist positions along the western edge of the city—exactly where they were heading. The fighting sounded more intense than it had been even a few minutes earlier, and it was clear a major attack was under way.

Captain Trius nodded slowly. "Yes, sir," he forced out, barely a whisper. "As you command."

"No." Astra's tone was cold, resolute. "We're not leaving anyone behind, Major."

"It is the only way . . ." Bolton winced in pain as he forced the words out. "We're done for, Lady Lucerne. We'll never make it out. But without us, you still have a chance. There's no way to know how long General DeMark can hold his position. And securing your rescue is our only priority."

"That's not how this army functions, Major. You knew my father better than that."

"But . . ."

"That's final, Major." She turned toward a soldier standing next to her. "Help the major, Corporal. All of you, let's get the wounded out of here now. Either we all get out of here, or none of us do."

Astra held the assault rifle in one hand, its stock resting on her leg. She'd gone through half the clips she'd taken off the enemy corpse. It had taken considerable fighting to get as far as they had, and Astra had been in the thick of it all. Her riotous mass of hair was tied roughly behind her head with a scrap of cloth, and her face was grimy and twisted into an angry scowl.

She'd be damned if she would hide in the rear like some spoiled princess when good men were making those kinds of sacrifices for her. And considering Bolton had led four hundred soldiers on a mission to rescue her, and barely eighty of them were left, it didn't take a tactician to know her gun was as needed as anyone's.

And they still had a long way to go.

"How far to General DeMark's position, Major?"

"A little over five kilometers, Lady Lucerne." His discomfort at her decision was clear in his tone.

She ignored it.

They both turned around at the same instant, reacting to the sound of footsteps approaching. Astra had her rifle ready, her finger pressing softly against the trigger. But the man in her sights stopped cold and began waving his arms. It was one of the scouts Bolton had sent out ahead of them.

"There's an enemy patrol up ahead, Major. Fifty strong, I'd guess. They've got the road blocked off. There are other checkpoints to either side. We'll have to go at least five kilometers out of our way to get around."

Bolton sighed. "We can't risk going straight, not with Lady Lucerne . . ."

"We go straight ahead. We have numbers and surprise . . . and we don't have the time to waste running all over the city looking to avoid a fight." Astra's eyes blazed with determination.

"But, Lady Lucerne, the risk is . . ."

"Acceptable. You know I'm right, Major. And I told you I will not be treated like some precious princess. I am my father's daughter, and that is all I will say on the subject." She turned around toward the group of soldiers clustered behind her. "Get ready, we attack in one minute."

She turned back toward Bolton. "And, Major . . . for the love of Chrono's hairy armpits, please stop with the Lady Lucerne nonsense. Call me Astra."

The soldier looked uncomfortable, but finally he nodded.

She pulled a fresh clip from her belt and slammed it hard into place. "Are we all ready?"

"Midnight," DeMark spat like a curse. "We have to hold until midnight! At all costs!" The sounds of war were all around, shells bursting everywhere and the staccato taps of assault rifle fire coming from just down the street.

It was dusk, and the last rays of sunlight were quickly fading. The enemy had launched a fresh attack an hour before.

DeMark's soldiers had held stubbornly for most of that time, but now they were pulling back across the line, leaving half their numbers behind, dead in the grim defense against an enemy that outnumbered them at least three to one.

Trevannes stood beside the commander, staring off in the same direction, toward the last-ditch defensive line their soldiers were desperately forming. "There is no way, General," he said. "There are just too many."

"We can't pull back until Major Bolton gets back with Astra," DeMark said.

"Rafaelus . . ." Trevannes grabbed his commander by the shoulders. "I don't know where they are getting all these fresh troops, but we haven't got a chance here. We're going to be overrun any minute now, and then it's over. Do you want to see Carteria in the marshal's uniform, sitting in his chair?"

He paused for a few seconds, staring hard at his old friend. "We have been comrades for years, Rafaelus. I feel the same way about Lady Lucerne as you. By Chrono, all of us do. But if we don't pull out now, we won't have an army. We will hand Carteria the victory he needs."

DeMark stood silently, hearing the words of his second in command. He understood the truth in Trevannes's argument, the certainty that only defeat and total destruction awaited if he maintained his position. But issuing the order to withdraw meant giving up on Astra. He could hear the sound of his heartbeat in his ears, feel the twisted knot in his gut.

I understand now, my friend, he thought, an image of Marshal Lucerne in his head. *The weight that was always on you, the terrible need to make decisions like this. How did you endure it? How will I measure up to the strength you gave to all of us? And what did that cost you?*

He looked away, off into the growing gloom of night. He couldn't face Trevannes. He couldn't face himself. But he would not fail the army, the marshal's legacy.

"The army will retreat. All units will prepare to withdraw to the north of the city."

"There are just too many of them!" Sergeant Timmons was crouched behind a concrete embankment, his assault rifle leveled in front of him. He was almost out of ammo—they all were—and he was choosing his targets carefully.

"I know, Sergeant," Astra said, her tone still one of unbowed defiance. "Just keep firing. Do the best you can."

Major Bolton was dead. So were most of the officers. Perhaps thirty of them were still alive, and half of those were wounded. Against all odds, they'd managed to fight their way through to the rendezvous point by midnight—but DeMark and his soldiers were nowhere to be found, only hundreds of new enemy troops, clad not in Celtiborian gray but in strange brown uniforms she'd never seen before.

Astra pulled off the heavy ammunition belt she'd been carrying, and she tossed it aside. She'd just loaded the last cartridge into her weapon. *This is it. We'll be overrun soon. Better to die in arms than let them capture me.* She glanced back at Lys. Her friend was badly hurt, her shoulder grotesquely swollen where the rifle butt had struck her. *Lys will die too.*

Where the hell is DeMark?

She wasn't surprised to not find the general here, at least not once she got past the initial disappointment. She had allowed herself a bit of hope, and she was paying for it now. The enemy was clearly too strong here.

Rafaelus DeMark would understand the importance of

keeping his army in the field . . . *even if the cost was leaving me behind. I'm sure he pulled back to a stronger position to regroup. Pretty sure, at least.*

Carteria . . . that miserable traitor. Was he the one who planned my father's death? Could he be the architect of all that has befallen us?

No. He is not capable of something like this. He could not have outwitted my father, suborned so many soldiers to his side. Not alone. And she thought about the last few years, and all that had transpired since Blackhawk had rescued her off Kalishar. A thread connected everything that had happened since, and now led to a single thought:

The empire is here. Somewhere.

She tried to maintain her focus on the fight. If she was going to die here, she would take every enemy she could with her. But there was one person she couldn't banish from her thoughts.

Where are you, Ark? Are you caught up in this, or did you escape? Please, she thought, *let him get away from here.*

Not that it mattered. Even if he had crossed the Void, even if he had traveled a thousand light-years from Celtiboria, if he heard she was killed—and Astra had very few illusions she was going to make it out of here alive—Blackhawk would find out.

And then there would be no force in the Far Stars that could restrain him.

What will my death do to him? Will he remain Arkarin Blackhawk? Or will it be Frigus Umbra, the legendary imperial general, the stone-hard, cold-blooded incarnation of death itself who wreaks vengeance on my killers . . . and anyone else unfortunate enough to be close by?

A strange noise interrupted her thoughts, and she cursed her sentimental musing. It sounded like an explosion, but it was softer, hollow. Then another, closer, and she felt a shock wave slam into her.

Some kind of stun shells. *No,* she thought, even as she dropped her gun. *I can't let them take me alive.* But there was nothing she could do. She fell to the ground and couldn't move. She just lay on the street at the edge of consciousness.

In the distance she could hear voices. "Take the Lucerne girl and the other one to the palace."

"Yes, sir. And the soldiers?"

"Kill them."

CHAPTER 13

"ANTILLES CONTROL, THIS IS LUCAS LANCASTER ABOARD THE spaceship *Wolf's Claw*. I request expedited authorization to land at Charonea spaceport Gold Sector. We have a medical emergency and request immediate assistance."

Ace was standing behind Lucas. As the acting commander, he'd normally have spoken for the ship, but he wasn't a member of the planet's most powerful family like Lucas. The *Claw* had been two days in hyperspace, and Blackhawk's condition hadn't changed. He was exactly as he had been, alive but barely so. His body temperature had plunged, and his skin was cool to the touch. His herculean heart was beating barely four times a minute, and neither Doc nor the *Claw*'s medical AI had so much as a guess at what to do.

"*Wolf's Claw*, you are authorized to approach and land at Gold Sector Three. We are clearing a path for you through existing orbital traffic. Emergency medical services will be standing by when you land."

"It's good to be a Lancaster, isn't it?" Ace smiled for a few seconds, but it fell from his face almost immediately. No one was in the mood for humor, not even him. *Katarina . . .*

"You better strap in, Ace. I've got expedited clearance, and I'm going to get us on the ground as quickly as possible."

Ace just grunted his acknowledgment as he turned and walked across the bridge toward his chair. He couldn't get his mind off Katarina, but he knew he had to focus. *There is no time for this. Katarina can take care of herself . . . probably a lot better than you can.* But he couldn't clear his mind, no matter how hard he tried.

He plopped down hard in his chair and reached down for the straps of his harness. Then he punched a key on his comm unit. "All personnel, prepare for immediate atmospheric entry and landing."

He sighed softly, wondering for an instant where Katarina was, but he quickly pushed it aside.

"Okay, Lucas. Bring us down."

Blackhawk was drifting in and out of the darkness. Memories were floating through his consciousness, a confused jumbled mess. Thirty years of struggle, of combat and strife. Pain. Love. Regret.

What is happening to me?

It appears your advanced bodily systems have created a deep coma state to concentrate all your strength into withstanding the effects of the poison that was

introduced during the attempted assassination. Your
ability to engage in cognitive thought and to access
memories in a coordinated manner—what you would
call consciousness—appears to be intermittent, as
your bodily resources are allocated as needed to
sustain your life.

It took Blackhawk a moment to recognize Hans, and there
was a sense of relief as if he were welcoming an old friend. The
AI had been with him for many years, through many battles.
But there was something else there too, another presence, one
even older. Not a friend.

Who are you?

You know who I am. The voice came from the depths of his
mind, from a part he'd long fought to ignore. It was cold, dark.

You are Frigus Umbra.

I am you.

No, he thought, *you are not me. No longer. Years ago you were, but
no more. I have become someone else, and I have turned my back on you
and all you represent.*

*Indeed, you call yourself Blackhawk, and you tell yourself you have
changed. But we both know that is not true. It is a fantasy, one others
may believe, but not you. Not really. If it is true, why did you lie to your
friends for so long? Why are you not with Astra Lucerne right now?
Because you know you are still me, that we will always be one.*

*No. I will never be you again. I have left you behind, forsworn all I
once was. And I did so of my own free will. I will not submit to serve a
master as I once did. Not ever. You are my past. Not my future.*

A dark figure stepped forward into his consciousness. Tall,
muscular, clad in black body armor. Blackhawk saw himself.
Younger, in his midtwenties. And he radiated darkness. He was

an angel of death, assured in his purpose, untroubled by guilt, by doubt.

He hated the man he saw, the inhuman creature who had killed so many on the orders of his imperial master. But he envied his younger self too. Twenty-five years of struggle had exhausted him—fear and guilt so profound it racked his mind day and night. That was Arkarin Blackhawk. It was the price he'd paid to atone for his sins, to strive to be a good man. Frigus Umbra had no such weaknesses, he faced no self-inflicted burdens.

You despise me yet you envy me, Blackhawk. How is this? You pride yourself on becoming what you are, but nothing you do eases the guilt, the burdens you carry. You must even deny yourself the woman you love. All to keep running from me, from what you really are.

Images of Astra flashed before him. He felt an irresistible anger that he couldn't be with her. But most of that rage was directed at the man staring at him, the creature who lived inside him—who was him. *You are why I cannot be with Astra. For twenty-five years I have run from you, fought to banish you from my mind. But still you are there, haunting me.*

I do not haunt you. I am you. We served the empire together once. We can still fight together, for whatever cause you wish. The marshal, your friend, is dead. And Astra is there, on Celtiboria. What awaits her? Death in a power struggle? Marriage to a man she doesn't love, a political expedient made necessary by your refusal to honor Lucerne's dying wishes? You make me the villain in your inner thoughts, but it is you who have made these choices. I am here, always here. Let me help you, Blackhawk. Add my strength to your own. Destroy Lucerne's killers. Save Astra from whatever terrible fate awaits her. Make her yours, and rule the Far Stars together. Only you are strong enough now that Lucerne is gone. Only you can stand up to the forces of the empire. Destroy Kergen Vos and his minions. Take your rightful place. Before it is too late.

No, Blackhawk thought, *I can't . . .* but he felt his resolve weakening. He had fought so long, made so many sacrifices. Yet what if he had been sacrificing all along the one thing that could help him defeat Vos? Avenge Augustin?

Save Astra?

He had fought the Umbra side of himself for so long. But Frigus Umbra was strong. And Blackhawk needed that strength now—more than he ever had.

"Well, Doctor?" Danellan Lancaster stood next to Blackhawk's bed, staring at the small cluster of medical professionals standing along the edge of the room. Ace and Shira were behind him, radiating concern.

"There isn't much I can tell you, Mr. Lancaster. He seems stable, though at a level of life signs we can only categorize as critical. His condition resembles a medically induced coma, though it is far more extreme, almost approaching something I would call suspended animation." Doctor Anterus Cravis was the best Lancaster money and influence could obtain. A brilliant surgeon and a master researcher, Cravis had been at the forefront of Antillean medicine for a generation.

And he was stumped.

"So there is nothing you can do?"

"There are things I can do, Mr. Lancaster, but I'm not sure they would help. They may even cause harm. Captain Blackhawk clearly has an enormously strong constitution. We have been able to analyze the neurotoxin. It is 100 percent fatal in humans, normally within a period of several hours. The fact that he is still alive three days later is extraordinary on its own."

Cravis turned and looked at the bank of medical monitors along the wall. "We could give him a complete blood transfusion, put him on accelerated dialysis . . . there are a dozen things we can do to try to clear the toxins from his system. But none of them would have saved a normal human being, even if you had brought him here immediately after the incident. Yet Blackhawk has somehow survived, and that's why I'm loath to take any further action."

"Why is that?"

"Because all the detox procedures are hard on the body. In attempting to help, we could weaken his body's own systems, interfering with whatever has been keeping him alive in the first place."

"So all we can do is wait?"

"I'm afraid so, Mr. Lancaster. Anything I do now is as likely to kill him as help him. I'm sorry. But my suggestion is to let his own body keep doing what it has been doing . . . and hope for the best." He paused a minute then added, "Indeed, I might be able to offer one bit of hope. Blackhawk's brain scans have shown periods of extreme activity. Almost like he was having intense dreams or something similar. I cannot explain it. It is not something I would expect in this situation, but the data is definitive."

"Thank you, Doctor. That's good news, I guess."

"It is, Mr. Lancaster. It is a sign that Captain Blackhawk has not suffered significant brain damage, which is always a concern when bodily function reaches such low levels."

"Very well, Doctor Cravis. May I assume you will continue to personally monitor the captain's condition?"

"Of course, Mr. Lancaster. I have had my schedule cleared completely. Captain Blackhawk is my only patient."

Danellan nodded, and he watched the doctor turn and leave the room. "So," he said, looking toward Ace and Shira, "we wait. And see if our extraordinary friend manages to survive."

"But what do we do about Celtiboria?" Ace asked.

News of Marshal Lucerne's death had spread quickly, and now word of the civil war that had erupted was beginning to reach Antilles. It was all vague, sketchy. Reports of scattered battles and of wholesale slaughter in the streets of the capital, much of it unreliable.

"I don't know, Ace," Danellan said softly. "I . . . I just don't know." He'd come a long way since Blackhawk had pulled him from the clutches of Kergen Vos's agents, but he found it difficult to sustain his newfound courage without the adventurer's support.

"We can't just stay here, waiting at his bedside," Shira said emotionlessly. "Ark would want us to go back to Celtiboria. Astra is there somewhere, in the middle of all this. He would want her to be safe. We owe it to him to get her out of there."

"I agree," Ace said, "and believe me—I want to return as much as anyone. Katarina is there too, Shira; but how the hell can we go back? We don't know who controls the system or what is going on down on the ground. If we run right back there, we'll just get the *Claw* blown to bits."

"What about the Antilleans?" Shira turned toward Danellan. "Can you convince the Antillean Senate to dispatch an expeditionary force?"

Danellan sighed. "There is so much fear and uncertainty in the wake of Marshal Lucerne's death. They will not want to commit to anything." He paused for a few seconds. "Nevertheless, I am not without influence . . . and I know a secret or two about a few key senators. I just may be able to get approval to send a naval squadron. But the Antillean army is a defensive organization, more of a planetary militia than anything else. We don't have any ground troops to send to Celtiboria . . . none capable of making a planetary assault, that is."

"And without a landing force," Ace said grimly, "we can't intervene in the civil war on Celtiboria . . . or help Astra or Katarina."

"But what else can we do, Ace?" Shira said. "We can't just sit here and do nothing! Maybe we can fight our way through with an Antillean task force and get the *Claw* on the surface at least. Or sneak in with the field."

"Can Lucas even land the *Claw* with the field on?" Ace asked. Landing was one of the most energy-intensive operations of any ship, and they all knew the field drew an enormous amount of power. But if it was possible . . .

"No." The voice was soft and weak, but it was clear—and it was one they all knew.

Everyone in the room spun around, looking back toward the bed. Arkarin Blackhawk's eyes were open, staring back at them.

"Not Celtiboria," he said, his tone strengthening with each word. "Not yet.

"We have somewhere else to go first."

CHAPTER 14

"ASTRA, I MEAN IT." LYS SPOKE SOFTLY, LEANING TOWARD HER
friend as she did. They were sitting on the cold stone floor of one
of the palace's dungeon cells. "Don't let them use me to force you
to do anything. It's not what I want. Even if they torture me. Even
if they kill me." She paused, taking a strained breath.

"Lys . . ." Astra could see her friend was still in considerable
pain. She was pretty sure the impact of the rifle butt had broken Lys's collarbone, but she hadn't said a word about the agony
Astra knew she was feeling. The two of them had grown up
together, shared most of the experiences of their lives together.
Astra knew Lys was smart and capable, but now she was getting
a true glimpse at how strong and resilient her friend truly was.

"I'm serious, Astra. Your father took me in when I had

nobody. He made a home for me, treated me as his own child. And you . . . have always been a sister to me." She paused, taking another labored breath and forcing back her tears. "I will not be the tool used to enslave you. Not even to save my life."

A tear streamed down Astra's cheek, quickly followed by another . . . and then a torrent. "You are my sister, Lys," she said, her voice heavy with grief. "You are a Lucerne, and as strong as anyone I've ever known."

Astra's mind raced, trying to think of a way out, something that could keep her from the terrible choice she knew she would face. But there was nothing. Lys was right. Carteria and whoever else was behind this coup would try to use her to legit-imize their power grab. They wouldn't kill her, or even hurt her too badly. They needed her, the legitimacy she could give to a regime. But Lys was expendable. And everybody knew how close the two of them were.

"Then, promise me, Astra. As my sister. *Please.* I don't want to live knowing you yielded to save me. Too many lives are at stake, entire worlds. You can't sacrifice the Far Stars for me."

I can do exactly *that for the people I love.*

But she knew, even as she thought it, it wasn't true.

So instead Astra nodded. "We'll get out of here, Lys. I don't know who besides Carteria is behind this, but my father still has loyal officers out there, men who served with him for decades. They will fight against this junta. Their forces will retake the capital and break through to us."

"I hope you are right, Astra, but . . ."

They both heard the sounds of the door opening, and they turned to see who was coming through. "Astra . . ." Lys spoke softly but with great urgency. "Remember what I said."

"I will," she gasped, barely getting the words out. "I promise."

The door swung open, and half a dozen guards walked into the cell. "Come, Lady Lucerne," the commander said. "General Carteria wishes to see you."

"General Carteria can eat shit." Astra stared back, without moving a centimeter. Her glare was as cold as space itself.

The officer didn't respond to Astra's taunt. He turned back to the small column of soldiers behind him. "Shackle her. And bring her along." He stepped to the side, making room for the troopers to move forward.

Astra struggled, punching and kicking at the soldiers, but there were too many of them. They pulled her arms behind her back and attached the shackles.

The officer nodded and gestured toward Lys. "And the other one. Bring her as well."

"We have come full circle, my friends. Back to where the marshal began his quest over thirty years ago." DeMark spoke softly, the fatigue weighing on his words. He had been defeated, and thousands of his soldiers had died for a lost cause. They'd held out for hours, desperately hoping Bolton would return with Astra, but in the end they had lost the fight, the capital, and the marshal's daughter.

"We must assume Major Bolton and all his people have been killed or captured. And Astra Lucerne is Carteria's prisoner." DeMark was staring into the flickering flames of the small campfire as he spoke. The survivors of his battered army had marched almost constantly for three straight days. They were exhausted, hungry, cold—and many of them were wounded. Finally he'd had to give them a night's rest. They were veterans, tough and loyal, but they were still only men.

"At least the army is safe for the moment," Trevannes said.

"We're almost a hundred kilometers from the capital, Rafaelus. Scouting reports suggest we are being pursued, but we're at least fifty kilometers ahead of their lead elements." DeMark's aide sat across from him. If anything, he looked worse than his commander. He'd been wounded in the final stages of the fighting, and he'd marched that hundred kilometers leaning hard on a makeshift cane. DeMark had tried to get him to ride in one of the army's few vehicles, but Trevannes had refused, declaring he would walk at the head of his soldiers and do anything he ordered them to do.

It was brave . . . and foolish. But that had been the marshal's legacy for much of the early campaign, too.

And maybe it's the example we'll need to see us through this new one.

"Still," he said to Trevannes, "we have a long way to go before we reach the temporary refuge of Riverlands. And each day's march takes us farther from Astra."

He looked out into the distance, and the horizon had never been more daunting.

DeMark had never been so completely exhausted. His arms were heavy, and his legs felt as though they were full of lead. He mourned for the soldiers lost, and his mind raced wondering where Astra was.

But he wasn't defeated.

Never defeated. He would lick his wounds, regain his strength. And he could come back. Carteria would pay for what he had done. *And I, Rafaelus DeMark, will nail him to a cross in front of the palace before this struggle is done.*

Katarina crept down the alley, her movements the epitome of stealth. She'd been tracking her quarry for days. He was good, the best she'd ever hunted. She'd almost lost his trail twice, but now she had him. There was no way out, at least no way quick enough.

She pulled one of her pistols out slowly, her hand gripped tightly around the weapon. The assassin she was after was dangerous, that was obvious. She'd only have one chance, a fleeting instant. If she failed, she would be the prey. *This enemy can kill you in an instant,* she reminded herself. *This is no petty dictator or corrupt politician. This man is an artist, just as you are. This is your greatest challenge.*

Katarina reveled in it. She felt the resolve inside, the laser focus driving her. She had to find this man and kill him. He was too dangerous. If he had failed to kill Blackhawk, he'd come back. Assuming he had failed, that is. She had no idea what had happened after she'd chased the assassin from the rotunda. Yet she had heard nothing of Blackhawk, no news of his death, nor any word of him at all, in the hospitals or anywhere else on Celtiboria, and she took some small measure of hope from that.

Except it would also mean that this wasn't over. Elite killers didn't abandon their missions. She had to dispatch this man before he had another chance to kill the captain.

He had been elusive, and it had taken all her skills and dedication to lead her here. Now it was time.

You will never leave this alley.

She crept up to the corner, her moves achingly slow. Each footstep was purposeful, deliberate. She avoided the garbage strewn around—dried-out leaves, loose gravel—anything that might make a sound and give her away.

Katarina brought the pistol up slowly as her body leaned forward. Two shots to the head. She had reconnoitered this spot. There was nowhere her victim could escape, no place to hide. He had finally made a mistake. And now he would pay the price.

Leaping around the corner, gun in hand, her eyes locked onto the end of the alley like two targeting lasers. There was a pile of debris, about a meter high, piled up at the far end. She saw a shadow.

His head!

She pulled the trigger, firing one shot—then a second. Her victim's head exploded in a spray of . . .

That's not blood, it's . . .

Katarina felt a wave of adrenaline surge through her body. Her legs acted unconsciously, by instinct, pushing her backward, even as the thought echoed through her mind. She knew immediately her bullet had struck a decoy, perhaps a melon of some kind. And that meant . . .

It's a trap . . .

She clenched her abdominal muscles, whipping her body back, around the corner just as an explosion ripped through the air. She heard the blast, felt the pain as jagged bits of metal tore into her legs.

She hit the ground and rolled, the momentum taking her the rest of the way around the corner. She slammed hard into the far wall and fell. Her ears were ringing, and her entire body hurt, but she ignored it all, pulling out her other pistol and straining to focus. She didn't think her enemy was anywhere near, but she wasn't going to take any chances. If he was, this was when he would come at her.

You are a fool, Venturi. Falling for this ambush like it's your first quarry.

She shuddered to think what her teachers would think to see her now.

The Sebastiani pulled herself up, slowly, painfully. Her legs were covered with blood, and her arm ached where it had slammed into the wall. She ignored the pain, focusing on her body, on her injuries. They were bad, but not critical. Scanning the area again, Katarina searched for threats. Nothing. She was alone—just as she had been since she entered this alley

She reached down and started removing the shards of metal from her leg. She'd been hit half a dozen times. If she'd been the slightest bit slower, the bomb would have torn her to pieces.

Removing the shrapnel was agonizing, but she was barely aware of the pain. Her Sebastiani discipline was in total control. Her thoughts were focused, looking ahead. Her enemy had won the first round, though she had survived his trap. She was dealing with something new . . . and it was going to take everything she had to prevail in this contest.

For the first time in her life, Katarina Venturi felt outmatched by an enemy. She didn't like the feeling.

"Ah, my dear Astra." Carteria's voice was friendly, but Astra could hear the menace beneath the surface. She'd hated the piece of shit since the day her father had granted him his life in exchange for surrendering the last of his own father's army. She'd argued with the marshal that day, more vehemently than she'd ever done before. She knew one day Carteria would become a problem, a traitor, and she had said so. But Marshal Lucerne had been adamant. Fighting to the bitter end would have cost him thousands of casualties, and she knew the decades of losses had scarred her father and influenced his decision.

Now it looked like his humanity, the part of him that mourned those killed in his wars, had been responsible for his worst mistake, and it bothered her how much she wanted to tell her dead father, *I told you so.*

Astra had expected trouble from Carteria much sooner, and when nothing happened, she wrote off the delay to cowardice. The piece of stegaroid excrement had never had the guts to face her father. Yet he was here now . . . and she very much wanted to know what—besides the marshal's death—had caused Carteria's sudden burst of courage.

"What do you want, Carteria?" she said.

"I want only good things for you. Indeed, for all Celtiboria . . . and the Far Stars Confederation. Your father built something extraordinary, Astra, and it falls to us—to you and me—to see that it endures."

"To be clear, there is *no* you and me, and there never will be. More important, there is no place for *you* in the confederation. None. You are a petty usurper, a traitor and a murderer. Nothing more."

"Your words are unfortunate, my dear Astra."

"I'm not your 'dear' anything."

"I mean it as a courtesy," he said smoothly. "I have nothing but respect and admiration for you. So much that I must insist you accept a role in the new order I am forging." Carteria looked at her and smiled.

She was sickened by his attempt at a pleasant expression, and she glared back with a withering intensity. "You think I am going to help you? To ally with you?" She laughed coarsely. "The only thing I'm going to do is piss on your bloated corpse after General DeMark and his soldiers crush this little rebellion of yours."

"Please, my *dear* Astra, such statements are beneath your dignity. And I am afraid General DeMark's forces are outnumbered and low on supplies, trapped in the lowlands near your father's ancestral home. It is only a matter of time before these traitors are defeated . . . and Rafaelus DeMark pays the price for his crimes."

Astra felt her stomach clench. She had no idea of the status of DeMark and his resistance or whether Carteria was telling the truth, and that had her worried. If DeMark had been able to hold out until midnight, Bolton's people would have gotten Lys and her away from Carteria's control. She'd known DeMark since she was a little girl, and she couldn't imagine the stubborn warrior pulling back unless it had literally been the survival of his army in question. And that didn't suggest things were going well.

"I guess we shall see, Carteria. But there is nothing that will make me work with you."

"Work with me?" Carteria stood in front of her, clad in a meticulous dress uniform, one that looked disturbingly similar to the regalia her father wore on formal occasions. He hadn't yet begun to call himself Marshal Carteria, but he was clearly moving closer.

"You obviously misunderstand me. I don't want you to work with me, sweet Astra . . ." His tone was soft, gentle—and every word of it was mockery to her.

"I want you to marry me."

"Marry you?" she spat back, incredulous. "Are you insane?"

"Not at all. I assure you I'm quite serious."

"I'm sure you are. But that doesn't change the fact that I'd marry a Kalishari slime worm before you. You are a detestable piece of human filth, Carteria. I don't know how you managed to lure so many Celtiborian soldiers to your schemes, but I will never be a part of your treason."

"Boldly spoken, Astra. You are indeed your father's daughter. Nevertheless, you will marry me. And you will give me children . . . heirs. And you will help me reunite the fractured Celtiborian army, and destroy any traitors who oppose us."

Astra laughed bitterly. "Never," she said simply, her voice as frozen as space. "I will *never* marry you."

Carteria turned and looked over toward the far wall, where two soldiers were holding Lys. Astra's friend was clearly in pain, but she hadn't said a word. She was slumped over, supported only by the viselike grip of her two captors. Her legs were shaking, and her face was pale.

"I had initially intended to use your friend here as a tool to persuade you," Carteria said, his tone changed. It was darker now, feral.

"No, Astra," Lys shouted. "Remember what I said. No matter what they . . ."

One of the guards punched her injured shoulder hard, and she howled in pain. Astra turned to run toward her friend, but another of Carteria's soldiers grabbed her. She jammed her elbow hard behind her, into the man's stomach. He fell back and released her, just as she spun around and hit him in the knee with a savage kick. He crumbled to the floor, as Astra turned back toward Lys. But there were almost a dozen guards in the room, and three of them were on her before she could take another step. They grabbed her arms and legs and held her tight.

"Please, Astra, allow me to finish." Carteria pressed a small button on his desk. An instant later, two men walked into the room. "As I said, I was going to use this woman to prove my intent. But I think there's an easier way. Allow me to present Mr. Bartholomew and Doctor Zarin." The two men nodded toward her.

"What is this, Carteria? Are these your mysterious allies?

Have they provided you the resources—and the spine—you needed to pull this?"

"Indeed, Astra, they are allies. And Doctor Zarin here is somewhat of a specialist. We were discussing the situation, and I lamented the difficulty I expected in securing, shall we say, the proper cooperation from you."

The condescending smirk on his face stoked her rage, but she controlled it, standing quietly and listening. She had to know what was going on before she decided on her next move.

"I am extremely fond of you, my dear Astra, but after all, you are also a spoiled, undisciplined, willful brat, aren't you? I understand your father's guilt, especially since he left your mother to wither and die all alone, but he should have used a bit more discipline with you, I fear."

She glared back at him, her mind racing, wondering if she had a chance to get to him before the guards could stop her. But her will was stronger than her rage, and she stood stone still, not giving him the outward reaction he wanted.

"As it turns out, however, Doctor Zarin is an expert at, shall we say, influencing human behavior." He paused a few seconds, staring at Astra. "His methods are gentler than those of, say, an interrogator . . . though they are not without side effects. I'm afraid that over time you will . . . lose . . . the troublesome parts of your personality. Permanently, I'm afraid." He turned back toward Zarin. "Isn't that right, Doctor?"

"Yes, General Carteria. My therapies are varied, as are the side effects. Generally, the more independent and defiant subjects tend to fare the worst. Their psyches fight against the conditioning, forcing me to use higher dosages. In the end, they can approach somewhat of a partially vegetative state, though that usually takes several years to present itself."

"That is an unfortunate aspect of these methods, especially in your case, my obstinate young bride," Carteria said, turning back toward Astra. "Nevertheless, the doctor's treatments will make an obedient wife and consort out of you. I will enjoy your new submissiveness. You will be so much easier to deal with. Once Doctor Zarin is done, you will stand beside me and urge our forces on to victory . . . and you will moan like an appreciative whore when I visit your bed at night. You will bear my child, my heir, and you will enjoy every moment of it. And if you remain a good and obedient wife, I may even allow you to live to see our children grow up, vegetable or not."

"You are completely mad, Carteria. There is nothing that could make me marry you. And the thought of you touching me makes me sick, much less bearing your hellspawn."

He smiled. "Maybe so, at least for now. But soon enough, you will no longer care. The doctor's methods are highly effective. But there is one unfortunate aspect of the plan, I am afraid—other than you becoming a mindless slave, of course." He pointed to Lys.

"It renders your friend here extraneous."

Astra felt a cold chill rip through her body. "No!" she screamed, as Carteria made a gesture to the guards holding Lys. One of them reached down, pulling a shortsword from its sheath. "No, please—!"

But it was too late.

Astra watched in horror as the soldier pulled the blade across her friend's throat in one swift motion. She stared, mesmerized as a torrent of blood poured from Lys's neck. The soldiers held her up for a few more seconds before they let go—and her lifeless form crumpled to the ground with a gentle thud.

"NO!" Astra screamed, throwing herself toward Carteria,

lunging for him with her bare hands. Her mind was focused on one thing, and she dove right for her enemy's neck. But then she felt herself being pulled back, Carteria's soldiers grabbing her, holding her in place. She struggled with all her strength, lashed out, kicking, biting. But it was futile. There were too many of them, and they held her fast.

Lys, she thought, feeling as if her guts had been torn out. *I'm so sorry, Lys.* The emotions threatened to overwhelm her. *First my mother. Then my father. Now my sister . . .*

She heard words, distant sounding. That hated voice. Carteria.

"Now that we've taken care of that, why don't we proceed with the first round of injections? After all, my bride to be is here now . . . and amply restrained."

"Very well, General Carteria."

Astra heard the footsteps, felt the sleeve of her shirt pulling as Zarin sliced it open. Then a pinprick, nothing really . . . until the drug hit.

She felt herself floating. She lost track of time and space, drifting into a strange waking dream. It all seemed unreal, but she knew it wasn't. Not all of it. Lys was dead. She wanted to cry for her friend, her sister. But she couldn't. She could feel her consciousness slipping away with one last thought of her own, burning in her mind like a plasma torch.

I will kill you, Carteria, whatever it takes . . .

CHAPTER 15

"ARK!" SHIRA ALMOST SQUEALED, THE FIRST TIME ANYONE could remember a sound like that coming from her. She ran across the room and leaned down, hugging Blackhawk and planting a big kiss on his cheek.

The others were right behind her, and a second later Blackhawk's bed was surrounded by his crew, their grateful cries creating a wild ruckus in the otherwise serene critical care unit.

Blackhawk had pulled himself up, and he was sitting in bed, his eyes bright and wide open. "There is a civil war on Celtiboria?" he said, bypassing the usual bedside chatter. His voice was growing in strength with each word. "And Astra is trapped there . . . somewhere?"

"Yes," Shira said tentatively. "How do you know that, Ark?"

He pulled himself up the rest of the way, twisting his head and stretching. He thought for an instant, as if he had to think about the answer. "I remember everything that was said around me. Since the rotunda."

They all stared back at him with surprised looks on their faces.

"Chrono, Ark. You were deep in a coma." Ace managed a smile. "And now you're sitting there talking to us like we're on the bridge of the *Claw*." Ace's eyes flitted around, checking Blackhawk out from head to toe. "Are you sure you're okay?"

"I'm fine, Ace. The poison is out of my system. I'm a little tired, but that's the worst of it. That, and I'm hungry enough to eat half a megasaur." He sighed softly and made a face. "But I suspect the food in here tastes like shit."

"Actually, this is Danellan Lancaster's hospital, so the food is pretty spectacular," Ace said. "At least in this VIP unit."

Blackhawk turned toward Ace and smiled. Then he moved his head, looking at each of his people in turn, seeing one doubtful expression after another. "Really—I'm good. I promise."

It took a moment for anyone to say anything, but finally, Shira broke the silence. "You said we have someplace to go. Where?"

Doctor Cravis came running into the room before he could answer. "Captain Blackhawk," he said, his own surprise evident in his tone. "I am delighted to see you awake." He turned to the aide following on his heels. "Wenton, I want a complete body scan, a deep brain resonance workup, a full blood analysis . . ."

"Doctor, I appreciate whatever you did for me while I was unconscious, but I'm afraid I don't have time for all that right now." Blackhawk swung his legs over the edge of the bed. "I can assure you I am quite well. But I have work to do." He looked around the room. "We all do. Now, if someone could tell me what happened to my clothes, I will be on my way."

Cravis stared back, a stunned expression on his face. "Captain Blackhawk, you were just in an extremely deep coma, the result of being poisoned by an exceptionally deadly substance. Indeed, you may be the first person ever to survive this level of toxicity. Leaving now is out of the question. We have to do a full workup before we can determine . . ."

"I'm really not asking your permission, Doctor."

"But—"

"Doctor, I'm sure you are the best at what you do, but I know myself, my body." He turned toward his crew, staring back into their concerned expressions. "That poison almost killed me, but it didn't. My body metabolized it, rendered it harmless." Blackhawk didn't explain further—mostly because he couldn't. He didn't really know precisely how many of his own extraordinary abilities worked, and he was just repeating the AI's explanation to him. In the end, it didn't really matter how he survived. What mattered was getting moving.

"I. Am. Fine," he said, emphasizing each word in a tone that didn't invite argument. "Now, we have much to do." He turned his head back and forth, looking around the room. "Clothes?"

"Ark, are you sure about this? You really were in pretty bad shape." Shira put her hand on his shoulder. "We thought we lost you there for a while." Her voice cracked a bit, something else her colleagues had never heard before. But then they'd never come quite so close to losing Blackhawk either.

"I'm fine, Shira. You know me. Don't I look fine?" He gave her a mischievous smile. "You guys need to see me do some calisthenics before you get off me so we can get back to work?"

She looked back for an instant, and then slowly the worried

frown slipped from her lips. She didn't answer his question, but she nodded.

Blackhawk stood up next to the bed. He was a bit tentative at first, but then he nodded and put his full weight down. He stood still for a few seconds, testing his balance. Then he turned toward Lucas. The pilot had been standing off to the side with a worried look on his face. "Lucas, I need to talk to your father. Can you call him and tell him we're coming to Lancaster Tower now?" Blackhawk paused a few seconds then added, "Let's say in an hour. Maybe we can stop on the way and get a couple sandwiches somewhere. I'm fucking starving."

"Sure, Ark. Of course."

Shira walked slowly around the bed. "So you said before we're going someplace else before Celtiboria. Where?"

"Saragossa," Blackhawk said. "We're going to Saragossa. We left a whole army of mercenaries stranded there when we left before. I think it's about time we go get them."

He turned and looked around the room, his face twisted into a frustrated knot. "I'm going to ask one more time . . .

"Where the hell are my clothes?"

"I am thrilled to see you on your feet, Arkarin." Danellan Lancaster walked across the room and embraced Blackhawk.

"Thank you, Danellan. I understand you were deeply involved in securing the best possible care for me at the hospital. I am in your debt."

"Hardly," the magnate said. "I consider you a friend, a very good friend. And I owe you much, Arkarin Blackhawk. You will find my gratitude is quite sincere. Besides, it appears your amazing constitution did all the work, not the medical team I assembled. I suspect you would have fared just as well had I put you on my office sofa and let you sleep it off."

Blackhawk smiled and nodded. "Perhaps," he said with a small chuckle, "but the kindness of a friend is still to be appreciated. And I know you have your share of problems now. So I will just say thank you again." He extended his hand, shaking with Lancaster.

"You are most welcome, Arkarin. And things are going better than I'd anticipated. The Antillean government has guaranteed a large bond issue. It doesn't solve the problem of dealing with the bank's actions, but it will keep us afloat for the foreseeable future."

"That's wonderful, Danellan. You've done a tremendous job. But I am afraid I am about to make your finances more difficult—and put your gratitude and friendship to the test. I have a considerable favor to ask of you, one that will be extraordinarily expensive—and perhaps disruptive to your already fragile operations."

"If I can do it, I will." Lancaster's expression was solid, his voice firm. "No matter what the cost." Blackhawk realized the formerly arrogant and spoiled Antillean magnate, the product of a lifetime of shelter and privilege, had at last found his courage and his integrity.

"I need your ships, Danellan. Vestron Shipping's vessels to be specific." He paused for a second. "All of them. Or at least all that can be gathered on short notice."

Danellan stared back for a few seconds, a look of surprise momentarily on his face. But he just nodded and replied, "Like I said, Ark, anything. Whatever the cost." He paused again. "Where do you want them to go?"

"Saragossa."

"But Saragossa is still under a guild interdict." Danellan frowned, and the concern was obvious in his tone. "Vestron's ships are all guild registered. The crews will refuse to go there."

"We have no time for guild rules or other bullshit. I don't care if we need guards on every ship holding a gun in the captain's mouth, Danellan, but I need those vessels on Saragossa. There are soldiers there I believe I can rally to our cause, and I need the transport capability to get them to Celtiboria." He turned to face the others, and he took a deep breath.

"I have decided to accept Marshal Lucerne's Final Orders," he said. "I intend to take command of the Celtiborian armed forces and to put down Carteria's rebellion. Then I plan to lead them against the imperial stronghold on Galvanus Prime. I will kill the governor and chop the head off this entire imperial incursion."

The room was silent, every stunned eye on Blackhawk. They were all familiar with his past, with the reasons he had initially declined the marshal's final request.

"I know, I know," he said. "I said a hundred times I couldn't . . . I wouldn't. But there is no other option now. I expected Astra to step into her father's shoes, not for a usurper like Carteria to seize power. And I sense the hand of the governor in this. Carteria is neither capable nor brave enough to try something of this magnitude on his own. And that means his victory will give control of Celtiboria to the empire, which obviously can't happen. If we lose Celtiboria, we will lose the Far Stars eventually. And I will do whatever I must to prevent that from happening." There was a strange darkness in his voice, something none of them had heard before. But they'd never been in a situation this dire, either.

He turned back toward the Lancaster patriarch. "There is an army on Saragossa, Danellan, some of the best mercenary companies in the Far Stars. They've been trapped there for the last few years, unable to arrange transport because of the guild interdict. I need the Vestron ships jury-rigged to carry soldiers. And I need them now."

"Do you think you can make a deal with them," Ace asked, "transport off Saragossa in return for backing you on Celtiboria?"

Blackhawk nodded. "Yes. Carano and the other merc commanders are desperate to get off that stinking rock. And Carano knows me; he understands I wouldn't waste his time with bullshit.

"I think we can rally a lot of the Celtiborian soldiers once we get there, but we can't drop down in the middle of a civil war without our own forces. And we have no way of knowing which Celtiborian expeditionary forces have been compromised. We can't go sticking our noses in one hornet's nest after another. We don't have time."

He shook his head. "No, we need to go right to the center of things, Celtiboria itself. DeMark is fighting for his life there. He probably retreated to Riverlands, falling back on Lucerne's traditional strongholds. I doubt we'll be able to get to him without landing in force ourselves. And even if we do, just reinforcing him could be dangerous. Carteria could kill Astra if he feels threatened enough.

"We can't very well bring the *Claw* down alone in the middle of Carteria's junta. We need some power behind us. And there is no way to know what Celtiborian forces we'll be able to rally quickly. But the units on Saragossa have been isolated. They're mercs, neither confederation troops nor imperials. And they owe me a favor. They're the safest bet right now."

"If you can convince them." Ace had a skeptical expression on his face.

"Oh, I think I can convince them," he said. "I'm betting Elisabetta Lementov has worn out General Carano by now." His grin widened into a full-blown smile as he remembered the Saragossan noblewoman, and her various . . . charms. She was a very attractive woman—and he suspected a wildcat in bed—but she was an unrepentant schemer as well. No doubt she followed every assignation with a laundry list of plots designed to increase her wealth and power. "He'll probably agree to anything for a ticket off-planet. Even going right into another battle."

He turned back toward Danellan Lancaster. "There is going to be a battle, though, especially when we get to Celtiboria. Which means we're going to need naval support too, enough to get through whatever ships have rallied to Carteria."

"I will address the Senate immediately, Ark. I'm sure they will give me what I want." The Lancasters had always been enormously powerful on Antilles, and Danellan's associations with Marshal Lucerne and Arkarin Blackhawk had only increased that influence. Any senator who might oppose Lancaster's requests would worry about angering the Celtiborians—or worse even, Arkarin Blackhawk. No one but his crew—and Astra and Danellan—knew Blackhawk's terrifying true identity, but even his public reputation in the Fars Stars was fearsome. No wealthy, comfort-loving Antillean politician wanted Arkarin Blackhawk as an enemy.

Especially now that he was taking control of the Far Stars Confederation.

"My thanks, Danellan." He took a deep breath and sat on the edge of the desk. "Things are going to get crazy, my friends. This is a tougher situation than we've faced before, and the stakes are much higher. Astra is on Celtiboria, and Katarina, too. They are our friends, part of our family, and if anyone thinks we would ever abandon them, they're *going to get a painful lesson.*"

Those around him nodded.

"We *will* get them back. And Rafaelus DeMark, too. He's a good man, and loyal. And right now, he's fighting alone. So we're going to help him. Whatever it takes."

He could feel the eyes on him, and some of the nods were augmented by fierce grins. First Shira, then Ace. Then the others, even Danellan Lancaster. They were all behind him, all ready to do what had to be done.

The fatigue inside Blackhawk was heavy, crushing, but he ignored it completely. There was no time for rest, for hesitation. The fight they had predicted, that they had feared, was upon them. It was time to determine if the Far Stars would continue as the one place in all of inhabited space men resisted the crushing boot of imperial tyranny—or if the deadening hand of empire would hold all mankind in its thrall.

Blackhawk slid off the desk and stepped forward. "Into battle," he said, extending his arm in front of him. "Victory or death."

Shira put her hand on top of her captain's "Victory or death," she repeated.

Ace was next. "Victory or death," he growled, slapping his palm on top of Shira's hand. Then the others joined in, surging forward, thrusting their arms one at a time into the scrum.

As one they chanted their battle cry.

"Victory or death!"

Vos tried to take me out of the equation.

Instead, he awoke the monster.

CHAPTER 16

WILHELM'S SHIP SWOOPED LOW OVER THE CITY. THE IMAGES ON the display showed the fruits of months of clandestine operations on Nordlingen—terrorist attacks, funding of shadow organizations, economic disruption. A plume of thick black smoke rose above a block of burning buildings, and he could see a freight train on its side next to the tracks, a burned-out wreck. Everywhere, he could see the flashing lights of emergency vehicles racing through the streets.

It was the scene of Vos's plans coming to fruition.

Eich Morgus was one of Wilhelm's most trusted agents, and he'd proven his worth yet again. His efforts had pushed a nearly pacified world like Nordlingen into almost open rebellion. The acceptance the Celtiborians had gained when King Gustav had rallied to their side was nearly gone now, replaced by anger and resentment. Even Loren Davanos, the disgraced—and executed—prime minister had become somewhat of a martyr, and those who had once cursed his name began to revere him as a patriot, as a man who had been strong enough to stand up to the invaders when the king caved in to their demands.

Things had escalated steadily, a torrent of imperial coin feeding every hint of anger among the population, fanning the flames of discontent into a roaring conflagration. There were incidents every day now—and a growing death toll, both among the Nordlingeners and the Celtiborian garrison. Every civilian killed fed the resentment of the people. And every dead soldier increased the severity of the reprisals.

The Celtiborians struggled to stamp out the terrorism, to prevent attacks that killed Nordlingeners alongside their own soldiers and to restore peace to the streets. But they'd been forced to employ increasingly aggressive methods: curfews, house-to-house searches, intense surveillance. The people resented the infringements on their freedoms while blaming the occupiers themselves for the terrorist attacks.

There had been no significant unrest on Nordlingen before the Celtiborians had come to force the planet into their confederation, no bombings in the streets, no politically motivated shootings in its cities. All that had come with the Celtiborian soldiers.

At least that is how it appeared to the average citizen . . . especially with Morgus's encouragement.

Rafaelus DeMark had tried to win the hearts and minds of the people, appearing with King Gustav on telecasts, reminding the citizens that the Celtiborians had come with the approval of the planet's monarch, that war had only come as a result of Davanos's treachery. But then Marshal Lucerne was murdered, and General DeMark was forced to return to Celtiboria, leaving the deteriorating situation on Nordlingen to his overwhelmed officers.

Propaganda had spread like wildfire, despite the best efforts of DeMark's subordinates to get their own message out. The soldiers of Augustin Lucerne were branded as occupiers, invaders. King Gustav spoke frequently, urging calm, reiterating his full support for the Far Stars Confederation. But the whispers in the dark began to accuse him of failing his people, of selling them out to a foreign enemy . . . again. The monarchy, universally accepted for centuries on Nordlingen, began to lose popularity. Images of the king wearing a Celtiborian uniform began to appear, caricatures showing him stepping on his people with grotesquely large boots. Criticism of his rule spread, and calls for his abdication drifted from the shadows to the mainstream.

Gustav's security forces moved to stamp down on the dissent, even as the Celtiborians were kicking in doors and trying to find the terrorist cells wreaking such havoc planetwide. Nordlingen had become a tinderbox, waiting for a spark to explode.

Mak Wilhelm had come to deliver that spark.

He had one hundred thousand imperial troops waiting in orbit, fresh from the training depots on Kalishar. The new legions had invaded four worlds, conquering them all in short lightning campaigns. But this was the first time the imperial Far Stars–raised soldiers would face off against Celtiborian regulars. Lucerne's soldiers were widely regarded as the best warriors in the Far Stars—and a match for the veteran legions of the empire proper. But the forces on Nordlingen were already at their limits, spread thin trying to stamp out the widespread resistance.

And they are only fifty thousand strong. I have twice that. And my forces are fresh, well supplied. The defenders' line of supply stretched back to Celtiboria, and since Carteria had assumed tenuous control of that world's capital city, not a rifle cartridge or canister of grain had been sent to Nordlingen—or any of the other worlds with expeditionary forces.

The black-and-gold banner of imperial might flew over twelve planets now, twice as many as when Kergen Vos had first arrived with little more than a plan and the promise of the emperor's support. Even that was but a start, barely a tithe of the hundred planets Vos had sworn to conquer in the name of his imperial master. Operations were under way across the sector, invasion fleets en route to half a dozen planets, bringing armies of conquest to the next wave of imperial worlds.

Even without actual invasion, those planets were prostrate, their economies stalled, starvation and destitution spreading rapidly through their demoralized populations. Vos was using his control of the Far Stars Bank masterfully, and his machinations were triggering catastrophic depressions throughout the sector. Credit was frozen, production was coming to a halt. By the time the legions arrived, the fringe worlds of the Far Stars would be helpless—and once they were all conquered, Vos would launch the final phase of his plan: the systematic conquest of the six Prime worlds.

No, Wilhelm thought with a wave of satisfaction. *Five Primes.* Celtiboria was already as good as taken. Carteria was nothing but a puppet . . . even if he didn't know it just yet.

"And now Nordlingen will fall," Wilhelm whispered to himself. He was clad in his field uniform and body armor, ready to join his army on the ground. It had been quite some time since he'd been placed in a purely military role, and he found himself looking forward to it. He was a spy at heart, but even a hardened agent could appreciate a break from all the conniving and deceit. There was something cathartic about the straightforward nature of an invasion, the pure application of overwhelming force to solve a problem.

He leaned back in the bolted harness, waiting for the dropship to touch down. He was in the second wave, and he knew thousands of troops were already on the ground.

The Celtiborians thought they had problems before? Wait until they meet true imperial might.

"Wherever we pull troops from patrol duty, incidents go through the roof. There were a dozen bombings in Calipurna yesterday, less than thirty-six hours after we drew down the troop strengths there. We need to beef up the patrols, sir. Before things get even worse." Colonel Ghallus stood in the middle of the headquarters, clad in fatigues and full body armor.

"I understand that, Colonel," Javis Kalin said, "but what do you propose we do? Ignore the hundred thousand invading soldiers who are advancing on the capital? That's a bigger problem than the insurgents." Kalin had inherited command when General DeMark had been compelled to return to Celtiboria. Kalin hadn't wanted the command even then, but now everything had gone completely to shit. The planet was virtually in a state of rebellion, his troops were critically low on supplies—and now a new invading army had landed, one that appeared to be large and well supplied.

"I'm sorry, Brigadier." Colonel Ghallus's voice betrayed his fatigue. "I understand the needs on the front line. But the situation in the cities is critical as well."

"I know, Colonel," Kalin said softly, "I know." Kalin was no less tired than Ghallus. Indeed, he was probably even more.

It had been three days since he'd gotten any sleep at all, and weeks since he'd enjoyed a full night's rest. He was running on stimulants and nutrition bars right now, and it didn't look like that was going to change any time soon.

The invasion had been the last straw. The Celtiborian fleet patrolling the space around the planet had been recalled weeks before, drawn into whatever power struggle was tearing Celtiboria apart. Kalin had very sketchy information on what was happening back home—and far too much to deal with right on Nordlingen to worry about it.

He stared down at the figures on his display. He'd been trying to hold back as large a reserve as he could, but it was clear his forces were losing on both fronts. Kalin had no idea who the invaders were. He assumed they were either imperials or troops from one of the other Primes trying to take advantage of Lucerne's death. Not that it mattered. Wherever they'd come from, they were steadily pushing back his outnumbered forces. And he'd virtually lost control of the cities entirely. The terrorists and revolutionaries had been joined in the streets by common criminals and opportunists. Looting and rioting ran rampant, and even when there were soldiers available to put down the troubles, the normal citizens jeered and threw stones at them.

King Gustav maintained his support for the Celtiborians and the confederation, but that carried little weight. The monarch's popularity had plummeted, from record highs in the 80s immediately after he was rescued from captivity to single digits in recent polls. Most of the Nordlingener army units had already deserted, many joining the rebels, and Celtiborian soldiers had been dispatched to supplement Gustav's meager number of loyal guards to protect the king in his palace.

The iron discipline Marshal Lucerne had instilled in his men had been the only thing keeping the beleaguered soldiers from opening fire on the civilians harassing them. But Kalin knew that would only last so long. Even the legendary Celtiborian veterans were only human. Sooner or later, a mob of civilians would push his people too far, and the streets would run red with blood. *If we even last that long,* he thought.

"Okay, Colonel, I want you to take personal charge of the anti-insurgency effort." He stared at his subordinate with sympathy in his eyes. "I know this is a booby prize, Fin, but I need you to do the best you can. I will give you one of the reserve regiments, but that's all I can spare."

"I understand, sir. I'll do the best I can."

"I know you will. And while you are doing it, I am going to take the rest of the reserve forward and launch a counterattack on the invading forces."

"Are you sure that's wise, sir? We're heavily outnumbered."

"I know, Fin. But the math is clear. If we stand and defend we can bleed them, but we can't win in the end. There are just too many of them, and we don't have the supplies for a long campaign. Our only hope is a surprise attack, one thunderous blow to split their forces and shatter their morale." It's not much of a hope, but there's no reason to tell Fin that.

"Yes, sir." A pause. "Are you sure you don't want me up with the attack, sir?"

"I'd love to have you with me, Fin, but I need you to hold down the cities. If we end up with an army of revolutionaries on our rear, we're finished. I'm counting on you to buy us some time before it all goes completely to crap."

"Yes, sir. I'll do my best."

"I know you will, Fin. It's all any of us can do."

"Keep up that fire," Gregor Zel shouted into his comm. He had half a dozen autocannons positioned along a low ridge flanking the dense columns, and he wanted to rake the enemy as hard as possible before they managed to maneuver out of the kill zone.

The soldiers his people had been fighting were well trained, but it seemed clear they were also rookies. He suspected they were mostly unblooded units on their first assignment. That didn't mean they couldn't win this war, Zel knew, but it did mean his veterans would use every trick to try and offset the enemy's superior numbers.

"If we maintain this rate of fire, sir, we'll be dry in five minutes. These guns will be nothing but expensive decorations."

"Fuck," Zel muttered under his breath. "All right, Lieutenant. Maintain full auto for one more minute then switch to aimed bursts." He paused then added, "And make sure to save enough for two minutes at full auto. Just in case these fucking cherries dig up enough balls to charge us."

"Yes, sir."

Zel looked out over the broken plains west of Nordlingen's capital. The ground had always been rough, but now it was pockmarked and ravaged by days of shelling and combat. The enemy forces had been pushing steadily forward for days, taking terrible losses from the well-prepared Celtiborian defenses, but in the end overwhelming their foes with sheer numbers. It was above Zel's pay grade, but he'd done the calculations himself, and he knew the current loss ratios were not going to end well for the outnumbered Celtiborian army.

Zel was a major now, though the loss of the supply line had denied him the correct uniform insignia . . . as well as food and ammunition. *Figures*, he thought. *A major wearing captain's bars . . . and occupying a colonel's billet.*

The officer had taken charge of the regiment when Colonel Martine had moved up to command the brigade. The increase in responsibility had been somewhat mitigated by the crippling losses the army had suffered, and the regiment was only marginally larger than the battalion he'd led into battle just a few weeks before.

The comm unit crackled to life. "Major Zel, Colonel Martine here."

"Yes, Colonel?"

"I need you to prepare your regiment to attack, Major. In one hour."

Zel felt his throat dry up. "Colonel, sir, half of my units are down to the ammo they'd got on them, and the rest aren't much better off. We've been putting up a strong defense when attacked, but I don't think taking the offensive . . ."

"Stow it, Major. I agree with everything you're saying. So does the C-in-C. But it doesn't change a thing. I know you—you've done the calculations the same as I did. We're inflicting a lot of casualties, but we're still losing the battle. This is a gamble, but that's part of war. The fleet's gone, there's no way off this dump of a planet . . . and we're almost out of supplies. And when the last ammo is gone, those heroic defenses of yours will collapse.

"Might as well put it to good use."

Zel still couldn't believe the order—but he couldn't argue with the colonel's logic, either. Maybe, just maybe, they could hit hard enough and break the enemy morale. That might not win the war, but it could buy time, more time than holding fast with at best another few days' ammunition.

"Yes, Colonel. My people will be ready."

"I know I can count on you, Major. The marshal's spirit will be with us on this attack. Martine out."

Zel stood for a few seconds, looking out over the blasted ground, the morass of mud and shell holes his troops would soon be picking their way across.

He flipped the switch on his comm. "Lieutenant, cease fire immediately. I want the crews to save every round they have left." His eyes were fixed on the disordered clusters of enemy troops in front of his position. They looked like shit, units running into each other as they attempted to retreat. *But there are a fuck lot of them down there.*

"Have your people get their guns packed up and ready to move, Lieutenant. You won't believe this . . ."

"General Wilhelm, the Celtiborian forces are continuing their attack. They've pierced our lines in four places, sir. Our forces are retreating with heavy casualties." The orderly stood at attention before the imperial general.

Wilhelm sighed hard. He was covered in dust, his body armor scuffed and the sleeve of his fatigues torn from the elbow down. He'd been up to the front three times, keeping a close eye on his forces. The troops Lord Tragonis had sent him were trained well enough, but they were gun-shy. Too many units had been routed when the Celtiborians counterattacked. Each retreating formation opened a gap in the line and compromised the units on either side. That was how an army got defeated in detail.

"They're exhausted, low on ammunition, and outnumbered across the line, yet we can't stop them at any point." He was frustrated. The last ground force Mak Wilhelm had led had been a ground force of veteran imperial legions. Tragonis had done an impressive job of turning the human detritus of the Far Stars into a large army, but they were no match for Lucerne's veterans.

Wilhelm was about to give the order for a full-scale retreat. It was the obvious call. Pull back and regroup, take advantage of numbers. Time wasn't on the side of the Celtiborians. As long as Carteria controlled their home port, there would be no new supplies. They might make up the food locally, but Nordlingen didn't have any factories capable of producing ammunition for the Celtiborian weapons.

His hand moved to the comm to give the withdrawal order, but something stopped him. *Lucerne is dead. Whatever veteran troops he has left on worlds like this, they are finite—and Tragonis is turning out one hundred thousand new bodies a month.*

And the ones who don't fall here will be all the stronger for it . . .

He stood still for a few seconds, thinking. Then he turned toward his aide. "All retrograde movement is to stop immediately. I want kill squads deployed behind all line units. Any soldiers running from the enemy are to be summarily executed. The army will stand in place and fight it out across the line. To the last."

The Celtiborians don't have the supplies they need. A few more hours of sustained combat, and they will exhaust the last of what they have. It doesn't matter how many of my soldiers they kill, they don't have the resources to destroy the entire army. And when their guns fall silent, it will be over. My forces will be on them, and Nordlingen will fall.

"Move all reserves forward, Captain. If the Celtiborians want a fight to the finish, that's exactly what we'll give them."

The aide hesitated before replying with a startled, "Yes, General Wilhelm."

"Assemble my bodyguard. I'm going up to the front."

"Yes, sir."

"The cities are to be abandoned. All personnel assigned to patrol and anti-insurgency duties are to assemble for deployment to the front." Kalin knew the metropolitan areas were going to explode. Violence and crime would be rampant. Thousands would die, and most of those would be innocent civilians. But it wasn't his decision anymore—the imperials had forced his hand. If he didn't keep an army in being, Nordlingen was lost, and his detached units in the streets would be rounded up by the invaders if they weren't overwhelmed by the rioters.

The patrolling forces had better logistics than the units in the line. They hadn't been expending ammunition at a rapid rate, and most of their units were still fairly well equipped. He would deploy them where his people at the front were running out of ammunition. They could plug the gaps, buy more time. At least until they burned through their own supplies.

But that's a problem for then.

"Yes, sir." The aide was sitting at the heavy comm station, and he turned to issue the orders.

"And, Lieutenant . . . recall Colonel Ghallus to headquarters."

"Yes, sir."

Kalin was pacing back and forth across his headquarters. He knew the battle was lost, or at least soon would be. But Marshal Lucerne's soldiers didn't yield, they didn't give up a fight. Not while they still had breath in their lungs and blood in their veins.

"As soon as the patrol units are redeployed to the front, I want all forces completely out of ammunition to proceed to the Nordlingener armories around the palace. They are to discard their weapons and reequip with locally produced guns and ordnance." The Nordlingener rifles seemed barely above bows and arrows relative to those the Celtiborians normally used, but they were a hell of a lot better than nothing, and at least there was a large supply of ammunition to sustain them. A shitty gun with reloads was better than the best weapon with an empty cartridge.

Kalin briefly thought about ordering his troops to search for the advanced weapons the locals had used when resisting the initial invasion, but those seemed to have disappeared once peace was declared. The imperial agents had destroyed the weapons, or at least successfully hidden them. A few had turned up in the hands of terrorists, but the Celtiborians hadn't found any of the hidden caches.

"Brigadier Kalin . . ."

The instant he heard the aide's voice he knew something was horribly wrong. He turned and faced the communications officer.

"The recall orders have been issued to all units on anti-insurgency duty. They all acknowledge receipt." The officer's voice was shaken.

"And?" Kalin knew there was more.

"Colonel Ghallus got caught in a firefight in the capital city, and he was shot."

Kalin knew before the aide even said it.

"He's dead, sir."

CHAPTER 17

"SARAGOSSA," ACE SAID, HIS VOICE WEARY. HE WAS STARING AT the bluish-white planet on the main display and shaking his head. "There's a filthy shithole I didn't expect to see again so soon."

"I didn't either, Ace, but the planet's lack of appeal works in our favor now. We come offering a way out to thousands of the best fighters in the Far Stars. I am just as glad we don't have to lure them from the golden pleasure houses of Sandaria . . . or even the dusty casinos and filthy fuckhouses of Kalishar. I want them bored and frustrated . . . and willing to do anything for an escape."

Even Carano has to be tired of his dalliance with Elisabetta Lementov . . . if she hasn't already given him the boot. It wasn't that

Blackhawk doubted the seductive Saragossan noblewoman could be a pleasant diversion, a suitable companion for a short stretch of sex-drenched R&R. Indeed, he'd come close himself to experiencing her indisputable charms. But he suspected her constant machinations and scheming would quickly grow tiresome. He'd be shocked if she and Carano weren't at each other's throats by now.

Unless I'm very wrong, the good general will jump at a chance to get his soldiers off Saragossa—even if it means going right into another fight.

"Approaching orbit, Skipper." Lucas glanced over at Blackhawk. "Where do you want me to bring her down?"

"Might as well go right to the center of things, Lucas. Land us behind the Lementov estate. I'd be surprised as hell if good old Elisabetta isn't still at the heart of the action. And she did invite us back, after all. We wouldn't want to spurn the lady's hospitality, would we?"

"Got it, Skip. The Lementov estate it is. At least this time we won't be coming in both turrets blazing."

Blackhawk switched on the shipwide comm. "We're entering Saragossa orbit. Everybody strap in, and prepare for landing."

His mind drifted back to the last time the *Claw* had visited the planet. They'd been on the run from Kalishar, hard hit from battle and looking for a hyperdrive core to replace their damaged unit, but instead they'd landed in the middle of a civil war. It had taken a lot of fighting to get out of that one.

Blackhawk felt a pang of sadness. His whole family had been together on Saragossa, and they'd all come away from that debacle, more or less intact. It was practically the last time that would be the case.

Blackhawk knew the *Claw* had long been a lucky ship. For all the desperate fights his people had gotten themselves into, and the magnet for trouble they sometimes seemed to be, they had gone a long time without a fatality. Most of them had been wounded, some multiple times, but for a long time, everybody had pulled through.

The Twins . . . how many times had he called them that? Now Tarq was dead, and it was one more reminder that the past was just that: the past.

And the dead were the dead . . . no matter what the living did. But that was a lesson Blackhawk had never quite been able to accept.

"Commencing final atmospheric entry sequence now. We should be on the ground in fifteen minutes, Skipper."

Blackhawk just nodded, grateful for Lucas's voice distracting him from his daydreams. It was time to focus on the mission.

Back to Saragossa. The universe must have a sense of humor.

"Arkarin Blackhawk, what a great pleasure it is to see you again. When they told me a spaceship had landed on my newly culti-vated flower gardens, I had a passing thought it might be *Wolf's Claw.* But I didn't really believe it. Not until this very instant." Elis-abetta Lementov walked into the drawing room, a big smile on her face. She wore a pale red gown of imported Sebastiani silk, and her hair was tied up in a monstrously complex style, held in place by a series of small silver clasps. She was a beautiful woman by any measure, though as Blackhawk had noted on his previous visit, there was an iciness to her, a calculating quality that would be admired in a man but that many found unsettling in a woman, especially in a highly traditional society like Saragossa.

Not that she had let such conventions stop her, which Black-hawk couldn't help but admire.

"Lady Lementov," Blackhawk said with a smile on his face. "It is always a pleasure to visit a woman of such surpassing beauty and intelligence." He reached out and took her hand, leaning forward and pressing his lips softly against her fingers.

"Ah . . . you are the charmer, Arkarin Blackhawk. And what is this Lady Lementov nonsense? I am always Elisa to you."

"Alas, Elisa, I have come to Saragossa on business. Seeing you is merely a pleasant added benefit."

"I must accept what good fortune I have, Arkarin." She stepped toward him and took his arm. "Come, let us sit on the terrace. I will order some refreshments." She turned and looked back at Ace and Shira, standing silently behind Blackhawk. "For all your people, of course. Come, it is a lovely day outside. Spring has come, and old friends are visiting. Let us celebrate."

"Thank you, Elisabetta. We would be most happy to enjoy your hospitality. Briefly, though, I'm afraid, as we have much to do while we are here and very little time. Where is General Carano?"

Lementov looked at Blackhawk with a sour expression. "I'm afraid the good general and I are not as close as we once were. With the cessation of hostilities, we no longer had the need to work so . . . *intimately*."

"So the peace has held?" Blackhawk had pushed for a truce between the warring nobles and workers before he'd left the last time.

"Yes, it certainly has. Both sides were too exhausted to continue the fight. The workers rebelled against the party overlords who had become so free in spending their lives on the battlefield." She paused and made a face. "And General Carano and the other commanders were unwilling to exploit the disorder in the enemy's ranks. I'm afraid we had no choice but to negotiate a peace. Many of our properties were returned, though the animals virtually destroyed everything they touched. And we agreed to a series of new laws offering various protections to the workers."

"I am happy for you, Elisa. The war you were fighting wasn't going to lead anywhere except to the destruction of both sides."

Lementov nodded, but she didn't say anything. Blackhawk knew part of her felt her side could have done better. He also knew the best and most lasting agreements were those that truly satisfied neither party.

"So back to General Carano . . . is it possible to arrange a meeting? I have matters I must discuss with him immediately."

"Why certainly, Arkarin. I will have my chamberlain contact him at once. Vladimir and I are not as close as we once were, but he is still my occasional . . . guest. And no doubt he will be as eager as I to see you again." She glanced back over her shoulder at Blackhawk. "Well, perhaps not quite as eager . . ."

Blackhawk smiled back. *Another time, another place,* he thought wistfully. But all Blackhawk could think of was Astra Lucerne, trapped in the middle of whatever was happening on Celtiboria.

One beautiful, powerful, complicated woman is enough for me.

He followed Elisabetta out onto the vast stone terrace behind the manor house. She motioned to a large table with chairs, just as several servants appeared carrying trays.

"Please, all of you . . . sit, rest. I have no doubt you are all exhausted from whatever adventures you plunged into after leaving us. We will enjoy a few pleasant hours while my people fetch General Carano for you."

"You have the ships here? Now?" Carano sat across the table from Blackhawk, a stunned look on his face. The mercenary general had harbored a grudge against the *Claw*'s captain for almost a decade, the result of a dispute that had ended with Blackhawk's sword buried in Carano's shoulder. But the two men had resolved their differences when the *Claw* had last visited Saragossa, and they'd fought side by side in the final battle against the workers' army. They weren't quite friends, but they at least weren't at each other's throats.

"They are in the outer system. Mostly freighters, I'm afraid, hastily configured into troop transports. I fear the accommodations will not be the most comfortable your people have experienced." Blackhawk stared at the surprised mercenary. "Still, it will get you off Saragossa."

"And you are sure these captains and crews will land despite the guild interdiction?" Carano still looked skeptical. He'd been trying to arrange transport for more than two years, with no success. The best he'd been offered was a smuggler's vessel to sneak his top officers off the planet. But leaving behind his entire army would not only have been an act of unspeakable treachery, it would have utterly destroyed twenty years of relentless work. No one would follow a general who had left his men behind while he escaped.

"I am sure, Vladimir. There are Antillean soldiers on board each vessel with orders to space any crew who do not obey orders." That was a bit of an exaggeration. Danellan Lancaster had gotten the Senate to provide the soldiers, but he'd told Blackhawk there was no way he could get such a drastic directive approved as one instructing the soldiers to execute freighter crews. The troops would arrest any of the spacers who resisted and confine them, but that was all. Still, Blackhawk figured spacing sounded a lot better—and he wasn't above a little white lie about cold-blooded murder to close the deal. Besides, he was prepared to go to the first ship that refused to land and throw the officers out the airlock himself. This wasn't the time for guild nonsense, and Chrono help the fool who tried to pull that shit now.

"There is enough room for everyone? The other companies as well?"

"Of course, Vladimir," Blackhawk replied. "I need all of you. Your Black Helms, Vulcan's Tigers, the Silver Swords. All of them."

"So what is this mission you want us to perform in return for transit?" There was suspicion in the mercenary's voice.

"Marshal Lucerne was assassinated. There is a civil war on Celtiboria to determine who will succeed him." He looked right into Carano's eyes as he spoke. "Lucerne's Final Orders declared me his successor. But I need more strength before I can go to Celtiboria and establish myself."

Carano stared back silently, his expression blank with shock. "That is a lot of information, Ark, so I want to make sure I understand. You want *us* to land on Celtiboria and fight *against* Marshal Lucerne's veterans? And in the process, seize control of the capital?"

Blackhawk looked across the table at the mercenary. "That is precisely what I want you to do. Though you will be fighting alongside many of his veterans against a pretender."

Carano laughed. "What's the point of getting off Saragossa only to go get killed on Celtiboria?"

""You don't understand, Vladimir. Most of Lucerne's veterans are off-planet, garrisoning worlds newly added to the confederation. The battle there is being fought mostly by reserve units and new cadres." Blackhawk's voice was firm, his confidence radiating with every word. "I know what I am proposing. And I know exactly how to attack Celtiboria and take control."

"*How* do you know, Arkarin? You are a tremendous warrior and an adventurer of great skill. But I am a soldier. I have led armies before. Do you understand the logistics of what you're proposing? The difficulty of invading a world as well defended as Celtiboria?"

"Yes, I understand." Blackhawk paused, the firmness of his voice failing for just an instant. "I am a soldier too, Vladimir. A general. Or at least I was, many years ago."

"I've never heard of you leading any armies in the Far Stars," the mercenary blurted out. "Where did you command these . . ." Carano hesitated. "Chrono," he said softly. "Were you an imperial general? Is that the great secret, the shadowy origin of Arkarin Blackhawk?"

Blackhawk stared back coldly. "Yes. My name was Frigus Umbra, and I commanded vast armies. I destroyed rebel planets, defeated the most heavily defended forces. So when I tell you I know how to take Celtiboria, I mean it. And when I tell you my secret, I do so to prove just how important this mission is for me." He regarded Carano with an intensity that made the hardened merc look down at the table.

"Frigus Umbra," Carano croaked. "I know of you." There was an undercurrent of fear beneath his words. "It is said you died almost twenty-five years ago . . ."

"Many things are said that are not true, my friend. But in a sense, I did die all those years ago—I am no longer that man. I am Arkarin Blackhawk now. But the knowledge and experience lives on, I assure you. Join with me, Vladimir Carano, and I will get your men off this godforsaken rock. And together we will save the Far Stars."

Carano nodded. It was slight, almost imperceptible, but Blackhawk knew he'd hooked the mercenary leader. "I have to speak with Vulcan and the others." He nodded again, more forceful this time. "But I am with you . . . General Blackhawk." He rose and extended his hand.

The *Claw*'s captain stood up himself, reaching out and clasping hands with his newest follower. *General Blackhawk*—he heard the cold voice in the back of his mind repeating it with grim satisfaction. He pushed back, tried to slam the door in his head shut. But he couldn't. *General Umbra,* he heard faintly, a whisper from the depths of his consciousness.

The voices were still there. And they were getting louder.

CHAPTER 18

"CITIZENS OF CELTIBORIA, IT IS ON A MATTER OF GREAT IMPOR-
tance that I address you." Carteria stood before the cameras,
resplendent in a spotless and perfectly tailored uniform. It had
the basic look of the dress blues that Marshal Lucerne had
always worn for such broadcasts, but it was different too, the
cut, the details. It set him apart from the other officers without
giving the appearance that he had seized the marshal's place.

"I, like you, have mourned the loss of Marshal Augustin
Lucerne. The news of his death was a great a shock to me, as
to all those who loved and respected him. We mourn together,
all true Celtiborians . . . and the millions upon other planets,
worlds whose people have joined us in confederation. But now I

must share with you a truth I myself have been loath to believe." His voice deepened, and he spoke slowly.

"Marshal Lucerne was taken from us not by outsiders, by enemies from another world seeking to strike against us, but by treachery from within. It is with a heavy heart and a feeling of great personal sadness that I must tell you all that General Rafaelus DeMark planned the assassination of Marshal Lucerne."

He paused, eyes briefly downcast, staring at the podium, a convincing look of sadness on his face. "But General DeMark's treachery does not end there. No, for he also launched an attack on the rest of the high command. General Callisto is dead . . . and Generals Quoras and Balmazar as well. The traitor knows no bounds, no limit in his lust for power.

"It is only by fortune's grace that I survived the massacre, and that I was able to rally enough loyal forces to gain control of the capital . . . and force the usurpers into the countryside. General DeMark is still at large, camped in Riverlands with an army of traitors. I have taken action to pursue him, to destroy his rebel force and bring him to justice for his horrific acts.

"This burden was not one I chose, nor was the position of acting marshal one I desired. But my obligation to my fallen leader—and to my people, the millions of Celtiboria, and the billions of the confederation—is clear. I will do what is necessary to destroy the traitors and to restore order and tranquility to our beloved world."

He turned, looking to the side and extending his arm as he continued. "And I am pleased to deliver some happy news amid such misery and despair as we have all suffered." He paused and smiled while a woman stepped onto the stage. She was clad in a black dress of mourning, but she was beautiful nevertheless, tall, with waist-length blond hair. Astra Lucerne stared straight ahead as she walked slowly to the podium, her eyes fixed, unmoving. Carteria took her hand and led her the last few steps to the podium.

"It is with great pleasure that I announce our beloved marshal's daughter, Astra Lucerne, has agreed to assume her father's offices as the head of state of Celtiboria and of the Far Stars Confederation. We all know Lady Lucerne grew up at her father's side as he united first this world and then much of the sector behind his dream for the future . . . a dream Astra will now see to its completion."

He paused again, turning to glance briefly at Astra. Her eyes were unfocused, unmoving, her face almost expressionless. Zarin had warned him of the potential side effects of overdoses of his drug cocktail, but Astra had been extremely resistant to the normal course of treatment, fiercely clinging to her defiance and individuality. He'd had no choice but to double the doses—and then triple them. She had eventually succumbed to the drugs, but she existed now in a surreal state of partial consciousness, almost sleepwalking through her day. It was inconvenient for Carteria's purposes, but he feared if he reduced the dosages, she would regain control of herself.

"I am further pleased to announce that Lady Lucerne has also agreed to become my wife. I have pledged her my sword to maintain the confederation . . . and my heart to help fill the great hole in her own, the chasm of grief the usurper and his followers have created with their unspeakable actions.

"Lady Lucerne is still too distraught for any lengthy addresses, but she insisted on coming out here with me, and appearing before you all." He'd intended to have Astra speak, but he'd decided it was too risky now. He pulled her closer to him, and she raised her arm, waving to the cameras, exactly as he had commanded her.

He turned toward her and pulled her closer, kissing her gently and then looking back toward the camera as an officer helped Astra off the stage.

"The wedding shall take place in one month in the rotunda, and it is my wish that it serve as a new beginning for all Celtiborians and, indeed, the entire confederation. For one month, we will celebrate our lost leader. We will give thanks for all he did to unite us, to make us strong and secure against all threats. In the time between now and then, my soldiers will hunt down the traitor and his forces. The man who would have made himself your master, who would have brought us back to the days of servitude, will be brought to justice. That is my promise to my bride to be . . . and to all the citizens of Celtiboria."

He stood silently for a few seconds, and then he continued, "I bid you all a good night, and I leave you with one last thought. Marshal Lucerne loved his people above all, and I know he would have wanted us to look forward, not behind. To pour our strength and resolve into facing the future, not mourning the past. Let us honor him not by endless grief, but by seeing his dreams realized. Let the prosperity and the security of the Celtiborian people—and the confederation—be our monument to him."

He stood still, waiting for the lights on the camera to go out. He knew the live telecast was being replaced by an image of Marshal Lucerne, a final attempt to connect the dead leader with the man who would succeed him.

"You are clear, sir," one of the technicians said.

Carteria walked slowly across the stage, thinking about his

plans. He wasn't worried about the telecast. The people were foolish and easily led. They would believe what he had told them, especially since they had seen Astra standing at his side.

But DeMark was still out there. He was outnumbered and outgunned, certainly—and hopefully the propaganda war Carteria had just launched would deplete his support among the populace. But Rafaelus DeMark was no enemy to be underestimated. DeMark knew the truth, not the work of fiction Carteria had just read to two hundred million people. And he was a dangerous soldier, one who could very well rally enough support to challenge the new regime.

But Carteria was worried about more than DeMark and his soldiers. His backers had assured him that Arkarin Blackhawk was dead, but he wasn't sure he believed them. Blackhawk's people had taken him back to their ship and escaped. Perhaps the great adventurer had succumbed to his wound, but Carteria would have been happier if he had seen a body.

He'd only met Blackhawk a few times, but Lucerne's mysterious friend had made a deep impression on him. General DeMark, for all his searing rage and lust for vengeance, was a man built in Lucerne's image. He would fight to the last, but he would be slow to put innocents in danger, and he would weigh himself down with the constraints of mercy and fairness.

But Carteria didn't think Blackhawk was cut from the same cloth. There was a darkness to the man, one he'd felt even on their short acquaintance. If Arkarin Blackhawk wasn't dead— and despite imperial assertions otherwise, Carteria knew too much about the man to accept reports of his death without physical proof—he would come back to Celtiboria. He would come to free the people, to support DeMark. He would come to avenge his friend. But perhaps most of all, he would come for Astra. And when he came, he would hold back nothing. He would do what was necessary to win the victory, even if the prize was a world turned into a graveyard.

He will come to kill me.

"The enemy has launched another offensive. They're coming through the farmlands between the rivers, about two hundred kilometers south of Aighboro." Brigadier Trevannes was pointing down to a spot on the map he had spread out on the makeshift table. "Rafe, the scouts are reporting thousands of the brown-coated troops with Carteria's forces."

Rafaelus DeMark sighed. "Casualties?"

"The reports are incomplete." Trevannes hesitated. "At least ten thousand, sir. Maybe more. But we've given out as many as we've taken."

"We can't trade casualties with them, Marius. Especially not when they're getting all kinds of unidentified reinforcements." He looked up at his second in command. "We need time, Marius. We're getting the old veterans back, despite Carteria's fucking propaganda campaigns . . . and we've got enough supplies thanks to the marshal's forethought in stocking the reserve depots. We'd be getting stronger every day if we weren't losing so many troops on the line."

"It's these reinforcements they're getting. We've worn down Carteria's regulars. I doubt they'd be capable of remaining on the offensive without these browncoats. They're close to half his numbers now, and we still have no idea who they are."

"C'mon, Marius. There's only one thing they can be. You know that as well as I do."

"Imperials." Trevannes said the word reluctantly, as if his merely suggesting the fact would make it true.

DeMark had no such compunction. "Of course it's the imperials! Who else could it be? At first I hoped it was some mercenary company he'd hired, but there are too many of them for that. One of the other Primes could probably have managed it, but why would they have? Carteria has no interstellar credibility. Even if one of our allies wanted to intervene, I can't imagine them trusting someone like him."

"But why would the empire trust him any more than one of the other Primes?" Trevannes asked.

"Because they aren't looking to take control, Marius. Not really. They want us to destroy each other, for civil war to rage until Celtiboria is prostrate, its veteran soldiers dead on a hundred battlefields." He took a deep breath and stared off in the direction of the front lines. "Whoever wins will be weak, exhausted. Easily swept away when they make their bid for control." He realized at that moment, too, that something even bigger might be afoot.

"And we can't forget that we're just one world. While we murder each other on Celtiboria, the rest of the confederation is hanging in the wind, with no central leadership. No supplies, no reinforcements. More than anyone, who gains from that?"

"The imperials."

"Exactly."

"But what can we do? The constant fighting favors them. Indeed, as casualties mount, Carteria's new allies become a larger portion of his forces. If it goes much farther, they will control him as a puppet, their dominance enforced by their soldiers on the scene."

"You are correct, old friend. But we will stop that from happening. We just need time. Time to recruit. Time for things to happen. We have no idea what is going on with the fleet—or on all the occupied worlds. There are hundreds of thousands of troops on those planets, the cream of the army. I can't imagine Carteria suborning many of them."

Though his influence over Astra is dangerous. Many of them might follow her orders. Is she really allied with Carteria? It doesn't make any sense. Astra hates that bastard, more even than I do. They must have some kind of control over her, some way to force her to play this role.

And that could be our undoing, a hazard far greater than a hundred thousand veterans in the field.

"We need to slow them down," DeMark continued, "force a lull while we get ourselves organized."

"So how can we do that? If we pull back, they'll be on our heels. They're not going to just give us the time we need."

"No, Marius. They will not. Which means we'll have to take it." He paused for a few seconds. "That is why we're going to open the dikes."

Trevannes stared back for a few seconds with shock on his face. "But, sir . . ."

"It's been done before in time of war."

"Centuries ago, Rafe. The floods will obliterate the farms, sweep away hundreds of villages. It will destroy Riverlands."

"To save Celtiboria, Marius." DeMark's voice was grim, firm. "To save the Far Stars."

"So that is the choice we have come to, as a last resort to stave off total defeat?"

"I wish I could offer a better option."

"And I wish I could think of an alternative, but you're right. Still, thousands will die, Rafe, no matter how much we try to aid them. Some will refuse to leave their farms. And we will destroy this year's crop and wash away most of the farmland. There will be starvation. All at our hands."

"You think I haven't thought of that? That I would do this if we had options? Yes, they will die, as our soldiers do now. This is now the people's war, Marius. Every Celtiborian is a frontline soldier. There is only victory . . . or death. For everyone."

Trevannes said nothing, but DeMark could see the difference in the officer's posture, in his bearing. Not hope, exactly, but not defeat, either.

"And we need to get Astra away from them," DeMark said, his tone determination itself. "I have no idea how they are making her behave the way she has, but I refuse to believe it is voluntary. Failing to rescue her while we were still in the capital is proving to be disastrous to our efforts."

"It's not like we didn't try, sir," Trevannes replied. "We lost Hain Bolton and his entire battalion."

"We've lost twenty times that many in the field, and now Carteria has the marshal's daughter to add credibility to his claim. I should have ordered an all-out attack. Astra was worth any number of casualties." DeMark hated thinking of his soldiers as some kind of macabre currency, with goals assigned a value in dead men. But whether he hated it or not, that was war. He was enough of a veteran to know that.

"The old grumblers, the veterans," he continued, "they will never follow Carteria. But what do you think the average Celtiborian sees, watching the vid with Astra standing next to him, with hearing that they are pledged to be wed?"

"We are not alone, General. We have allies. Admiral Desaix is out there, the troops in the expeditionary forces. Time may not be our enemy. Perhaps help is even now on its way."

DeMark stood and looked out into the hazy dusk sky. "Perhaps, Marius." DeMark wasn't one for optimism and blind faith. Reinforcements might come. Desaix and his fleet had probably remained loyal, though they could do little to influence the struggle on the ground—not unless things got so desperate they decided to bombard Celtiboria. There was another source of hope, though . . .

Blackhawk, he thought. *Are you still alive, my friend?*

If he was, Ark would come—DeMark was sure of that. The adventurer would never abandon Astra. Never. And as much as DeMark hated Carteria, he actually felt a moment of pity for the usurper when he thought of what Blackhawk would do to him if he hurt Astra.

If he was still alive.

There were rumors, stories that Blackhawk was dead, that he had been assassinated just like Lucerne. DeMark didn't believe it. No, he would accept that Blackhawk was dead when he saw the body and not before.

But still, the doubts gathered in the dark places in his mind.

CHAPTER 19

"TRANSITIONING TO NORMAL SPACE IN TWO MINUTES. ALL VESSELS lock onto my nav data and stay tight on our signal." Lucas's voice was hoarse, fatigued. The voyage had been hard on them all. Saragossa to Celtiboria was an enormous trip for a single jump, but Blackhawk had insisted. He had no idea what was happening on Celtiboria, but he knew Astra was in Carteria's clutches.

And that was all he needed to know.

The trip had been interminable. The *Claw* was capable of blasting through the alien dimension at an enormous velocity, but now she was leading over a hundred civilian freighters and liners, ships that couldn't have hoped to complete such a long jump without being tied into the *Claw*'s data net. But even Lucas's expert guidance couldn't make the old rust buckets any faster. He'd pushed them as hard as he could, but they were still slow.

"Very well, Lucas. Bring us in as close as you can. We need to get on the ground as quickly as possible." None of them had any idea what to expect around Celtiboria. They had an Antillean naval squadron with them, but if Admiral Desaix—or enough of his ships—had declared for Carteria, Commodore Hammerleigh's dozen Antillean frigates weren't going to have much of a chance.

"I'll do my best, Ark, but these tubs are a bunch of pigs. I could get the *Claw* practically in orbit on transit, at least with a reasonable risk factor, but if I come in too tight, half these freighters will end up getting torn apart by the grav fields around the planet."

"And if we don't come in close, we risk getting blasted apart on the approach. It's dangerous either way, Lucas. Bring us in tight . . . even if we lose a few freighters."

Lucas stared back across the bridge. "Yes, sir," he replied, holding his gaze for a few more seconds. Blackhawk could guess about Lucas's concern, but that's because the young pilot had never had to dismiss six hundred potentially preventable deaths as inconsequential.

That's because you've never met General Umbra, Lucas.

You have now.

"Attention, all vessels. We will be executing a precision transit, entering normal space far closer to the planet than any of you are used to. It is essential that you follow on my mark, and utilize the exact nav data I am transmitting. There is no room for error." *Great, Lucas . . . scare the shit out of them. That will help. Maybe you should just ask if any of them can become better pilots in the next half minute or so.*

But he had to admit Lucas had gotten their attention. A trip this long through hyperspace played havoc with attentiveness and efficiency. The alien space affected people in different ways, but all of it was counterproductive to executing precision maneuvers. And that was just what Lucas was demanding of them all.

Maybe he understands command better than I give him credit for.

"Transit in fifteen seconds . . ."

"I have ships emerging from hyperspace, sir." The officer spun around and looked toward Captain Rhageth. "They're very close to Celtiboria, sir. Less than 250,000 kilometers."

Rhageth's head snapped around. "That's impossible, Ensign. Check your instrumentation."

Rhageth had been *Hillcat*'s first officer when he'd accepted Carteria's coin and led the mutiny that added the ship to the usurper's fleet. He'd never been a loyal follower of the marshal, and he'd still harbored resentment for the destruction of his old master, the warlord Undarra. He'd never expected to have a chance to strike back at those who had destroyed his old commander, but events had taken an unexpected course. The fact that his new employers had also paid him enough coin to fund a fairly comfortable retirement was just a bonus.

The ship was understaffed, as were most of the others. Carteria's people had managed to suborn many key officers in the fleet, but large portions of the crews remained loyal, even on the ships most heavily penetrated by Carteria's agents. The mutineers had surprise on their side, and they'd been armed and ready when the signal to strike went out, but the fighting was still brutal. Rhageth had found it more difficult than he'd expected to open fire on his former comrades, but once the fighting had started, he broke through the doubts. In the end, he'd ordered the last few survivors executed. His losses had been heavy, and he didn't have the personnel to spare guarding prisoners.

When the mutinies were over, about a third of the Celtiborian home squadron had defected to the Carterian cause. Rhageth was certain more ships would have switched sides, but Admiral Desaix was back in the system, home for the marshal's funeral. Desaix didn't have many ships with him, but he acted decisively when the mutinies began, limiting the spread of the damage.

It hadn't helped that the Carterian agents had bypassed the captains of the ships, targeting instead officers who had served the more recently defeated warlords, men likely to harbor lingering resentments toward Marshal Lucerne and his top officers. While it was certainly effective in creating turncoats, it left the new Carterian fleet without any senior officers—and a former first officer like Rhageth in command of the entire force.

"All instrumentation checks out, sir. We have ships transiting 250,000 kilometers from Celtiboria. They are between us and the planet."

Rhageth felt his stomach clench. There was no way this wasn't bad news. "Strength of enemy fleet?"

"Unknown, sir. Forty-five so far. They are still transiting. All transports so far."

Rhageth slapped his hand down hard on his command chair. The side of it was still stained with the former captain's blood. "Prepare to come about and engage the . . ."

"More transits, Captain. On our outward flank, sir. Looks like ten to twelve vessels, all frigates."

"Fuck," Rhageth said, mostly to himself. "All vessels full alert. Prepare for battle."

Twelve frigates was a tough match for his own force. Many of his ships were damaged during the fighting with Desaix's loyalists. And the large imperial fleet that had chased the Celtiborian admiral and his forces from the system had since left, leaving only eight ships to support Rhageth's tiny armada.

He thought about fleeing, but then he thought about the agents aboard his ship, watching his every move. He understood exactly why they were there, and he felt an involuntary twinge between his shoulder blades.

I betrayed Admiral Desaix, and now I find myself in the thrall of far harsher taskmasters.

But what was done was done. And his only hope of survival was winning this battle.

"The fleet will prepare to close."

Blackhawk held on to the armrests of his chair. He tolerated hyperspace and the shock of transiting in and out of normal space well, but he wasn't looking forward to emerging this close to Celtiboria's gravity well.

The *Claw* shook hard, but only for a few seconds. Then everything was still, and half a minute later the ship's systems began coming to life, and the forward display lit up. There was a small bluish circle almost dead center in the middle of the screen. Celtiboria.

"Well done, Lucas." Blackhawk was amazed at the smoothness of the transit. He knew his pilot was one of the best in the Far Stars, but he was still surprised sometimes by the way Lucas controlled the *Claw*.

"Thanks, Skip," the pilot said, but his attention was elsewhere.

His eyes were fixed on his scope, watching the fleet of freighters turned troop transports. He'd sent them all meticulous plots, but it was still up to each pilot to execute the reentries.

"We've got ten ships transited and reporting satisfactory condition." Lucas's face was pressed down on the scope as he spoke. "Twenty." Then, an instant later he yelled, "We lost a ship. The *Fazaria*. It looks like she transited into too much particulate matter."

Ace sighed hard, but he didn't say anything. Blackhawk saw his number two turn to stare across the bridge toward Lucas's station, probably hoping it was the worst of the news.

It never is.

As if to confirm his thought, Lucas said, "We lost *Hampton* too. And *Veragia*."

Almost two thousand dead. Lucas looked to Blackhawk, then to Ace, his eyes pleading. Ace could only shake his head.

Blackhawk did nothing at all.

"All ships are to accelerate toward the planet as soon as systems functionality returns." Blackhawk's voice was cold, his eyes peering intently at the display. He paid no heed to Lucas's reports of ships lost. War was war, and he knew how to win. Soldiers died, ships were destroyed. What mattered was whether they were lost in victory or in defeat. And Blackhawk had no intention of having those lives wasted. His mind was filled with memories of battles, of thousands of troops landing on hostile planets, columns of perfectly drilled soldiers moving forward, driving the enemy before them.

I will honor them in victory. That is the only acceptable response to losing soldiers: destroying those who would have destroyed you.

It had been many years since Blackhawk had commanded an army, almost a lifetime, but it was flooding back to him. He felt adrenaline surging through his body, and his mind was crisp and alert. *This is what I was created to do,* he thought. He heard Lucas calling off ship names, more vessels lost to his tactic of inserting so close to Celtiboria. But they were numbers to him, statistics. *Only a fool hesitates during a fight to mourn the dead,* the voice from deep inside said.

"All ships transited," Lucas said, his voice heavy with fatigue and sorrow. "We lost nine vessels, all heavy freighters."

Ace took a deep breath. "That's over five thousand men dead," he said grimly. "And we don't have soldier one on the ground yet."

"Let's focus," Blackhawk snapped. He knew Ace and Lucas had seen their share of adventure, and they'd fought their way out of a good number of close scrapes, but this was their baptism of war. *There is no room for weakness now, nor for sympathy. There is only victory or defeat, life or death.*

Blackhawk knew he was letting go, allowing his discipline to slip away. But he needed the old thoughts, the old ways.

The old *discipline.*

He felt his mind adapting, part of it relaxing even as the rest remained tense and focused. He tapped into that hidden darkness, almost eagerly. Slowly, steadily, he could feel the parts of him he knew as Frigus Umbra slipping out of their cage. For twenty-five years he had struggled to forget what he had been.

It was a struggle, but I kept Umbra a distant memory. It was you, Vos, who pulled him from his place in the deep darkness. You and your puppet Carteria, who dared to put Astra at risk. Now you will reap what you have sown.

You want war? I will show you war that will give even you nightmares.

"Bring the fleet in, Lucas." His voice was frozen like deep space. "It's time to go see General Carteria."

"Captain, our scanners are picking up massive activity around Celtiboria." The officer was hunched over the scope, and his surprise was evident in his tone. "It looks like a whole fleet emerging from hyperspace, sir." He turned and looked toward the captain. "But they are less than 250,000 kilometers from the planet."

"Can you confirm that distance, Lieutenant?" Captain Korn replied, a touch of surprise in his tone.

"Confirmed, sir. We have almost one hundred ships on the scanner now . . . and some spiking energy readings too. If I had to guess, I'd say they lost a number of ships in transit."

Korn leaned back in his chair. Why would a fleet come in that close to the planet? Nav error? But that didn't seem right. Most fleets would transit at least ten million kilometers from a planetary body. Any navigational mistake could put them off target, but the chances of that placing them right next to a planet—the planet of interest in this system—were infinitesimal. It had to be intentional.

But to take such a risk . . . ?

It might make sense for an invasion fleet, but only if the commander was willing to accept heavy losses just entering the system, to trade the lives of thousands of soldiers to gain surprise. Yet it *would* be quite the surprise. It *was* quite a surprise, because that new fleet was between the planet and its defensive vessels, and the troops on the ground would have less than an hour to prepare their defenses before the invaders would be on them.

And if they would sacrifice thousands to get past Carteria's ships, that would mean . . .

"Lieutenant, prepare the ship for transit, and set a course for Rykara." Admiral Desaix had left Korn and his ship behind to keep an eye on things in the system. They'd been powered down hiding in the asteroid belt ever since the rest of the fleet withdrew. His orders were to stay in place unless he had something vital to report.

"Yes, sir. Engaging power up sequence now."

That is an invasion fleet, I'd bet my last copper on it. I don't know who would be hitting Celtiboria right now, but it's not the imperials. Carteria's got the spaceport all sewn up down there, so they could just land reinforcements normally. They'd have no reason to take such crazy chances as jumping in right next to the planet. No, it has to be someone here to attack Carteria and his forces. That makes them friends, at least after a sort. And that makes getting word to the admiral pretty fucking vital.

"Expedite the sequence, Lieutenant. We have to report this to Admiral Desaix as soon as possible."

"Yes, sir!"

"But that's insane!" Carteria roared. "It's just not possible!" He was pacing across the massive room he'd taken as his bedchamber, an oversized goblet of gold and silver in his hand. He'd taken one look at the small, plain quarters Lucerne had chosen, and he'd rejected them out of hand, ultimately selecting the living space of the last Celtiborian king, from the presenatorial era. If he was going to be marshal and rule over the Far Stars, he was going to live the part. Augustin Lucerne's Spartan tastes had been amusing affectations, but it was not an affliction his self-appointed successor shared.

"Nevertheless, Gen— . . . Marshal Carteria, there are ninety-seven vessels currently moving into suborbital landing positions." Carteria hadn't officially taken the marshal's title, at least not for public consumption. He'd decided to make that announcement at the end of the week—after he wed Astra

Lucerne in a ceremony broadcast across the planet. But that hadn't stopped him from having his soldiers begin getting used to the new rank.

"What about the defensive fleet? The warning systems? How could we have no notice?" Carteria was tense, bordering on panic.

"The defensive fleet is engaged with a squadron of frigates accompanying the invasion vessels, Marshal. The entire force of transports apparently transited inside our defensive perimeter, less than 250,000 kilometers from the planet."

"But that's impossible," Carteria said again, throwing the half-full goblet across the room.

"Nevertheless, Marshal," the nervous officer continued, "it is the case. The orbital fortress remains out of action due to damage suffered in the initial fighting there. We have no close in-ground defenses available and in working order, so there is no way to prevent the landing. We project they will be on the ground in less than thirty minutes, sir."

"I want all units on full alert right away. Any landings are to be met. All enemy forces are to be engaged as soon as they touch ground."

"Yes, Marshal." The officer saluted and turned to leave.

"And, Major . . ."

"Yes, sir?"

"Advise Mr. Bartholomew and Mr. Houser that I wish to see them immediately."

"As you command, Marshal."

"General DeMark, I am sorry to wake you, sir."

DeMark swung his legs over the edge of the field cot. He could see the officer's hesitancy. It was something he was notic-

244 — JAY ALLAN

ing more and more, his people acting strangely around him. He didn't like it, the deference, almost like worship. He'd seen it before around Marshal Lucerne.

Seen it? You probably did it yourself.

His own recollections of his dead commander were heavily skewed to the positive. Augustin Lucerne had been a good man, and a great commander. But he'd made mistakes too. Men had died because of his errors. But those who had followed him rarely acknowledged such failings, preferring instead to create an image of the perfect warrior, the infallible leader. *Now I understand, Augustin. I understand the weight that you were always under.*

"Don't worry, Captain, I wasn't sleeping." *If only he knew how long it's been since I truly slept at night.*

"There are unidentified ships inbound, sir. They appear to be freighters, but they are coming down over the Cimaron Plateau west of the capital."

"Freighters? Attempting belly landings outside the spaceport?" What kind of lunatic would try something like that?

"Yes, sir, almost a hundred of them."

DeMark stood up abruptly. "A hundred?" He took a deep breath, his mind racing to imagine who could bring so many vessels to Celtiboria. "I have no idea who they could be, Captain, but they must be allies. Or at least enemies of our enemies. Carteria controls the spaceport in Alban, so there's no reason any friends of his would risk such a crazy landing."

He reached out and grabbed his coat. "Bring the army to full alert, Captain. I have no idea who is trying such an insane fucking landing, but the enemy of my enemy . . ." His voice trailed off, and he thrust his arm into the coat.

"Yes, sir."

"Break camp. I want everybody ready to move out in one hour." DeMark walked toward the flap of the tent and looked out over the encampment. The dawn light was just beginning to come up over the horizon. "If this is some force about to attack Carteria, we're not going to let them fight alone." He turned and looked at the captain, his face twisted into a feral glare. "We're going to help them. We're going to hit Carteria's forces across the line."

It's time, he thought grimly. *Time for the battle to succeed the marshal. The battle for Celtiboria and the future.*

Katarina stared at the screen, her eyes sore and red. She had been searching for days, weeks, trying to regain the trail of her prey—the assassin who had attacked Marshal Lucerne and Blackhawk, and who had almost taken her down as well.

She had monitored all departures from Celtiboria. If her target went off-world, she needed to maintain contact or she'd never find him again. But she was pretty sure he hadn't left yet. So she had turned her attention to tracking where he had come from. Perhaps that would lead her to his current location.

Katarina had always been highly unemotional when practicing her trade. She had many kills to her credit, mostly vile human beings who had been in sore need of killing. But emotion had never played a part in her actions, even with the most hideously evil targets. She had been a professional, and she had conducted herself as such.

But this was different.

She had respected Lucerne and looked up to him as so many others had, but his was still just a death at the end of the day. Blackhawk, though—the captain she loved. He was one of the few people she'd ever met who truly understood her. He'd treated her as one of the family from the start, creating for her the first real home she'd ever known. He'd even humored her need to indulge in a charade of independence, playing along as she made a show of paying for her passage and staying somewhat aloof from the others. Above all, he had been something she never thought possible: her friend.

And now she didn't know if he was alive or dead.

There was nothing she could do to change that fact, no way to help Blackhawk, wherever he was. But she could find the man responsible for the attack, and she could put him down for good. If Blackhawk was dead, she would avenge him. And if he was alive, she would kill this assassin before he could try again.

It had taken her a while, and she'd had to spread some crowns around, but she was finally into the Celtiborian immigration and customs system. She had access to all data on anyone who'd arrived on Celtiboria over the past several months. It was possible to sneak onto the planet, of course, but she knew that was actually riskier than simply traveling with an alias. No, she was fairly certain her target was in these files, one of the thousands of people who had arrived at the spaceport in the weeks before Lucerne's death.

She'd been paring down the list of prospects. A fair number of those who'd arrived in her target time period had left already by the time of Blackhawk's attack. She eliminated others for various reasons. She knew her target was a man. She didn't have a good idea of his age, but she could discount children and the elderly. Then she began verifying the names on the list, removing anyone for whom she could find reasonable identity confirmation.

It was long, tiresome work, but it was what she'd been trained to do. The actual killing was a small part of her profession. Soldiers focused on combat, expecting others to worry about the time and place of the battle. But an assassin had to track down her prey, a task that was often extremely difficult. And almost impossible when you're after someone with your own skill set.

Now, however, she'd eliminated all but four possibilities. There were two business executives whose identities she couldn't confirm, and a disreputable-looking character she suspected was some kind of petty criminal.

And a Taralian monk.

It made perfect sense. Taralian pilgrims were not that uncommon on Celtiboria. It was the kind of alias she would create for herself. She'd dug deeper and discovered that this particular monk had disappeared shortly after he had arrived. No transactions, no accommodations registered to him. Nothing.

And that was really all the confirmation she needed.

It was still a hunch, but she knew that every battle came down in the end to acting on a combination of knowledge and instinct. And she was willing to bet she had found how her assassin had gotten onto Celtiboria. It was a clue.

Now I just have to find him.

"Lady Lucerne?"

Astra Lucerne looked up dreamily at the face above her head. She was lying on her bed, and her body felt heavy, stiff. She wasn't asleep, but she was groggy, and her thoughts felt slow.

"Lady Lucerne, please. You have to wake up." The shadowy figure grabbed her arms, shaking.

Astra tried to focus her eyes. The face . . . it was blurry, hard to see. But it was familiar. Someone she knew . . . a friend. "Lys?" she said softly.

"No, my lady," the voice responded. The tone was somber, sad. "Lys is dead. They killed her."

Astra struggled with the words. *Dead? Lys?* Then the memories came back, the images of that room, that terrible moment. The order being given then . . . the knife slicing across Lys's throat, her friend's last gasps for air, blood pouring down her body. Then nothing.

The images of Lys sent a shock through her, clearing her mind. She could think, she could remember. It felt like she'd been asleep for weeks, living in a trance, trapped deep in her own mind, unable to see or hear or speak.

"Rasa?" Her voice was still weak, but her vision was clearer, the face above her becoming recognizable. Rasa Dinari. Her personal aide.

"Yes, my lady. We must get you out of here, now."

"What happened? I feel as if I have been asleep for weeks." Astra tried to raise her head, but she moved too quickly and a wave of dizziness took her.

"They were drugging you, my lady. There is this horrible man who prepares the drugs. But Doctor Vaughn and I . . . we were able to switch the last few injections."

"Drugs?" Astra raised her head again, slower this time. "Yes . . . I think I am starting to remember."

"They have been making you do things, my lady. The telecasts. Your engagement."

"Engagement?" Astra's voice was shrill, her expression one of shock.

"Yes, my lady. You are to be wed to General Carteria in five days. That is why I must get you out of here. But we must go now. You are under constant surveillance. You still have friends in the palace, though. One of our allies is disrupting the live feed from this room, recycling old footage. But that will not remain undiscovered for long."

Astra felt the heat in her face, the tension in her muscles as her fists clenched. The memories were coming back now, all of them. Carteria ordering Lys's murder. Standing next to him in front of the camera. Kissing him during the broadcasts.

She felt horror, then revulsion. She wanted to lean over the edge of the bed, empty her stomach, but the nausea was rapidly replaced by panic and regret. How many loyal soldiers had died fighting Carteria while she appeared next to him, helping him win support? What had they thought, her father's steadfast veterans, seeing her stand next to a worm like Carteria?

But mostly she felt anger. *No, that's not the right word.*

How about overwhelming, homicidal rage.

They had killed her oldest friend. She would never forget the image of Lys, already badly hurt, as Carteria's henchman cut her throat.

She sat up, throwing her legs over the edge of the bed. She paused a few seconds, catching her breath. She stared at the wall, an angry scowl on her face.

"Here, my lady, drink this. Doctor Vaughn says it will give you energy and help to cleanse the brainwashing drugs from your system."

Astra reached out and took the vial from her servant's hand. She put it to her lips and tried to gulp it in one big drink. But she couldn't get it all down, and she coughed and spit some back up. She took a deep breath and drank again, a sip this time.

"Thank you, Rasa. For everything you have done." Her mind was becoming clearer with each passing moment, and she began to appreciate what a terrible chance her aide was taking—had been taking for days now. "I will never forget this."

"Anything for you, my lady. But we have to go. Now. We must get you out of the city before the interference with the security system is discovered." There was extreme urgency in the servant's voice, and fear too.

"Wait . . ." Astra was beginning to realize—whoever was in the security office buying her time to escape was on a suicide mission. When Carteria's people discovered the interference, they would follow it right back to the source. "Who is blocking the surveillance?"

"That is not important, my lady. He understands his part in this."

"To die?" Astra snapped back. "To be caught and executed while I flee to safety?"

"We must get you out of here, my lady."

"No." Astra slid off the bed onto her feet. She felt wobbly for a few seconds, but then she could feel her equilibrium returning. She drained the last of Doctor Vaughn's potion and she turned to face her aide. "You go, Rasa. Get down to the security office and get our friend there. The two of you slip out of the city. Use whatever route you had planned for me."

"No, my lady. I must get you out!" Rasa's voice was shrill, and she was on the verge of hysteria. "Please, we must go now."

"I am not going, Rasa. But I order you to go. Both of you."

She walked over to her closet, pawing through the clothes and pulling out a black shirt and pair of pants.

"My lady, how can we leave you? I beg you . . . we must go now." There were tears streaming down Rasa's face.

Astra took a deep breath. Her memories had flooded back into her consciousness, and as they did she became more and more certain of what she had to do. Her father was dead, murdered in his quarters. And Lys too, killed in front of her on the orders of a man to whom her enemies planned to see her wed. And Blackhawk. She remembered Carteria telling her he was dead too, killed by the same assassin who had murdered her father.

She didn't want to believe anything a usurper and murderer like Carteria told her, but she knew Blackhawk would have come for her if he was still alive. *Ark would never leave me here,* she thought, tears streaming down her cheeks. But she held the grief in check, controlling herself with all her remaining strength.

She turned toward Rasa. "Go . . . now." She wiped her face, gritting her teeth and willing the tears to stop. "Now!" She pushed Rasa toward the door. "That is what I want. It is my order. Save our ally in the security office, and get the hell out of here." She slapped her hand on the door's locking mechanism, pushing Rasa out into the corridor. "Go," she said again. "I will never forget you, Rasa Dinari, but you must trust me when I say this is for the best. You have my everlasting gratitude." She pressed her hand over the mechanism, and the door slid shut.

She turned and leaned against the door for a few seconds. Her world was gone, everyone she cared about taken from her. Now there was only one thing for her to do, one last task to complete.

Then I can be with you all, she thought. She stood for a moment, eyes closed with images dancing in her mind. Her mother. Blackhawk and her father. And Lys. She felt the tears coming again, but she clamped down on them. Astra Lucerne had never been a soldier by trade, but she was a warrior at heart, a fighter who would never yield. And now it was time for her last battle.

She had a promise to keep. She would kill Carteria.

CHAPTER 20

"YOUR WORK HERE IS TO BE COMMENDED, AGENT MORGUS." Wilhelm sat across the makeshift table from the agent. The command post was far from the normal ostentatious affair of an imperial army headquarters. Rather, it was just a compact portable shelter with a desk on one end, and the small, scratch-built table on the other. Lord Tragonis was steadily turning out trained soldiers on Kalishar, but transport capacity was still a serious problem, even with Vos's newly established control over the shipping guilds. There was barely enough capacity to carry men and supplies, so luxuries had been cut to the bone. And that included a plush shelter to serve as the C-in-C's headquarters.

"Thank you, General Wilhelm. I must admit, I was shaken after Agent Calgarus's unexplained death. I feared we had some previously unknown enemy on Nordlingen, but that has not proved to be the case. Our operations have exceeded our highest targeted parameters. Simply put, the Nordlingeners are quite stupid. Manipulating them is not at all difficult."

"I wouldn't say stupid, Eich. Easily led, perhaps. As are most people. Nevertheless, I daresay your operation is a greater danger to Celtiborian control of the planet than my army."

The invasion force had come close to defeating the Celtiborians, but Lucerne's army held on despite everything Wilhelm had managed to throw at them. Then they abandoned the cities, diverting all their strength into a last-ditch attack. Wilhelm did his best, but his rookie soldiers didn't have what it took to stand against crack veterans like the Celtiborians. Their lines crumbled, and they fled back into the hills. He'd finally managed to stabilize things and establish a fallback defensive line . . . sacrificing many of his own soldiers to accomplish even that.

Things had been fairly static since. Both sides were exhausted. They had suffered heavy casualties, and the Celtiborians were still low on ammunition. But Wilhelm knew the stalemate wouldn't last. The Celtiborians had filled some of their supply gap by seizing storehouses of Nordlingener weapons, primitive compared to their own equipment, but far better than empty guns. And in the hands of those grim veterans any weapon was deadly dangerous.

"Eich, my forces are stuck where they are. The Celtiborians are weakened, but there is no way I'll be able to mount an offensive any time soon. I need you to ramp up your efforts. I don't care what or why or how, but we need to push this planet over the edge. A pure military conquest is out of the question, at least until we get reinforcements or wear the Celtiborians down more. And your operations are the best way I can think of to sap their strength." He looked across the table at the agent. Wilhelm was the military commander on Nordlingen, but he was also Morgus's superior at imperial intelligence. Other than Vos and Tragonis, there wasn't a man or woman in the Far Stars who outranked him.

Morgus sat silently for a few seconds, then he stared back at Wilhelm. "What are you authorizing me to do?" Wilhelm understood what Eich was asking. Morgus had been sent to Nordlingen with a fairly wide set of operational parameters, but he hadn't had a blank check. Calgarus had been on the planet to assess Morgus's operation and to decide whether to expand or upgrade his mission parameters. But Calgarus ended up dead, and Morgus had continued in accordance with his original mandate.

"I'm taking off the shackles, Eich. I'm authorizing you to do whatever you wish. Your only orders are to create as much disruption as possible. Consign this planet to hell. I don't care what you do, Eich, and I don't care what it costs.

"Just give me chaos."

Vos walked slowly down the dimly lit hallway. In three years as governor on Galvanus Prime, he'd only been down in these catacombs twice before. There were mostly storage areas in the lower levels of the imperial capitol, filled with artifacts of little interest to him. Dusty old artworks and other relics of Galvanus Prime's mediocre past bored him mightily. But the archives were down here as well, and the chief archivist had sent word that he had discovered something of note.

He walked through the open door into the small office. "I have come to you, Professor Orash, as you requested. I hope this is worth my time." He let the unspoken threat hang there.

Vos had ordered Dun Orash to research a number of matters, and he'd been singularly unimpressed with the progress he had seen. Vos was a man of action, and he expected quick results. So far, he hadn't gotten them . . . and he didn't plan on giving the man much more time.

"My thanks, Your Excellency," the archivist said meekly. Dun Orash was a frail man, thin, of average height. He motioned toward a chair he had set up at a small table. "Please, Your Excellency, sit. I can assure you that you will be interested in what I have for you."

"You've said that before," Vos said, but sat down. "So tell me, Dun, what have you found?"

"I have been researching the origin of Arkarin Blackhawk for several years, as you know."

"Yes, Dun, I *do* know. And in all that time you have been able to tell me nothing other than the fact that all trace of him disappears almost twenty-five years ago." Vos glared at the archivist. "You've told me every place he's been since, every man he's killed, every woman he's bedded. But nothing about where he came from."

"Until now, Governor."

"Oh?"

"I believe I can now answer your questions about Blackhawk's origin. Or at least offer a strong hypothesis."

Vos's eyes widened. *Finally* . . . "By all means, Dun. Tell me what you have found."

The archivist nodded, and he pick up a handheld control unit, turning on the wall display. "By all accounts, Arkarin Blackhawk arrived in the Far Stars somewhere between twenty-two and twenty-four years ago. There was no way to be certain if he has always lived in the Far Stars or if he came from the empire; however, the complete lack of any prior records has suggested he is not native to the sector. I have recently been exploring the possibility that he is a refugee or fugitive of some kind from imperial space—"

Vos stared at Orash. "Yes, I know all this. I do not have time to waste. Get to the point."

Orash was flustered a bit by Vos's interruption, but he nodded and replied, "Yes, Your Excellency." He punched a button on the controller, and an image of Blackhawk appeared on the screen. He appeared to be in his midthirties.

"This is Blackhawk less than three years ago. It is an image taken from the security cameras of the Far Stars Bank headquarters. It is the clearest capture we have. It has been surprisingly difficult to secure images of the man. To call him camera shy would be a gross understatement."

Vos was staring at the archivist. "This is fascinating, Dun, but I have seen this image, and I know where it is from. I repeat: Do you have anything new for me?"

"Yes, Your Excellency, but it is only a theory. I need to explain so you can follow my thinking."

Vos frowned, but he nodded and said, "Very well, but make it quick."

"Yes, Your Excellency." He gestured toward the image on the display. "You will notice that the man in the image appears to be much younger than we know Blackhawk must be. His exploits over the past twenty years are fairly well documented—and even in his earlier adventures, he was clearly extremely capable and well trained. One of our greatest mysteries has been his youthful appearance when we can deduce that he must be at least fifty years old."

Vos sighed. "So Blackhawk is vain. He has had cosmetic surgery. That is your great discovery?"

"Or, Your Excellency, he is a man who naturally ages at a reduced rate."

"What are you talking about, Dun?"

"There have long been secret imperial initiatives involving genetic engineering. Indeed, it has been suspected for some time that several top soldiers and operatives of the empire have been the creations of such programs."

"Continue . . ." Vos was getting interested.

"This, as I'm sure you realize, is nothing but supposition. So we proceeded to examine the evidence. The appearance of slow aging is one possible trait such a genetically engineered individual might exhibit, but Blackhawk's youthful look is hardly proof that he is the product of an imperial genetics program. Still, I moved forward based on the assumption that this was indeed his origin, and I tried to find corroborating factors."

Orash turned toward the screen and pressed the button on his controller again. A chart appeared. "These are the results of a computer analysis of Blackhawk's known combat capabilities, and the results of battles he has fought for which there are adequate records to support study.

"We analyzed Blackhawk opponents against a series of human norms, adjusting for stochastic factors to establish a probability for fighters of various skill levels to defeat the enemies Captain Blackhawk has vanquished."

Vos stared at the chart for a few seconds, but then he turned toward Orash. "Decipher this for me . . . what did your analysis show?"

"Even using the parameters for human warriors in the first percentile of ability, the AI projected win percentages of less than 1 percent in eight instances, and less than 5 percent in twenty. And that is based only on the combats for which we have significant data on Blackhawk's opponents."

Vos stared back, his look a combination of interest and confusion. "So that proves . . ."

"It proves nothing, Your Excellency. However, it provides strong mathematical evidence that Arkarin Blackhawk possesses physical abilities far beyond those of even the very best human specimens. Indeed, the incident where he defeated the Kalishari ka'al's champion and the stegaroid he was riding is a single example of extraordinary defiance of probability—less than one chance in four thousand by the AI's estimate. But all incidents taken together suggest the likelihood that Blackhawk is a human being with abilities derived even from the highest ends of the naturally occurring gene pool is less than one in seven hundred billion."

Vos stared back across the table. "One in seven hundred billion?"

"Yes, Your Excellency. For all intents and purposes, we can assume that Captain Blackhawk is a genetically engineered being . . . the product of a highly advanced laboratory and not a traditional conception or birth."

"That explains his abilities," Vos said, his tone quiet, thoughtful. "But how does it help us learn about his past?"

"Genetic engineering of this sort is extremely rare. Indeed, based on this data, we can assume almost with certainty Blackhawk did not originate in the Far Stars. The processes that created him are beyond the science of any world of the sector."

"So he is from the empire?"

"Almost without question. And even in the empire, no privately run laboratory could have produced him. Genetic engineering of this sort is prohibited in the empire, and the punishment for engaging in it is death by torture for all involved."

"So he's—"

"Yes!" Orash said. Vos ignored the interruption, too interested in what the researcher had discovered. "It means Captain Blackhawk was almost certainly produced by a clandestine imperial program."

Vos stared at Orash, his eyes focused like two lasers.

The scholar continued. "And the processes used would have been enormously expensive. Cripplingly so, even for the empire itself."

"So he must have been someone significant. A high-ranking operative or a soldier . . ."

"Precisely, Your Excellency. Based on that assumption, I began a search through the records seeking any imperial officers or agents of note reported missing in the approximate time period of Blackhawk's arrival in the Far Stars."

"And you found something?"

"Yes, Your Excellency, I did. The initial search yielded four individuals of sufficient stature missing during the five-year period preceding Blackhawk's first recorded activity in the Far Stars. I was able to eliminate three of them fairly easily, leaving only one potential.

"I had a strong belief this candidate might be the identity we were looking for, so I had my staff search data records from locations he had visited, focusing specifically on that five-year period, attempting to discover evidence from the other side, as it were."

"And what did you find?" Vos demanded. He was starting to lose his patience again.

"We found Arkarin Blackhawk." Orash looked across the table into Vos's confused expression. "Not Blackhawk the Far Stars adventurer, but Blackhawk the middle-aged engineer turned revolutionary on Deltara. A man who was killed when the imperial forces arrived and crushed the rebellion."

"You're losing me, Dun. Blackhawk isn't dead." *Not unless Rachen has managed to finish him off by now.*

"Yes, Your Excellency. Arkarin Blackhawk is dead. The man in the Far Stars, the captain of *Wolf's Claw,* took the name of a deceased rebel and engineer, but that is not the identity he was born—or, more accurately, created—with."

Vos stared across the table, his gaze focused on his subordinate. "So then who is he?"

"The man who disappeared without a trace from the fighting on Deltara. An imperial warrior presumed dead in the battle, his body lost somewhere in the rubble." He paused. "I believe that Blackhawk is none other than Frigus Umbra, the most feared imperial general of his day."

Vos sat still, in stunned silence. *Umbra,* he thought, feeling the heat inside him rising, hatred long buried pushing its way out. Frigus Umbra had been the scourge of the empire, a military genius, a man without fear, without pity. He had invaded many worlds, crushed millions under his iron heel. On Deltara certainly . . .

And on a planet called Belleger.

Vos sat quietly, his thoughts drifting back through the years. Belleger, where he'd watched Umbra's soldiers murder his parents. Where he'd seen the refugees, the orphaned children like him die in the streets. Where he'd become . . . what he'd become. Frigus Umbra had been the architect of it all, and Vos's sole comfort had been to imagine the vicious general lying dead and unburied in the ruins of a rebel planet. But to find out Umbra wasn't dead, that he had escaped . . . it was almost too much to bear.

"Are you okay, Your Excellency?"

Vos heard the question, but he didn't answer, not for a long while. All he could do was sit there, his fists clenched and his body literally shaking with rage. One name kept running through his mind, clear, inescapable.

Frigus Umbra.

CHAPTER 21

"WE DON'T HAVE TIME TO DISCUSS OUR LOSSES IN TRANSIT AND on landing. There are enemy forces less than ten kilometers from our position, and I need you to deploy two of your battalions in a defensive line while we unload the Tiger Company's tanks." Blackhawk's voice was firm, almost imperious.

Carano had started giving him shit the second they hit ground. Between the unorthodox close-in transit and belly-landing the transports, the mercenary companies had lost ten percent of their strength before even exchanging shots with the enemy. The merc general was livid about the losses, and he had let Blackhawk know about it in spades.

The plain presented a bizarre view, dozens of massive freighters, set down all across the flat grasslands. Soldiers poured out of the ships, forming up into columns and shaking down into battle order. And plumes of thick black smoke rose from the locations where four ships had crashed on landing. Two of them were total losses, everyone on board killed instantly. But half the occupants of the other two had survived, and even now they were forming up around their stricken vessels, tending to the wounded and trying to organize around the gaps in their formations.

"Fuck this shit, Blackhawk. When you sold me on this scheme, you didn't tell me you were going to throw my men away on insane jumps and crazy landings." Carano was shaking with rage. Blackhawk understood—and he knew Carano was going to catch hell from the others, who'd signed on mostly because he'd convinced them. But there was no time for bullshit like this. Not now.

"Enough, Carano. This is war, not a fucking picnic. Men die. But the losses pale next to what they will be if we lose this fight. We didn't have time to waste, so we had to risk the close-in transit. And the enemy controls the spaceport. We don't have any dropships, so how the hell did you think we were going to get down to the surface?"

Blackhawk's voice was deep, and there was a strange force to it, almost a compulsion to obey. Carano was enraged, but he hesitated and stared back silently, his urge to argue fading away. "But so many dead already . . ." the mercenary finally managed to force out. The intensity was gone, however, his will to resist Blackhawk's orders clearly weakened to impotence.

"We have surprise on our side, Vladimir. We are on-planet and in position without giving the enemy time to prepare. Is it better to lose ten percent to gain that advantage? Or forty percent launching assault after assault against an entrenched enemy?"

Blackhawk's eyes were intense, and they bored into Carano's. "Now do as I say, and get that defensive line in place. The enemy is probably going to hit us with whatever they can get here quickly . . . which is just what we want. They will launch piecemeal attacks, and your line will repulse them. And when they have exhausted themselves, we will counterattack." Blackhawk spoke with conviction, without a trace of doubt in his voice. "And then we will not stop . . . not until the capital is ours, and the enemy is utterly destroyed."

It has been so long, he thought, breathing deeply and feeling the power inside him. Yes, they had taken losses, but he had gotten his army on the ground faster than anyone would have believed possible. He had won the initiative at the cost of a few ships full of mercenaries, soldiers who would have died anyway, fighting a more prepared enemy. *Carano doesn't understand. The battle is half won already.*

They don't understand, Blackhawk, but I do. We do. We fought once for the empire, now we battle against it. But the gods of war care not, because the choice is still a stark one—victory or defeat. The exhilaration of battle is the same, the elation at triumph. And the cost of victory, it too is the same . . .

Blackhawk pushed back against the voice in his head, against the part of him that would completely erase Arkarin. But he knew what it told him was true, and the voice was pushing back just as hard the deeper he found himself in the fight.

He also knew another truth: that Astra was out there, Carteria's prisoner. Blackhawk had seen the videos, watched her stand next to the foul creature, smiling, her hands clasped on his arm as he spoke of the two marrying . . .

Truth or not, if I must become Frigus Umbra again to save Astra, then so be it . . . I shall become Frigus Umbra. And Carteria and his people will see the true face of war and despair.

"All gunners, target the first three ships of the enemy formation." Ian Hammerleigh stared coldly at the display, watching the Celtiborian ships as they approached. The fleets had made two passes already, and losses so far had been fairly equal. The Antilleans had one ship destroyed and three seriously damaged. The Celtiborians had lost two vessels outright, but they had only one other with significant damage. Overall, the fight was pretty even, which meant victory would go to the side with superior tactics and leadership.

Hammerleigh held out hope that would be his fleet.

Still, it felt strange fighting Celtiborian vessels. He'd been a squadron commander months before, when the massed fleets of the two Prime worlds had almost clashed in what would have been the largest naval battle ever in the Far Stars. Disaster had been averted then, but here he was now, barely six months later, gunning down Celtiborian warships.

This is a usurper, *though,* he thought. *There are loyal Celtiborian ships out there too, somewhere.*

"All vessels report targeting systems locked and ready. Awaiting your command to fire, sir."

"Very well, Commander." Hammerleigh was glad to have Barstowe as his tactical officer. The young man was one of the best in the Antillean service. Already Barstowe was reviewing the plots of each of the ships . . . and then double-checking the data. Hammerleigh hadn't ordered him to do the check—he didn't have to. That's what made the young spacer such an excellent officer.

"Enemy coming into firing range, Captain."

"Very well . . ." Hammerleigh was staring at his own display, waiting.

"Incoming fire, sir." The urgency in Barstowe's voice clicked up a notch, not an uncommon reaction to being fired upon. But Hammerleigh was going to give his young officer a lesson in staying cool under fire. The Celtiborian mutineers could blast away at long range, but the Antillean squadron was going right down their throats before they fired.

"*Barrick* and *Autara* report hits, sir."

"Very well. Stand by . . ."

The seconds ticked away. The Celtiborians had fired everything they had, and they'd scored half a dozen hits, but nothing that took any of Hammerleigh's ships out of the fight. And the Antilleans were still closing. Before the Celtiborians could recharge their lasers and fire again, Hammerleigh's ships would have completed their attack run.

At point-blank range.

"Captain . . ."

"Stand by, Lieutenant . . ."

Hammerleigh was focused on the screen, his eyes locked on the three small circles at the front of the enemy formation. He could see the range figures dropping on the display. Thirty thousand kilometers, twenty thousand, ten . . .

"All vessels open fire," he said calmly but loudly.

"All vessels, fire!" he heard Barstowe repeat, with rather more enthusiasm in his voice.

The lights dimmed as the ship fired its lasers at full strength, and Hammerleigh knew his other ships were doing the same. In space, the deadly blasts ripped toward their targets at the speed of light, invisible except where they traversed clouds of particulate matter.

At a range under ten thousand kilometers, the weapons were extremely accurate, and they impacted before their power dissipated to any significant degree. The three targeted ships were all hit by multiple shots, and the deadly energy ripped into their hulls, tearing the ships apart. The heavy damage from the lasers triggered chain reactions of secondary explosions that turned all three vessels into clouds of plasma within a matter of seconds.

Cheers erupted all around Hammerleigh as the crew saw the damage reports streaming in. The battle wasn't over, not yet. But there was no doubt . . . they were winning.

"Contacts emerging from hyperspace, Captain." Barstowe's voice cut through the celebrations, and in an instant the bridge was silent again.

Hammerleigh didn't respond. He just stared down at his display, waiting for the scanning report. He had no idea who these new ships were, friend or foe. But he knew the outcome of the battle was riding on that answer.

Katarina walked through the crumbling streets of the ghetto the Celtiborians called the Back Streets. It was a nasty slum by any reasonable standard, though it occupied a place in Alban's societal hierarchy above that of the notorious Hidden City— one could at least live indefinitely if not comfortably in the Back Streets, and many who found themselves relegated there ultimately managed to climb back out. It wasn't a plush existence by any means, but there were cheap rooms available and vendors in the streets selling food and other necessities. The whores were disease-ridden, but they could be had for half an imperial copper, and the plentiful Velurian "leaf" offered a cheap high for those who wanted to forget their troubles.

Not the worst place, as far as shitholes go.

The neighborhood was a home to the lowest class of workers in Alban—and a varied assortment of fugitives and petty criminals. It was the perfect place for those who didn't want too much attention.

It was where she would be if it was her on assignment. She was pretty sure her target was still on-planet, and that alone was surprising. It gave her hope that Blackhawk had survived the attack. Why else would his assassin have remained behind except to complete the job? But that left her with another question: Was Blackhawk still on Celtiboria?

But all hell broke loose on the planet almost the instant Ark was attacked. The others would have gotten him back to the *Claw* and off-planet. Ace wouldn't have hesitated.

Ace . . .

Katarina was on a mission, if a self-appointed one, and her mind was a focused tool right now. But her frozen resolve wavered just a bit as she thought of the *Claw*'s first officer. Ace Graythorn was a pain in the ass, cocky and irritating. But she'd come to realize that was only on the surface. She'd begun to see beyond that image Ace projected to the man below: loyal, brave to a fault, and smart as a whip. And something more too. Katarina had long eschewed personal relationships. They didn't mesh well with the life of a Sebastiani assassin. But it was also becoming clear that such a life—as a lone wolf killer—was almost certainly behind her. She was a member of the *Claw*'s family now.

And that was letting her see Ace in a different way than she had before . . .

She pushed her thoughts aside. When her target was dead, when she returned to the *Claw,* and they were all past this crisis—then perhaps. But not now. Now it was time to kill.

The streets were filthy, full of litter and human waste. City services in the Back Streets were sparse, and many buildings just dumped sewage and wastewater in the open ditches on either side of the road. But an assassin as skilled as the one she was pursuing would pay no heed to such things. Katarina had been trained to disregard discomfort, foul stench, pain, and hardship, and she didn't doubt her adversary had as well.

It was a crime-ridden place too, plagued by thieves and wandering gangs, but that would be no concern to her prey either. A petty thief or thug for hire who assaulted an assassin of such caliber would quickly find he'd made a fatal mistake.

She turned and wandered into another building. She'd been checking out all the flophouses and hole-in-the-wall inns. Her instincts told her she would find her target hiding in one of them. And she was determined to find him—if she had to rough up the clerk in every stinking shithole in the Back Streets.

"Colonel Vulcan, I want those tanks on the move. Now!" Blackhawk was standing just below the lead vehicle of the Tiger Company column. It was three meters high, covered with dark paint in a camouflage pattern. A large main gun protruded from the front and two racks of rockets flanked the turret. A half-dozen smaller guns rounded out the vehicle's awesome armament. It was an astonishing testament to the materiel of war, a killing machine almost without equal.

Vulcan's mercenary company was known for its armor, even though the colossal main battle tanks were enormously expensive to produce and operate. Most mercenary units were purely infantry, easy to equip and transport. But Vulcan had targeted his own niche, and his people had one of the most fearsome reputations in the Far Stars. It cost a king's ransom to hire the Tigers, but they promised a weapon few enemies could match, and that was a priceless advantage in war.

The Tigers had never been many, even before the pro-tracted fighting on Saragossa had cost them far greater losses than they'd expected. But now they had an open field in front of them. The Celtiborian forces were highly efficient and well armed, but they were mostly infantry. And the speed of Black-hawk's attack had denied them the time to dig in and build fortifications. It was a textbook example of the perfect situation for armor on the battlefield.

The nature of the decades-long struggle on Celtiboria had dictated the composition of its armies. The warlords had ruled mostly over agricultural villages and small cities with limited industry. Celtiboria was the most populous world in the Far Stars, but its centuries of disunity and internecine combat had relegated it to a second tier of economic development. Large factories and manufacturing plants capable of producing mili-tary aircraft and vehicles were rare—and they had always been massive targets for enemy aggression.

Marshal Lucerne had negotiated alliances with the other Primes, and few of the lesser worlds in the sector had the eco-nomic might to field armies equipped with large air forces or complements of tanks. So his vaunted army, by far the most feared fighting force in the sector, had remained primarily an infantry formation, with no real need to expand beyond its his-torical proficiencies.

We've got the armor now, though. And we're going to use it.

"You want us to head straight for the city, General?" Ariano

Vulcan had a reputation as a hothead, a man who argued with commands as often as he followed them. But he hadn't questioned a single order from Blackhawk. He clearly responded to something in his new commander's tone, a strength, a force of will. Whatever it was, Blackhawk's strange charisma on the battlefield seemed to affect martinets and argumentative officers with an even greater force than it did more reasonable commanders.

"Yes. Don't stop for anything. Carano and the other companies will be behind, moving up to protect your flanks, so just cut a corridor through the defenses. I've got ten thousand picked infantry behind your tanks. You drive to the city limits, and they will take the place . . . block by block if they have to."

"Yes, General Blackhawk." Vulcan turned around, looking back over his shoulder at the forty tanks stacked up and ready to go. Then he nodded to Blackhawk and disappeared inside the massive turret. A few seconds later the hatch slid shut, and the heavy tracks began to move. The immense beast of war surged forward, its 160 tons of armored mass digging deep into the ground, spitting mud behind as it slowly accelerated.

Blackhawk stood and watched for a few minutes as the battle tanks rumbled slowly, widening their line, forming up eight abreast. Then he turned and walked toward Carano's command post. It was time to get the rest of the army moving.

DeMark walked slowly through the waist-deep water. He was soaked to the bone, and the crisp dawn air chilled him to his core. He knew the entire army was just as miserable, that half of them were probably cursing him for his orders to fall out and prepare to launch an offensive.

So be it. If every commander cared about the curses of his men, they'd never get anything done.

Opening the dikes had stopped the Carterian forces cold, turning the fighting along the battle line into a waterlogged quagmire. It had been an extreme strategy, one that would affect the inhabitants of Riverlands for generations to come. But it had been a necessary action to save the loyalist army, and DeMark had used well the time he'd paid so dearly for, building up his forces and preparing for the rematch he was now setting in motion.

He wasn't sure what to expect from the locals if his forces were able to break through and drive to the capital. Carteria's propaganda campaign was raging without a pause, accusing him of Lucerne's murder. And the usurper had repeatedly featured Astra in his addresses. She stood next to him, holding his arm, and mostly looking passively into the camera. DeMark knew there was something wrong with her, some kind of coercion at work. She looked strange, unnatural—and anyone truly acquainted with Astra Lucerne knew she was *anything* but passive.

Still, DeMark was sure the act worked for the majority of the people, sitting in their homes for the most part, programmed to believe what they heard. They saw the marshal's daughter standing next to Carteria, bestowing her credibility on him, and they looked no further. He controlled the capital. He controlled the broadcast facilities. It wasn't hard for the citizens to begin to accept his rule as legitimate. They wanted peace, not civil war and a return to the days of the warlords, and they would give their loyalty to anyone who promised them just that. By the time they realized what a monster had taken Lucerne's place, it would be too late. They would be slaves.

And Carteria will be just as much a slave. DeMark knew his enemy wasn't strong enough to pull off what he had managed alone, that he must have imperial backing. No one else was strong enough, no one else had the nerve to try something like this.

And that nerve was paying off. Carteria was quickly winning the contest without even fighting. The people of Celtiboria were becoming accustomed to him, and the lack of fighting had made his rule seem all the more normal. They were starting to believe him and accept him as their leader.

Except in Riverlands. The inhabitants of Lucerne's ancestral homelands were made of sturdy stuff. They were tough and independent, and they knew Astra Lucerne, well enough, at least, to be sure she'd never voluntarily support a piece of slime like Carteria. In the weeks since he'd flooded Riverlands and destroyed thousands of farms and countless villages, the people had nevertheless rallied to DeMark's cause.

Retired soldiers—men in their sixties and even seventies, who had served the marshal in his earliest campaigns—straggled into camp, bringing old rifles with them . . . and as often as not, sons as well. As the days passed, more recruits trickled in, the men of the Great Plateau a hundred kilometers upstream, where Lucerne had settled thousands of mustered out veterans.

Supply was a problem, but thanks to the storehouses Lucerne had set up years before, it was a manageable one. DeMark had no production facilities to speak of, but there was enough of a stockpile to support his army for a few months. He'd wondered how long he should wait before making a move. His forces were still outnumbered, and the flooded Riverlands would impede his own offensive, just as it had his enemy's. Those one hundred ships decided it for him.

"Marius . . ."

Brigadier Trevannes was a few meters ahead, talking to a small cluster of officers. A column of soldiers marched off to the side. They looked profoundly miserable, but they were moving forward nevertheless. They held their weapons over their heads, cartridge belts wrapped around the assault rifles. They were veterans, and they were going into battle. They might be wet and frozen to the bone, but their guns would be ready, by God.

"Yes, sir?" Trevannes turned to face the army commander. The other officers looked on nervously at the sight of DeMark.

Stop that, he thought. *I'm just one of you.* But he knew the hero worship was useful too, however uncomfortable it made him.

"I want to launch the attack in one hour." DeMark walked the last few meters and stood right next to his executive officer.

"Sir . . . we will only have half the frontline units in place by then. Perhaps we should wait . . ."

"No," DeMark snapped back, more brusquely than he'd intended. "Time isn't on our side," he said, reining in his tone. "We have no idea who landed or how large their force is, but we'll never have a better chance than this. If we wait, and the newly arrived force is defeated fighting alone, we will have lost our best opportunity to destroy Carteria. And if they're enemies—which I doubt—then we need to strike them before they can establish a firm foothold on the planet."

Trevannes nodded. "Very well, sir. I agree. I will move forward and take command of the lead units."

"No," DeMark said sternly.

"Sir?"

"I will take command of the attack. I want you to direct the advance, keep the reserves moving forward through this morass . . . whatever it takes."

"General, you can't expose yourself to that level of risk," Trevannes said, his voice thick with tension. "We need you. You are not expendable."

DeMark just smiled, and he put his hand on Trevannes's

shoulder. "We are all expendable, my old friend . . . and this is something I have to do." He looked forward, in the direction of the front line. "That's an order, Brigadier Trevannes," he said simply.

"Identity confirmed, Captain. They are imperial ships." Barstowe was doing his best to stay resolute, but his voice wavered nevertheless. They all knew they'd been fighting to unify the Far Stars against imperial aggression, and in recent weeks it had become evident their enemies were being supported by agents of the empire. But this was something different entirely. It was no machinations behind the scenes, no covert financial support. They were staring straight at an imperial battle fleet.

"Open a line, Lieutenant." Hammerleigh took a deep breath. *This is above my pay grade,* he thought grimly.

"Open, sir."

"Attention, imperial commander, this is Commodore Ian Hammerleigh of the Antillean navy, acting on the direct authority of the legitimate Celtiborian authorities."

Okay, that's a bit of an exaggeration . . .

"You have entered the sovereign space of the planet Celtiboria and the Far Stars Confederation. You are directed to depart at once." He ran his hand under his neck, signaling Barstowe to cut the connection.

He knew he was wasting his time, but there wasn't much else he could do. His pathetic little cluster of damaged frigates didn't stand a chance against the large fleet that had emerged.

"The fleet will power up engines and prepare for maneuvers, Lieutenant." He didn't know yet what he was going to do. He might be able to get far enough from the planet and the enemy fleet to jump back to Antilles, but at least a couple of his ships were too damaged for that. Retreating home meant leaving them behind.

Yet staying means losing the entire fleet.

"I want all ships to retreat at flank speed. Damaged vessels are to keep up the best they can."

"Yes, sir," Barstowe replied.

Hammerleigh leaned back in his chair, deep in thought. The idea of fleeing the system made him sick to his stomach. He'd come here to support Blackhawk and his mercenaries, and he wasn't the kind of man who could live easily with turning tail and abandoning allies. But if the imperials were moving openly, things had just gotten a lot grimmer—and Antilles was going to need every ship she could get. Especially if the Celtiborians were going to fall.

"I don't feel any thrust, Lieutenant."

"Coming, sir. Just a second."

An instant later, Hammerleigh felt the familiar g-forces. His ships were on the move. He still wasn't sure what he was going to do, but he was certain he wanted as much time as possible before he had to make a final decision.

The massive main battle tank was moving forward at forty kilometers an hour, crashing through the undergrowth and small trees like they weren't even there. The gigantic turret pivoted, and the main gun fired, loosing a shell that would travel almost ten thousand meters to obliterate its target.

The Tiger Company's tanks had moved ahead without pause. Carteria's soldiers had been unable to even slow them, despite their best efforts. They'd planted mines, dug hasty tank traps—everything they could think of to slow the monsters of war. But they'd only managed to take four of them out of the line, and only one of those had serious damage. The other three had just had their tracks thrown—and two of those were already repaired and back on the line.

Blackhawk watched from a small hill as a pair of tanks opened up on an enemy battalion. Each tank brought two heavy autocannons to bear and fired on full auto. The defending soldiers were crouched down in a hasty trench, but the big hypervelocity projectiles tore easily through the small berms they'd thrown up. Dozens fell, and the rest of the unit returned fire, their bullets bouncing harmlessly off the tanks' heavy armor.

A few small groups raced forward out of the trenches, handpicked teams making semisuicidal charges, trying to throw explosive satchels onto the tracks of the tanks, disabling the monsters and buying time for their compatriots to swarm the things. But the Tiger Company had its own infantry, trained to work closely with the armor and protect the flanks of the great tanks. They stayed close by, gunning down the satchel teams as their big brothers continued to rake the enemy lines. After a few minutes, the survivors of the battalion, no more than half its original strength, began to pull back. At first, they held their order and moved in formation. But the autocannons kept on them, and they began to come apart, soldiers racing in different directions, trying to escape the deadly fire any way they could.

The tanks continued forward, but they came to a halt at the edge of the enemy's former position. There was a deep trench, and it was too wide for the tanks to cross.

Blackhawk turned, and he saw the support units moving forward. The bridging vehicle was even larger than the tanks, and it carried a twenty-meter-long platform of reinforced hypersteel, a bridge to stretch across the gap, providing a path for the tanks to resume their advance. Still, the enemy had bought themselves a little time to regroup. Blackhawk knew it would be close to an hour before the bridging unit had their equipment in place. An hour was a long time in the middle of a fight, but then Vulcan's tanks would be on the move again. With any luck, they'd hit Alban by nightfall. But his forces had more than luck on their side.

He took one last look before he turned and walked back toward HQ. His mind was constantly analyzing the battle and the nonstop stream of reports.

Luck is important in any fight, but lazy commanders attribute far to much to uncontrollable factors. They are lazy, stupid, cowardly . . . they don't understand war. At least not like I do. Information wins battles—the ability to process it quickly and make quick decisions based on changing data.

Of course a division of main battle tanks doesn't hurt, especially when the enemy doesn't have any.

The most recent report came through from one of the drones he'd sent out—this one from the north. *More fighting in that direction,* Blackhawk thought. *That has to be DeMark. He knows we're here and he's driving down to link up with us. Good, Rafaelus. Good.*

Probability that Rafaelus DeMark is in command of loyalist forces 76 percent +/-7 percent. Further probability that DeMark would order an attack after detecting your landing 94 percent +/-3.5 percent.

There it was. He and the AI agreed. DeMark was the likeliest successor to Lucerne, the most able of an extremely talented pool of officers. And he was extremely aggressive, not a man to wait for events to develop around him.

He was a man Blackhawk could depend on to cover his northern flank, even though he didn't know he was doing it.

Blackhawk jogged back toward his command post, taking care to avoid the deep, muddy ruts where Vulcan's tanks had come through. There were bodies everywhere, mostly the enemy. Supported by the fearsome armored spearhead, the mercenaries had suffered far lower losses than their enemies— and their support services had managed to evac most of the wounded very quickly.

Blackhawk had been almost three full days without sleep, but he was awake and alert. He'd forgotten the excitement of battle, the surge of energy he got from leading soldiers into the fight. It was like a drug, watching the broken formations of the enemy flee before his advancing forces. The perfect high, the ultimate feeling of achievement.

He was the perfect warrior, his mind totally focused. Save one thing.

Astra.

He could see her in his mind, and he imagined her captive inside the palace. He saw visions of the end of the fight, Carteria and his top officers gathered in his headquarters, the sounds of shelling getting closer and closer. Blackhawk knew the usurper would never harm Astra while his cause lived. He needed her to sustain his legitimacy. But what would happen when all was lost, when his last adherents were gathered together awaiting their final fall?

They will kill her. When they know it is over. When they are facing defeat and destruction, they will kill Astra.

> **Probability Carteria will order the death of Astra Lucerne if his forces are defeated, 83 percent +/-14 percent. Unusually large error factor due to incomplete data on subject Carteria.**

"Lucas," Blackhawk yelled into his comm unit. "Get the *Claw* ready to take off."

"You got it, Skip. Where we going?"

"Not far. Just to the palace." He cut the line and turned toward Carano. The mercenary general was leaning over a table, studying a map displayed on a large tablet.

"I have to apologize, Blackhawk," Carano said. "You were right. We lost heavily getting here, but we caught them flat-footed. They're retreating across the line. If we can keep them from regrouping and setting up another line, we should reach the capital in twelve hours. We would almost certainly have greater losses if we'd given them time to dig in."

"No apology necessary," Blackhawk replied. "And they won't get another line formed. Nothing solid. Not with Vulcan's tanks on their tails."

I've got to get there before they realize they've already lost. Or Astra is as good as dead.

"I need some of your troops, Vladimir. A platoon of your best."

Carano nodded. "Of course, Ark. Where do you want them?"

"At the *Claw*. As quickly as possible."

Carano stared back with a look of surprise on his face. "Are you going somewhere?"

"Yes," Blackhawk answered, his voice devoid of emotion. "I'm going to the palace. I'm going to kill Carteria."

CHAPTER 22

RAX FLORIN SAT ON HIS THRONE, ALONE AND DEEP IN THOUGHT.
He'd been drawn into the plot to overthrow the previous ka'al,
and to take the office for his own, to rule Kalishar.

The lure of power, he knew, was a drug to most men, an
addiction that ruled their minds and souls. Florin had felt the
same urges, the impulse to reach out and grasp the throne his
new imperial friends were offering. But it wasn't greed in the
end that had pushed him into accepting the mastery of Kalishar. It was fear.

The old ka'al had long been suspicious of Florin, wary of a
well-known pirate who had retired and settled on Kalishar with
nothing to do but bed his mistresses and covet the throne. The

ka'al had also been a famous buccaneer in his day, even a popular one, at least among those of his curiously insular profession. Tarn Belgaren had been a clever man, and a wildly successful pirate in his youth. He'd been the scourge of a dozen systems, and when the opportunity to make himself a monarch presented itself, he was unable to resist. Years later, as an old man, obese and corrupt, the strength and energy of his youth gone, he'd feared that Rax Florin presented the same threat that he had so many years before, a younger, more aggressive rival.

Or so the ka'al had seen it.

In fact, Florin had no designs whatsoever on the ka'al's position. Not until the monarch's suspicions created them out of necessity. Florin was a different kind of man than Tarn Belgaren, intelligent and well educated for a pirate. He had come into his illicit profession by a fairly circuitous route, and he'd never become as comfortable with brutality and bloodshed as most of his peers.

That was not to say he wouldn't do what needed doing. But he didn't find bloodshed the *only* answer.

Florin had been perfectly content to spend his time bedding his mistresses and *not* plotting to take the throne. In the end, though, Belgaren's growing animosity had left him no choice. He was not going to sit around, waiting for Belgaren's guards to come murder him on their lord's order.

And so I sold myself to the empire.

Florin had done what he'd decided he had to do, taken the steps he deemed wisest. He'd negotiated hard with the empire, at least, setting a high price on his bondage. But bondage it was nevertheless. And a quagmire that continued to swallow him whole, pulling him deeper and deeper into servitude to the empire.

He'd insisted on a large imperial garrison, part of his price for allowing the governor's minions to turn a vast swath of Kalishari desert into a massive military training facility, one that was now churning out soldiers at an astonishing rate. He'd felt the garrison was necessary for his safety. If his neighbors found out he was allowing the empire to train soldiers on his world, they would not react well. And Kalishar's own armed forces were stretched thin enough keeping control over the mobs of drunken and partying pirates that drove the planet's economy.

The imperial soldiers virtually guaranteed Kalishar could resist an attack, at least one from any of the planets located nearby. But Florin was no fool, and he realized his protectors were also his jailers. And with the importance of the training facility, Kalishar had become far too crucial to the empire to allow the wishes—or even the continued existence—of the local monarch to interfere with imperial plans.

Florin had been pondering his situation for months now. The deal he'd made was one he could live with . . . as long as he lived, at least. But he wasn't foolish enough to believe the imperial guarantees he'd received would outlive their usefulness to the empire. All it would take was for Tragonis or another high-ranked imperial to decide they were better off without a ka'al on Kalishar—and that would be the end. The one hundred thousand imperial soldiers assigned to him to protect the planet would sweep his tiny army away. Then they would drag him from his throne room, straight to his death.

And imperial methods of execution tended to be theatrical . . . and extremely unpleasant.

It all added up to one thing: he had to make a move at some point.

I just wish I had an idea of when.

He'd been waiting, watching events and hoping for some change that served his purposes, but things had only gotten worse. Marshal Lucerne was dead, the confederation caught up in a succession crisis. Things were getting worse, not better. He had to do something. Now.

That was why he'd called for Bevern. Illus Bevern had been Florin's friend for a long time. A Kalishari native, and the master of several less than fully respectable businesses, Bevern had met the current ka'al years before, when the young pirate Rax Florin had been looking for a reliable way to sell stolen goods. The two formed a tentative partnership, one that quickly solidified and stood the test of time. They'd both made millions of crowns from Florin's extraordinary career as a pirate, but their relationship had been purely social for several years now. *Almost* purely social.

Florin got up from the throne and walked slowly across the room. He'd almost asked Bevern to come to him at the palace, but he hadn't. He understood the empire and its ways, at least as well as a Far Stars pirate could, and he suspected he was under a considerable amount of surveillance. Certainly, he assumed his throne room was monitored, and he wouldn't have been surprised to discover he was being watched in his study, in the shower, even in bed with his women.

Because of these suspicions, he had kept up a charade since the day he made his deal, one he thought might be useful at some point in time. To all observers, the ka'al was a man fond of long walks in the desert.

Long solitary walks.

As a monarch, he couldn't just go wandering alone anywhere he chose, so he had created a preserve, a large expanse of desert, surrounded by a security fence and patrolled by his soldiers. And every day, without fail, he'd gone for a walk, usually alone, but occasionally with an old friend or acquaintance. It was an affectation, something that became normal to the legions of onlookers who surrounded a monarch—and to anyone else who was watching as well.

That was just what Florin wanted. He detested the cursed walks; they bored him senseless. He never understood those who saw beauty in the barren desert, and he'd much rather have been back at the palace, lying on a pile of cushions while one of his concubines massaged his back. But it was the only way to spend time with a contact far from whatever prying eyes and ears infested the palace.

He walked through the double doors of the throne room, out into the wide hallway beyond. Four guards fell in behind him as he passed their post at the doorway, and they followed him down the corridor.

"I am going to take my walk," he said. "Lord Bevern will be joining me."

"Very well, my ka'al," the commander of the guard detachment replied robotically.

"I am planning an expansion to my living quarters, and Lord Bevern's construction firm will be doing the work." Florin knew the guard captain didn't give a shit, but he spoke loudly, for the benefit of anyone else who was listening in.

"Shall I dispatch a detail to escort Lord Bevern to you, my ka'al?"

"Yes, Captain. At once."

"So you are ready to make a move?" Bevern's response was slow, his fatigue evident in each word. The sun was strong, and the desert hot, with little shade. He was older than Florin, and heavier. But he understood the need for privacy. What they were discussing could get them both impaled.

"Yes. We've been over this before. Imperial domination doesn't end well for me. I'm a convenience right now, but they'll eventually want an imperial governor on Kalishar, not a ka'al." He turned and looked at Bevern. "And an imperial regime won't bode well for you either, my friend. I don't see them allowing you to continue operating your businesses."

"I have to agree with you, but what can we do about it, other than flee? There are hundreds of thousands of soldiers on Kalishar now. You have what? Ten thousand men?" Bevern was almost gasping for breath as he forced out the words.

Florin slowed his pace. "Less than ten thousand. Just a bit over ninety-five hundred, in fact. And I suspect the ranks of my soldiers are riddled with imperial spies. But I have a plan, old friend . . . one I'm afraid asks a great deal of you."

Bevern stopped completely and looked at Florin. "What would you have me do?"

"I want to get a message through. To Arkarin Blackhawk."

"Blackhawk?" Bevern said, a hint of confusion in his voice. "He's a mercenary, an adventurer. He humiliated the old ka'al, I grant you that, but I don't see what he can do for us."

"That's because you don't know all that I know about him. Arkarin Blackhawk was close friends with Augustin Lucerne. He is almost certainly deeply involved in the succession dispute going on now. And he is a survivor. I'm betting whatever side he backs will prevail."

"And that helps us how?" Bevern asked.

"Whoever succeeds Lucerne will lead the Far Stars Confederation. And the last thing they want is an imperial operation recruiting on a dozen fringe worlds and turning out a hundred thousand trained troops a month."

"You want them to intervene? To attack Kalishar?"

Florin nodded slowly. "That is precisely what I want."

"But does that help us? How do you know Lucerne's successor will be any more kindly disposed to us than the empire?"

"I don't," Florin said simply. "But I consider it almost a certainty the imperials will eventually dispose of me . . . of us. So what do we have to lose? Our only option for long-term survival is to make the effort. I want you to deliver an offer. You travel frequently for your business, so it shouldn't draw undue attention for you to take a trip. And once you are off Kalishar, no one will be the wiser about your true destination."

Bevern stared expectantly at his friend, nodding slightly.

"We can provide them detailed maps and information on the imperial fortifications, camp, facilities. The strength and location of all military forces. We can agree to intervene with our own forces at a key moment to support their invasion."

"And in return you would want . . ." Bevern let his voice trail off.

"Pardons for both of us . . . and all our key people. A guarantee that my position as ka'al will be respected and that Kalishar will be admitted to the Far Stars Confederation with minimal interference in our internal affairs. Assurances that we will be provided with adequate protection until the fighting against the empire has concluded."

"So this is what we have come to? Begging for help from Lucerne's successors? Joining their confederation?"

Florin sighed. "It's better than getting a spear shoved up your ass in front of the new governor's headquarters. Or finding yourself nailed to a cross. The empire isn't usually gentle in its methods of execution. Painless deaths don't make as strong an impression on the population. And the imperials are all about show."

"Okay, you convinced me." Bevern sighed loudly. "I will do my best."

"That's all any of us can do at this point. Let's head back. The sooner we get you off-planet, the better I'll feel."

CHAPTER 23

ASTRA WALKED SLOWLY DOWN THE HALL. HER HEAD WAS POUNDING, and she was fighting off spells of dizziness. She could feel rivulets of sweat running down her neck, her back. Rasa's intervention had pulled her back to reality, put she still felt the effects of the drug conditioning. She had control of herself, of her thoughts again, but it was still a struggle to maintain it. Memories were flooding into her consciousness, things she had said and done while under the influence of the conditioning.

It was overwhelming, and it took all her considerable will to stay focused. She was nauseated and unnerved to her core as she recalled how she had behaved under the drug's influence. But she had to be at her best now. She had a job to do, and she'd be damned if she was going to fail. And she had to do more than maintain control . . . she had to convince anyone she saw that she was still under the effects of the drugs.

She tried to walk calmly, slowly, as she remembered herself doing under the influence of the drugs. The guards and the rank and file had no idea she'd been drugged, of course, but if anyone who did know realized she had control over herself again, that would be the end. They'd have her in the dungeon at the very least—and possibly much worse.

No, she thought, *nothing worse. Not yet, at least. That piece of shit still needs me. But I hope to Chrono that Rasa and her ally were able to escape. They saved me. Please, don't let them die for it.*

There were guards everywhere in the corridor, rushing around with considerable urgency. Astra had heard the sounds of battle, the explosions. There were only distant rumblings at first, but it had come closer over the last few hours. *They are losing,* she thought, suppressing a wave of excitement. *Is that DeMark out there? Has he fought his way back to the capital?*

She was surprised. She had figured DeMark was struggling to survive. When Bolton's people had gotten her to the extraction point, the loyalist army was gone, driven back. She hadn't expected a major reversal. Not so soon, at least. Not with all the added strength Carteria had gotten from his mysterious brown-coated allies.

She turned the corner and headed toward the control center. Carteria would be there. And she had unfinished business with the miserable pile of excrement.

"Are you well, Lady Lucerne?" A passing officer stopped and looked at her. "May I be of any assistance?"

"I am well," she replied, trying to emulate the pleasant tone she remembered from when she was drugged. "Thank you, but

I do not need anything. I am going to the command post to see the general."

She felt the tension inside, wondering if the officer would notice anything different about her behavior. She struggled to stay calm, to prevent giving off any signals that would raise the officer's suspicion.

"Very well, Lady Lucerne." The officer stood at attention for a moment and saluted, clicking his heels as he did.

"Thank you, Captain," she said, turning to continue down the corridor. Her back was soaked with sweat now, and she pushed her shoulders up, trying to keep the material of her dress from the wet skin.

She walked up to the command center door and waved her hand over the scanner. The hatch slid open, and she stepped inside, trying to look like she was staring straight ahead while her eyes snapped back and forth, scanning the room.

There he is.

Carteria was toward the front of the room, speaking with the two imperial agents and several of his officers. He turned his head and noticed her.

"Astra, my dear," he said, his tone cautious, but not quite suspicious.

"I heard the shelling," she said, her voice hollow. "I came to see if everything was okay." She could tell from his expression things were far from okay. Carteria had always lacked the sort of quiet courage most of her father's commanders possessed, and now he looked like he was on the verge of panicking.

"Yes, my sweet," he said, redoubling his effort to sound calm.

Fuck you . . . gutless coward . . . I can smell the fear on you.

"I am glad," she forced out, as she continued forward, moving closer to him. "May I stay with you for a while?"

Carteria sighed. He looked like he was about to send her away when one of the agents leaned in closer and spoke to him softly. No doubt he thought the drugged Astra couldn't hear what he was saying, but she listened carefully and caught every word. And what she heard made her stomach heave.

"Perhaps you should marry her now, General," Bartholomew said. "We must get the people to rise up, to challenge the invaders for every meter. Only the daughter of Marshal Lucerne can accomplish that. Marry her now, and address the people as one."

"How can she rally the people? She's like a child since she's been taking the drugs." There was a frown on Carteria's face.

"That is symptomatic of the early stages of the conditioning, General, but even now she should be regaining some limited— and tightly controlled—cognitive ability. She may very well be capable of a short speech now, if it is written for her."

"Perhaps you are right," Carteria said. "There is nothing to be lost by trying." His voice became darker, more threatening. "And it makes sense to keep her close. If we cannot stop the enemy advance, I will not allow her to fall into my rivals' hands."

He turned toward one of the guards. "Go and get the senior adept of the temple. Bring him here at once."

"Yes, sir." The soldier turned and hurried to the door.

"Astra, my love," Carteria said softly. "Marry me now, so we may lead our people through this crisis as husband and wife." He moved toward her and put his hand on her cheek.

She fought back the urge to take his hand off, literally. Then she struggled with another, even stronger compulsion—to drop to her knees and vomit. She managed, though, turning her head slowly and smiling at him. "Yes," she said calmly, a childlike cadence to her voice. "I think that would help give the people strength." *And it is a distraction, one that leaves me standing right next to you.*

And that's where you will die like a pig, howling in fear as you bleed to death at my feet.

"The engines are cold, Skipper, so it's liable to be a rough ride." Lucas's hands were flying over his station, working through the expedited preflight process at incredible speed.

He'd left the comm line to engineering live, and a second later Sam's voice blared out of the speaker. "Don't you worry about the engines, Lucas. Do what you've got to do, and I'll make sure the *Claw* gives you what you need."

"Thanks, Sam," Blackhawk replied into his own comm unit. He looked at Lucas. "You heard the lady."

"Yes, sir!"

Blackhawk was sitting in his chair, and he now pressed a button on the armrest, opening a line to the entire ship's PA. "Everybody, we're going in quick and dirty, so I want all of you to hang on to the ropes we've got set up. We're probably going to have a hell of a fight on our hands, but nobody gets hurt on the way in . . . got me?"

The *Claw* was packed full of Carano's handpicked veterans, a makeshift platoon of forty of the best soldiers in the army. There weren't even close to enough chairs and acceleration couches, so most of them were sitting on the floor, both hands gripping a net of cables strung around the lower deck. The trip to the palace would be short, less than a minute. But even a few seconds was enough time to get bounced off the walls and deck.

"My boys will be okay, General." Carano was seated at the reserve workstation, looking across the bridge. Blackhawk hadn't wanted the commander of the Black Helms to come along—it didn't make sense to risk so much of the chain of command in so desperate an operation. But Carano had insisted, and there hadn't been enough time to argue about it.

"Let's go, Lucas." Blackhawk nodded toward his pilot. He was perched uncomfortably in his chair, more or less leaning sideways. His heavy ammunition belt and body armor were making it a tight fit, and keeping him from truly sitting down.

He had his trusty pistol on one side of the belt, a well-worn weapon about as heavy as a handgun could be. On the other side, an even older implement of war hung in its sheath. Blackhawk's trusty shortsword had seen decades of battle with him, and he had slain countless foes with its razor-sharp edge and point.

His armament was rounded out by three frag grenades clipped to his belt, and a heavy assault rifle propped next to his chair. He was armed and equipped for a fight to the death. And that was just what he planned. He would come out of that palace with Astra Lucerne at his side . . . or he wouldn't come out at all.

"Hang on," Lucas shouted through the comm. A few seconds later, the *Claw* lurched upward, its positioning jets blasting it a hundred meters into the air before the main engines fired. The g-forces kicked in as Lucas drove toward the palace at full power.

Blackhawk could feel the stress, the crushing sensation of five times his body weight as his ship accelerated toward it target. "Now, Ace," he forced out, turning his head slowly to face his first officer.

"Got it, Ark." Ace was hunched over his station, struggling against the g's. "Needle gun engaging," he rasped as he grabbed the controls and pressed his finger over the firing stud.

The *Claw's* needle gun was a highly focused laser designed to deliver maximum power over a small target area. It could be used to destroy specific systems on a ship or to hit small targets in close proximity to friendlies. But now it was tearing apart the exterior walls of the palace, killing any defenders on the ramparts and opening the way for Blackhawk's small strike force to get inside.

The g-forces reversed direction as Lucas slammed on the braking jets and brought the *Claw* down at a sharp angle. The massive palace, a huge section of its northern wall now a smoking ruin, was growing quickly on the main display.

He's coming in too fast, Blackhawk thought. *No, Lucas knows what he is doing at those controls . . . better than you ever did.*

But it sure as hell looks like he's coming in too fast.

He slapped the comm unit and yelled, "Everybody, prepare to disembark as soon as we're down." Blackhawk's own hand was on the latch of his harness, waiting.

The *Claw* came down hard, one last lurch of g-forces before she sat still, less than five meters from the pile of rubble that had been the palace wall.

Blackhawk threw his rifle around his back, and he leaped out of his chair, running to the ladder. He slid down the rails, his feet never touching the rungs, and he raced across the lower deck, now full of Carano's men forming themselves into a rough column. He sprinted down the hall and into the cargo hold, just as the ramp was lowering to the ground.

He ducked low, taking a quick look around for any enemies. There were a few bodies mixed in with the rubble, but no live soldiers he could see. He heard the others behind him, following him into battle once again.

He charged ahead.

DeMark stared down the sights of his rifle, gently pulling the trigger. An enemy soldier fell out of the black cypress tree, a huge splash marking where he sank under the water. DeMark knew he'd been lucky to pick off the sniper. His enemy had been careless for only an instant, but that had been enough. The brief reflection off his scope had sealed his fate—at least when he faced a marksman as capable as Rafaelus DeMark.

"Let's go, it's all clear." He was talking into his comm, but he was waving his arm too. He had two companies with him, chest-deep in the murky water that had flooded the country for kilometers in every direction.

He knew as army commander he had no place this far forward, but he didn't give a shit. Trevannes had tried to talk him into falling back half a dozen times, but he'd refused, the last time with a degree of firmness he trusted would prevent another attempt . . . at least for a while.

A man could only take so much, though. He'd mourned his friend and commander, seen his comrades of twenty years murdered in an ambush when they had met to discuss the future. He'd watched the fruits of thirty years of conflict and struggle crumble away, the great army of the confederation scattered throughout the Far Stars, and the parts that remained home savaging each other in civil war. He'd sent Hain Bolton and four hundred picked men to their deaths . . . and he'd still failed to rescue Astra. It wasn't smart for him to be out with the forward pickets doing a lieutenant's job, but he also knew he couldn't live with himself if he did anything else.

He also knew there were uses for it, too. His cynical side was well aware that good leadership involved a fair degree of manipulation. It was stories like this that created a persona soldiers followed into hell itself. There were more than a few tales of the exploits of the young Augustin Lucerne, crazy acts of personal bravery still spoken of decades after they happened.

"Marius, deploy all reserves," he said into his comm unit as he trudged forward through the deep water, holding his rifle over his head. "The entire army will advance and engage the enemy across the line." Carteria's forces were wavering under the intense assault, and now it was time to put everything on the line and risk it all on a breakthrough.

DeMark pushed forward, ignoring the burning in his legs. Every step was an effort, his waterlogged boots sinking into the deep silty mud below the floodwaters. The fighting had been brutal, but the area to his immediate front was silent, the few survivors of the defending force now moving back in wholesale retreat. But he could hear the sounds of a fierce battle to the west, where his forces had hit a strongly held ridgeline. He stopped and pulled out his small, portable tablet, checking on the status of his troops in that sector.

Things were a mess. The enemy was deeply entrenched on the high ground, raking his forces as they moved slowly forward through the floodwaters below. Casualties were high, and getting worse every minute. His people had launched three assaults, but each had been beaten back by the enemy's relentless fire. He needed to do something, or his entire advance would break up on that strongpoint.

He turned toward the small column formed up behind him. "Let's move out, boys. Our comrades need us." He turned and started walking west, waving his arms for the soldiers to follow. "Let's take those bastards on the ridge in their flanks." His voice was gritty, angry. "No long-range fire," he yelled. "We just move in and sweep them away."

He held his rifle above his head, and he heard the wave of cheers from behind him. Then he trudged forward and headed west.

"All units, maintain full thrust." Hammerleigh hated running, but it was the only way he could keep even a tiny force in the system. If he'd stayed near the planet, his people would all be dead now. Over a hundred warships had transited into the system, and they'd headed straight for his tiny armada. They'd have blown every one of his ships to dust if he'd let them get in range.

Besides, truly running would be jumping back to Antilles, he thought. And he hadn't done that. It was the smart play, the only option he had that made any real sense. But he just couldn't bring himself to do it. Ian Hammerleigh wasn't the kind who ran from danger. He'd escorted almost sixty thousand soldiers to the system, and they were all on Celtiboria, every one of their lives hanging in the balance. Tactical reality or no, bolting and leaving them behind to their fates seemed like the basest cowardice to the Antillean officer.

"They've detached a squadron, Captain." Barstowe's voice was cool, controlled. He was proving Hammerleigh's confidence in him to be well placed. "It looks like they're positioning the main fleet near Celtiboria. The detached force is on an interception course, and they are accelerating at eight g's."

"Reposition thrust vector to move directly away from the approaching vessels." His ships were as fast as their pursuers, or nearly so at least. He could play cat and mouse with them for hours, probably days. Or at least he could force them to deploy fully, using their massive numerical superiority to hem him in, cut off escape routes . . . and stay away from what was happening on Celtiboria.

"Yes, Captain. The fleet is . . ." Barstowe's voice faded to silence, and he stared at his screen for several seconds. When he continued, his tone was grim. "Captain, we have more ships transiting into the system, approximately four million kilometers from the planet. It looks like another big fleet." He turned and stared at Hammerleigh. "They're between us and the pursuing squadron."

"Very well," Hammerleigh said. His thoughts were a great deal more colorful, but he kept them to himself. He was already facing one massive fleet. But this one would be a lot closer. He glanced down at the display. Not only closer, but positioned to cut off his escape vector from the pursuing squadron. *It couldn't have been worse, if they'd landed right on top of us.*

"Plot adjusted vectors, Lieutenant. Most efficient course away from both." *Waste of time. You'll buy an hour, maybe two. Then one or the other of them will be on you.* He sighed hard. *It's time to jump. Staying to support the ground troops is one thing. Throwing away the lives of your crew with no hope of accomplishing anything is something else. You owe them your first loyalty.*

"Lieutenant, all ships are to prepare hyper . . ."

The main comm unit burst to life, interrupting his order. "Attention, all vessels in Celtiborian space. This is Admiral Emile Desaix, commander of the Far Stars Confederation navy. All ships must identify themselves at once. All units engaged in mutinous and unlawful activities—and all hostile foreign vessels—will be destroyed."

The bridge was silent, its crew stunned. The new ships weren't enemy reinforcements! Admiral Desaix had rallied the Celtiborian navy—and he'd come home to destroy the traitors and their foreign support. Finally, a broad smile began to take shape on Hammerleigh's face. "Lieutenant, open a channel to the admiral's flagship." His smile morphed into something else, something feral. "It's time to settle things here once and for all."

CHAPTER 24

BLACKHAWK CROUCHED BEHIND THE CRUMBLED PILE OF STONE.
It had once been a statue or a gargoyle of some kind, part of the
palace's ancient façade. But the *Claw*'s needle gun had brought
it down, along with most of the wall. Blackhawk's best guess
was a dragon—or what some Celtiborian artist had imagined a
dragon to be eight hundred years before.

He was firing three-round bursts from his assault rifle. Most
of the others were on full auto—there were a lot of enemy
troops facing them—but that was a waste for Blackhawk. His
genetically enhanced eyes zeroed right in on any visible target.
If he couldn't take it down with three bullets, it wasn't hittable.

"Blackhawk, look out . . . to your left." Carano's voice was loud and clear, though it was odd to hear it both through the comm and directly at the same time. The mercenary general was only a few meters away, behind his own piece of shattered palace wall turned into cover.

"Thanks," Blackhawk snapped off as he spun around to the left, dropping the enemy soldier with a single burst. He'd seen the threat himself, of course, and he'd already been moving to take his shot. But there was no harm in letting his comrade think he'd been of help. Carano, despite their troubled history—and the terrible losses his people had taken as a result of Blackhawk's seemingly reckless orders en route—was proving to be a good ally. The Frigus Umbra presence expected that of any subordinate—on pain of death. But Blackhawk was still in control—mostly—and capable of gratitude to his allies. Still, he wondered which persona would emerge when someone failed to follow his commands.

Let's hope it doesn't come to that.

"Ace," he yelled into his comm unit. "We're pinned down. See if you can clear some of these bogies out with the needle gun." It was close quarters for that kind of attack, but Blackhawk had seen Ace man the weapon for years, and his accuracy was uncanny.

"You're awfully close, Ark. You sure?"

"Yes, I'm goddamned sure; now just follow my orders." He regretted the outburst and tone the instant the words escaped from his lips. Feelings and motivations were running wild in his mind, things he hadn't dared to allow out of their dark prison in a quarter century. But he knew he needed some of what had been Frigus Umbra to defeat this enemy. He just hated unleashing that on his allies, and certainly not on a friend like Ace.

That said, it got Ace moving.

He could hear the small gun emplacement positioning, the creaking of metal on metal as the *Claw*'s precision gun took aim.

A second later he heard the loud whine, the weapon releasing its accumulated charge. Normally, the laser would be invisible, but the collapse of the wall and the fight that followed had churned up a massive cloud of dust, and the argon-ion laser beam left a brilliant blue streak, visible for several seconds, as the turret vibrated, spreading the point of destruction around the enemy position.

Ace's aim was as true as ever, and after only a few shots, at least half the enemy soldiers were down, most of them cut to pieces by the high-powered laser beam. The rest were falling back. It wasn't quite a rout, but Blackhawk wouldn't have called it good order, either. However it was characterized, though, it didn't look like anything was going to make the defenders hold their positions while the *Claw* built up another charge.

"Forward," Blackhawk cried, whipping around his chunk of stone and charging into the depths of the palace. He was firing on full auto now, caring more about spraying projectiles in front of him to suppress the enemy rather than to score hits.

He could hear the others behind him. Carano and his crack platoon. Sarge and his men—Ringo, Von, Drake, and Buck. Shira. But not Tarnan. Blackhawk felt bad about that. He'd insisted Tarq's brother stay behind on the *Claw*. The big man had argued, putting up quite a fight. It was just about the only time Blackhawk could remember anything but straight obedience from the giant. But the *Claw*'s captain had pulled rank and held firm. Tarnan had enough dealing with his brother's loss, and Blackhawk couldn't bring himself to risk the last survivor of that invincible unit the *Claw*'s family had so long called simply the Twins.

Blackhawk knew it was his own guilt over Tarq's death at play as much as anything, and that weighed even more heavily on him, but he'd still left the giant behind.

Ace had argued like hell, too, but Blackhawk had shut that down immediately. He needed Ace on the needle gun, and in command of the *Claw* in case he didn't make it back. He'd left his exec with clear orders: *If the ship is in danger, get the hell out.* They could always come back and do a pickup, but Blackhawk had been clear the safety of the *Claw* was the paramount concern. And there was no one he trusted in command of his beloved ship more than Ace Graythorn.

Blackhawk ran deeper inside the palace. There was a large section of roof that had fallen when Ace's shots had taken down the structural supports along with the outer wall. But once they'd gotten about ten meters farther into the massive building, they were past the worst-hit sections.

There were no enemy soldiers in the hallway. Blackhawk suspected most of the units on duty in this section had deployed to face his people. *And now they're dead or running, victims of Ace and the needle gun mostly. But they won't be the last we see.*

"Eyes open, everybody. And be careful. A lot of the marshal's household staff is probably still here. They're loyal Celtiborians who got stuck here and couldn't get out. So be sure you're targeting an enemy before you shoot."

Is that really what you want to tell them? Aren't such people expendable . . . at least in the scheme of things? Do you really want your meager force hesitating before they pull the trigger? To save some scribe or housemaid?

Shut the fuck up, Blackhawk thought . . . to himself, he supposed. He didn't want to think too much about what the Umbra psyche was saying. Especially since a lot of it made sense to him.

He heard sounds coming from around the corner. He waved his arm, gesturing downward, and he held his rifle at the ready. The noise was getting closer, and then two people came running around and toward Blackhawk's team. They didn't look like enemy soldiers, and he snapped out, "Hold fire."

It was a man and a woman in the hallway, and they stopped dead, staring at the armed force with a look of terror on their faces.

"No, please, don't shoot us." It was the woman, and she was near hysteria. But an instant later she shouted, "Captain Blackhawk? Is that you?"

Blackhawk stared back. She looked familiar. He couldn't place her face, but he'd definitely seen her before.

Rasa Dinari. One of Astra Lucerne's personal servants.

Of course! He had seen her before, though he didn't think the two had ever spoken.

"Rasa?" Blackhawk ran forward to the terrified woman. "I am here for Astra. Do you know where she is?"

"Yes, Captain. Thank Chrono you are here. My lady is in grave danger. I tried to convince her to leave, but she would not come. She sent me away, told me to sneak out of the palace. But I could not go without her. So I stayed, waiting for the chance to help her."

Blackhawk felt a wave of adrenaline. Astra was in danger, imminent danger from the tone of Rasa's voice. There was no time to waste.

"That chance is here, Rasa. Tell me where she is . . . and what danger she is in."

Katarina slipped into the dark room, slowly, carefully. *Do not underestimate this adversary,* she reminded herself. *He is at least your equal, and probably . . .*

She let the thought trail off. There was no point in allowing self-doubt to interfere now. She would do her best, use all her training and experience to defeat this enemy. If that was not enough, she would die. But she would never allow fear to influence her decisions . . . even though she felt a cold dread deep inside.

She'd ransacked rooms throughout the Back Streets. She'd paid informants, beaten what she needed out of flophouse clerks and street vendors. She suspected she was the terror of the Back Streets right now, and she'd left a trail of bruises and broken bones behind her. But they'd told her all they knew. She was sure of that. She just wasn't sure it was enough.

This is the assassin's room. I am sure of it. She'd chased down a number of false leads, but now she felt certain. She was on the right trail.

She looked around the room, searching for clues, for any idea where her elusive adversary had gone. But there was nothing. Nothing at all . . . save a hair. She took one look at it, and she felt a cold chill. It was long and soft, and it was a deep black, and she'd found it on the mirror, clearly left there for her to discover.

It was hers.

She spun around, scanning the room again—for enemies, for traps, but she found nothing. He must have gone back to the bombing site. That's where he got the hair. Her enemy had already gotten the better of her once. Indeed, it was only by the slimmest of margins she had escaped his trap. And now he was playing with her, leaving mysterious clues. Katarina had always been the hunter, but now she wasn't sure who was truly tracking whom.

The Sebastiani assassin looked across the room. The window was open, the ancient wood frame covered with a last few flakes of peeling paint. *He went out that way,* she thought, moving slowly toward the wall. *It's the only way he could have gotten out.*

She realized she wasn't following clues and was probably walking into a trap. But it was all she had to go on. She looked around the window frame, searching for anything dangerous. An explosive, a well-deployed blade—even a poisoned needle could finish her in an instant. But she couldn't find anything.

Katarina eased her way out slowly, looking carefully up then down. Nothing. Where would he have gone? *He is leading me, luring me in. Up,* she realized. *He wants me on the roof.*

She slid out of the window, grabbing onto the casing along the outside to hold herself in place. She stood, her feet on the windowsill, and she reached up and grabbed on to a small row of bricks protruding from the wall.

Her fingers gripped tightly, aching as she moved her foot upward, putting more pressure on her handhold. The old building had a series of small ledges and masonry decorations. It wasn't an easy climb, but it was doable. At least for someone of her training. Or that of the man she was following.

She worked her way slowly upward. The room had been on the third floor, but the building was six stories. She knew she was exposed, that her enemy's best chance to gain an advantage over her was while she was climbing, but that was a risk she was willing to take. Trap or no, this was her chance to face off with her target. Whatever opportunity she had—would ever have—it was now.

Grabbing a small ledge just below the roof, Katarina climbed up with her legs until they were only half a meter below her handhold. She took a deep breath and threw her arms over the edge of the roof, thrusting with her legs and leaping onto the flat surface. She twisted hard and rolled to the side, pulling out her pistol as she dove behind a small masonry chimney. She peered around the edge, looking across the roof. There was a small penthouse about six meters away. While she was panning her eyes over it, a voice came from around the corner.

"Welcome, Sebastiani." It was low pitched, unsettling, but it wasn't overtly hostile. That was a surprise.

"And you are of the Exequtorum," she answered, using all her discipline to keep her tone calm, unemotional.

"Excellent. Your skills are considerable, Sebastiani. I offer you my respect. I could have finished you on the wall, or left another explosive in my room, but you deserve better. There is, in our curious profession, a certain honor, is there not?"

"There is," she replied. "Though I am not sure I would extend it to a murderer. An imperial killer."

"You disappoint me, Sebastiani. My order is more disciplined even than yours. We kill only on imperial command. Your brother and sister adepts likely terminate far more targets than my brothers and I, and less discriminately. Morality, ethics . . . these are variable concepts, subject to radically different inter-pretations. We may exist on different sides of a political struggle, but our honor is the same. It is measured in how we approach our own obligations, how true to our oaths we remain."

"Why did you kill Marshal Lucerne?"

"Because my master ordered it," Rachen replied. "The same reason I attempted to kill Blackhawk. Why I will kill Blackhawk. Indeed, your friend has returned to Celtiboria. As soon as we have completed our business, I will finish him as well."

"Not if I can help it, you won't." She squeezed tightly on the grip of her pistol.

"We need not do this, Sebastiani. I have not been charged to attain your death. I cannot allow you to leave and warn Blackhawk, however, so if you yield to me, I will stun you and leave you here. You need not add your death to his."

"That will never happen. Your road to Blackhawk extends through me." Her voice was icy.

"Very well, Sebastiani. Again, you have my respect. We shall do what we must."

Katarina breathed slowly, deeply—calming herself, preparing for the contest about to begin. She recited the Sebastiani mantra in her head. *My mind and body, they are one. I am the angel of death, and none can stand before me. I am my mission and my mission is me. As long as I draw breath so shall it be.*

All the years of training, of meditation. A life spent honing my skills. All for this . . .

"All units, fire at will." Desaix was standing in the center of *Glorianus*'s flag bridge. It was a strange affectation, but he preferred to stand during battle. It wasn't always possible. High g-force operations and wildly evasive maneuvers drove him back to the cushioned support of his chair. But now his fleet was nearly in free fall, almost at a dead halt, standing toe to toe with the enemy and blasting away.

The Celtiborian flagship was barely a midsize cruiser by imperial standards—at least on the other end of the Void. But in the Far Stars, *Glorianus* was a behemoth, an unmatched war machine, the pride of Marshal Lucerne's united Celtiboria. She was the strongest ship in the sector, larger by a third than the mightiest of the imperial vessels Desaix's people were facing. And he no longer had any doubt that the enemy fleet was imperial in origin—and that it represented a major portion of Governor Vos's naval strength.

Glorianus shook as she fired her heavy torpedoes. They were her strongest weapons, ship killers capable of taking out anything smaller than a frigate in a single shot. But Lucerne's ship wasn't shooting at gunboats or even frigates. She was squared off with two light cruisers, locked in a death struggle with a pair of the strongest vessels in the imperial fleet.

She shuddered again, this time as an enemy laser ripped into her hull. Her armor was thick, but they were at point-blank range now, and the enemy cruisers mounted heavy laser cannon. *Glorianus*'s damage control parties were working at capacity, fighting internal fires, rerouting severed conduits and data lines, replacing fried components. The ship was seriously damaged, but thanks to the tireless efforts of her crew, she was still in the line, firing almost at full effectiveness.

Her two opponents were harder hit. One of the enemy cruisers was almost out of the fight, her hull holed in a dozen places and bleeding atmosphere and fluids. Her fire had diminished until only a single battery was still active, and even that was shooting only sporadically. Desaix felt the urge to finish her off, but he didn't interfere. The fleet was his, but Captain Josiah commanded *Glorianus* in battle. And there was no one Desaix trusted more in a fight to the death than Flavius Josiah.

Josiah had directed all his fire toward the other enemy vessel, and Desaix's trust in his flag captain was not misplaced.

The second enemy ship was the greater danger, and *Glorianus* hung now on a cusp. If she could win the duel quickly, she'd still be something close to operational, and she could continue to lead the battle. But if she took too much additional damage, her status would decline rapidly—and Desaix would be compelled to transfer the flag to a less battered vessel. And Josiah was directing all his weapons at the ship that was still strong enough to really hurt his own.

Desaix stared at the tactical display. The ships of his fleet were shown in blue, small triangles arrayed in a tight battle formation. The enemy ships were white circles, and they were matched off against his vessels. The display was less dense than it had been. Both sides had taken losses, and more than forty ships had been destroyed outright, blown into lifeless hulks or obliterated when their reactors lost containment and they turned briefly into miniature suns.

There was another group of ships on the screen, the six red ovals of Commodore Hammerleigh's Antillean command. He'd lost half his vessels, in the fighting before the Celtiborian fleet arrived and in the combat since.

Hopefully our arrival has at least made those losses not in vain.

Desaix's forces had hit the squadron chasing Hammerleigh shortly after transiting into the system. They unleashed a hellish broadside that wiped out half the enemy ships in an instant—and left the rest damaged to varying degrees. The enemy force had intended to overwhelm and destroy Hammerleigh's small squadron, but the massive Celtiborian attack had given the Antilleans the upper hand. Desaix wanted to stay and finish them off, but the main enemy fleet beckoned, and the Celtiborian admiral reluctantly left the mop-up to Hammerleigh and his six ships.

Desaix knew victory would be decided in the struggle between the main fleets, and not in a minor peripheral fight. He was determined to crush the imperials, to drive them from Celtiboria, and he had closed hard, weapons blazing. The battle had been going on for hours now, and it still raged, undecided.

"Admiral, Captain Nortel reports *Warrington* is bracketed by six enemy vessels. He requests immediate assistance."

Desaix's eyes flashed to the display. "Order *Ragnor* and *Hephestus* to . . ." His voice stopped cold as he watched the icon representing *Warrington* disappear from his screen. He felt a coldness in the pit of his stomach. Jeran Nortel had been one of the best officers in the Celtiborian navy, the kind of man everyone liked, his crew, his superiors . . . everybody. And now he was dead, another name on the massive roster of those who had given their lives to Marshal Lucerne's quest to keep the empire out of the Far Stars.

Lucerne was right all along, Desaix thought grimly. *I doubt even he could have imagined just how right. Here we are, the confederation half formed, our forces scattered all across the Far Stars—and we're fighting the war he feared all along. Too soon. It happened far too soon, and if we're going to win it, I'm afraid the price will be terrible.*

No time for mourning now. Nortel was a friend, and a brave officer. He must not have died for nothing, for defeat.

Honor in victory.

"All ships, prepare to initiate thrust at two g's . . . commencing in thirty seconds." They were engaged at close range already. But Desaix was going to take it to knife-fighting distance.

Let's see if you have the stomach for that . . .

"Are you certain, General?" The senior adept of the temple stood before Carteria, as erect as a man of his advanced years could manage. The Celtiborians as a people were not enormously religious, and the temple remained more as a tradition, a vestige of the past that still served to encourage a basic moral code.

But tradition had its purposes, even more for usurpers and pretenders than those duly empowered to lead. And Carteria wanted to exploit every scrap of sentiment, of belief, of pride in tradition the Celtiborians had. Anything that legitimized his power grab was useful. His marriage to Astra had to put the people firmly behind him immediately, or he risked losing all.

"Yes, yes," he snapped back. "I am sure."

The invaders were about fifty thousand strong, a force he could defeat given time. But that's one thing he didn't have. The enemy was all concentrated just a few kilometers from the city, and thousands of his own soldiers—and his mysterious brown-coated allies—were detached to the north, fighting DeMark and his loyalists. He had thought them hemmed in by their own actions—opening the dikes—but DeMark had somehow managed to push his own people south, through the flooded quagmire, and now fiercely engaged his surprised forces.

And that didn't even take into account this new army that had somehow landed so close to the city.

Carteria was desperate. *I just need* one *thing to go right.* And for him that meant this marriage. *If the people start to rise up in support of Astra and their new marshal, there's a chance.*

His new friends had promised more support, both military and financial. *But I have to hold out a little longer . . .*

Then when the enemy reached the capital, the streets would be full of partisans, men and women urged to resistance by Astra, by the daughter of their beloved leader.

Human shields. Let DeMark and his mysterious allies shoot their

way through throngs of civilians . . . and then the people will be mine.
All of them.

"Very well." The adept turned toward a cluster of technicians along the wall. "Begin broadcast."

He paused while they worked at the controls, nodded as one of them gestured for him to proceed. "Hello, my fellow Celtiborians," he said, slowly, overpronouncing every word, an affectation his lifetime of inflated self-importance had slowly developed.

"Amid the strife of war, the terrible spectacle of treason and murder and General DeMark and his criminals . . . and his off-world allies, it fills me with happiness to announce that Astra Lucerne, the daughter of our beloved and greatly mourned leader, will marry General Carteria. This joyous ceremony will take place not in five days as previously announced, but now. Not in the temple, nor in the vastness of the Great Rotunda, but here, in the command post where they have together been leading the loyal Celtiborian forces in their heroic defense against those who would enslave us all. This is Lady Lucerne's wish, her desire to show her support and affection for the man now fighting to preserve her father's legacy, and defeat those who would see it destroyed."

The adept turned and reached out a hand. Astra smiled and extended her own, allowing him to guide her into place. Her will was iron, and she stood still, giving no signs to anyone that she was in control of her own thoughts . . . and that those thoughts were murderous. Her eyes moved, quickly, glancing around, taking stock of the area, but that was it.

You are a filthy traitor, adept. I will see you hanged from the rafters of your temple.

She saw Carteria walk slowly to her side. He was smiling, but it was forced. She knew this wasn't how he'd imagined his triumphant ascension to the marshalate.

I don't think this wedding is going to go like you imagine, either, bastard.

She heard the sounds as the adept began the ceremony—he was using the full text, of course, not the mercifully short version most normal people used for weddings. *The old fool,* she thought. *He was boring when I was a child. Age has done nothing to improve that situation.*

"And thus, I ask you, Astra Eliane Lucerne, daughter of our illustrious and departed marshal, rightful heir to his offices and positions, do you . . ."

It's now or never, she thought. She struggled to focus, to push back the fear. It was one thing to plan a move, to accept a course of action you knew would end in your own death, and quite another to stare into the blackness and leap. She was human, and it was inbred in the species to fear the mystery of death. But in every way possible, she was ready. Images floated through her mind. Her father, Lys . . . Blackhawk. There was nothing left for her in life, save duty. *And what duty is more important than ensuring a monster like Carteria never rules Celtiboria?*

Her eyes darted quickly toward the soldier standing just behind her. She took a breath . . . then another, and she steeled herself. *It is time.* And then one other thought flashed through her mind. *I love you, Ark. Always.*

She raised her leg and drove it back suddenly, her foot smashing into the kneecap of the guard behind her. He howled in pain and began to fall, even as she steadied herself. She turned around, reaching back, grabbing the heavy combat knife from the stricken guard's sheath as he collapsed to the ground.

Her blood was now surging with adrenaline as she swung herself back forward, the knife held firmly in her hand. Her move had surprised everyone, and they all stood frozen for a brief instant, stunned and unsure how to react. It wasn't long, but it was the time she needed.

She lunged forward toward Carteria, just as the treacherous general began to react. His face was a mask of fear, and he tried to move back, to escape her blow.

Too slow.

Thrusting hard with all her strength, Astra drove the blade into his chest, twisting it as she did. She felt his hot blood pouring out of the gaping wound, covering her hands, her arms, and she looked into his eyes, watched the very life drain from him. He screamed one last time as she jerked the knife savagely, and then his legs buckled, his body sliding down to the floor and landing with a lifeless thud.

She savored every second.

Astra stared at the camera, still broadcasting the entire scene across the planet. "I am Astra Lucerne," she screamed. "Carteria was a traitor. General DeMark is a true and loyal officer. You have been lied to, but now I tell you the truth. I beseech all of you to support DeMark and destroy this nest of traitors!"

"Kill her!" a voice screamed from the other side of the room.

But no one moved.

The voice belonged to Bartholomew—an imperial agent—and the soldiers in the room were Celtiborians, sworn to Carteria's service. They reacted slowly to the command, uncertain what to do. Their leader was dead, and his murderer stood before them, holding the blood-soaked weapon in her hand. But she was Astra Lucerne, the daughter of Marshal Augustin Lucerne, and they stared at her and hesitated. Only for a few seconds, but once again, that was enough.

An explosion ripped through the room, blasting the entry door to bits—and an instant later men came pouring in, their weapons blazing, taking down Carteria's soldiers in a hail of gunfire.

And in the center, she saw a shadowy figure emerging from the smoke, and she knew immediately. It was Arkarin Blackhawk, standing like a bronze statue, pistol in one hand, shortsword in the other.

CHAPTER 25

"YOUR FRIEND BLACKHAWK IS AN EXTRAORDINARY MAN. IT IS extremely rare that a target escapes my first attack, and I am intrigued by his abilities. He survived the jackalfish venom, and I have known of no other human who has matched his feat."

The Exequtorum assassin's voice came from the same area. He hadn't moved yet, at least not far. "He is back on Celtiboria now, and I will go finish my job shortly. It is regretful that you feel you must die for your friend, for it will serve no purpose." He paused then added, "Yet I respect your steadfastness. Your death will bring me no joy. So . . . now we shall have our dance, no? We are creatures of a kind, you and I. Your skills are exceptional. Indeed, you may be the best I have encountered outside my own order."

"I am good enough to kill you," she answered coldly.

"No doubt some part of you believes that, but you have never faced a member of the Exequtorum, so you have no frame of reference. Your Sebastiani guild is impressive, your lore powerful. But the Exequtorum is something else entirely. The empire is vast and ancient, yet we are older still. And for all the centuries the emperors have ruled, we have been there, the final arbiter to enforce their commandments. Where the navy and the imperial armies could not succeed, the brothers of the Exequtorum have gone. And never have we failed."

Until now, Katarina thought, though she knew she didn't believe it. She'd been in danger before, many times, but she'd never felt as she did now. She was outmatched. She would fight with every scrap of courage and strength she could muster, but deep down she knew she was facing her death.

"Very well, Sebastiani. Let us begin."

The voice went silent. Katarina froze, listening carefully for any sounds. She knew her enemy would move quietly, and she strained to catch anything. But there was nothing.

How will he come at me? She looked around the roof, checking for any covered approaches toward her. The one side of the penthouse came about five meters from her position, but there was nothing but open roof between there and the chimney she crouched behind.

She tucked herself into a tight crouch. She knew her opponent would not miss if she gave him any target at all. Her hand was wrapped tightly around her pistol. It was the only weapon she had, save for two of her throwing knives.

I can't just hide back here. Surrendering the initiative to an opponent like this is suicide.

There was a small structure behind her, a doorway leading

to the stairs back into the building. She imagined it in her head, visualizing it, estimating the distance. Her legs were tight, poised.

Suddenly, she lunged toward it, pushing off with all her strength. She twisted in midair, adding randomness to her trajectory, making herself as difficult a target as possible.

She heard the first shot, even as she was still in the air. Then a flash of pain as it grazed her thigh. She was thrown off, lost her concentration for a second, and she slammed hard onto the roof.

She snapped her head around, making sure she was completely behind cover. Then she stared at her thigh. There was blood soaking through her pants, but she realized immediately it was only a flesh wound. Still, she was shaken. *How did he know I would go that way?*

She scrambled to her feet. The staircase enclosure was taller than the chimney, giving her more room to operate. Where would he be? She held the pistol at the ready as she crept to the far side of the small structure. *Do not underestimate this man . . .*

He makes no sounds, leaves no clues, she thought. *You must fight him with instinct, initiative. You must feel where he is.*

She let her mind go free, to imagine her enemy's actions, location. Then she bolted suddenly, leaping back for the chimney, firing at the roof of the stair enclosure as she did.

The imperial assassin was crouched on top of the structure. He spun around, dodging her fire and shooting back as he tumbled from his perch.

Katarina scrambled around the chimney, just as her enemy's return fire slammed into the far side of it, shattering the old brick and creating a cloud of dust. But before she ducked her head behind the cover, she saw her adversary dive from the stair enclosure—trailing blood behind him.

She felt a wave of elation, but she slammed it down immediately. There was no time. *I hit him,* she thought, but she hadn't been able to tell how badly. *Should I charge him?* That would be suicide if he was ready for it, but if he was badly hurt, stunned . . .

No. He'll be dangerous until he is dead. She crept around the other side of the chimney, crouched low . . . only to find her opponent was already on the move. She fired, but it was too late. He slammed into her, and they both tumbled onto the middle of the roof. Her hand lost its grip on her pistol, and it went skittering away, out of reach.

She moved her arm around, running now on pure instinct. Her enemy was leaping up, bringing his own gun around to fire. Her hand was on her midsection, feeling around . . : there it was, the cold steel of one of her throwing knives. She didn't think about it. She wasn't even consciously aware of her action, but her hand grabbed the knife and threw in one motion.

He did the same, clearly reacting on instinct and throwing up his arm in a blocking motion, and yet the blade still sunk deeply into his forearm, sending his own gun flying through the air . . . and bouncing off the edge of the roof.

Her body was racked by pain. She was sure she'd broken a couple ribs, and the gunshot wound throbbed and continued to pour blood down her leg. But she'd taken a toll on her opponent as well, and she wasn't finished yet.

She forced herself to her feet, but he was already rushing toward her, and she barely had time to brace for the impact. The two of them grabbed on to each other and rolled across the roof, arms and legs scrambling wildly in a confused melee.

Katarina felt his arm slip over her shoulder, around her neck, and she thrust back hard with her elbow, wriggling free before he was able to establish the choke hold. But she heard her second knife fall, hitting the roof and bouncing away, out of reach.

They both climbed to their feet, facing each other, now unarmed. Katarina lunged forward, landing a hard punch to her opponent's midsection. But his response was lightning fast, and his fist smashed into her chest. The breath was forced from her lungs, and she felt more ribs breaking. The pain in her chest was almost unbearable, despite her Sebastiani mantras.

Trading blows for several minutes, the two expert warriors struggled with all they had to give, parrying and circling each other, seeking an opening to strike. Katarina had hurt her opponent, more she suspected than anyone else ever had, but she knew she was losing. Her breaths were raspy, painful affairs, and the pain in her thigh was almost as bad. She knew she was close to the end of her strength.

And that he wasn't.

Desperation invaded her mind. She continued fighting— she was a professional, and she would never give up—but she was also an expert warrior, and she realized the contest was over. She had finally met her match, an adversary she couldn't defeat. She had done all she could, and she knew her final battle had been the best she could manage. But defeat was defeat, and its taste was bitter.

The Sebastiani assassin lunged again, one last attempt to deal her enemy a crippling blow. But he was stronger than her, his fatigue a degree less severe. He moved first and spun around, delivering a savage kick to her stomach.

She stumbled backward, and he was on her in an instant. He punched hard to her chest . . . then again to her face. She stumbled back as he struck again and again, unopposed, her limbs too weak to even attempt to block the attacks.

Katarina struggled to stay on her feet, and she stared at him one last time. There was no hatred in his eyes, no anger—not even satisfaction about his imminent victory. She wanted to hate him . . . she did hate him for what he had done. But she realized he was just doing a job, not as unlike her as she wanted to think. Death was his vocation, as it had been hers for so many years. And beneath the fear, the pain, the struggle to survive, part of her couldn't help but respect a job well done.

He paused an instant, sharing that last glance with Katarina. Then he swung around and delivered a hard kick to her midsection, sending her flying off the roof—and down twenty meters to the street below.

Blackhawk stood just inside the door. "Capture the two imperials, Sarge," he said. Then, turning toward Carano's men, he added in a frigid tone, "Kill the soldiers. They are traitors." Half of Carteria's guards were already down, but the others had begun to drop their weapons and put their hands in the air.

"I said kill them," Blackhawk repeated, his voice like something from a nightmare. "Kill them all." He raised his pistol and pulled the trigger, blowing the head off the nearest soldier. "Death to the traitors."

"You heard the man," Shira yelled, whipping up her assault rifle and firing. The soldiers flanking Blackhawk glanced at her briefly and opened fire, gunning down the Celtiborian turncoats, while Sarge's crew moved forward, weapons trained on the two imperial agents.

"Ark!" Astra screamed with joy and shock. "I thought you were dead!" She ran across the room and threw her arms around him. "I thought you were dead," she repeated tearfully.

"It's not that easy to kill me," he said, closing his own arms around her, at least as much as he could with his weapons in his hands. "I was so worried about you." He held her for a few more seconds, savoring the feel of her body against his. "But we've got to get going. We're here for you, but there's still a fight going on, and our forces haven't reached the palace yet." Blackhawk had no idea how Carteria's troops would react when they found out he was dead—or what his imperial allies would do.

Blackhawk took a half step back from Astra and looked into her eyes for a few seconds. Then he leaned in and kissed her. He pulled back and smiled at her. "I could do that all day, but we have to get the hell out of here."

"I'm with you, Ark." She reached down and pulled a gun from one of the dead soldiers. "Let's go."

"Nice job, by the way," he said, motioning toward Carteria's corpse. "It's a good reminder never to piss you off too much. It looks like you cut his heart out."

"Not out," she said, smiling at him as she did. "Just chopped it up a little. And yes, it's a good reminder not to piss me off . . ."

He held his smile for a few more seconds, then the serious expression returned to his face. "C'mon," he said. "I have to get you out of here."

"Get us out of here, you horse's ass," she snapped back.

"Us," he said, smiling as he put his hand on her face. "Us."

He turned toward the soldiers milling around the room. Carteria's men were all dead, and the two imperials were shackled, each of them flanked by a pair of Sarge's men. They were both alive, though they looked a bit worse for the experience.

"Let's go," Blackhawk yelled. "Carteria may be dead, but this palace is still full of his men." He motioned toward the door, watching as Carano and half his troops took the lead. Sarge's men followed with the two prisoners, with Blackhawk and Astra right behind, and the rest of Carano's mercenaries bringing up the rear.

"How did you know where to find me, Ark?" Astra asked as they moved out into the hall.

"I figured you had to be somewhere in the palace, and I was ready to tear the place apart to find you. But then we ran into Rasa, and she told us. You had her scared to death, you know. She was sure you were going to get yourself killed. And she was right, wasn't she? What the hell were you thinking anyway? I understand you wanted to kill Carteria, but if we'd been a few seconds later . . ."

"I know, Ark, but it was all I could think to do, the only way to make a difference. I couldn't let the bastard marry me and use that to cement his hold on power." Her eyes filled with tears. "Ark, they killed Lys. They cut her throat in front of me."

"I'm so sorry," Blackhawk said somberly, taking Astra's hand in his. "I know how close the two of you were."

"And I thought you were dead," she said. "I needed to do something, to strike back somehow. I felt like I was alone, that everyone I loved was gone. It was the only way I could think to stop Carteria."

Blackhawk just nodded. He was still trying to accept how close she'd come to being killed. He understood her logic; indeed, he would likely have made the same choice had he been in her shoes. But he couldn't bear the thought of her sacrificing herself. Anyone else, but never her . . .

They were running down the corridor, back the way they had come. There were bodies in half a dozen places, the spots where they'd gotten into firefights on the way in.

"Is Rasa safe, Ark? She switched the drugs they were giving me. Without her, I would have stood there and married that creature and not resisted at all."

"She's fine. I had one of Carano's men take her back to the *Claw*."

"Ark . . . I think I understand. At least better than I did." He felt her hand tighten its grip on his as they moved down the hall.

"Understand?"

"The conditioning, Ark. How it feels to be trapped inside your head, screaming at your body as it ignores your commands, hearing the words coming out of your own mouth, not being able to stop them. What they did to me was a tiny copy of what happened to you. I can't imagine how you face it, how you deal with it every day."

"It gets easier with time," he lied. "But . . ."

He stopped suddenly as a burst of gunfire erupted up ahead. He leaped to the side, grabbing Astra and pushing her down, out of the line of fire. "Stay here," he said. "We've got to get you out of this place. Besides the fact that I love you, you're the only one who can stop this madness. Things have gone too far. No one will listen to anyone else. Even DeMark. Without you, he'll have to crush the opposition . . . and probably a lot of civilians tricked into supporting Carteria."

Blackhawk pulled his pistol out of the holster and moved slowly forward, Shira with him, her rifle at the ready. "Status?" he yelled as he pushed his way toward the front of the small column.

"Just a small patrol, General," Carano answered. "Four guards. We took them out."

"Casualties?"

"Two wounded. Both of them are ambulatory."

"Good," Blackhawk said. "Let's keep moving. We're almost out of here. I suspect they're disorganized as hell now, but they'll pull it together eventually, and I'd just as soon be back on the *Claw* by then."

"You and me both, Blackhawk." The mercenary commander looked a little harried. With the Black Helms as the biggest merc company in the Far Stars, he was used to fighting full-scale wars, not racing through the halls of an enemy-occupied stronghold.

"Ark." Blackhawk's comm unit crackled to life. "Ace here. We had to lift off. We've got enemy all around the LZ. Looks like a couple companies at least. Your exit's blocked for sure."

Shit. "Ace, we're almost to the LZ. Any other egress routes look better?"

"Not really, Ark. They've got troops all over, streaming back from the front lines. It looks like the mercs have really got 'em on the run. I can see a dozen battalions heading your way. They're pretty shot up, and they're definitely disordered, but it's no rout. Not yet, at least. We need to get you out. Now."

Blackhawk sighed. It was good news overall that the mercenaries were pushing Carteria's forces back, but it was also damned inconvenient right now.

"I can blow 'em away pretty good, Ark," Ace continued. "It doesn't seem like they've got any ground-to-air capacity. Lucas can hover the *Claw* right over 'em, and I can blast away with the needler, maybe clear the area long enough to set down and pick you all up. But you still may have some fighting to do to make it out of the palace."

"Do it, Ace. I'll get everybody to the exit point, whatever we have to do. Blackhawk out." He looked forward. "Vladimir, we're going to have to fight our way out. We've got heavy enemy concentrations at the LZ. The *Claw* is airborne, and Ace is going to try to clear the area with the needle gun. But we may still have a firefight before we can make it to the ship."

"We'll do what has to be done, Ark." Carano slammed a fresh cartridge in his assault rifle. "Because that's what we do."

CHAPTER 26

KATARINA LAY ON THE HARD PAVEMENT OF THE STREET, HER BODY broken. She was bleeding from a dozen places, and there was a pool of blood all around her. The pain had been intense, unbearable, even to the veteran Sebastiani assassin. But now it was gone, all of it. She felt nothing. Not pain, not the cold hardness of the street beneath her. Nothing.

She was vaguely aware. She could hear something, not individual sounds perhaps, but just a general noise. She could tell there were people around her, running over toward where she lay. But it was all hazy.

They probably think I'm a suicide. Perhaps I am, of a sort. I knew I couldn't win, deep inside I was certain of it. But I couldn't run, I couldn't back down. Not when my friends' lives were at risk.

Katarina Venturi had been a Sebastiani assassin as long as she had been an adult, and most of her childhood had been spent in the hallowed halls of the guild as an acolyte, learning the ways of the order. It had been her life; indeed, she had been born into it, pledged to the guild from birth.

But though I have lived my whole life as an assassin of the guild, I will not die as such. No, I am no longer what I was, the guild no longer my master, my life. I am part of a different family now, the family of Wolf's Claw. My comrades, my friends . . . my brothers and sisters, they are all that truly matters to me.

There was commotion around her, people moving about, talking, yelling . . .

I am sorry, Arkarin, she thought sadly. *I tried to stop him.* She wondered what would happen when the assassin of the Exequtorum finally met up again with Blackhawk. The imperial killer was dangerous, the deadliest fighter she had ever encountered . . . perhaps save one. If Blackhawk saw his enemy coming, she knew he could win. She'd never seen anyone who matched Blackhawk's raw physical abilities. He was the greatest warrior she had ever known, and the only one she'd ever met to whom she would swear allegiance. *Yes, Blackhawk can beat the imperial assassin . . . if he sees him coming . . .*

She could feel herself fading, her contact with the outer world slipping away. But she could still sense the people around her. It seemed strange. A jumper in the Back Streets couldn't be too uncommon. Yet it felt like there were literally dozens of people crowding around her. *Nothing to see here, folks . . . just a woman dying on the street . . .*

She drifted deeper into thoughts, memories . . . Ace lying on the *Claw*'s sick bay cot fighting for his life. She remembered how scared she'd felt, how helpless, watching Doc work on him, not knowing if he would survive.

Her existence had long been a solitary one. It was the only choice for a Sebastiani assassin. Attachments were weaknesses an enemy could turn against you. She'd seen it with Blackhawk, and his love for Astra. They'd never discussed it, but the pain his feelings caused him had been clear to see. An enemy could lash out at Blackhawk by harming Astra, kidnapping her. It was a vulnerability.

Katarina had always tried to stay sharply focused, unemotional. But her time on the *Claw* had worn away her defenses. She could pretend all she wanted, but those people had come to mean a great deal to her. She loved them all, and it was they she would miss, they she longed to see once more before death took her. And Ace most of all.

Ace. She tried to place when she'd first felt the way she did about him, but she couldn't. She suspected it had been further back than she imagined, but it was looking down at him in that bed that had made it all real to her. The thought of watching him die, of seeing him slip away without the chance to tell him how she felt hit her hard. It had told her all she needed to know.

Damn you, Ace, she thought. *Damn that cocky, arrogant persona of yours. You make it take so long to get to know you . . . the real you. Perhaps we could have had more time . . . the years we wasted.* But she knew that was unfair. Ace had his own defenses, his personal aversion to emotional involvements, just as she did. They were both to blame, just as they both suffered the loss of the years they could have had together.

As different as we are, we are so alike in ways. I am sorry, Ace. Sorry for what we could have had but won't now. Sorry for failing here, for leaving you . . . without even telling you how I truly feel.

Katarina could feel the blackness enveloping her, taking her. She wanted to fight it, but she knew she was spent. *I'm so sorry, my friends, sorry I was too weak . . .*

The imperial cruiser shook hard as *Glorianus*'s lasers ripped through its hull, vaporizing armor, destroying systems, severing conduits. The two ships were five thousand kilometers from each other. That wasn't close, it wasn't even point-blank.

It was grappling.

The Celtiborian flagship mounted the biggest laser broadside in the Far Stars, and at this distance the fearsome weapons struck at almost full strength.

This last shot had been dead-on, a thrust through the heart. The imperial vessel lost power almost immediately, and she sat there in space for perhaps half a minute. Desaix watched from his flag bridge, his eyes locked onto the display as the last imperial ship larger than a frigate hovered there, just a few thousand kilometers away.

Desaix imagined the craziness going on inside the imperial vessel, the frantic damage control crew struggling to restore power, to keep their ship in the fight. But he didn't think they were going to make it. He'd watched Captain Josiah's perfect shot gut the enemy vessel, and, after that thirty seconds of nothing—that brief period of last-minute efforts to save the ship—the imperial cruiser erupted with the fury of uncontrolled nuclear fusion. The ship didn't fall apart, it didn't even blow apart. It simply vaporized, leaving in its place, for a few fleeting seconds, a miniature sun. And then it was gone.

"Nice shooting, Captain," Desaix said into his comm

unit. "Now bring us around behind that cluster of frigates at 135.180.090."

"Yes, sir," came the immediate reply.

The battle had been a close-run affair, and a bloodbath for both sides. The forces had been more or less equally matched, and it had largely become a contest of leadership and raw tenacity. And slowly, at great costs, the Celtiborians had gained the upper hand.

Glorianus had destroyed the imperial flagship—and then the second ship to carry the commanding admiral. The empire's fleet was scattered now, divided into separate squadrons and functioning without effective overall direction. The Celtiborians, on the other hand, had Emile Desaix, and he was fully in command.

"Admiral, we're picking up energy readings throughout the enemy fleet." A short pause. "They're activating their jump drives, sir. They're running!"

"All ships, maintain fire. Let's blow as many of these bastards to hell as we can before they jump."

All across the line the Celtiborian ships closed on the enemy ships, firing everything they had. The imperials had diverted all power to their hyperdrives, so Desaix's vessels were free from incoming fire as they poured all they had into the enemy.

Desaix could see icons disappearing, enemy vessels destroyed by his fleet's final frantic attacks. The imperials lost a dozen ships before their survivors began to jump into hyperspace. Ten ships were gone . . . then twenty. But still, the Celtiborians blazed away at the remaining vessels. Thirty . . . forty.

Forty-two enemy vessels had jumped into hyperspace. But that left fourteen behind, ships with damaged hyperdrives. Some of them were almost completely crippled, and they broadcast their surrenders at once. Perhaps half were still combat capable, and they tried to pull back conventionally, fleeing toward the outer system. But Desaix wasn't about to let any of them escape, and half the Celtiborian fleet pursued. A few shots were exchanged, but the imperial captains knew they didn't have a chance, and they chose surrender over certain death.

The largest space battle in the history of the Far Stars was over.

"No," DeMark said into the comm unit, his voice like iron. "No stopping, no regrouping. We stay on them, day and night." He half expected the officers on the other end to argue, but his tone silenced their complaints. DeMark knew he was asking the impossible from his men—but he had also just realized that was how wars were won. The marshal had done the same thing many times. Something had happened, some event that had shaken up the Carterian forces. DeMark didn't know what it was, but he intended to exploit it to the fullest.

The browncoats, as Carteria's unidentified allies had come to be called, tried to plug the gaps and hold the line, but they weren't strong enough to stand against DeMark's advance, not without their Celtiborian allies.

Now is the time to hit these imperials and bleed them white. There was no solid evidence to suggest that the mysterious soldiers were from the empire, but they were too many, and they were too well equipped to be anything but. And if they were imperial troops, DeMark knew he'd only have to face them again if he let them escape. Because one thing was clear: *This battle isn't just for Celtiboria.*

It's for all the Far Stars.

DeMark walked across the crest of a small hill, a spot that gave him a good vantage point over much of the position. He wouldn't call the ground he was on dry, exactly, but it wasn't covered with a meter of water, either. His uniform was still soaked through, but he'd managed to change into a dry pair of boots, at least.

He'd finally pulled back from the front lines, much to the relief of Marius Trevannes and the rest of his officers. He'd found being up in the fight, standing alongside the privates and corporals, and the others who did most of the fighting, to be cathartic. It was easier to send men into dangers you shared with them, and nothing was better for morale than the troop seeing a general up on the front lines.

But he also had an army to run, and he couldn't do that in combat, not effectively, at least. A hundred thousand soldiers awaited his orders, counting on him to lead them. And now it looked like they might break through with enough effort. With any luck, they'd trap Carteria's disorganized army between their advance and the invading force around the capital. Though he'd kept it to himself, DeMark had been despondent just two weeks before, despairing of his chances of stopping Carteria's coup. Now, he felt that victory was there for the taking. As long as his exhausted soldiers could keep moving, keep fighting.

"General DeMark!"

He turned around. Marius Trevannes was running up the hill, clearly excited about something.

"What is it, Marius?"

"It's Blackhawk, sir. He's back. Ace Graythorn managed to get a transmission from *Wolf's Claw* through the enemy jamming. Blackhawk is behind the landings near Alban, sir. He's got sixty thousand mercenaries, and they're advancing on the city."

DeMark smiled. Part of him had refused to believe Blackhawk was dead. The man was just damned hard to kill. "That's good news, Marius. Good news by any measure."

"That's not all, sir. Blackhawk led an advance team into the palace to rescue Astra Lucerne. He's got her, and he is on the way back. And Carteria's dead. Apparently, Lady Lucerne killed him."

DeMark stood motionless, silent, staring back at his second in command for a few seconds. He had trouble processing all he had just heard. "Well, that changes everything," he finally said. "Doesn't it, Marius."

"Yes, sir . . ." Trevannes had a big smile on his face. "I'd say it does."

"Let's make an announcement, Marius. Let's let the men know why they're pushing so hard, why they're not getting any rest. It's time to send these traitors and their imperial masters straight to hell!"

Blackhawk moved slowly down the corridor. The power was out in this section of the palace. He didn't know if that was intentional, some effort by their enemies to impede their progress, or if they'd taken out a conduit or some other critical infrastructure during the fighting. However it had happened, they'd been making their way through the inner corridors with a handful of flashlights. But now, Blackhawk could see hints of sunlight reflecting off the walls ahead.

The trip back had been bloodier than the one in. Five of Carano's soldiers were dead, and the mercenary general himself had taken a shot in the foot. It wasn't a grievous wound, but it was painful as hell, and damned inconvenient when they were racing to get out of the palace as quickly as possible.

They'd killed at least twenty men, all but a couple of them

imperial browncoats. Word of Carteria's death seemed to have spread, and Blackhawk figured his Celtiborian forces were paralyzed, uncertain what to do next. Blackhawk had no hesitation on that score.

I don't care what you do, you're all finished. There's only one way to deal with traitors.

He didn't know how much of that thought was from the Blackhawk side and how much from the Umbra side. Neither of his personas had much pity for turncoats.

Astra was right behind him, rifle in her hand, and two ammunition belts crisscrossed over her chest. He'd tried to keep her back, in the middle of Carano's men. He told her she was the only one who could end the strife and unite Celtiboria again. He reminded her she was still partially under the influence of the drug conditioning the imperials had used on her. He'd even tried ordering her to stay back. But all he'd managed to do was remind himself of the utter futility of trying to tell Astra Lucerne what to do.

Chrono, she's a pain in the ass, he thought. But even as he did, he knew he loved her more for her pigheadedness, if that was even possible. They were alike in so many ways. He suspected that would be their biggest challenge if they ever had the chance to be together.

A big if.

"Ark," Ace's voice crackled through on Blackhawk's comm. "The courtyard is full of enemy troops, mostly the browncoats. I'm going to open fire and clear a place to land, but we've got thousands of enemy soldiers moving back toward the palace, so you've got to move quickly once we're down."

"Got it, Ace. Go ahead. I'll make sure we're there. Blackhawk out." He turned back toward the group. "All right, let's move. Whatever's in our way we charge right over—I don't care what it is. We either get out of here in the next few minutes . . . or we run right into the entire enemy army retreating back to the palace."

"We're ready, Ark," Carano answered, managing to keep most of the pain from his voice. "Let's do it!"

Blackhawk spun around, his rifle thrust forward. He almost tried to get Astra to fall back again, but he stopped himself. It was a waste of time. *You love her, you fool. You have to take the whole package. And she's as stubborn as you are.*

"Let's move!" He headed forward, moving swiftly, not quite a jog, but a very fast walk. He reached the end of the hallway in a few seconds, and he turned to the left. The sunlight was bright in the room. It wasn't the way they'd come in, but he knew it had to be close. Most of the exterior wall was gone, and he could see the courtyard beyond. There was screaming, and men were running around, diving for cover. He got hit with a wave of stench. Burning flesh, he realized. Ace was blasting away with the needle gun, clearing an LZ for the *Claw*.

There were soldiers in the room too, a couple dozen, taking shelter from the *Claw*'s fire. But they turned around with surprise as Blackhawk and the mercenaries poured in, diving for cover and firing.

Blackhawk moved to flip over a table with a polished metal top. It was enormously heavy, and his enhanced muscles strained to turn it over. But Astra dropped her rifle and slid in next to him, grabbing on with both hands. The table's legs slowly lifted from the floor, and it tipped over with a loud crash. They both ducked behind, just as several enemy soldiers fired their way.

Astra grabbed her rifle from the ground and peered over

the table. She leveled the weapon and squeezed off half a dozen shots, taking down at least two of the enemy before she ducked back down.

Blackhawk dove onto his stomach, extending his rifle around the end of the table. His eyes focused quickly, his mind assessing targets almost subconsciously. He pulled the trigger, firing a three-shot burst. Then again. And again. And each time he pulled the trigger, an enemy died.

The firefight raged for a minute, perhaps two. Blackhawk and his people were having the best of it, but they'd lost two more of Carano's men. It was a fair loss rate for the twenty enemy soldiers they'd taken down, but it was never easy to lose your own.

"All right, Ark," Ace screamed through the comm. "Now!"

"Now!" Blackhawk roared, leaping over the table as he did, and running forward toward the shattered wall. He was firing on full auto now, blasting away at anyone in his way. He could feel Astra right behind, hear her fire zipping past him. He had a cold pit in his stomach, a fear that she would be hit, that he would lose her here, so close to her rescue. But there was nothing to do but keep going. He'd only put her at greater risk if he stopped now.

He ran out into the courtyard. The once pleasant spot had become a nightmare, chunks of enemy bodies strewn everywhere. The reek of death, of seared, cooked flesh hung heavily in the air. But Blackhawk saw only one thing: *Wolf's Claw,* sitting in the middle of the scene of carnage, its ramp open, with Tarnan standing on it, blasting away with his autocannon.

"Inside, everybody," Blackhawk yelled. He savored the feeling of his boots on the *Claw*'s metal ramp, and he stopped alongside Tarnan, waving to the rest of the group to get inside the ship.

"Shira, get to the lower turret, just in case we need some serious firepower."

"On my way, Ark." She raced up the ramp.

Blackhawk stood firm, firing away, even as he pushed Astra up the ramp. He was standing next to Tarnan, and he would until everyone else was on board. He knew he should get to the bridge, but he didn't care. He'd be damned if he was going to leave Tarq's brother alone. Not until the fight was done.

The rest of Carano's men scrambled aboard, carrying the wounded with them. Blackhawk slapped Tarnan's back and said, "Let's go, big man." Tarnan turned and looked at Blackhawk for an instant. Then he nodded, and the two of them raced up the ramp and into the *Claw*.

CHAPTER 27

"I DON'T KNOW HOW, SIR, BUT SHE'S STILL ALIVE." THE MEDIC was crouched over the still form, staring up at the lieutenant. "She's so torn apart, I'd be afraid to even move her."

Lieutenant Drango stared down at the woman lying in the street. There was blood all around her, and her left leg was twisted outward at a grotesque angle. She was still alive—he could see her chest moving slightly when she took a shallow breath—but it was obvious she was in bad shape. He almost told the medic to move along. According to the map on his tablet, his company was in the Back Streets section of Alban. He remembered the name from the preflight document, a notorious slum, one where a dead body—or an almost dead one—wasn't that rare a find.

But there was something wrong, something that didn't quite make sense. First, she was beautiful. Not just attractive, but drop-dead gorgeous. Her mane of thick black hair was twisted in knots and caked with dried blood, but even lying in the street horribly wounded, he could tell this was no ghetto dweller.

Her clothing was another clue. She wore rags, a costume perfectly in keeping with the norms of the neighborhood. But underneath there was a black unitard. Most of it was soft and skintight, but some spots had hardened, where some chemical reaction had changed the composition of the material. This was no slum dweller's costume; it was high-tech body armor, a suit that probably cost more than anyone in the Back Streets made in a lifetime.

"Is there anything you can do to help her?" Drango continued looking at the woman for a few seconds before turning back to face the medic.

"I could give her some fluids, a few basic drugs. Painkillers too. If she's got any awareness, I can't even imagine how much she's suffering." He stared back at Drango. "But I don't see it doing much, sir. She's in a bad way. As far as I can tell, these injuries are mortal."

"Maybe so, Corporal, but she looks like someone important to me, so do what you can, and call in a medivac team. Let's get her to the field hospital and see what they can do for her." Chrono knows what someone important was doing in this shithole.

"Whatever you say, sir." The medic still sounded doubtful, but he opened up his kit and started pulling out his equipment.

Drango stood and stared at the still-unmoving form. He'd been a soldier all his life and part of General Carano's outfit for five years. He'd seen fighting on half a dozen planets, and more dead and wounded soldiers and civilians than he dared to count. But this one was different. *She doesn't belong here.*

Who could she be?

Blackhawk ran across the lower deck. He was about to tell Doc to help the wounded, but the *Claw*'s resident medic was already at work. He'd drafted a couple of Carano's men to help with triage, and he had his patients spread all across the deck.

"We'll try to keep things as smooth as possible, Doc, but we need to get out of here fast."

"Do what you need to do," Doc grunted, his attention focused on the wounded man he was hunched over.

Blackhawk raced up the ladder. "Get us off the ground, Lucas." His head snapped around. "Stay on the needle gun, Ace. Shoot at anything you think looks dangerous. I've got Shira in the lower turret, just in case we need serious firepower."

His two companions acknowledged his orders as he ran across the deck and flopped down into his chair. Astra had come up behind him, and he motioned toward the reserve workstation. "Get strapped in, Astra," he said, as he was dropping into his own seat.

"Liftoff in ten seconds," Lucas said into the shipwide comm. "Everybody hang on."

Blackhawk had one belt of his harness on, and he decided that was enough. He flipped on his display, staring at the feed from the *Claw*'s belly scanners. They were dark now, buried in the ground under the ship, but as soon as they lifted, the sensors would give him a view of the battle taking place in the city. From the numbers of enemy troops that had retreated to the palace, he knew things had to be going well.

The *Claw* lurched hard, and Blackhawk could feel the g-forces of liftoff. He knew Lucas was trying to keep things as smooth as possible, but blasting off from a planet's surface was a rugged endeavor, even with a master pilot at the helm.

Blackhawk could see the ground receding below the *Claw* in his display, and in a few seconds, they were five hundred meters up and Lucas had engaged the main engines. He kept the thrust light, nothing like the wild ride in, when maintaining surprise had been so crucial.

Blackhawk was amazed as he gazed into his scanner. He'd expected the Tiger Company's tanks to be useful against the Celtiborian infantry formations, but now he got an idea of just how successful the attack had been. The tanks had already reached the city limits, and several had moved into the urban area itself, supporting the advancing infantry. Huge sections of the city were burning, and he could see the lead elements were only a few kilometers from the palace itself.

"Lucas, bring us down just outside the city, and drop us off. Then you can take Astra and the wounded back to the LZ."

"No, Ark, I'm not going back to the LZ."

Blackhawk was completely unsurprised by Astra's objection. "Astra . . ."

"Don't 'Astra' me, Ark. I need to go into the city with the army. We need to retake the media center and establish that I am in control . . . and who the true enemy is. We can't even guess what the people are thinking after that broadcast."

Blackhawk sighed. Trying to protect Astra was proving to be one of the more difficult projects he'd ever tackled. "Fine, but I want you to stay back from the front line." He stared across the bridge at her. "If it's not enough that I love you, if you get yourself killed, we'll never be able to end this fight without a full-out bloodbath."

Astra stared back for a few seconds, then she just nodded. She had a sour look on her face, like she didn't enjoy her own argument coming back at her.

"Setting down in one minute, Ark."

Blackhawk nodded as he unhooked his harness. "Ace, take over the *Claw*." He turned and looked across the bridge. "Let's go, Lady Lucerne," he said.

She made a face and unstrapped herself from the chair, following him to the ladder and climbing down to the lower deck.

"Shira, Tarnan, you ready?" Blackhawk knew he couldn't leave the big man behind again.

They both nodded. Shira had her customary pair of assault rifles, and Tarnan was holding the massive two-man autocannon he used as a personal weapon.

"Sarge?"

"We're ready, Captain." His men stood behind him, clad in their usual nondescript fatigues and body armor. They each had an assault rifle, and they carried half a dozen grenades on their shoulder straps.

"We're coming with you, Ark." Carano stood at the edge of the deck, with the twenty of his men who'd come through unhurt. "We're in this thing together." The merc commander himself was favoring his injured foot, but his expression dared anyone to make it an issue.

Blackhawk just nodded. He'd been using Carano and his people for his own purposes, because they were the only large military unit he'd been able to rally on short notice, but he'd begun to respect them all. They fought like hell, and they'd done their duty.

"Everybody hang on," he said, grabbing one of the handholds along the edge of the deck. He stood silently for a few seconds, then the ship shook hard and came to a halt.

"We're down." Lucas's voice blared from every speaker in the ship.

"All right, let's go." Blackhawk turned and walked down the main corridor, heading toward the ramp.

"Sergeant! Bogies along the tree line!" Clive's voice was loud and shrill, and it sliced into Sergeant Paras Bodine's ears like a razor-sharp spear.

Bodine whipped around, bringing his rifle to bear, just as he heard his men open fire. He saw the enemy, just in time to watch all of them fall, victims of his squad's accurate shooting. He ripped off a few shots himself, but he was late. All the targets were down.

"Nice shooting, boys," he said, real gratitude in his voice. He'd thought he had seen something off to the right, and he'd focused all his attention on it . . . and he'd missed the four browncoats hunkered down in the small wood to the left. They'd have picked him off for sure if it hadn't been for Clive and the others. "Saved my ass there, you did."

Bodine and his squad were a crack unit. They'd been part of Marshal Lucerne's household regiment, stationed at the palace until the tragic events that had precipitated civil war. Bodine had loudly declared he would dive into a vat of shock-tail scorpions before he would serve Carteria, and most of the rest of the household troops shared that opinion. When things turned bad, about half of them fought their way out to join DeMark's loyalists. Bodine didn't know for sure if the other half of his comrades were dead, but he had a bad feeling about it.

"Hey! You were right, Sarge. We got troops coming in from the right too."

"Get down, boys. Grab any cover you can." Bodine dove down to the ground, crawling forward half a meter toward a large stump. It wasn't great cover, but it was a hell of a lot better than nothing. He brought his rifle around in front of him.

He watched as eight figures moved across the ridge, followed half a minute later by at least twenty more.

"Fuck," Bodine muttered, as even more soldiers came up over the hill.

"We should get out of here, Sarge. That's a lot of troops coming through there."

"Yeah, let's—" Bodine started to reply. But then he stopped. "Wait a minute. Those aren't browncoats. And they're not Celtiborian uniforms, either."

He reached around, pulling out a small pair of binoculars. He stared across the field, focusing on the lead cluster of soldiers. They were wearing camouflage fatigues, with dark gray body armor.

"What do you make of them, Faring?" Bodine handed the binoculars to his assistant squad leader.

"I don't know," the corporal answered. "They don't look like . . . Chrono's balls, what the hell is that?"

Bodine was staring straight ahead as the giant vehicle rose up, cresting the ridge, its tracks slamming down on the hillside as it continued forward. The thing was huge, nothing he needed the binoculars to see clearly.

"Some kind of tank," Bodine said. "But it's the biggest fucking thing I've ever seen." He reached behind him and pulled out his comm unit. "HQ, this is Sergeant Bodine, Company A, Lucerne Household Regiment. We've made contact with . . ."

"Calm down, Sergeant. They're allies," the voice on the comm said. "Our lead elements are running into them all along the line. We had no warning because of the enemy jamming. You are to make contact and hold your position until further notice."

"Yes, sir." He turned toward his men. "You're not going to believe this, boys . . . but it looks like we've run clean out of enemies to fight. At least for the moment."

"Go, Ace. Go find her." No one on the *Claw* had heard a word from Katarina since she took off that day in the rotunda, hot on the heels of the assassin who'd come a hairsbreadth from killing Blackhawk. Ace had followed Blackhawk's orders and made sure the *Claw* got back behind the lines and landed safely, but then he hitched a ride forward on a supply truck. He wasn't the kind to sit back in the ship and wait for the others to return.

And to be fair, Ace wasn't the only one concerned about Katarina. Blackhawk was worried sick about her. Indeed, the *Claw*'s captain suspected they were dealing with a member of the Exequtorum. To most of his crew—and to virtually all those who'd heard the name of that shadowy organization, it was myth, legend. But Blackhawk was well aware the emperor's personal assassins were very, *very* real. Indeed, he'd seen their handiwork up close. He had enormous confidence in Katarina, but he knew she'd gone after an enemy orders of magnitude more deadly than any she'd faced before.

However good we are, there is always someone better . . .

And besides the caliber of her adversary, she'd been wandering around in the middle of a war zone, not exactly prepared for so desperate a fight. Wherever she was—assuming she was still alive—she could probably use some help.

"Thanks, Ark." Ace stood still for a few seconds then added, "I'll find her." There was more hope than certainty in his voice, but sometimes hope is all you have. Blackhawk's own mind had more trouble with mechanisms of that sort. He'd been designed to be a capable leader, every chromosome in his body selected and manipulated to make him clear-minded in a crisis. Fooling himself was a difficult thing to do. He knew Katarina was probably dead, and he couldn't pretend otherwise, at least not in any way he'd believe. But while there was even a chance, he owed it to her—and Ace—to see everything that could be done was done.

He watched Ace turn and start to walk away, and he yelled after him, "Wait, Ace . . . take Sarge and the boys with you." There was still a lot of fighting going on in the city, and it was anyone's guess how many of the enemy were still dug into positions all around. Letting Ace go prowling around alone was just asking to add his death to the likely loss of Katarina.

"I will." He paused and nodded slightly. "Thanks, Ark." He turned around and headed over toward the *Claw*'s resident troop of soldiers.

"Katarina?" Astra walked up behind Blackhawk. She didn't know much of what had transpired while she was held captive, but Blackhawk had told her about the attempt on his life, and Katarina's pursuit of the would-be assassin.

"Yes," he answered sadly. "I knew there was something going on between them, but I hadn't realized how serious it was."

"You think she's dead, don't you?" Astra put her hand on his arm.

"I'd never count Katarina out until I was sure, but I know what she went up against . . ."

"I'm sorry, Ark."

He put his own hand over hers. "I'm just surprised. I'd never have guessed . . . Katarina and Ace? That's not one I would have predicted."

"We don't pick who we fall in love with, Ark." She leaned around, looking up at him with a smile. "You can't possibly think I would have picked you, can you? Like I couldn't have found someone easier to deal with?" She held a snarky grin for a few seconds. "Or that you couldn't have found some beautiful maiden somewhere who couldn't wait to do every stupid thing you told her to do without an argument?"

"There have been a lot of beautiful princesses. Maybe I should take a closer look . . ." He smiled and nodded. "No, you're right. But still, I'm surprised by it." His cheerful expression faded quickly. "I just hope he finds her. In one piece."

He paused for a few seconds, then he shook off the melancholy.

"Whatever happens, we've got work to do. We need to get to the broadcast center. If we don't get you on the air soon, this whole planet is going to ignite like putting a torch to dry straw."

Rachen crept through the rubble of a semicollapsed building. There had been heavy fighting in Alban, as Blackhawk's mercenaries pushed deeper into the city. It looked like most of Carteria's Celtiborian soldiers had slipped away after the death of their commander, but the imperial browncoats were still mounting serious resistance. The chaos was helpful in sneaking close to Blackhawk, but it was frustrating as well. He'd been stalking the adventurer turned general for hours now, waiting to catch him alone, but he'd been with someone every moment.

Taking out Blackhawk with his followers and allies so close was dangerous. He'd taken a serious risk in the rotunda, attempting an assassination in the midst of such a large crowd, and it had allowed Blackhawk's Sebastiani friend to track him down. She'd been an impressive warrior, and the pain from his wounds reminded Rachen that he hadn't defeated her by the kind of comfortable margin typical to his encounters. Indeed, his injuries were slowing him down, which made going after Blackhawk like this even more dangerous.

But none of that mattered. Brothers of the Exequtorum did not fail missions. They did not pull back because they were injured or conditions were difficult. Whatever the risk, he had no choice. He had to make his move now.

Blackhawk had just detached six of his people, including his second in command. He was perhaps twenty meters away from the mercenary soldiers who were with him. He finally stood alone . . . almost. The blond woman, Lucerne's daughter. She was there too.

She is Blackhawk's weakness. He has affection for her. It will disrupt his logic, slow his response. I will kill them both. Her first, and then him. She is not on my mandate, but the death of both of them will throw Celtiboria into total chaos. It will ease my escape path . . . and mandate or no, it will serve my master's interests.

Rachen was lying behind a large chunk of the building's wall. He'd been there for ten minutes, lying dead still, watching the scene before him. Motion was his enemy, as it made it far easier for someone to spot him. Far better to wait for the prey to wander into your grasp than to jump around chasing him.

He had an assault rifle out in front of him, one he'd pulled off a dead soldier. It wasn't ideal for use as a sniper's weapon, but it would serve his purpose. He hadn't risked retrieving his own gear. The battle with the Sebastiani assassin had been more difficult than he'd expected. And the Sebastiani had been in his quarters. It was possible she'd alerted someone as to his identity, or even left a trap for him.

No, going back would have been too large a risk.

Delaying the attack wasn't an option either. The battle on Celtiboria was almost over, and Blackhawk had pulled victory from the jaws of defeat. The adventurer could leave the planet any minute, and once he buttoned up in his ship and blasted off, Rachen would be back to the beginning. He'd have to reestablish contact, and that could take months.

The assassin slowly moved the weapon into place, his eye fixed on the small aiming sight. He was targeting Astra. *Just take her down, one shot to the head. Then Blackhawk. There's something about him, some kind of toughness. He survived my venom somehow. I have to be sure this time. Three shots to the head. Then I get out of here.*

He held still, slowing his breath at first, then holding it altogether. He took one last look down the rifle, and he squeezed his finger slowly, methodically . . .

"The main broadcast center is about a kilometer in this direction." Astra was pointing to the southwest. "It's that tower there . . . the one with the blue glass." She turned and looked at Blackhawk. "It's the only place besides the palace where we can get a signal out planetwide . . ."

Blackhawk had been listening to her, but he felt something, a coldness, the sixth sense he so often had in battle. It wasn't anything mystical, just the subconscious reaction to his enhanced senses. Sometimes his eyes or ears caught something, and he reacted before his conscious mind had time to consider the threat.

In the rubble over there. Movement. A reflection.

He grabbed Astra and began to throw her hard to the ground.

"What the . . ." she began, but Blackhawk wasn't listening. He saw the threat, and he knew immediately what it was. Another assassination attempt. And this time Astra was in the line of fire.

He heard the gunshot, even as he was drawing his pistol. He saw Astra lurch forward, heard her protestations cease, her words replaced by a yelp of pain.

He fired his pistol repeatedly, unloading the cartridge as he ran forward toward the threat. He wanted to stay with Astra, longed to check her injury, to make sure she was okay, to hold her in his arms. But his instincts were in total control . . . and they knew only one course of action.

Neutralize the threat.

"Help Astra!" he screamed, with a volume and firmness of command that grabbed the attention of everyone within fifty meters. He was peripherally aware of people running behind him, toward her. *Help her, please.*

He had covered half the distance before he'd emptied his pistol. He doubted he'd hit his enemy, but he'd forced him to duck behind the wall of the broken structure. And that's what he wanted. Blackhawk was running on pure rage, Frigus Umbra uncaged, feeding his need to kill his opponent.

This would be close-in work, not an extended firefight.

This man is Exequtorum. I could lose this fight . . .

He tossed aside the pistol and drew his blade, grabbing the end of the half-collapsed wall and leaping up, swinging himself around. His enemy was there, and ready. He'd dropped the gun when he'd hurriedly pulled himself out of the line of fire, and now he stood facing Blackhawk with a sword in his own hand, a weapon plucked from one of the dead soldiers lying nearby.

"You are a capable man, Arkarin Blackhawk," the assassin said, as the two moved slowly, each evaluating his opponent.

"Capable enough to kill you," Umbra said, Blackhawk allowing his alter ego to step forward, face his enemy. "I have never killed one of the Exequtorum, but I will remedy that now."

"So you know of my order?" The assassin was moving as he spoke, as was Blackhawk, each seeking an opening to press his attacks. "You continue to surprise me, Arkarin Blackhawk. You are not at all what I expected to encounter out here in the Far Stars."

"Not everything is as it seems. You appear to know me, but I find I'm at a disadvantage."

"Ah . . . indeed. I am known as Lord Rachen, Captain Blackhawk."

"Well, Lord Rachen, you killed my friend. Augustin Lucerne was a good man, and he deserved better than to be murdered in his quarters." Blackhawk's eyes narrowed, his mind taking stock of his adversary. "And now, I will avenge him."

The two men faced each other, each staring into the other's eyes. They held their weapons aloft and moved slowly, cautiously.

Blackhawk felt Umbra's rage inside him, the supreme arrogance of the undefeated imperial general. But he tempered his alter ego's rash anger. Rachen was no normal enemy, and if he made even the smallest mistake, the deadly assassin would vanquish him.

The two had almost circled each other when Blackhawk lunged forward, thrusting his battleworn blade toward his enemy's chest. But Rachen wasn't there. He'd seen Blackhawk's strike and quickly shifted to the side, evading the blow and positioning himself for his own attack.

Blackhawk felt a coldness move through him, a warning. He realized immediately that he had committed himself too aggressively, that he'd allowed his foe to gain an advantage. His instincts took control, and he felt his arm moving, his blade ahead of his conscious thought.

Pain. Rachen's blade bit into his flesh . . . barely. Then his own blade clanged against the assassin's, pushing it aside amid a small spray of his own blood.

Blackhawk could feel the sweat pouring from his head, down the back of his neck. He'd almost given his opponent a killing blow.

He sucked in a deep breath as he pulled back, watching Rachen as the assassin watched for another chance. *No,* he thought. *I underestimated you once . . . my own folly. I will not do it again.*

The two continued their deadly dance. There were few warriors anywhere that would be a match for either man. Death was their trade, and they were among the most skilled of its purveyors.

And after this struggle, there'd be one less in their elite ranks.

Rachen sprang forward, his motion as rapid as it was unexpected. Yet Blackhawk was ready. He saw the assassin's approach, knew where the blow would come. He slashed with his own blade, parrying Rachen's blow with a loud clang. But the imperial wasn't deterred. He swung again . . . and again, and each time his sword met Blackhawk's.

The two traded blows, each successfully blunting his enemy's attacks. Blackhawk could feel the adrenaline pumping into his arteries, his heart pounding in his ears. He channeled his determination—and Umbra's rage—into each strike, but still Rachen matched him at every turn. Blackhawk had faced death before, many times . . . but he couldn't remember the last time he'd feared defeat fighting a single opponent.

He's favoring his left leg, Blackhawk thought, noting the slightest hitch as the imperial assassin stepped aside to counter his blow. *Use that. You need everything you have to defeat this man.*

Blackhawk lunged again, bringing his blade in from the right, forcing his opponent to step to the left.

Yes, that leg is definitely injured.

Blackhawk took a step back, maintaining his defenses. *He's too skilled . . . I'm not going to catch him napping. This is a war of attrition, and I need to wear him down.* He felt the slickness of blood on his side. His wound was nothing of consequence, more a reminder he'd allowed his enemy to draw first blood. It was painful, but he ignored that, and he channeled his frustration, the anger at his own carelessness, into his attacks.

Rachen lunged forward once more, swinging his sword with a primal ferocity. The blade slammed hard into Blackhawk's, and he felt the impact all the way up his arm. But his sword held firm. Again, the assassin struck . . . and again, striking at Blackhawk's weapon with all the strength he could muster.

Blackhawk winced as yet another blow slammed into his sword. His armed ached, from the impacts, from the fatigue . . . but he held firm.

The enemy's blows are weakening. He is becoming fatigued. Now is the time to press your attack.

You think I'm not tired?

You are weakening as well, though more slowly. Your genetics are your advantage. Your adversary is as skilled as you are . . . perhaps even more so.

He felt a rush of injured pride. *Better?*

Immaterial at present . . . and nearly impossible to accurately measure. But your advantage in stamina is clear. You are becoming fatigued, but he is tiring more quickly. Use that.

Blackhawk felt a burst of anger toward the meddlesome AI, but even as he did, he realized Hans's advice was sound.

He leaped back, vaulting over of a pile of rubble that had once been part of a wall. Rachen was surprised, but just for an instant. Then he came at the captain, stabbing at Blackhawk over the wall.

That's right . . . you think I'm retreating, that I'm too weak to continue. You think it is time to finish me. So come . . . come at me with whatever you have left . . .

Rachen thrust again, but Blackhawk sprang back, away from the wall. The assassin followed, jumping over the shattered masonry in a single bound. And something else . . .

Blackhawk caught the move out of the corner of his eye, the imperial grabbing a chunk of broken stone as he glided over the wall. He landed and threw the rock in a single motion. Blackhawk ducked, dropping down as he felt the projectile just scrape the side of his head.

Chrono, he's good . . .

And then Rachen was on him.

His blade brushed aside his enemy's, but the assassin's body slammed into his, and the two fell together, rolling painfully across the debris and shattered masonry of the ruins.

Blackhawk sucked in a deep breath and pulled his knee up hard into Rachen's stomach, rolling away as his enemy fell back.

He leaped to his feet and brought his sword around, but the imperial managed to scramble back to his feet and get back in a defensive position.

"You are a highly skilled warrior, Arkarin Blackhawk . . . far more formidable than any I expected to encounter out here."

"I am Arkarin Blackhawk . . . here. But I am not from the Far Stars, no more than you are. I came from the empire, just as you did."

Blackhawk paused for an instant, and the two faced each other, unmoving. Deep inside himself, Blackhawk surrendered, allowing the monster to come fully out of its cage, in all its brutal savagery. "Prepare for death, dog, for you face Frigus Umbra, not some pirate or petty adventurer from the fringe of human space." Blackhawk's eyes blazed, and he could see the reaction in his opponent . . . the fear.

Rachen paused. It was just for an instant, a momentary shock at hearing such a familiar name, but it was enough. Blackhawk/ Umbra lunged forward, hand tightly wrapped around the worn hilt of that deadly shortsword. The imperial agent reacted, pulling back, trying to avoid the strike as he brought his own blade up to parry. But that single instant of distraction had been too much. His efforts avoided the killing blow, but Blackhawk's sword plunged into his shoulder, sinking in deeply, and slicing to the side, freeing itself from his flesh in a spray of blood.

The Exequtori stumbled back, bringing up his sword, maintaining a fighting stance. He appeared to be oblivious to the pain, but his side was covered in blood.

There was no thought on either side that surrender was an option. No consideration of mercy or quarter.

Blackhawk/Umbra pressed on, swinging mightily at his

enemy. Rachen parried every blow, but Blackhawk could tell his opponent was weakening. The shoulder wound wasn't mortal, but the assassin was losing a lot of blood. And any weakness in a fight like this was fatal.

Blackhawk felt like he could smell his enemy's blood. He could feel victory, the kill, within his grasp. He wasn't a soldier now, not an adventurer, not even a pit fighter in some gladiatorial spectacle. No, he was a predator, pure and simple, a feral beast locked into the hunt. There was nothing in his mind now, no thought, no feeling . . . nothing at all, save the death of his enemy.

He swung again, with all the strength he could manage, and his sword clanged loudly as it slammed into Rachen's. The assassin struggled to continue the fight, to parry Blackhawk's deadly blows, but eventually he stumbled, falling to one knee.

Blackhawk swung his sword down viciously, knocking the blade from the assassin's hand. He could feel his heart beating in his ears, like some drum calling him to war. His hand gripped his blade like a vise, and every muscle in his body was tense, ready to finish the battle.

Rachen tried to put up an arm to protect himself, but Blackhawk's sword struck hard, severing it just below the elbow. Blood poured from the hideous wound, yet even then, the assassin was silent. He was Exequtorum. Blackhawk knew he would not show pain or fear. But he didn't care about the pain.

Just as long as the bastard feels it.

He slashed the blade across Rachen's throat in a motion so quick it was barely visible; his sword was already through when the torrent of blood began to pour out. But he wasn't done. He brought his sword around again, and he rammed it hard through Rachen's chest, shoving it through his opponent's heart with all his strength—until the hilt slammed into the breastbone, and ten centimeters of bloody blade protruded from the dead assassin's back.

He stood there for a moment, Blackhawk and Frigus Umbra, for a brief instant one and the same. He was covered in his enemy's blood and holding the assassin's body up with his sword. Then, in a blinding motion, he ripped the blade back out, and Rachen's body fell to the ground.

He remained where he was, his fist clenched around the sword, and inside he struggled, pushing the Umbra side back, fighting to remain himself. To remain Blackhawk.

Slowly, at least it felt that way to him, though no more than a few seconds passed, he regained his composure. He was again Arkarin Blackhawk. He stood covered in his defeated foe's blood, and he realized he was surrounded by Carano's stunned soldiers. They stood and stared, shocked at the spectacle they had just witnessed. But there was only one thing Blackhawk cared about.

"Astra!" he screamed, as he spun around and ran back to where she had stood.

CHAPTER 28

"ONE OF OUR ADVANCE ELEMENTS FOUND HER. WE HAVEN'T BEEN able to identify her yet. I'm afraid most of the Celtiborian information systems are still offline. I don't know if she is your missing crew member, but she fits the general description you provided." Major Danforth was one of Carano's senior staff officers, overseeing the operation of the field hospitals. Carano had personally called and ordered him to cooperate with Blackhawk's people.

"Just take me to her," Ace snapped, the edge in his voice unintentional. He didn't know if the mystery woman in the field hospital was Katarina, and from the description Danforth had given him of her injuries, he wasn't sure he hoped it was. The thought of finding her just in time to watch her die . . .

"Sorry, Major. I've been searching for almost forty-eight hours, and I'm a little raw, I guess."

"I understand." The major kept walking, Ace following right behind. The building had been some kind of hotel or residential complex, but the fighting had cleared it out, and the Black Helms medical services had moved right in. There were field hospitals spread across the battlefield, but this was the main semipermanent facility, the place seriously injured soldiers were sent once the field units had done all they could.

Danforth stopped and gestured toward a door. "She is in there, Mr. Graythorn. I'm afraid she has not regained consciousness yet." There was a man standing about a meter and a half from the door. "This is Doctor Maastrict. He has been caring for the patient." He turned toward the white-coated surgeon. "Doctor, this is Ace Graythorn, one of General Blackhawk's people. He believes our mystery patient may be one of the general's crew."

Maastrict nodded and extended his hand. "I am pleased to meet you, Mr. Graythorn, though I wish the circumstances were less grim."

"Thank you, Doctor." He reached out and grasped the offered hand. "May I?" he asked, but pushing his way through, not waiting for a response.

"Of course, Mr. Graythorn."

Ace walked into the room, Maastrict following behind. There was life support equipment everywhere, machines piled on top of machines. He moved toward the bed, listening to the sound the respirator made as it drew breath for the woman lying motionless, most of her body covered in bandages and other dressings.

He took a deep breath and walked the rest of the way, staring down. Her hair was gone, shaved off, and a heavy bandage covered most of her head. Her eyes were closed, and the heavy tube from the respiration unit covered most of her mouth, but Ace knew immediately. He felt a wave of weakness in his body, and for a few seconds, his legs wobbled. Then a surge of anger took him, and he stood there shaking, his hands clenched tightly into fists. He wanted to charge out of the room, find whoever had done this and kill him. Slowly and painfully. But he knew that wasn't an option. Blackhawk had already killed the assassin.

Oh, Kat, he thought, struggling to keep his mind in focus. *Why? Why did you run off by yourself? You were alone so long, but no more. I would have gone with you. This was our enemy, not just yours.*

The sight of her so helpless, so grievously wounded, was more than he could take. He'd seen her injured before, but nothing like this. She was the strongest person he knew, save Blackhawk. And now he'd seen them both utterly helpless, facing death. *Blackhawk survived,* he thought. *She will too.* She *has* to.

And yet, Katarina, for all her abilities, wasn't a genetically engineered warrior designed from dozens of carefully selected parents in some imperial lab.

He heard footsteps behind him, and he spun around, his hand dropping to his pistol. He caught himself and stopped, but there was no question his combat reflexes were in control now.

"Sorry, Doctor," he said softly. "I'm afraid it's been a difficult few days." *For all of us,* he thought, as he saw the bloodstains on the surgeon's scrubs.

"I understand, Mr. Graythorn."

"Please, everybody calls me Ace."

"Very well, Ace. Please call me Ivan."

Ace's eyes widened. He didn't know the makeup of Carano's Black Helms all that well, but he'd heard the name of their senior medical officer. By all accounts, he was an extraordinary surgeon, one Carano had bribed with an enormous cut to come aboard and run the Helms' medical services. "Thank you for all you've done."

Maastrict nodded and sighed softly. "You are welcome, Ace. So I assume our mystery patient is your lost crew member?" It was clear from his tone he realized she was more than just a member of the crew to Ace. "I am sorry that we haven't been able to do more. I was almost certain her wounds were mortal when I first saw her, but she has so far survived. I don't want to give you false hope—she is in extremely grave condition. But her chances of survival increase with each passing day."

"Is there anything you need, Doctor? Anything at all?"

"No, Ace. We have done all we can, I'm afraid. We will just have to wait and see what happens. She is obviously a very strong woman. If she lives, that will be why."

"Yes, she is very strong." *You have no idea, Doctor.* "I'll stay here for a while if it is okay. I'd like to sit with her." Again, it wasn't actually a question.

"Of course, Ace. You can stay as long as you like." Maastrict paused, then he said, "I'll leave you alone. Just call if you need anything."

"Thank you, Ivan." Ace stepped to the side of the room, grabbing a chair and moving it next to the bed. He sat and looked at her for a long time.

Come back to me, Katarina. To all of us.

"I told you I was fine, Ark." Astra sat up on the cot, wriggling around, trying to get comfortable. "I'd say let's get out of here and go down to the broadcast center, but I suspect you'd put up a fight."

"You're damned right I would. You are not leaving this hospital. And this isn't something I'm going to argue with you. There are guards at all the exits, so stay in bed, and do what your doctor says."

She sighed and leaned back on the pile of pillows behind her back. Rachen's bullet would have taken her head off if Blackhawk hadn't reacted as quickly as he had. He'd shoved her hard, but not enough to get her completely out of the way. The shot had entered her back and existed from the front of her shoulder. It was painful, and it had been a bloody mess, but it was a clean wound. It was already fused and wrapped in a clean dressing. In a few days she'd be as good as new.

"You're so stubborn," she said, glaring at Blackhawk. She tried to look mad, but a smile forced its way through to her lips. "But seriously, we need to make a broadcast. We have to assure the people that there is a leader they trust, that this fighting can stop."

"I've got that in hand, my dear. We're setting up a relay to the broadcast center. You can speak from right where you are." He gestured behind him. "Sam's outside, hounding the engineers. By the time she's done, you'll probably be able to transmit clear across the Void."

"Well, if I'm going to be on a planetwide broadcast, can I at least get some clothes?" The doctors had cut her shirt off her, and she was lying in the bed wearing only a flimsy hospital gown, one that was too big and kept slipping off her shoulder.

Blackhawk couldn't help but notice her effort to stay covered. "I don't know, I kind of like this look."

She made a face. "There's nothing under this flimsy thing you haven't seen before, Arkarin Blackhawk, but let's try not to extend that to all of Celtiboria."

"Oh . . . okay. I suppose we could find you something more appropriate." He turned and scooped a package off a small table. "I sent for this already. A perfectly respectable Celtiborian business suit. Stylish even. Do you think you can change by yourself, or do you need some help?" He stared at her mischievously.

"Yeah, and that would help keep us on our broadcast schedule," she said, winking at him. "I think I can manage." She waved her hand toward the door. "A bit of privacy, please, General Blackhawk."

Blackhawk nodded and flashed her a smile before turning and walking toward the door.

"Ark . . ."

He stopped and turned to look back.

"They told me what you did to the assassin . . ." Her voice was soft, hesitant. "Was that you . . . or him?"

Blackhawk took a deep breath, and for a brief instant he considered lying to her. But he wouldn't do that. Not to her. Not about this. "It was both of us."

He tried to offer her a brief smile, but it died on his lips. He just looked into her eyes for a few seconds, and he turned and walked through the door.

He was relieved to see her acting so normally. He'd reacted immediately when she'd been shot, making the decision that he needed to deal with the threat first. The fight with Rachen had been a dangerous and deadly one, but the hardest part had been trying to stay focused, wondering if Astra was dead or alive. If he had been only Blackhawk, he wasn't sure he could have done it—and against an enemy like Rachen, one small distraction would have been enough. For years he had fought against his past, as he knew he would again, for the rest of his life. But he had to acknowledge, to himself at least, that Frigus Umbra had saved his life out there.

It doesn't make it any easier to accept.

Blackhawk stood in the control center of the palace, lost for a moment in thought. Augustin had commanded from this room. He had launched his expeditionary forces. After thirty years of warfare to unite Celtiboria, he had stood here and given the orders, followed through on his dream, his quest.

And all it brought him was death. Three decades of struggle to die in his bedroom at the hands of an assassin. Blackhawk felt a sadness deep inside him. Pain at the loss of a friend, certainly, but it was more than that. Augustin Lucerne had deserved a better death, a hero's death.

He knew Lucerne had been drunk when his killer came upon him; DeMark had told him that. Blackhawk was one of the few people who truly knew how much the decades of pressure and war had worn down the iron will inside the great man. Augustin Lucerne carried a lot of sadness around with him, a lot of regret. And every man had his limits.

Eliane's birthday. When he'd first heard of his friend's death, he hadn't remembered. It had been days later when it occurred to him. Blackhawk had never known Eliane Lucerne. She had died several years before he'd come to the Far Stars, when he was still Frigus Umbra, the terror of imperial space. But he understood his friend's deep sadness, how terribly his wife's death had affected him.

"General Blackhawk . . ."

He turned toward the communications officer. *I wish they'd stop calling me general.* He had never claimed the title. Carano and his people had bestowed it upon him spontaneously, and it had stuck. And spread. There was already a general inside of Blackhawk, one he was struggling to control. *And none of you want to see him here, I can promise you that.*

"Yes, Lieutenant?"

"We have a message from Admiral Desaix, sir. He is on his way to the surface now. He has a visitor with him, an emissary."

Blackhawk's face twisted into a frown. "An emissary? From where?"

"From Kalishar, sir. From the ka'al."

Blackhawk was silent for a few seconds. The ka'al was possibly the last person in the Far Stars he expected to hear from. He and the new ka'al had crossed paths once or twice years before, but they'd never had a conflict of any kind. More important, Blackhawk had figured the empire had Kalishar all sewn up by now. They'd turned Belgaren into their puppet, and he couldn't imagine they'd allowed Rax Florin to succeed him without sinking their hooks into the new ka'al first.

"What does he want?" Blackhawk finally asked.

"Admiral Desaix is coming down with him, sir. The admiral says he doesn't want to discuss the matter over an open comm line."

Blackhawk just nodded. *What could Rax Florin want from me? It has to be some kind of trick . . .*

"Bring them to me as soon as they land. I'll be in the marshal's office."

"Chrono's balls, I'm glad to see you in one piece, old friend." Blackhawk leaped out of the chair and walked around the desk. It felt strange using Lucerne's old desk—and somehow right too. He was doing all he could to see that the marshal's legacy survived, and he wanted to be as close as he could to whatever essence remained of the great man.

He walked over and threw his arms around the dusty, disheveled form of General Rafaelus DeMark. "I'm glad you made it through, you broken-down old warhorse." DeMark had just come from the battlefield, and he looked it. The fighting had died down to a few pockets of imperial diehards, but they were surrounded and cut off from reinforcements and supplies. The battle was essentially over, and Celtiboria was liberated . . . again.

"It's good to see you too, Ark. I wasn't too sure it would ever happen. I didn't think I was going to make it back for a while. And there were all kinds of rumors flying around that you were dead. But I knew better, at least most of the time. There's not a harder man to kill in the Far Stars."

"I don't know about that, Rafe, but for now, let's just say I got lucky." He gestured toward one of the guest chairs. "You look exhausted." He turned his head and looked back at the desk chair. "Or sit back here, Rafe. It's probably more rightfully your place than mine."

"No way, Ark." DeMark sat in the guest chair. "You're his chosen successor. The one he wanted to lead after he was gone. And I'd be the first to line up behind you and give you my sword if you took the marshal's star cluster."

"We'll see, Rafe. But that means a lot coming from you. Right now, we've got work to do. We beat the enemy back here, but the empire is on the move, everywhere in the sector. I'm afraid we've underestimated Kergen Vos, my old friend, and he's stolen a step on us."

"So what do we do about that?" DeMark asked defiantly.

Blackhawk walked to a small counter on the side of the room, and he poured two glasses of water from a large pitcher. "We take back the initiative, that's what we do. We steal a step on him now, and by the time he realizes what we're doing, it will be too late."

He handed one of the glasses to DeMark. "I'm thinking this is the strongest thing we should be drinking for a while now. We need to stay clear-minded, totally focused. We have to do this right, Rafe. We've got one chance, one opportunity to end this now, short of a holocaust. If we fail, the Far Stars will see death and destruction unlike anything in its history."

DeMark nodded and took a deep drink. "I'm with you, Ark. So what do we do? What is that chance?"

"We take the head off the snake. We strike at Galvanus Prime."

DeMark stared back, a stunned look on his face. "The imperial sector capital? Do we have the strength?"

Blackhawk stared back at his friend. "Whatever we have must be enough. It is the only way to end this quickly, before billions have died."

DeMark nodded, but he still looked doubtful. Blackhawk understood. Galvanus Prime was a well-defended planet, the toughest invasion target in the Far Stars.

"You have to trust me, Rafe. I know imperial tactics. Better than anyone else in the Far Stars." Blackhawk didn't offer anything else, and DeMark didn't ask.

"I trust you, Ark. I'll support anything you think makes sense. You can count on me. Always."

CHAPTER 29

"THE TARGET IS GALVANUS PRIME, THE IMPERIAL SECTOR CAPITAL. The world that for one thousand years has claimed to be the center of government for the entire sector. The base of the imperial governors, a planet that for a millennium has been a threat to Far Stars independence."

Blackhawk stood at the head of the table, just in front of the large display screen. Rafe DeMark and Astra sat flanking him, and next to them Admiral Desaix and General Carano. A few other Celtiborian and mercenary officers, along with Shira and Sam, rounded out those in attendance.

Blackhawk wished Ace was present too, but he was still in the hospital standing vigil over Katarina. Against all odds, her condition had begun to improve, and Ace wanted to be there if she woke up. Blackhawk had agreed completely. Katarina was part of his family, and he wanted a familiar face there when her eyes opened.

"General Blackhawk, Galvanus Prime is impregnable to any force we can muster," Admiral Desaix said. "The planet's two orbital platforms are immense fortresses, and between them, they cover every approach. Every ship in the fleet would be blasted to dust and plasma before we got into our own firing range." Admiral Desaix had been looking at Blackhawk while he was speaking, but now he glanced around the table.

Blackhawk reached down and pressed a button on the table. The screen behind him flickered for an instant and then displayed a schematic of Galvanus Prime and its vaunted weapons platforms.

"Admiral Desaix is correct, as usual. Any conventional assault on Galvanus Prime is doomed to failure. For centuries, the planet has been defended by its orbital platforms. The two structures are like nothing else in the Far Stars. They are each over ten kilometers in length, bristling with heavy weapons. Their arsenal outpowers and outranges anything we have. They can destroy every combat vessel we possess, and every troop transport trying to land on the planet."

"So how can we attack, General?" DeMark asked. "If we can't get a ground force through, Galvanus Prime is invincible."

"So it would seem, General." Blackhawk looked out over the table. "Which is why we are going to destroy the platforms."

"How?" Desaix blurted out. "We can't even get into firing range before they blow us apart."

"I propose that we use two nuclear weapons. Not the normal warheads all the Primes keep in their reserve arsenals, but weapons many times more powerful. I want to construct two enhanced fusion bombs, each with five hundred megatons of destructive power." He looked down the table. "Sam, can you put those together quickly if I get you the raw materials?"

She'd been glancing down at the table, as she usually did when she was around people she didn't know well. Now she looked up at Blackhawk. "Sure, Ark. Get me the tritium I need and a couple fusion warheads for triggers, and I'll build your bombs."

"That's all well and good, Ark. And I have no doubt Sam here can construct the weapons. But how do you plan to deliver them to the target? Any vessel carrying them will be targeted and destroyed before it gets close. And the platforms carry enormous defensive batteries. Even if we could rig up some very long range missiles, they would be intercepted long before they got close enough to damage the stations."

"You will just have to trust me on that, all of you. I will deliver the bombs with *Wolf's Claw*. And once we clear the way, the invasion fleet will have an open approach. The imperial Far Stars fleet was badly hurt in the battle in this system last month. They will not have had time to make significant repairs—and they also have vessels detached all across the sector escorting invasion fleets. Vos has limited naval strength, especially at Galvanus Prime. He had to draw what he needed from somewhere, and with the weapons platforms, I'm betting he figured Galvanus Prime was already adequately protected. But we will turn the tide on him. Without the fortresses, I believe Galvanus Prime is as weakly defended as it has been in five centuries."

"Again, though," Desaix said, "how can you possibly get past their defenses, even with *Wolf's Claw*?" The admiral looked at Blackhawk, a confused expression on his face. "Your ship is quite formidable for its size, General, but there are weapons on those platforms that could destroy *Glorianus* with a single hit . . . and the flagship has twenty times the mass of *Wolf's Claw*."

"Well, Admiral, I guess the secret will be getting through without getting hit, won't it?"

"Rafe, come on in."

DeMark walked into the office. He was the last to arrive. He'd run back to what was left of the front lines to check on his positions after the last meeting. Then he'd hurried back to his quarters for a quick shower and a change into a new uniform. Meeting with Blackhawk covered with mud and the detritus of the battlefield was one thing, but greeting a foreign dignitary required a higher level of decorum whenever possible.

About a dozen chairs were set up in front of the desk. Astra was sitting in one, with Desaix next to her. Shira was standing in the back, behind Blackhawk, looking out over the room with her usual suspicious scowl. Most of the people in the room were unarmed, but she had a pistol on each hip.

There was another man, dressed in a strangely ornate fashion, at least by Celtiborian standards. He sat off to the side, waiting quietly for Blackhawk to introduce him.

"Thank you all for coming," Blackhawk said as DeMark sat down. He gestured toward the stranger. "Allow me to introduce Lord Illus Bevern, an ambassador sent to us from the ka'al of Kalishar."

The room was silent, but everyone present wore an expression that betrayed some level of surprise and confusion. All except Shira. She stood behind Blackhawk with the same scowl on her face. She had been to Kalishar before, and she looked like she'd have been just as happy if she never heard of the stinking dump again.

"Thank you, General Blackhawk," Bevern began. "I'd like to begin by congratulating you all on your victory on Celtiboria. You have saved this world from imperial domination, a worthy and commendable goal." He paused and glanced around the room for a few seconds.

"My own planet is not so fortunate. Our previous ruler, Ka'al Tarn, sold himself to agents of the empire. He had mismanaged the economy, and he found himself desperate, in need of imperial gold to prevent total economic collapse—and likely a rebellion that would have ended with his head on a spear outside the palace. Unfortunately, while the imperial aid satisfactorily addressed the initial problem, it quickly led to others."

Bevern looked at Blackhawk then at Astra, clearly trying to hide his discomfort. "You all know the ka'al was behind the abduction of Lady Lucerne, and the cause of considerable hardship for many of you present. On behalf of my master, Ka'al Rax, I offer you our heartfelt apologies for all you went through."

Blackhawk looked over at Astra with a quick smile. "Well, Lord Bevern, based on what you and I discussed, I believe Lady Lucerne and I are prepared to let bygones be bygones. And my crew as well." Most of them, at least. Shira was directly behind him, but he could have sworn he felt the intensity of her stare on his back.

Astra leaned over and looked toward the Kalishari. "Yes, Lord Bevern, if what you have told us is true, all is forgiven." She sat back and continued, "Perhaps you can repeat what you told us for the benefit of those who were not present at our first meeting." Those who were not present meant everyone but Blackhawk, Astra, and Desaix. The others were staring expectantly at Bevern.

"Very well, Lady Lucerne. As most of you suspect, Ka'al Rax

has been compelled to cooperate with the imperial authorities on Kalishar. As noted, the previous monarch had been deeply in debt to the imperials, and they were instrumental in aiding in the coup that replaced Tarn Belgaren." He paused. Florin had taken imperial coin to help him seize the throne. It was challenging to make that sound sympathetic, especially to this audience.

"It is the level of this cooperation that brought me here . . . to seek your aid, and to offer ours. The empire must be stopped on Kalishar, and when I tell you what has happened, I am certain you will all agree."

Blackhawk nodded. "Please continue, Lord Bevern."

The Kalishari nodded. "Things began slowly, but then the governor's agent began a widespread recruiting program, building imperial units from the lowest levels of society along the fringe. And he demanded the use of a large tract of the Kalishari desert to build a training facility."

"A training facility? Is that where he is getting all the soldiers he has deployed?" DeMark asked the question that had been on everyone's mind. The best estimate had been seventy-five thousand of the browncoats killed in the fighting on Celtiboria. And seemingly every day word came of another world invaded by a huge army of unknown origin. Even DeMark's old command on Nordlingen had sent drastic appeals for reinforcements, reporting a massive enemy invasion.

"Yes, I am sure that any soldiers you have encountered have come from the facility. They have expanded the operation continuously. It is now a truly vast encampment, with hundreds of buildings stretching over a hundred kilometers of the deep desert. Our best estimate is that they are now graduating nearly one hundred thousand trained soldiers per month."

"What are they doing with all those troops?" DeMark asked. "How are they even transporting them?"

"I think I can answer that, Rafaelus." Blackhawk looked around the room. "I just received this communiqué from Danellan Lancaster. He is privy to this information through his ownership of Vestron Shipping. Apparently, Kergen Vos has somehow gained control of several of the shipping guilds. Through these machinations and the influence of the guilds, he has been able to obtain the exclusive use of nearly three hundred transport vessels."

The room was silent for a few seconds, everyone present shocked by the news. Kergen Vos had scored a coup seizing control of the Far Stars Bank, one that had terrifying implications. Word that he had added two of the four shipping guilds to his list of conquests only made things worse.

Bevern cleared his throat. "So that is how they have been moving the soldiers off-planet." He paused for a few seconds. "Things are worse than I imagined. But I believe we can do something to strike back. I have been sent to offer the ka'al's covert aid if you are willing to launch an invasion of Kalishar to destroy the imperial facilities and garrison."

"He will help? In return for what?" DeMark asked.

"The ka'al requests a pardon for himself and all his lords and servants. He wants General Blackhawk's assurance that he will retain his throne after the empire is defeated. He requests admittance into the Far Stars Confederation, and he is prepared to respect and enforce its laws on Kalishar."

"Kalishar is a pirate stronghold," Desaix said. "Is he prepared to give that up as well? I don't see a planet earning its keep on criminal activity being welcomed into the confederation."

"Yes, he is prepared to forswear piracy and support for such activity . . . provided General Blackhawk agrees to provide assistance in developing an alternate economy."

Blackhawk had been quiet, giving everyone a chance to ask their questions. But Bevern had told him of the ka'al's terms, and he'd already decided what he was going to do.

And no one else got a vote.

"I have accepted the ka'al's offer," he said matter-of-factly. "Lord Bevern has brought considerable evidence of the existence of the imperial facility. This knowledge both explains the source of the mysterious soldiers we have encountered, and it uncovers a tremendous danger. If Governor Vos is allowed to conquer more worlds, it will be almost impossible to roll back his forces. We must strike Kalishar, and we must do it as quickly as possible. Every month that passes produces another hundred thousand enemy troops we will eventually have to fight."

"So the offensive against Galvanus Prime is canceled then? We will divert our resources toward Kalishar?" DeMark was nodding as he spoke. "I agree completely, General."

"No." Blackhawk could feel every eye in the room on him.

"What do you mean, General?" Desaix asked. "Are you saying no to an invasion of Kalishar?"

"No, Admiral. That is not what I am saying. We will invade Kalishar. And Galvanus Prime. Both." Blackhawk's voice was firm.

"But how is that possible?" Desaix asked nervously. "We don't have the resources to sustain two major attacks."

"It is possible because it is what we must do," Blackhawk said. "There is no advantage to be gained by endless debates, no purpose to pointless handwringing about resources. We must move quickly against both worlds, or we risk ultimate defeat. Therefore, we will find a way. We must."

Blackhawk turned and looked at Carano and the other mercenary generals. "That is why I called you all here. You have discharged your debt to me, provided the promised service in return for transport off Saragossa. Now, I ask you to fight another battle. I would hire your companies to aid me in the attack on Galvanus Prime. You will be paid from the Celtiborian treasury. I ask you to fight again by my side, to help me save the Far Stars. I propose to repair the belly-landed transports and reembark your forces. I also intend to confiscate every available vessel in the system and load them with the pick of the soldiers now on Celtiboria." He turned toward DeMark. "That's mostly going to be your veterans, Rafaelus."

Carano turned and leaned toward the other mercenary leaders. They spoke softly among themselves for a few seconds before Carano turned back to Blackhawk. "We are with you, General. All of us."

Blackhawk nodded. "Thank you all. You have my sincere gratitude."

"But that still doesn't explain how you're going to aid Kalishar," DeMark said. "If you're taking all our ships and soldiers from Celtiboria, who will be attacking the imperial training facility?"

"You, Rafe."

"What?"

"You will not join the forces going to Galvanus Prime. You will remain on Celtiboria. Danellan Lancaster has obtained an emergency resolution from the Antillean Senate authorizing the nationalization of all interplanetary vessels currently in the Antilles system, regardless of ownership. Even now, he is organizing this makeshift fleet and preparing to send it to Celtiboria.

"When the armada arrives, you will travel to Rykara and several of the other worlds with Celtiborian expeditionary forces on them. I leave the choice of destinations to your discretion. You will embark these soldiers, take command of the total force, and invade Kalishar."

Blackhawk gestured toward Bevern as he continued, "The ka'al will provide significant aid to your operation. He will arrange for the planetary defenses to be neutralized, so you will be able to land without opposition. And when the battle is under way, the Kalishari army will strike the imperial forces in their rear areas.

"You will have a large army of Celtiborian veterans at your back, Rafe, and with any luck, total surprise. You will destroy all imperial installations . . . and you will take no prisoners. Those who have taken imperial coin to fight against their brethren of the Far Stars will pay for that perfidy. And we shall set an example."

"Is that really necessary?" DeMark looked uncomfortable.

"Yes, Rafaelus, it is," Blackhawk replied, more of Umbra coming out in his voice than he liked. "This is a war to determine whether the Far Stars survives as the only place men breathe the air free of imperial oppression. And we could very well lose. Our enemy is extremely capable, and he has gained a march on us. There is no room for softness or pity."

DeMark didn't answer. He sat there with an uncomfortable look on his face for a few seconds. Finally, he just nodded.

Blackhawk turned and looked at Desaix. "You will accompany the fleet moving to invade Galvanus Prime, Emile. The *Claw* will destroy the two orbital forts while you eliminate any enemy warships. Once the system is clear of imperial fleet units and our ground forces have landed, you will depart at once. You will find DeMark's fleet of transports and you will link up to provide support for the invasion of Kalishar."

"Understood, General," Desaix replied. "But I still don't understand how *Wolf's Claw* is going to destroy the forts."

"You don't need to know how, Emile. Just that it *will*. The *Claw* will transit in ahead of your forces. We will sneak past any enemy ships on patrol and destroy the fortresses. Your arrival will be timed to match the moment we launch our attack."

Blackhawk sat behind the desk, as calm as he had been definitive. Everyone else in the room was looking at him like he was crazy . . . and maybe they weren't too far off the mark. The plan he had laid out was so far beyond audacious, it seemed downright reckless. But it was also brilliant, and Lucerne's veterans recognized that too. If they could pull it off, it would destroy the empire's two strongest assets in the Far Stars. There would be more fighting to do, but the rest of the struggle would be little more than mopping up.

Blackhawk knew Vos expected them to get bogged down in places like Nordlingen, to send fresh strength to combat the rebellions and unrest the imperial agents had cultivated. But Blackhawk wasn't going to play the governor's game—he was going to invent his own. He was going to abandon those worlds and strip them of their garrisons to build an army to invade Kalishar.

The withdrawal of the Celtiborian soldiers would give the affected planets over to empire-backed insurgents, and Blackhawk regretted the suffering that would result. However, nothing was more important than winning this war. The Blackhawk part of him understood the evil of the empire, and he realized that nothing was too great a price to pay to keep the Far Stars free. And deep in the back of his mind, where much of this daring plan had come from, the Frigus Umbra part of him didn't care at all. Victory was his mantra, and the suffering of millions of civilians was no concern to him.

"So do we all understand our roles in what is to come?" It was a question that did not need an answer. Lucerne's officers were veterans, brilliant soldiers all. He knew they understood his plan. And he wasn't soliciting opinions. If he was going to command, he would command. And no army had ever won a war taking votes.

And he'd never lost a war.

Blackhawk stood up, signaling the end of the meeting. He'd called them together to tell them of his plans. He had done that. And now it was time.

Time to end this.

CHAPTER 30

"THERE IT IS. GALVANUS PRIME." SHIRA WAS SITTING AT ACE'S station on the bridge. Ace had hesitantly approached Blackhawk with the idea of staying behind on Celtiboria, and the *Claw*'s captain had agreed completely that one of them should stay with Katarina—and clearly that person should be Ace.

Her condition had improved considerably, and she was expected to survive and even recover fully. But she was still in pretty bad shape, and Ark thought Ace's presence would help her get through the long recovery that lay ahead.

Besides, he knew his first officer would be a basket case worrying about her. And that's how even good warriors got themselves killed.

"Okay, Lucas, drop the mine."

The *Claw*'s pilot pressed a single button, and the ship shook slightly, almost imperceptibly. "She's away, Skip."

Blackhawk counted down in his head. The mine had a thirty-second timer. "Be ready on the field, Shira." He touched the comm unit clipped to his collar. "Okay, Sam. Twenty seconds."

"On it, Captain," she replied, her voice distracted, her tone a little irritated, as it usually was when someone interrupted her when she was working.

Blackhawk leaned back and waited. The mine was a thermo-nuclear device, but it wasn't one of the massive bombs they'd brought to destroy the enemy platforms. Its purpose was much simpler—to simulate the tragic failure of the *Claw*'s reactor containment.

Blackhawk had originally intended to engage the *Claw*'s distortion field and bring the ship right up to the enemy fortresses undetected. But there was no way to jump into the system with the field up, and he knew Galvanus Prime had the best detection grid in the Far Stars. The *Claw* would be picked up the instant she jumped in, and just disappearing without an explanation would have the enemy on full alert. He'd thought about trying to simulate an immediate return to hyperspace, but there was no way to fake the strange energy signature that a jump to alternate space created.

Simulating a catastrophic reactor failure, on the other hand, was easy.

It wasn't exactly common for a ship to lose containment jumping in from hyperspace, but it did happen. Often enough, at least, to make it appear like a perfectly normal accident. And that's what Blackhawk wanted the enemy to see. He wanted them calm and complacent, confident their massive fortresses made them invincible. Right up until the instant the things were vaporized by five hundred megatons of pure energy, and Galvanus lay open before his invasion fleet.

"Ten seconds, everybody," Lucas said into the shipwide comm. He'd used the ship's gas expulsion positioning jets to push the *Claw* far enough from the mine to avoid any damage. The ship was ten kilometers from the warhead now, with no detectable engine activity. As far as anyone would guess, she'd suffered damage on the jump in, and her reactor blew half a minute later.

"Now," Shira said, as she activated the field. There was no obvious effect to the passengers, but to an observer reading scanning data, a massive explosion occurred that appeared to vaporize the ship.

Blackhawk sighed softly and stared at the screen. The ship's radiation detectors spiked, a blast of gamma rays from the mine explosion, easily blocked by the *Claw*'s shielding.

"Distortion field activated and functioning properly," Sam's voice said loudly on the comm unit.

"Any sign of enemy activity, Shira?"

Her face had already been down on the scope, checking the data. "No, Cap. No sign of any reaction. It looks like they've got about forty warships in the system, Ark. Maybe ten on patrol and the rest positioned near the planet. If I had to guess, a lot of the ones near the planet are damaged, queued up for repairs."

Blackhawk nodded. That was a strong force, but nothing Desaix's fleet couldn't take. "Very well," he said with a small grin on his face. They were in Galvanus Prime's system, and as far as the enemy was concerned, they were invisible, a phantom. So far so good.

"Let's accelerate toward the planet, Lucas. Keep it moderate, no more than 25 percent engine output." The distortion field was an extraordinary device, but it wasn't perfect. It created near invisibility, and it blocked detection of almost all energy output. But firing the engines at full blast would be a risk, one Blackhawk had no intention of taking.

"Engines at 25 percent, Skip. Estimate three hours, eleven minutes to Galvanus Prime orbit."

"Very well." Blackhawk sat silently, still. *Three hours. A little over three hours, and then it begins. You are a brilliant man, Kergen Vos, a worthy opponent. But there's no way you'll see this coming.*

"Twenty minutes until scheduled transit, sir."

"Very well." Emile Desaix stared out over the flag bridge. He could feel the tension in the air. His people knew they were going into battle, and that was part of it. But it was more than just the prospect of combat. His crews were veterans, all of them battle tested, and while that didn't mean they weren't afraid, it did mean they'd be ready for the fight. Galvanus Prime, though . . .

The planet was a target unlike any they had ever faced, so heavily defended it was commonly considered absolutely impregnable. At least until Arkarin Blackhawk decided to attack it.

Desaix had assured everyone that Blackhawk would destroy the fortresses, but he didn't know how convincing he was. He didn't even know how convinced he himself was. And if Blackhawk was wrong, if his mysterious plan failed, the cream of the Celtiborian fleet would emerge from hyperspace well within range of the fortresses' heavy weapons. By the time his ships were able to build up enough charge to jump away, most of them would be blown to plasma. They were betting their lives on Blackhawk.

Desaix had almost refused the order and demanded Black-hawk tell him more about his plan to destroy the forts. But there was something strange about the general, some bizarre effect even Desaix couldn't understand. He was so in command, so firm and utterly confident, it was hard not to obey him. Indeed, Desaix wondered if Blackhawk could give any order that he *wouldn't* follow.

He found that thought both encouraging and disturbing.

Desaix shook his head and looked around the bridge. He'd almost transferred his flag. *Glorianus* had been badly damaged in the recent battle at Celtiboria, and there had only been time to address the most crucial repairs. Most of her weapons were functional, but he knew she didn't have the backups and stay-ing power she did when she was fully operational.

Captain Josiah will get what he needs to from her. He's the best cap-tain in the fleet. And it would have been a betrayal to abandon *Glorianus.*

The ship was the pride of Celtiboria's navy, and she had been Desaix's flagship since Marshal Lucerne had appointed him to the top position. And Flavius Josiah had been his flag captain the entire time. Besides, most of the other potential flagships also carried damage from the recent fighting.

Desaix was a veteran spacer, but he found it difficult sit-ting in hyperspace, waiting to jump back to normal space and see if Blackhawk had pulled off his promised miracle. If he had, this might be a major turning point in Far Stars history. Galvanus Prime had been an imperial stronghold for over a thousand years, the rock on which the threat of empire had rested. If Blackhawk could destroy those forts, that was about to change.

If Blackhawk can destroy the forts . . .

"How's it going, Sam?" Blackhawk stepped into the cargo hold. It was chilly, well below the comfortable temperature of the rest of the ship. Heating the hold was a waste of energy, and it was an easy way to economize on power consumption, especially with the field on full power, sucking a huge percentage of the reactor's output.

"The bombs are fine, Ark. Just arming number one now. A fusion warhead isn't that complicated." She looked up for a second, staring across the hold toward the captain. "They'll work. Don't worry, I guarantee it."

"Sam, I doubt a lot of things in the universe, but your engineering skill is not one of them."

She smiled for a few seconds. Then she turned back to her work.

Chrono, she looks exhausted. He'd never seen anyone work as hard as Sam had over the past few weeks. As far as he knew, she hadn't slept longer than an hour or two a day, and she'd been popping stims like candy. He knew they worked for a while, but eventually there was a price to pay. He'd almost stepped in and ordered her to get a good night's sleep. But he realized the cold truth: he needed every bit of the effort she was putting in.

Building the bombs was the least of it. Once she had the materials she needed, it only took a couple days to finish the massive warheads. It was the transport fleet—the ones that had belly-landed on the high plains near Alban—that had consumed her every waking moment. Most of the freighters took at least some damage in the landing, and Sam had been in charge of the repair effort. Blackhawk had hoped to get 70 percent of the ships ready to launch for the invasion, but Sam had somehow gotten all but two of them patched together in time. If the invasion was a success, Sam Sparks would be as much the reason as any warships or unit of ground troops.

"These are ready to go, Ark. But as soon as the first one drops out of the hold, they're going to pick it up on their scanners. I've done everything I could to make it appear to be a pile of space junk, but it's still going to appear out of nowhere. It takes us what, almost an hour to orbit halfway around the planet? I wouldn't bet on them not figuring out it's a bomb, not with that much time. And if we detonate it too soon, they're going to be on full alert at the other station. The field's an amazing device, but it is not perfect interference. If they look hard enough, they can probably spot us. They won't know what we are, but they'll know something is there. And if the other station just got blown to atoms, my guess is they'll open fire with everything they've got."

"You're right, Sam. About all of it. But we're only going to need six minutes, not an hour."

She looked back up from the warhead. "Six minutes?"

"You forget. We not only have you down here . . . we've got Lucas at the controls. He's going to blast us out of orbit with about seven g's of thrust, and reverse it almost immediately, blasting us back into orbit . . . right next to the other station. And we'll get there a hell of a lot faster than we would just orbiting over."

"That's a lot of power, Ark," she said, her face twisted in a thoughtful expression. "It makes it a lot likelier they'll pick up some energy bleed from the field."

Blackhawk nodded. "That's true. Nothing's foolproof. But it's been a given for centuries that Galvanus's fortresses make the planet impregnable. Vos expects us to run around to Nordlingen and a half-dozen other worlds, putting down the rebellions he provoked and battling his invasion forces. The last thing he expects is a cobra strike at him. I wouldn't want to count on too much complacency from these imperials, but they're not expecting an attack . . . and I'm willing to bet that buys us the six minutes we need."

Sam nodded slowly. "You're probably right . . . I hope you're right. Because we're all betting our lives on this little stunt."

Kergen Vos was pacing back and forth in front of the governor's chair. He was alone. He'd chased the sycophants and courtiers out an hour before. He didn't have the patience for them. Not now.

He'd never based his plan on conquering Celtiboria so soon, and the failure to do so didn't set him back significantly. Still, it was frustrating to come so close only to see a great victory slip through his fingers.

Carteria had been an opportunity to be exploited, nothing more. But things had gone brilliantly at first, and the rogue Celtiborian had rid him of most of Lucerne's staff of seasoned officers. The head had been lopped off his magnificent war machine. Most of it, at least. Rafaelus DeMark had survived.

Vos knew DeMark was probably the best of Lucerne's generals, the only one whose abilities truly rivaled his master's. But even he had been defeated, driven from the city into the countryside. Carteria had the capital, he had Astra Lucerne, he had almost one hundred thousand imperial reinforcements. Vos had almost allowed himself to believe Celtiboria was his. Then Blackhawk returned.

No, he thought, not Blackhawk. *Frigus Umbra.* The butcher. The mass murderer.

The madman who ignored Carteria's power and resources like they were nothing . . . and destroyed the Celtiborian pretender as if he were swatting a fly.

Vos had not been hesitant to utilize force and butchery in his own rise to power, but Frigus Umbra had invaded his home world, killed his parents. Cast him out onto the street to die. The governor stood in the vast audience hall looking at the frescoed walls but seeing something different: images of his mother and father. Their broken, charred bodies lying in the wreckage of their destroyed home.

Vos knew he was being illogical, hypocritical. He'd served the same empire as Umbra, inflicted the same kinds of brutal punishments. If his body count had been far lower than Umbra's, he didn't really consider that a defense of his actions. This wasn't about morality or ideology.

This was personal.

Now I know why Rachen failed, why Blackhawk has been so capable an enemy. There is not a more dangerous man in space—in the Far Stars or, indeed, the empire itself.

He stared down at the floor, his hands clenched into fists. "I came here to reclaim the Far Stars for the empire," he said softly, speaking to himself. "And I will see that done."

He turned and walked across the room, heading toward the command center. "And I will kill Frigus Umbra. Blackhawk. But I do not do that for emperor, not for ambition or gain or the accumulation of power." His voice was pure venom. "I do it for me."

"Two thousand kilometers and closing, Skip." Lucas was staring at his screens with a withering intensity. This was precision work, even for a master pilot of his abilities.

"Depressurize the hold," Blackhawk said.

"Depressurizing, Cap." Shira had been doing an outstanding job of filling in, but Blackhawk still felt a brief rush of surprise every time he didn't hear Ace's voice responding.

"Eighteen hundred kilometers . . . decelerating now."

Blackhawk felt himself pushed forward as the *Claw*'s thrusters pulsed at just under two g's. It was a risky maneuver so close to the enemy fortress, but there was no other option. The velocity and trajectory of the bomb had been precisely calculated, and the *Claw* needed to be on an exact heading at the designated speed, or the bomb would detonate too far from the station to destroy it.

"Targeting solution entered into the AI, Captain," Shira said softly. "Warhead armed and ready. Awaiting authorization to engage."

Blackhawk stared down at the arm of his chair, and he switched on his connection to the comm unit. "Engage targeting solution one," he said.

Command order accepted,

the ship's AI responded.

Warhead release in forty-three seconds.

Blackhawk leaned back in his chair and took a big breath. He'd shown nothing but confidence around Desaix and the others; indeed, he'd been almost cocky, unconcerned. But that was all for their benefit. He needed Desaix and his fleet ready to go, and he needed Carano and his people—and the Celtiborian troops—focused on their part of the operation, not worrying about the orbital forts. But the truth was, even with the field, there was a significant chance the *Claw* would be detected. How soon that would be, and how quickly the forts could react, remained to be seen. But if either one responded swiftly enough to intercept one of the warheads, the invasion would be over before it began. *And we'll be back to playing Vos's game, chasing his invasion forces around the Far Stars.*

"Warhead release in ten seconds."

"Keep on that scope, Shira. If these stations show any kind of power spike or strange activity let me know. Err on the side of being fucking paranoid." He realized immediately that last part was unnecessary, at least with Shira. She was perhaps the only person he knew more cynical and untrusting than him.

"So far so good, Cap."

The *Claw* bucked softly. The warhead was released.

"Let's get the cargo door closed."

"Closed," Shira answered almost immediately.

"Okay, Lucas, do your magic. We're on a schedule."

The pilot just nodded. He was staring intently at his screens, his hands moving over the thruster controls. Lucas worked the *Claw*'s helm like a virtuoso playing a piano, but even he looked nervous now.

"Thrust in 3 . . . 2 . . . 1 . . ."

Blackhawk felt the pressure slam into him as the *Claw*'s engines blasted hard, accelerating the ship out of orbit on an angle that would position it for reentry on the opposite side of the planet. The thrust would last less than a minute, but the captain knew that kind of power output this close to a major enemy installation was pushing the distortion field to its limits. He'd planned everything meticulously, but no matter how he looked at it, they needed a little bit of luck too. Maybe more than a little . . .

"Reversing thrust now."

Blackhawk could hear the concentration in Lucas's voice, the intense focus. The whole op was timed to the second, and it relied on his precision piloting.

"How's it look, Shira?"

"Clear, Cap. Doesn't look like anyone's so much as put on an extra night-light in there." Her face was pressed against the scope, unmoving as she spoke.

Blackhawk tapped the comm controls. "Sam, everything good to go down there?"

"Yes, Captain. Second warhead is armed and ready."

"Approaching second station," Lucas said. "Decelerating in ten seconds . . ."

Blackhawk sucked in a deep breath and held it. If they got through the deceleration thrust without the enemy detecting them, they were home free.

"Deceleration . . . now!" An instant after Lucas's warning, the braking force slammed Blackhawk back into his chair. He pressed the comm unit again, activating the channel to the ship's AI. "Commence warhead deployment sequence. Engage targeting solution number two."

Command order accepted. Warhead release in one minute, eleven seconds.

"Ark, I'm picking up enhanced energy readings from fortress two." Shira's voice was tense. "It might not be anything, but . . ." Her head whipped around. "Massive power spike, Captain!"

Fuck! "Time until warhead release?" Blackhawk snapped.

"Forty-nine seconds," Shira answered immediately. "Too long. They're definitely powering up their weapons grids."

"And we're on a straight-in path. Even if they can't pick us up on their scanners, they have to know about where we are." Blackhawk turned toward the pilot's station. "Lucas, can we release the warhead now and still target the station?"

"Yes, Ark, but it will be going in awfully fast . . ."

"Do it. Now!"

Lucas moved his hands quickly over the controls. A few seconds later the ship shook lightly. "Warhead's away, Skip, but she's gonna slam into the station long before she detonates."

Blackhawk was already pressing the AI control. "Recalculate time for warhead to arrive on target and detonate five hundred meters before impact."

Understood,

came the emotionless reply.

"Lucas, get us the hell out of here or we'll follow that bird right in. And I don't want to be anywhere near that five-hundred-megaton blast."

Twenty-two seconds to warhead detonation.

"Hang the fuck on!" Lucas yelled as he angled the throttle and blasted the thrust hard, pushing the *Claw* toward a course along the flank of the station.

"Laser fire, Captain," Shira yelled. "Multiple batteries. Targeted on our previous approach and speed. They might have clipped us without the course change." She spun around and looked at Blackhawk. "Missile volleys too, Ark. On a wide trajectory, blanketing as much area as possible. They're definitely looking for us."

"AI, is warhead one close enough to the station to destroy it?"

Yes. Warhead one is three kilometers away from target. Probability of total destruction 64 percent.

Sixty-four percent was a number that made Blackhawk's stomach flip, but there wasn't any choice. "Detonate warhead one simultaneously with number two!"

He turned back to Lucas. "Distance from warhead two?"

"Seven kilometers, Ark. We're pushing out at full thrust, but we've got too much velocity along the warhead's vector."

Warhead detonation in eight seconds.

The AI's voice echoed throughout the ship.

"Lucas, do what you can . . ." Blackhawk knew the airless vacuum attenuated the effects of nuclear weapons quickly, but this was a big warhead. And it was still close enough to bathe the *Claw* with a lot of radiation . . .

"Hang on. This may give us away, but . . ."

Blackhawk felt himself slammed back hard into his chair. Lucas had blasted the engines at full thrust, almost ten g's.

"We have a pack of missiles after us, Ark," Shira said, forcing the words out through the intense pressure. "If they didn't know where we were before, they sure as shit do now."

Warhead detonation,

the AI announced. And an instant later,

Fortress two destroyed.

Lucas let out a loud cheer, and he cut the thrust to five g's. It wasn't exactly comfortable, but it was a hell of a lot better than 10 g's.

"Don't relax now," Shira snapped. "We've got half a dozen warheads on our tail."

"Don't worry . . . I'll lose them," Lucas said. The ship shook hard twice over about a thirty-second period, and then suddenly it went into free fall. "How are those missiles looking now?"

"Looks like they lost us. They're searching for targets, but they're heading off on their own vector." She looked across the bridge to the pilot's station. "How'd you manage that, Lucas?"

"I figured their onboard nav suite couldn't penetrate the field. With the station gone, it wasn't hard to shake them. Of course, if we didn't have the distortion field up, we'd be plasma by now."

"Bring us around the planet, Lucas. I want to see what happened to the first fortress." Their scanners were blocked by the bulk of Galvanus where they were.

"On it, Skip. Just take a few to get there."

Blackhawk sat back and stared at the data on his screen. The AI had detonated the warhead 473 meters from fortress two, essentially vaporizing the entire structure.

"Coming around Galvanus now," Lucas said.

"Scanning data coming in, Captain. Transferring to your screen." Shira's voice was calm, but there was something there, something unsettled. Blackhawk knew at once, and he looked at his screen. Fortress one was heavily damaged, and more than half of it was just gone . . .

But it was still there.

"Maybe we can bring the fleet around in the planet's shadow," Shira said. "Or . . ." She stopped suddenly. Circles began to appear on her screen, new contacts. Desaix's fleet, coming in just on schedule.

Right in front of the surviving fortress.

CHAPTER 31

"INITIAL SCANNING REPORTS COMING IN, ADMIRAL. IT APPEARS that one of the forts is gone, sir. Preliminary readings suggest it was destroyed by a nuclear explosion."

"One?" Desaix took a deep breath. His tactical officer's next few words would tell him if his fleet would survive or not.

"Yes, sir. The other fort is still there, at least part of it. It's hard to determine operational status, but it can't be in good shape. There's a ton of damage and a huge section is just gone. I'd estimate best case, 20 percent functionality.

"Twenty percent might be enough to destroy every ship we have, Commander."

Desaix sat silently for a few seconds, going over his options. He might be able to get his fleet back into hyperspace. The damaged fortress probably wouldn't be able to destroy most of his ships before they jumped. *But Blackhawk is right. This is our chance to win this war. If we fail here, we may never roll back the imperial aggression.*

"Commander, all vessels are to advance at full thrust and engage the fortress."

"Admiral, scanning reports coming in. Enemy ships approaching from behind the planet. Looks like twenty-five, maybe thirty-five vessels total. Mixed classes, nothing larger than a frigate. Sending the data to your screen."

Desaix sighed. *Well, you knew there had to be ships here. Be glad it's a fleet you can handle . . . at least if you can take the station out.*

"The fleet will divide. Squadrons A and B are to assault and destroy the station. Squadrons C and D are to engage the enemy fleet." Desaix's resolve stiffened with each word. There would be no retreat, no hesitation.

If the final battle for the Far Stars is to be fought, let it be here . . .

"What?"

"You heard me, Lucas. Bring us down. Right at the capitol. Bring us *through* the front doors of the capitol if you can."

"But, Ark, the troopships are with Desaix. And they won't be able to land until the battle fleet finishes off the fortress."

Shira added her concern to Lucas's. "You want to go down alone?"

"We need to kill Kergen Vos," Blackhawk said. "That's why we're here. If he escapes, we have failed. The imperial forces are extremely hierarchal. Taking Galvanus Prime will be a great victory, but cutting the head off the beast is our primary goal. And if we wait too long, Vos might escape and set up a new headquarters somewhere." He paused and turned to look first at Lucas then at Shira, his eyes burning with resolve.

You don't need to explain, the voice deep inside said, dripping with malice. *They are your subordinates. They exist to follow orders.*

No, Blackhawk pushed back. *I am not you. Your day has passed.*

Yet you use my strategies. You crushed the traitors on Celtiboria as I would have. You refused their surrenders and shot them down like dogs. You think you are different, but we are one, Blackhawk. And we always will be.

"No," he blurted out unintentionally. He turned to see both Lucas and Shira staring at him. "Sorry," he said. "I was just thinking." He took a breath, struggling to calm himself. "Bring us down, Lucas. Leave the field up. I don't care if you burn out every circuit on the ship, but get us down to the capitol . . . before Governor Vos decides the battle is hopeless and slips away."

"Got it, Skipper." But it was clear Lucas *didn't* quite get it, or why Blackhawk was acting this way. And he didn't have to turn around to realize that Shira was thinking the same thing. They all knew about his conditioning, but it was one thing to speculate about it, another to watch him unravel.

No, not unravel. I am Arkarin Blackhawk, and nothing will change that. Not who I was, not what I must do. Even a good man must sometimes make difficult choices, take harsh steps.

He felt a weak rush of resolve, but not the level of certainty he wanted. And in the background, he could hear Umbra laughing.

The *Claw* shook as Lucas angled down, tapping the thrust to push out of orbit and down toward the upper atmosphere. He'd never landed the ship with the field on, but there was a first time for everything.

"Sam," Blackhawk said into the comm. "We're landing with the field at full power, so I need you to do everything you can to keep us from blowing out half the systems or scragging the reactor. I know it's tough, but if anybody can do it, it's you."

"I'll do my best, Captain," she replied simply, her voice soft . . . and a little shaky.

Shit . . . no cockiness, no argument. She sounded like a meek little girl. And the thought of Sam Sparks feeling in over her head scared the hell out of him.

The ship bounced around as it skipped off the upper atmosphere. Lucas usually cut in at a deeper angle on landings, using the engines to slow reentry. But he was trying to use the minimum amount of energy possible. If they lost the field within range of any air-to-ground weapons, the *Claw* would be in serious trouble.

"Shira, get the needle gun ready. As soon as we're down, power up and blow a hole in the walls of the capitol."

"On it, Ark."

He flipped the comm channel. "Sarge, I want your boys and Tarnan ready to go the second we land. And the Black Helms, too." Blackhawk had asked Carano for two crack squads to supplement his people.

"We're ready, Captain." Sarge sounded a little shaky, but Blackhawk knew it had nothing to do with the looming combat. Sarge was a certified ground-pounder, and the *Claw*'s captain would have bet a pile of imperial crowns that Sarge was fighting to keep his breakfast down.

"Twenty kilometers, Skip. Looks like the field's holding."

Blackhawk just nodded in Lucas's direction. *That's good news. Now if it can just hold a few more minutes . . .*

The *Claw* banked hard as Lucas angled toward Galvanus

City. The capitol was the nerve center of the imperial bureaucracy in the Far Stars, and Lucas was going to put the *Claw* right outside the front door. Breaking into the capitol and getting to the governor before he had a chance to escape was a tough proposition for thirty-odd crew members and mercenaries, and once again Blackhawk was very happy to have Lucas Lancaster at the helm—he would have landed the *Claw* in Vos's bedchamber if it had been possible.

"Ten kilometers."

"Shira, I know you want to come with us, but you're going to have to stay on the needle gun in case we need it again."

She just looked back and nodded, a sullen look on her face.

"I'll do that, Arkarin."

Blackhawk turned to see Doc climbing up the ladder from the lower deck. "Doc . . ."

"I'm serious, Ark. I know how desperate a fight this is going to be. I was going to come along, but Shira will be much more valuable out there than me. And I'll take her place on the scope and the needle gun." He paused, but when Blackhawk didn't respond right away, he added, "Sam's going to be stuck down in engineering, and Lucas has to be at the controls in case the *Claw* needs to bug out. But I've got nothing to do, at least not until you get back all shot up."

"Okay, Doc." Blackhawk nodded. "Thanks." He turned toward Shira. "All right . . . go get your gear." She nodded and jumped to her feet, racing across the bridge to the ladder.

Doc moved over to take her place. He almost lost his footing when the *Claw* bounced suddenly, but he made his way to the chair and sat down, buckling the harness. "I'm not the fighter most of the rest of you are, but I'm a good shot with this thing."

Blackhawk smiled and nodded. Doc was right. He'd been

at the controls before, and he had a good feel for it. "Thanks, Doc. It'll be helpful to have Shira along," he said, climbing up from his chair and heading toward the ladder.

"Take command, Lucas." He paused for a few seconds, taking one last look at the bridge. Then he scrambled down the ladder to the lower deck.

"Keep up the fire. Reserve Squadron, escort the transports to the other side of Galvanus. A and B, maintain fire on the fortress."

The massive station had been nearly gutted by the massive nuclear explosion. Desaix guessed it was fighting at less than 10 percent of its normal effectiveness. But it had still taken down eight of his ships.

The losses hurt, each Code Black transmission cutting at him like a knife in the gut. Yet he knew his forces were winning the battle. The surviving sections of the station were racked with internal explosions, and the batteries and rows of torpedo tubes and missile launchers had mostly fallen silent. One more attack run was all it would take to finish off Galvanus Prime's last fortress. Then the great bastion of imperial strength, the impregnable stronghold of the governors, would lie defenseless before his invasion fleet. And the survivors of the force attacking the station could move to the support of the squadrons facing the enemy fleet. That battle had been a bloody stalemate so far, but that would change when Desaix led another thirty-five ships into the fight.

Desaix watched the wave of frigates moving across the screen, a cloud of small dots streaking out from them toward a large oval. He imagined the torpedoes as they blasted through space heading for their massive target.

He stared. *This should do it,* he thought, as he watched them close the final thousand kilometers. A cluster of small starbursts began to appear around the station's icon as the torpedoes began to impact. Desaix was silent, focused, waiting for the AI to update the station's status screen. But an instant later, the entire oval disappeared from the screen. The fortress was gone.

Blackhawk managed it, by Chrono! His plan worked. He destroyed the legendary defenses of Galvanus Prime. Close enough, at least . . . he needed a little cleanup from us. Now I better get these troops on the ground before he gets himself killed. Him and the two dozen lunatics down there with him.

"Reserve Squadron and transports are to commence the invasion of Galvanus Prime," he said firmly. "Squadrons A and B are to move to the support of C and D and engage surviving imperial ships."

"Yes, Admiral," came the tactical officer's reply.

Desaix flipped the switch on his comm unit, opening the direct line to his flag captain. "Flavius, if you would be so kind, bring *Glorianus* around toward the imperial fleet. We've got one more fight here . . ."

The *Claw* sat on the cobblestone square outside the capitol. She lay at a slight angle, atop the crushed statuary of an ancient fountain. She was less than five meters from the massive entry doors of the hulking imperial structure. Lucas had scored a bull's-eye.

Blackhawk looked back over the men—and one woman—stacked up behind him. He felt a rush of relief that Astra hadn't come along. She'd wanted to, but there was too much work to do consolidating the position on Celtiboria, and even Marshal Lucerne's stubborn daughter had to admit she was needed more behind a desk at home than with a rifle in her hand next to Blackhawk. It's not that he thought she couldn't take care of herself in a fight. He'd seen it before. But this operation was going to take everything he had . . . and he didn't have time to be worrying about her.

Katarina was a loss to the *Claw*'s combat power, too. Next to Blackhawk, the beautiful assassin was the deadliest fighter on board—and the perfect combatant for a mission like this one. But it would be months, if ever, before she was ready to step once again onto the field of battle.

And of course, her condition had cost the *Claw* Ace's services as well. The first officer was a handy man in a fight, and a tactician second only to Blackhawk. But he didn't dwell on what he didn't have. What strength he had would be enough.

It would have to be.

"Now, Doc. Blast open the doors." Blackhawk spoke firmly, calmly into his comm.

"Firing now, Ark," came the immediate reply. An instant later they heard the hum of the needle laser, and a few seconds after, a loud crash from outside the ship.

They were lined up in the cargo hold. Blackhawk hit the switch, and the ramp dropped down, allowing Galvanus's midmorning sunlight to stream into the gloomy space.

"Let's go," Blackhawk yelled, as he ran down the ramp and onto the rubble-covered pavilion. The great double doors were shattered, cut almost in half by the laser and lying on the floor, just inside the building.

Blackhawk ran right over them and into the capitol, assault rifle in hand. There were two guards, dead, crushed by the falling doors, but otherwise he saw no enemies.

His people had an element of surprise, and that was their greatest weapon, one he intended to use to the fullest. Once it was gone, he suspected his people would be outnumbered at least ten to one by the enemy soldiers in the capitol. But there were plans within plans in this operation, and another seven thousand soldiers would soon land right in the middle of the city and move to Blackhawk's aid. And before they were overwhelmed, the main army would land and destroy the imperial forces . . . and win the battle.

The hall inside the main doors was immense, over one hundred meters from side to side, and fifty deep. The ceiling soared thirty meters from the polished marble floors. The walls were covered with faded frescoes, filaments of gold and platinum worked into the extravagant artworks. The scenes depicted the emperors of the early days of the imperial history, in all their exaggerated glory, looming twenty-meter images of warriors clad in the full imperial regalia.

The mercenaries Carano had sent poured into the hall, dividing into two groups and flanking Blackhawk. They were Carano's men, but they had fought under Blackhawk on Celtiboria, and they were responding to his leadership.

"That will be the main reception area," he said, pointing toward the set of doors directly opposite the main entry. "Take those doors down."

Two of the mercenaries ran to the front carrying a heavy satchel charge. They moved up to the doors and dropped it in place, turning and racing back toward their comrades.

"Bogies," Shira yelled, an instant before she opened up with her weapons. She stood to the left of the group, a rifle in each hand, gunning down enemy guards as they ran toward Blackhawk's team. She faced the enemy alone for perhaps a few seconds, and in that time she took down a dozen of them with her withering fire.

Sarge moved first, swinging around to her side as he whipped his rifle toward the enemy and opened fire. His men were right behind him. They didn't have shit for cover, so they knew the best defense was to clear the hall as quickly as possible, pinning the enemy with their firepower, and clearing them out before they could close.

A few seconds later, Tarnan opened up, his giant autocannon tearing enemy soldiers into bloody chunks, his massive shells ripping right through his targets and slamming into the walls, sending shards of marble and plaster flying everywhere.

It had been a platoon of enemy troopers coming down the hall, but now there were no more than four or five still standing—and they had dropped their weapons and run for cover.

Blackhawk had moved to join his people in the firefight, but he quickly realized they'd already won the exchange. The enemy had barely gotten off a shot. One of the mercs took a bullet in the arm, but that was all. Blackhawk felt a wave of pride in his people, and relief as well. But he suspected the next exchange wouldn't be so quick or so easy.

The surprise is gone.

"Blow it open," he yelled, and an instant later the charge detonated, ripping the doors from their hinges and sending the twisted and mangled chunks of metal flying into the room.

"Let's move!" Blackhawk raced forward into the reception hall. It was larger even than the gallery outside, a massive hundred-meter-square room—and at the far end was the chair, the place where the governor sat when receiving the nobles and supplicants of the imperial demesne. He could see it was a magnificent work of art even from where he stood, an ornate gold-and-silver object of immense value. However magnificent it was, though, a governor who wanted to keep his head was sure to call it the chair, and never a throne. The governors ruled with more naked power than most monarchs in history, but they were always aware that they were merely the eyes and ears—and fists—of their master, the emperor. Those who forgot were likely to receive a visit from the Exequtorum.

Blackhawk sighed. He hadn't really expected Vos would make it easy, but part of him had hoped he'd find the governor in the chair. "Let's go," he yelled. "Spread out, look for nondescript exits, even secret passages." He suspected the governor had his own ingress and egress point . . . and that it would lead directly into his inner sanctum.

Glorianus was a big vessel by frontier standards, the largest warship in the Far Stars. She had led the force that retook Celtiboria from the imperials, and she'd been at the forefront of the final assault on Galvanus Prime's massive fortress. Now she had faced off against the remnants of another fleet of the empire.

She was battered, her hull pitted and pockmarked, sections melted away by the intense heat of enemy laser blasts. She was bleeding atmosphere, and fluids poured out of her broken pipes and conduits, freezing instantly in the frigid vacuum of space. Only one of her engines was still operating, and her reactor was running at 30 percent. By any measure, the last place she belonged was dead center in the battle line. But that's exactly where she was.

Half her weapons were silent, laser batteries blown into chunks of shattered metal, missile launchers fused shut and twisted out of shape. But she still spat death at her enemies, and she stood proudly alongside her brethren as the Celtiborian fleet fought a battle to the death with the last imperials.

Desaix had expected the outgunned enemy fleet to break off and flee. Without the fortresses they had no real chance to win the battle. But then he realized: Kergen Vos was on Galvanus Prime. And he would order the fleet to fight to the death before he would lay his world open to invasion and conquest.

Glorianus shook hard as her main tubes launched four torpedoes toward an enemy frigate. Her target was one of the biggest enemy ships still in action. The imperial vessel was as battered as Desaix's flagship, but she was still firing back with everything she had.

The torpedo volley was *Glorianus*'s last, at least until she could be resupplied—and that was not something that was going to happen on the battle line. The heavy weapons moved directly toward their target. The enemy's defensive fire was almost silent, her point defense batteries blasted to twisted rubble.

Desaix watched as the imperial vessel blasted its engines, using what little thrust she had left to try to evade the ordnance *Glorianus* had launched at her. But it was too little, too late. The Celtiborian admiral watched with a feral grin as two of his weapons scored direct hits.

Thirty thousand kilometers away, the torpedoes slammed into the stricken vessel, the massive explosions tearing apart sections of hull, twisting and severing the ship's main spine.

Like so many imperial ships before it, whole sections of this one were now losing structural integrity, their atmospheres sucked out through huge rents in the hull, the compartments turning into tombs of flash-frozen spacers who didn't get their survival gear on in time.

The few who survived such conditions would try to make their way to whatever escape pods or lifeboats the ship possessed. But most would be trapped, blocked by the ship's shattered structure or by the fires raging out of control in sections that still had oxygen. Damage control crews would work desperately to prevent containment failure in the reactor—those that hadn't already tried to flee themselves—and they would struggle to keep the conflagrations from reaching the ordnance in the magazines.

But Desaix knew their struggles would be in vain. His torpedoes had killed the frigate, and its desperate, panicking crew would die with their ship. He knew it for a certainty, and a moment later, when the vessel consumed itself in the fury of its own reactor, he sat and watched quietly, impassively.

"No lifepods, sir," the tactical officer said somberly.

Desaix just sat stone still and stared ahead. He'd already known that.

The freighters streaked through the late-morning sky, a bizarre sight to anyone on the ground. They trailed streaks of fire behind them as they ripped through the atmosphere at a far greater speed than they'd been designed to endure. But this was an invasion, not a delivery of trade goods, and while the heart of Galvanus's defenses had been the two orbital forts, there were still ground installations that could shoot down the makeshift troop transports. Indeed, the invasion fleet had lost three vessels already, along with the eighteen hundred soldiers aboard them. The survivors pushed it to the max, preferring to risk melting their hulls in the thickening atmosphere to being shot out of the sky by ground-based missiles.

General Carano sat strapped in on one of the makeshift benches, surrounded by several of his senior officers. He had his key personnel deployed to several ships, and the officers of the other mercenary companies were also scattered around. He couldn't leave the Helms completely leaderless if a lucky shot took down a vessel with the entire command staff.

Not just any planet, he thought. *Galvanus Prime.* They were invading the imperial sector capital. And doing it under the overall command not only of an old rival, but a former imperial general, a man famous throughout the empire for his martial brilliance—and his cold brutality.

He definitely knows how to plan a battle, though, Carano thought, listening to reports. *And he knows how to destroy his enemies. Which makes it that much better to be his friend . . .*

He stared at the small tablet in his hand, watching the reports streaming in real time. *The Celtiborians are already on the ground. Some of them, at least.*

Desaix had managed to scrape up a dozen proper troop transports, enough for seven thousand Celtiborian veterans to land directly in the capital, their maneuverable dropships bringing them down right on Blackhawk's heels, while the less-maneuverable freighters came down on a flat plateau fifty kilometers outside the city.

The rest of the Celtiborians were in the modified freighters and commandeered passenger ships, destined for the same rough belly landings.

The army's mission was simple: attack, attack, attack. Drive toward the city and link up with Blackhawk and the seven thousand Celtiborians—before they were overwhelmed and destroyed.

Easier said than done.

"Landing in two minutes." The voice of the ship's captain was loud in Carano's earpiece. He tapped the small control on the side of his head, connecting him to the general comm channel. "All right, boys, remember, this tub's gonna have a hard landing, but we ignore that. The second she's down we move out. I want all units to form up by platoons and be ready to go into action immediately. We've got weak intel on enemy ground forces near the LZ, so we need to be ready for anything. And even if the area is clear, we're moving out without delay. We've got seven thousand allied troops in Galvanus City, and they're gonna get scragged if we don't get there and link up with them."

He paused a few seconds then added, "We've been in many battles together. You are the Black Helms . . . and the Helms are the scourge of the Far Stars. This is the most important battle we have ever faced, against an enemy more dangerous than any that has stood against us. I know I can count on all of you, as I have for so many years. Black Helms forever!"

Blackhawk fired again, picking off the last of the fleeing enemy. The firefight had been short but sharp, and his small band had gotten the best of it. But they'd also taken their first losses. Two of the mercs were down. One was dead, but the other was still on his feet. Tarnan had also taken a hit to the arm, but the big man was strong and powerful, and it hadn't slowed him down at all. He still whipped the massive autocannon around like a normal soldier would an assault rifle.

"All right, let's go," Blackhawk said. "That was the last of them. But keep your eyes open. There will be more."

They were walking down a long corridor somewhere behind the audience chamber. They'd found a number of exits from the massive hall, but when Blackhawk saw this one he knew at once. It was Vos's personal entrance. And that meant it led to his office, his quarters . . . to anywhere he was likely to be.

He crept down the hall, moving swiftly, but still with caution. The others had trouble matching his speed, at least without making enough noise to wake the dead. But there was no time to lose. If Vos had an escape route, he could disappear. Galvanus was a planet, a highly industrialized one with a dozen major cities and over a hundred million people. If Vos slipped away, it would be a nightmare trying to find him again . . . and his minions might very well direct a large portion of their now-scattered forces toward a reconquest aimed at rescuing the governor. *No. Vos has to die. And we need to make sure the imperials everywhere in the Far Stars know their commander is dead.*

Blackhawk was gambling on speed and surprise to seize Galvanus, but he knew he didn't have anywhere near enough troops to hold the place against a large invasion. And Desaix's ships would be leaving as soon as they finished off the imperials in the system. Indeed, they might even be gone already. They had to get back to Celtiboria for some hasty repairs before setting a course to join the Kalishar invasion.

You can't postpone that, no matter how much you're tempted. You've got to shut down that stream of reinforcements. Give them another year, and even the Celtiborians won't be able to match their force.

He stopped abruptly outside a door on the left side of the hall, motioning for Shira to cover him. He pushed at the door, but it was locked. There was a small panel alongside the door frame, some kind of palm-activated lock. Blackhawk raised his rifle and smashed the butt hard against the glass panel, shattering it. He looked down, reaching inside, manipulating a small tangle of wires. The indicator lights above flashed, but the door didn't budge. Finally, he backed away and said, "Tarnan . . ."

The giant moved to the front and fired at the locking mechanism and the edge of the door next to it. The heavy autocannon rounds tore into the lock and the solid metal of the door as well. After a few seconds, he silenced his weapon and smashed his way in with a gargantuan kick.

The door ripped mostly from the frame, and it hung by one chunk of hinge, wobbling back and forth. Blackhawk moved quickly inside, his head turning rapidly, scanning for enemies. The room was huge, and the furnishings opulent. There were shelves and fine wood cabinets along the walls, and a huge desk at the far end of the room. It looked like it was built of some rare hardwood.

> **Cestian blood oak. Extremely rare. The trees experience a rapid growth surge once every eleven years, after which they quickly decay and return to seedlings. It is the only time they produce specimens of sufficient size to produce usable lumber.**

Blackhawk shook his head. *What a useless piece of trivia,* he shot back. *Can we focus on the matter at hand?*

> **Certainly. Based on projected market value of the items in the room, this is the governor's office. Probability 83 percent +/- 4.5 percent.**

So where the hell is he? The thought was mostly to himself, but Hans answered him anyway.

> **Based upon our knowledge of Kergen Vos and a projection that he is a subject of high intelligence also possessed of paranoid tendencies sharply above human norms—a common trait in specimens of extreme mental ability, I might add—I would theorize there is a hidden escape route from this office. Though I consider this likely, I do not have the data to compute meaningful percentage probabilities.**

"Look for a hidden exit," Blackhawk exclaimed. "A secret passage or something similar."

Sarge and his men moved to different sections of the room, searching the cabinets along the walls, pulling up the throw rugs and looking underneath. Within a minute or two, they had ransacked the place thoroughly, but they still hadn't found anything.

Blackhawk began searching the desk. He went through the drawers methodically, carefully. He felt around for a button or control in the drawers or underneath.

Then he heard shots in the hall. A few, at first, but seconds later things had erupted into a full-blown firefight. The mercs who had stayed in the hall were streaming back into the office, carrying three of their own.

"Enemy troops, General." Jav Guerrin was a Black Helms lieutenant, and the commander of the detachment Carano had sent with Blackhawk. He was a long service veteran, but he looked a little shaken nevertheless.

Blackhawk glanced up. "Get all your men in here. Flip over the rest of this furniture and get behind. Form up to cover the door." He was still moving his hands along around the desk. *There has to be something. Vos is the type to have an escape route . . .*

There it is! He'd slipped his finger into a groove next to the track for the central drawer. There was a small lever there. It was hard to reach, but he managed to get his finger over it and pull. He heard a creak as a section of wall behind him slid open.

He glanced over toward the front of the room. The mercs had tipped over the cabinets and bookcases, and they'd taken position behind. The door was a lost cause, so all they could do was cover the entrance—and blast anyone who tried to get in.

He turned around and stared through the now open section

of wall behind the desk. The doorway was less than a meter square, but the passage itself looked like it was a meter wide and maybe one and a half high. It was dimly lit—it looked like small lamps were placed every ten meters or so, not sufficient to truly light the place, but enough to cut the total darkness.

He turned around. "Shira, you're with me. You too, Sarge . . . and your men."

He turned toward Tarnan. "It looks like it's a little tight in there for you, big man. If you want to come, it's okay, but I'm sure these guys could use your firepower too. Your call."

Tarnan leaned down and looked into the tunnel, shaking his head. "I'll probably be more use here, Cap. You go get the bastard. We'll hold them off here until you get back."

Blackhawk put his arm on Tarnan's massive shoulder. "I know you will." He turned toward Lieutenant Guerrin. "You stay here and hold this room. I'm going to go get the governor."

"Good luck, General," the merc officer said. "Blow his fucking brains out."

CHAPTER 32

THE IMPERIAL SHIPS WERE ACCELERATING AWAY, AS QUICKLY AS their damaged reactors and battered engines could manage. The fleet defending Galvanus Prime was destroyed, save for half a dozen vessels running for their lives . . . and pursued by Desaix's victorious vessels.

Blackhawk was right, the admiral thought, shaking his head as he did. *I wouldn't have imagined anything like this was possible. But if the ground forces can win the fight, Galvanus Prime will be a world of the confederation, freed from its imperial shackles for the first time in a millennium.*

Desaix was exhausted. His ships were battered, his people asleep on their feet. He'd ordered stims for all crew members, but even with the pharmaceutical aid, he was glad his people were done with their part of the operation.

Still, he hated leaving the system. It felt like abandoning the troops on the ground. But that was part of Blackhawk's plan, too, and the fleet had done all it had come to do—now he had to get it back to Celtiboria. His ships needed repairs and refit so they could join up with DeMark's forces bound for Kalishar. That would be another fight, one that was just as vital to defeating the imperial aggression.

"Captain Varing reports his vessels are closing on the runners, sir. He should catch them in approximately one half hour." The tactical officer was as tired as everyone else, and even his best efforts couldn't keep it from his voice.

"Very well, Commander." Desaix leaned back in his command chair and took a deep breath. He knew what he had to do. Blackhawk's orders had been clear. But he still hesitated to issue the actual command, to order his ships to prepare to depart the system, leaving tens of thousands of friendly troops behind on the planet.

Finally, he slapped his hand down at his side and said, "All vessels will prepare to jump back to Celtiboria as soon as the final enemy units have been destroyed. We've got half an hour, so I want all ships to conduct emergency diagnostics during that time. I don't want to lose anybody in hyperspace because some conduit got shaken apart in the fight."

"Yes, Admiral," came the prompt but weary reply.

Desaix turned back toward his display. Galvanus Prime was just a dot at this range. He tried to imagine what was going on down on the planet's surface. He'd read the initial reports. The main force had landed with minimal losses, but that's all he knew. And it was all he was likely to know before he jumped out of the system.

Fortune go with you, Arkarin Blackhawk . . .

"Sergeant Wald, I want every one of those buildings searched from the cellars to the roofs. You got me?" There was a hard edge to Seth Marne's voice. He'd lost twenty of his men already to enemy snipers, and he was mad as hell.

"Yes, Major," the veteran noncom snapped back. He turned and shouted out orders to a cluster of troops standing to the side of the street. They broke into several groups and dispersed into the buildings.

Marne's battalion was leading the move through Galvanus City. Seven thousand Celtiborian veterans had come down right in the middle of the capital, and they poured out of their dropships and began moving toward the imperial capitol. They all knew Blackhawk was in that massive building with less than thirty men, and their mission was a simple one: get to the capitol and take control of the area before Blackhawk's people were wiped out. And then hold it until the main force arrived.

Simple . . . yet virtually impossible.

The imperials were disorganized, but Marne knew they had a hell of a lot more than seven thousand soldiers in and around the capital. So he'd pushed his people hard—and the enemy's snipers and ambush parties had made him pay the price. Now, he was slowing his advance, exerting more care, sweeping carefully for enemy positions. It would take longer to reach the capital, but he couldn't let the enemy keep picking off his soldiers. They'd need all their strength to hold on when the imperials got organized and launched a major counterattack.

He heard gunfire from inside the next building, and he crouched low, his rifle snapping up, by reflex more than anything. A few seconds later, his comm buzzed.

"Sergeant Weld here, Major. We cleared out a nest of snipers. You can move up through the next block now, sir."

"Good work, Sergeant. Your people are to move up to the next block. Same procedure."

He sighed. It was going to take all day at this pace. But there was nothing else he could do.

Blackhawk moved swiftly down the corridor, crouched down under the low ceiling. He turned and looked back over his shoulder. He could see his people struggling to keep up. "We can't let Vos get away. I'm going to chase him down. The rest of you keep up the best you can." He was rarely so open about his enhanced abilities, but there was no time for bullshit now.

Besides, it's not like my secret identity is really all that secret anymore.

He felt the surge of energy in his legs, the enormous wave of adrenaline powering him as he accelerated, taking off at a dead run no one there could match.

He'd been given all that power at the behest of the emperor, to enable him to serve the imperial will, and for a long time, that was just what he did. But now, things had come full circle, and his abilities were turned against the minions of empire.

The corridor was long and featureless, a winding gray concrete tunnel. Blackhawk knew he'd come at least several kilometers, but there was no sign of an end yet. He'd wondered if he was truly on Vos's trail, but now he was sure. A passage this long could have only one purpose—an escape route leading outside the city.

He had no idea how much of a head start Vos had, so he kept moving instead of stopping and searching for signs to confirm his enemy had come this way. But now he was passing through an area where the smooth concrete roof was cracked. Water had seeped in, and the ground was damp. He could see footprints ahead of him. Not one set, but at least ten. Vos had come this way, and he wasn't alone.

Blackhawk continued moving for another five hundred meters. Then he stopped suddenly. His acute hearing was picking up sounds ahead. Voices, footsteps. He took a deep breath, filling his lungs with oxygen, quickly banishing the fatigue from his run.

He's got guards, and they're probably his best. So the question is: Do I wait for the others? Or do I try to take them all out? He glanced around. *Where am I? How far have we come?*

You have traveled 4.6 kilometers since entering the tunnel. I estimate that you are under a position three hundred meters from the perimeter of the city.

Almost five kilometers. The exit has to be near . . .

He reached down and pulled a clip from his belt, replacing the half-full one he had in place.

No—he's too close to escaping. There's no time to wait.

Pillars of thick black smoke rose into the sky, great columns marking the spots where villages were dying. The sounds of explosions ripped through the air as two armies struggled for supremacy. The imperial troops had recovered from their initial surprise, and they'd set up a defensive line along a high ridge. Their positions covered every approach, exposing the attackers to withering fire no matter how they advanced.

The open plateau was covered with dead and wounded. The imperials had lost heavily in a pitched battle before they withdrew to the ridge, and then the invaders suffered heavy casualties during two failed assaults against that position. Now the invaders were trying a third time, a massive advance on the imperial center. And in the forefront of that attack came a column of massive war machines.

The tanks of the Tiger Company rumbled forward, their integral infantry units in close support, and a huge column of the Black Helms stacked up behind. The Celtiborians had borne the brunt of the battle and the first two assaults as well, and now the mercs were moving into battle. It was their turn. And they had the tanks.

General Carano moved forward, marching at the head of his formation. He watched the tanks rumbling forward, heading toward the ridge. The enemy had already opened up on them, firing everything they could bring to bear. But Vulcan's armored vehicles were turning aside everything the imperials could throw at them. The great tanks were almost impregnable, especially to the front, and they continued their relentless advance, firing their powerful main guns as they did.

Carano watched as two of the heavy shells impacted dead center on the ridge. Great clods of dirt were thrown into the air in all directions. He was too far away to see if any enemy soldiers had been killed, but from the location of the explosion he'd have bet parts of imperials were mixed with the flying turf.

Vulcan's attack was on a narrow frontage, intended to split the enemy line in two, and his people were concentrating their fire on a mere five hundred meters of the line. The heavy fire was creating a kill zone, weakening the soldiers who would have to stand before the relentless assault.

The Helms had their main force behind the tanks, but Carano had detached a regiment to each side, charged with protecting the armored column from any flanking move off the ridge. If Vulcan's monsters had a weakness, it was their suscep- tibility to track damage from flank attacks, and Carano had no intention of letting the enemy get that close.

He wondered how Blackhawk and his people were faring. He'd found himself completely under the general's spell, and he was amazed at the sheer fearless audacity of the man. The fool—hero?—had landed in the middle of the city, with his tiny crew and two volunteer squads from the Helms. That was insane, by any rational analysis, but Carano found himself wish- ing he was there. It was odd to think someone was crazy and in the same moment to feel the urge to join him.

Yet it wasn't just he who felt Blackhawk's pull. When he'd asked for twenty volunteers, hundreds of his soldiers had stepped forward. There was something about Blackhawk that defied easy explanation. And if his story was true, if he had been a merci- less imperial general, there had been a massive change in the man since. Carano wasn't a follower, and not many men won his respect. But Arkarin Blackhawk was one of those men. He had a true quality in him, Carano was sure of it. And it was nothing he could have gotten from being an imperial killer.

The tanks fired again. Carano moved to the side, getting a look around the looming vehicles. He could see his flank guards advancing, keeping up with the tanks. They had strict orders to stay back if the enemy remained on their ridge. There was no point in advancing into withering fire. But if the imperi- als came down from their positions to move against the tanks, his people knew what to do.

He felt a rush as he watched the tanks move ever closer. The enemy fire intensified—they were throwing everything they could scrape up, but the Tigers never faltered. A lucky shot had taken out one tank, but the others kept moving and shooting, coming closer and closer to the enemy line.

Carano saw the motion right away. At first he was worried the imperials were launching an attack, but then he realized . . .

He punched his comm unit, opening his channel to Colonel Vulcan. "Armando, they're pulling back! They're abandoning the ridgeline."

An instant later, Vulcan's booming voice erupted into Carano's ear. "Chrono's balls, you're right, Vladimir. Now is the time. This is where we destroy them."

Carano changed to the Helms' channel. "All units, the enemy is retreating. All regiments are ordered to attack along the ridgeline. Forward, Helms! To victory!"

"To victory!" shouted the Helms.

He looked back ahead as Vulcan's tanks kicked in their reserve power, moving toward the ridge at fifty kilometers per hour. *Go, Armando,* he thought, feeling the battle lust begin to consume him. *Break that line!*

Tarnan crouched behind the broken remains of the cabinet, barely managing to keep his massive frame under cover. Kergen Vos's furniture had been expensive and handcrafted, but even the dense hardwood was poor protection against modern weapons. The enemy had been trying to break into the room for almost an hour, but Guerrin's people had gunned down every attempt to force the doorway. Tarnan was slow to give trust and respect to new allies, but the mercs were acquitting themselves well, and it made an impression.

Jav Guerrin's troops were fighting hard, but the relentless attacks had taken their toll. Of Guerrin's original twenty men, seven were dead, and half the others were wounded. A few of those were serious, but the rest were still able to fight. Still, however he looked at it, they were down to half strength. And ammunition was running low too.

Now he could hear the enemy in the hall. They were trying to take down the wall so they could attack on a wider frontage than just the meter-wide doorway. But Kergen Vos's paranoia had inadvertently served his enemies well. The walls weren't just concrete, they were reinforced hypersteel. The enemy was cutting through with a plasma torch—Tarnan could see the glow burning through, but even so, it would take them a while to finish.

But they've been at it awhile, he thought grimly. *If Ark doesn't get back soon, we're . . .*

We're what, he thought to himself. *What is Ark going to do? You're trapped down here, all of you. Blackhawk might manage to kill Vos, but none of us are getting out of this.*

Tarnan loved and respected Arkarin Blackhawk, and for years he'd believed the great warrior could lead his crew through any challenge—and bring them all back alive. But that was before his brother was killed. Tarq had died in the *Claw*'s sick bay, while Doc worked to save Danellan Lancaster's life. Tarnan understood the situation, and he knew Blackhawk hadn't had any choice. But the pain was still there, as he knew it would always be. He was still loyal to Blackhawk, and he would follow him everywhere. But he knew things could never be the same as they had been. That unshakable confidence, the rock-solid belief—that was gone. Forever. Though that wasn't likely to matter. Tarnan didn't expect to live more than a few minutes longer.

"Tarnan?" Guerrin's called across the room.

"Lieutenant?" the giant responded.

"I think they're going to get through soon. Can you set your autocannon here? You should have a good field of fire when the wall comes down."

"Sure, Lieutenant." He crouched and set his gun down in front of him.

Just a few minutes now, and it will all be over. Tarq, my brother, I will be with you soon. We did our best, Ark. At least we bought you some time. I hope you used it well . . .

He looked down at his autocannon, double-checking, making sure his ammo feed was snugly in place. Then he heard gunfire in the hallway . . . and screaming.

Tarnan's head snapped toward the doorway. He could see imperial soldiers moving back and forth in front of the door. They were firing down the hall, and they were dropping to the ground. Someone was shooting at them! The fighting went on for perhaps half a minute, and then he saw soldiers running past the door. Celtiborian soldiers!

"General Blackhawk?" a voice yelled from the hall.

"It's Lieutenant Guerrin, Second Regiment, Black Helms. General Blackhawk left in pursuit of Governor Vos."

A gray-clad figure peered around the edge of the door before walking slowly into the room. He was a Celtiborian officer, and he walked in followed by a grizzled-looking sergeant and two privates.

"Major Seth Warne, Lieutenant." His head turned slowly, stopping when his gaze reached the massive figure with the autocannon. "And you must be the famous Tarnan. Glad to finally meet up with you guys." He paused and wiped his hand across his face. "I'm sorry it took us so long!"

Blackhawk stopped suddenly. The noises were getting louder,

and the tunnel turned sharply to the right. He crept up to the corner and peered around.

He could see soldiers moving swiftly down the corridor. He ducked back quickly before anyone turned around and noticed him. He'd caught a glimpse of the tunnel ahead, and it looked like it opened up into a larger, better lit room a few hundred meters ahead.

That's probably the exit. I'd bet this tunnel dumps out into some nondescript building, like an electrical grid station or a water pump house. That's how I'd design a bolt-hole.

Okay, Ark—no more time for caution.

He took a deep breath as he surrendered himself, let the battle trance take him as he had so many times before. And like so many times before, the odds were against him. He needed everything he could muster to have a chance.

Everything.

He felt the Umbra thoughts stirring deep in his mind, the cold anger toward an enemy, the relentless need to destroy all who opposed him. He would be Arkarin Blackhawk in this fight. *And* Frigus Umbra. His fatigue was gone, and his body twitched with anticipation . . .

He spun around the corridor, running as quickly as he could while still remaining almost silent. The line of guards was up ahead, but every second before he was noticed got him that much closer.

He'd covered about half the distance when the guard in the rear started to move his head. That slight motion, perhaps no more than a twitch, sealed his fate. Blackhawk didn't know if the man was moving to look behind him, but he reacted anyway.

His gun fired, and the top of the guard's head vanished in a spray of blood. He continued charging forward, firing as he did. There was no cover in the tunnel, so he rushed to take down as many as he could before they were able to react.

Even as he hurried, though, it was as if time slowed. His eyes and arms worked together, almost without conscious recognition. He sighted each successive target, and his rifle whipped around from one target to the next. His weapon fired again and again, and each time it did, it spat death.

As he fired another shot, he could see farther down the tunnel out of the corner of his eye. It looked like a small group of the guards were trying to turn to face him, while the others withdrew.

"No time to mess with rearguards," he mumbled to himself, reaching to his belt and grabbing a frag grenade. He whipped it around in one smooth motion, pressing the arming switch as he threw it down the hall. He dove forward, slamming hard to the ground, lying on his stomach with his rifle in front of him. He could hear enemy shots whipping by above him, and a second later, the grenade blew.

The explosion was contained by the tunnel, and he covered his face with his hands against the back blast. It was mostly air moving where Blackhawk lay, but up where the enemy rearguard had turned to make a stand, the explosion had released a deadly storm of shrapnel. The four guards were all down, and at first glance, it didn't look like any of them were getting up again.

Blackhawk leaped to his feet and ran down the tunnel, checking to make sure his enemies were dead before he continued on. He pushed himself even harder, since Vos obviously knew he was here now.

He ran another few hundred meters. He was almost to where the tunnel dumped into the larger room. Every tactical impulse he had was screaming at him to stop—bursting out into a large area full of enemies was foolish. But there was no other option. Either he plunged into the room recklessly, or he let Vos escape.

And Vos is too dangerous to let live. If he gets away, millions more will die than otherwise would.

Blackhawk popped the nearly spent cartridge from his gun and slammed a fresh one in place. Then he lunged forward without a second thought, running into the center of the room, his head whipping around, taking stock of the tactical situation.

The situation sucked.

There were at least fifteen guards in the room. They were slightly surprised by his wild charge, and he was able to take down four of them almost immediately. But then the rest were on him.

He felt arms grabbing him from behind, and he thrust back with his rifle butt, striking one of his assailants hard in the midsection. He could feel the soldier drop. But almost immediately another enemy moved up, and he felt a sharp pain as the newest attacker clubbed him with a rifle.

A normal man would have dropped to the ground . . . but Arkarin Blackhawk was not a normal man.

He turned quickly, taking one hand off his rifle and whipping his shortsword from its sheath. He fired the assault rifle forward on full auto—dropping it when the clip was expended—while he brought the sword around.

The stunned soldier didn't see the deadly blade coming, and Blackhawk cut his throat so deeply he almost decapitated the man. The other soldier who'd grabbed him from behind stepped back, freeing Blackhawk, giving him a momentary respite. But there were too many of them. He felt another rifle butt strike him from behind, and then a shock—some kind of stun rod.

He could feel his body responding, shaking off the damage. His powerful heart pounded hard, feeding oxygen to his straining muscles. His brain was focused, crystal clear. He fought on in an adrenaline-fueled surge, his deadly sword now joined by his pistol as he dropped one enemy after another. But they kept coming. He felt the stun rod again, and his body shook. The weapons were designed to knock out an ordinary human with one blow, but Blackhawk had taken two, and he was still in the fight.

It was a lot harder to ignore nine thousand volts assaulting his nervous system than a blow by a rifle butt, though.

Then he felt a third, and he staggered for an instant. The strength was draining away from him, his herculean stamina almost gone. But there was one thing left . . . a power yet untapped.

He felt the Umbra side burst out of its cage, a wave of pure malevolence sweeping over him. And with it came a last blast of strength. He shook off the effects of the stun rod, and he redoubled his attacks. His sword flashed through the air, its motion too quick to follow. And every time it did, one of his enemies fell in a spray of blood. Another stun rod hit him, but Umbra shrugged off the paralyzing effect with sheer force of will. Blackhawk seemingly watched his alter ego in wonder, realizing for the first time how much of his strength and perseverance came from the darkest part of his psyche.

But even the black fury of the Umbra side wasn't going to be enough. Another stun rod hit him. Then another. He dropped slowly to his knees, his sword slipping from his hands as his enemies continued to strike him again and again with the stunning weapons.

Blackhawk felt a new sensation come over him, one he'd never before experienced: failure. Defeat. He struggled to the last, refusing with every fiber of his being to give up . . . until he fell to the ground and blackness took him.

Water. He was in water, sinking, drowning. He fought to breathe, but there was nothing but the water. Then light, hazy at first . . . becoming brighter.

He was on the floor. No, the ground. It was soft, wet, mossy. He turned to try to get up, but he fell back down again. His hands were tied behind his back. Slowly, he began to remember. Galvanus.

Vos.

"I am pleased that you are awake, my old friend." A man stood over him, holding an empty bucket. He stared at Blackhawk with a smile that did little to hide his obvious hatred.

"Vos?" Blackhawk croaked, his throat dry and sore. He tried to straighten himself as much as he could. Every muscle in his body ached from the repeated electrical shocks and multiple beatings, but he pushed through, and he managed to work his way into a seated position.

"Yes, General Blackhawk, I am Kergen Vos." The governor paused, and when he continued, his voice was darker, more threatening. "Or should I call you General Umbra?"

Blackhawk stared back, his eyes still blazing with defiance despite his position. "I am Blackhawk. Frigus Umbra is no more. He was my past, not my present. Nor my future."

"I'm afraid you have very little future, General Blackhawk, so that's not really of concern. Your past, though, is of interest to me. You have opposed me in the Far Stars, with great success. You have been a worthy opponent, one I would have granted a quick and painless death in most circumstances." Vos glared at Blackhawk with a searing intensity. "But . . . I am afraid my grievances against your alter ego are more personal, and unfortunately, they transcend honor and respect among enemies."

Blackhawk sighed softly. He might be about to die, but he wasn't going to spend his last minutes humoring this fool on whatever vendetta he'd been nurturing for decades. Frigus Umbra had a lot of enemies. Indeed, Arkarin Blackhawk had his share as well.

He shrugged.

"This is not something you can just dismiss. No—I won't let you. Do you recall a planet called Belleger, General?"

Blackhawk sighed. "So that's what this is about? That's why you didn't just kill me?" He glanced around the room, taking note of Vos's men. There were more here than had been in the tunnels, at least another half dozen.

"So you do remember then? How your armies came, how they killed and rampaged, destroying everything in their path? The millions on Belleger who burned to death in their homes. The ones impaled on pikes by your soldiers. The women raped, the children murdered. Or, for those who survived all that, the slow death of starvation. No, General Umbra, I'm afraid I couldn't simply put a bullet in your head as you lay unconscious. For you there must be a more . . . fitting end."

"You don't look like you starved to death," Blackhawk said. "And I'd wager you weren't impaled either. Just another monster looking for someone else to blame for his detestable actions." He had tremendous sympathy and regret for the victims from his days as Frigus Umbra, but not for those who'd used their grievances to justify their own brutality.

"Indeed, General. I survived. Though the rest of my family was not so fortunate."

Blackhawk stared back at Vos, his expression like granite. "Perhaps they didn't embrace becoming a turncoat as you did. What did you do, Vos, to claim a place in imperial intelligence? Did you turn in your friends, spy on your countrymen?" He was working his hands around behind his back, trying to slip out of his bonds.

He could see Vos was becoming angrier.

Good. The more unbalanced he is, the better. And the longer this takes . . . Shira and the others will be here soon . . .

"No doubt you blame me for what you have become. Perhaps you feel you had no choice on Belleger. Maybe you decided your own life was worth more than everyone else's. But it's been more than twenty-five years, Vos, a quarter century, and here you are still grasping for more power. How many have died in this attempt you have launched to claim the Far Stars? How many will still die? Yet you feel righteous because my army invaded your world so long ago?"

Vos's face was growing red with each word, but still he didn't answer. Blackhawk knew the rage was a defense. He was striking Vos where it hurt. For all Frigus Umbra had done, for the terrible evils he had brought to so many worlds, Blackhawk knew he had lived as an honorable man for more than two decades. But Vos had remained a monster, long after he could have escaped.

He might have forgiven Vos for whatever he did to get off Belleger, even taken the blame for that. But not for the decades since. Vos had contracted the sickness that infected the empire and its minions: the irresistible lust for power. And for more than twenty-five years he'd justified his actions by blaming Frigus Umbra for it all. Blackhawk knew he might die here, but he'd be damned if he was going to let Vos continue this self-deception.

"And tell me more of your grand rebellion on Belleger, Vos. My soldiers did what they did, and they crushed any who opposed them. But your revolutionaries did not bring freedom to the people, even for a moment. They didn't even try. The leaders of the rebellion sought only power for themselves. Do you recall it that way? Or have you romanticized it all to justify all you have done?

"After the reconquest, we found hundreds of mass graves. The rebels inflicted their own reign of terror during their brief rule, and thousands of your people died at their hands before my fleet even arrived. So spare me your pretensions at moral outrage. I have faced what I did long ago and struggled to make my peace with it. But Frigus Umbra was far from the only evil that existed—that exists . . . inside the empire or out."

"Take him," Vos said, his voice wavering. Blackhawk could see the governor was shaking with rage.

"You don't enjoy facing your own demons, do you, Vos?"

"You will burn, Blackhawk," the governor said through clenched teeth, "as so many thousands did on Belleger. Your last sounds will be howls of pain, and they will be as music to me."

"Never. You will not hear a sound out of me."

Blackhawk was about to slip his hands out of the rope, to jump to his feet and make a lunge for Vos. It would be suicide, but he just might be able to take the governor down before the soldiers killed him. But he stopped himself, waited. He saw movement in the woods, leaves rustling despite the lack of wind. He waited a few more seconds, and *then* he leaped . . .

Shira came charging out of the trees into the clearing, her two assault rifles firing on the imperial soldiers. She'd taken down four or five in the instant before Sarge and his boys burst out behind her, their own weapons out, firing full.

Blackhawk's eyes went to a small pile of equipment. His belt was there. And his sword and pistol. He dove toward the pile, hitting the ground in a combat roll. Most of the guards were occupied with the attack of Blackhawk's crew, but two noticed him, and they turned and opened fire. But he was ahead of them, and their bullets hit the empty dirt. Black-hawk grabbed his pistol as he rolled past the small stack of supplies, and he sprang back to his feet. He fired twice, and both of his enemies dropped to the ground. Then he whipped his head around. Shira and Sarge's crew could finish off the guards. Blackhawk's mind was on one thing and one thing only.

Kergen Vos.

The governor had taken off into the woods, and Blackhawk raced after him. Vos had a head start, but it was no contest. The captain caught up easily and tackled the governor hard, jamming his knee into Vos's back and putting his pistol to his prisoner's head.

He whipped the governor to his feet, and he headed back to the small clearing, pushing his captive forward. There was no more gunfire. His people had finished off the imperials. But as soon as he walked back out of the woods, he could tell something was wrong.

Sarge and his boys were clustered together, kneeling over something. And Shira was standing off to the side, tears stream-ing down her face.

He felt a cold feeling inside. "What happened?"

Shira opened her mouth, but at first no words came. Finally, she croaked out a tortured whisper. "It's Drake."

Blackhawk shoved Vos to the ground hard. "Call the *Claw*. Lucas can probably be here in a few minutes with Doc . . ." But one look at her expression told him there was nothing Doc could do.

Blackhawk pushed forward, dropping down to one knee next to Sarge. The veteran noncom was hunched over, stricken.

"He's dead, Captain. Took a shot dead center in the heart."

Blackhawk put his hand down on Sarge's shoulder. He could

feel the Umbra part of him, the lack of sadness and pity it felt for a man who had served on the *Claw* for years, who had been a brother in arms. Blackhawk felt a wave of disgust for what he had been so many years before, and he pushed hard, slamming the Umbra psyche back into the depths of his mind. He knew his battle with himself wasn't over, but right now, with the body of his friend lying a meter away, the Blackhawk side was firmly in control.

First Tarq. Now Drake . . .

He stood up and regarded Vos with frozen eyes. He leaned over and pulled a sword from one of the dead imperials. "That man lying there was a brother to me. His loyalty and steadfastness are things a creature like you could never understand.

"And now you will die. For his death, and for so many others you have caused. For the good of the Far Stars."

Blackhawk could see the fear in Vos's eyes. The governor, whatever else he might be, was no coward. But facing Blackhawk this way, staring up at him, feeling the rage radiating off the legendary warrior's body, that was something Kergen Vos had not been built to endure.

Blackhawk threw the sword he'd taken at Vos's feet. Then he drew his own, casting aside his pistol. "Still," he said, his voice as cold and dark as space itself, "I will give you this for Belleger. Pick it up. Fight me. Die as a man, in arms. As you should have died on Belleger so long ago."

He watched as Vos paused for an instant. Then the imperial nodded once, slowly, and he reached out and picked up the sword. He got up slowly and stood, staring at Blackhawk without saying a word.

Blackhawk gripped his blade tightly, his eyes locked on Vos's. The governor lunged forward, and he struck hard. Blackhawk stepped to the side, parrying the man's blow and coming around with his own. His sword bit into the governor's side, and Vos howled in pain as a spray of blood erupted from a ten-centimeter gash.

Blackhawk watched as Vos staggered, trying to maintain his focus through the pain and fear. He came at Blackhawk again, but once more his attack was blocked. Blackhawk swung hard in response, Vos barely raising his blade in time to meet the deadly attack.

Blackhawk's crew was gathered around them, weapons in hand, but he waved them off. "No," he said. "He is mine."

Vos leaned forward slightly, telegraphing his next attack. Blackhawk waited an instant, and then he set himself in motion. He swung hard, pushing Vos's weapon aside, and he brought his arm back fast and thrust forward, driving his blade deep into his enemy's chest.

Vos gasped hard, and an instant later a torrent of blood erupted from his mouth. Blackhawk leaned over him, staring into his eyes for a few seconds.

"That was for Drake," he whispered in the dying man's ear. "And for Tarq." He jerked the blade up, and Vos gasped. "And that was for the marshal." He pushed forward, watching the governor's body slide off his sword.

He stood for a few moments staring down . . . exhausted, aching, heartbroken over Drake's death. Vos was dead . . . the serpent's head had been severed, and Blackhawk knew half the battle against the empire had been won. It was the primary reason he had come to Galvanus, and now it was completed. But there were still soldiers fighting, and the fate of the planet—of the Far Stars—still hung in the balance.

He turned and looked one more time at Drake's unmoving form. Walking over toward his fallen comrade, Blackhawk knelt down beside him, slipping his hand under the dead man's shoulder.

"Come," he said softly. "Help me carry him." He took a deep breath. "We have to go. We've still got a war to win here."

Blackhawk stood silently and watched as the column of soldiers marched down the battered main street of Galvanus City. The buildings on both sides of the thoroughfare were damaged, and the air still hung heavy with the smell of smoke. But the main army had broken through and linked up with the forces in the city. The last of the imperial troops had surrendered, and the confederation forces were firmly in control, at least of the areas around the capital. There were a few pockets of resistance in other areas of the planet, but with Vos gone, Blackhawk knew it was just a matter of time before Galvanus was totally pacified.

Blackhawk had initially refused to allow the Celtiborians and the mercs to accept surrenders. The voice inside him kept demanding he show strength by refusing any mercy—and Drake's death was like a hot blade shoved in his gut. He knew what imperial training was like, and he understood the mindset of the empire's soldiers. These men would never be anything but prisoners. There was no way to rehabilitate them, not most of them at least. But fighting to the end would have cost thousands more of the Celtiborian soldiers and the mercenaries who had served him so faithfully and loyally. In the end, the Blackhawk side of him had won out, and his desire to save the lives of his own soldiers saved the last of the imperials.

He walked across the wrecked pavilion in front of the capitol. Whole sections of the great building lay in ruins, the black-and-white marble that had covered its entire façade strewn about in broken chunks. The crushed remains of the fountain the *Claw* had obliterated stood in front of the destroyed main doors, its severed pipes still spraying jets of water five meters into the air.

Rows of soldiers were lined up in the pavilion. Carano stood in the front, along with Vulcan and the other merc commanders. Vulcan's arm was heavily bandaged. He'd suffered some bad burns when his tank was hit just as his forces were breaking the imperial battle line. He'd recover fully, except for a few scars, but he was still in considerable pain.

Next to the mercs, the Celtiborian officers stood at perfect attention. Lucerne's veterans had decided almost as one: Arkarin Blackhawk was the marshal's choice to succeed him—and now he was theirs as well. He had led them on an impossible mission, and he'd brought them victory. They would follow him anywhere he led.

Blackhawk knew he should be exhausted, but instead he felt invigorated. *You really were manufactured for war,* he thought sadly. The Celtiborians—and the mercs, too—were ready to accept his command, and despite his best efforts, the feeling swept through him, an excitement and pleasure, like sex or the high of a drug. He wanted to address the soldiers, to rally them for the next fight, hear them chanting his name as the conquered citizens of Galvanus looked on in stunned awe.

But what name would they shout?

Was he Arkarin Blackhawk? Or Frigus Umbra? He'd had a few moments of doubt, savored the thought of glory and military conquest, but then he rallied his discipline. He pushed the old thoughts back into their place.

These people are not conquered, they are liberated. And these soldiers are not yours. You cannot make yourself their sole master. You must help defeat the rest of the imperial forces, cleanse the Far Stars so Lucerne's confederation can have its chance. But you cannot be marshal. Whether you want it or not. It is not for you . . . unless you would again become a monster, a man with no friends, only a universe of terrified supplicants.

He stepped forward and nodded toward the assembled commanders. The war wasn't over, and he knew he would continue to struggle with his thoughts, his motivations. But today was for something else, and all the men and women who had died deserved his utmost attention.

The flagpole stood in the center of the gargantuan pavilion, rising thirty meters into the bright blue sky. For a thousand years it had flown the black-and-gold flag of the empire. But now that banner had been taken down, and it lay tattered and torn on the ground.

Blackhawk stepped forward and handed the folded cloth he held to the soldier standing by the pole. He stepped back and watched as the private—a man picked from the ranks for his bravery during the fighting—slowly raised it aloft.

Blackhawk stood silently, his neck bent back, staring up as the wind took the blue-and-silver confederation flag, unfurling the silky banner above the first world ever liberated from imperial control.

He stood where he was, silently looking up at the symbol of what they were fighting for.

I wish you had lived to see this day, Augustin. The flag of your beloved Far Stars Confederation flapping in the breeze of a world that has long stood only for imperial oppression. You may have fallen, my old friend, but what you created lives on. There are more battles to fight, but your people are united behind your ideals.

And nothing will stop us.

EPILOGUE

THE WAR IN THE FAR STARS RAGED FOR ALMOST THREE MORE
years, but for all the death and suffering it caused, the outcome was never in serious doubt. The imperial forces lost their
best chance at victory when Blackhawk killed Vos, cutting the
head off their entire organization. The imperials lost Galvanus
Prime too, and without their mastermind or their capital, they
were reduced to scattered forces fighting a series of unrelated
battles, desperate—and ultimately futile—defenses of the planets they had conquered. One by one, the grim Celtiborian veterans, backed now by the soldiers of the other Primes and the
former mercenary units, fought the imperials and liberated the
conquered worlds.

Kalishar had been the final hope for the empire's fortunes

after Vos's death. The pirate stronghold had been a major imperial fortress, but Florin's bold move had sealed the fate of Lord Tragonis and his soldier factory. Rafaelus DeMark had come himself, with Desaix's battle fleet and every transport vessel the allied Primes could supply.

Three hundred thousand of Marshal Lucerne's oldest, toughest veterans landed in the deep Kalishari desert, and they didn't stop the fight until every imperial soldier on the planet was dead. Lord Tragonis himself had been killed trying to escape, shot down by Admiral Desaix's vessels as his ship tried to sneak far enough from the planet to jump away.

There would be a glut of imperial titles left vacant beyond the Void.

DeMark had personally thanked Rax Florin, and he publicly confirmed his status as ka'al, subject now, of course, to the constitution and laws of the Far Stars Confederation. In the new, united Far Stars, piracy was likely to become a far more difficult profession, and a world that had earned its keep as a sanctuary for buccaneers and thieves was likely to need a new source of economic growth. Fortunately, Florin was an intelligent man, one DeMark fully believed could manage the task. And the vast stores of imperial crowns he'd hoarded would no doubt be of considerable help . . . along with the economic aid Blackhawk had promised to help pull Kalishar out of its poor—and highly disreputable—past.

The Celtiborian general and the Kalishari ka'al had spent several hours together discussing things, and when DeMark finally left, he did so with strong hope for the planet's future, and more respect for its ex-pirate monarch than he'd dared to imagine beforehand.

Hope, of course, was tempered with reality—hope was for

the future, but the present loomed over the Far Stars, where devastation was widespread. Planets had become battlegrounds, industry had been destroyed, populations had suffered horrific losses. Vos's machinations with the Far Stars Bank had caused unprecedented economic devastation across the sector, and a deep depression had settled in.

No one thought recovery would come easy or soon, but Danellan Lancaster had agreed to lead the confederation's economic team. The once spoiled and insular magnate had found his true talents, and already there were fragile signs of recovery, just a few green shoots poking above the snow and ice, perhaps, but a hopeful sign nevertheless. Lancaster had seen personally to the restructuring of the Far Stars Bank and the purging of imperial interests from that ancient institution. The bank was healthy and firmly back in local control, ready to finance the rebuilding on war-torn worlds throughout the sector.

Blackhawk had once been nervous about the Lancaster patriarch, hesitant to trust him with anything important. But Danellan had been true to his word, and Blackhawk had since come to trust him completely. He'd appointed Lancaster to the confederation's top economic post without a second thought and with the full support of Astra and DeMark.

The people of the Far Stars, so long splintered and warring with one another, found a common cause in the united defense against the empire, and they carried this spirit forward as the sector looked toward economic recovery and a brighter future.

Marshal Lucerne's true brilliance became apparent as the Far Stars Confederation absorbed all the systems of the sector. For the first time in its history, the Far Stars was united. Lucerne had conceived his confederation to respect the local laws and customs of its member worlds and to rule with a light hand. The sectorwide confederation provided protection, enforced basic rights for its citizens, and regulated free trade among planets, but beyond that it tread softly, respecting the local governments.

Lucerne had realized it was the only way to unite worlds so vastly different from one another in culture and tradition. The merchant princes of Antilles, the pleasure seekers of Sandaria, the ascetic priests of Aussellon . . . the people of the Far Stars were wildly different. Their forefathers had come to this distant refuge millennia before, many of them fleeing persecution at home. And centuries of independence had allowed those differences to grow.

Ironically, it was Governor Vos who had helped secure the success of the confederation in the end. His near conquest reignited the fear of the empire, something that had faded over the recent centuries of inactivity. By the time the last imperial-occupied world was liberated, 90 percent of the planets in the sector had agreed to join the Far Stars Confederation. The rest required a moderate amount of coercion, but there was little doubt they would also yield eventually.

And so, Lucerne's quest to unite the Far Stars succeeded, and in the process it saved the sector from imperial domination far sooner than even he had imagined. Millions had died to see it done, the great marshal included, but now the Far Stars was united, even the six worlds that had existed so long under the imperial yoke.

A new age had begun. There was suffering everywhere, and vast amounts of work still to do before peace and prosperity could take hold. But there was hope as well, hope for a bright new future.

Mak Wilhelm sat at the controls of the small, one-man speed-ster. It was a cramped and uncomfortable vessel for a trip as long and hazardous as one across the Void, but he had little alternative. Kergen Vos had come close to realizing his dreams in the Far Stars, but in the end he'd been defeated by Arkarin Blackhawk . . . and one by one his subordinates fell, yielding up not only the worlds they had conquered, but those that had always been part of the empire.

Wilhelm dreaded returning to the imperial court after such a disastrous defeat. He hadn't been in command, and that might save him from the scaffold, at least. But he didn't fool himself about his prospects. His career, at least, was likely headed for a sharp downward trajectory.

Most of Vos's lieutenants had died during the war, killed in battle or hunted down when they tried to flee . . . though he'd heard that Villeroi had killed Chairman Vargus and slipped away just before the confederation forces invaded Vanderon. Wilhelm had never liked the psychopath, but he wasn't sur-prised at the possibility that he was one of the survivors.

Wilhelm had held out on Nordlingen until the end . . . until General DeMark himself returned to the planet with two hun-dred thousand veterans of the war on Kalishar. There were countless legends of generals who had died valiantly along with their soldiers, fighting to the bitter end in lost causes. But Mak Wilhelm had no desire to be one of them. He'd stayed as long as there had been any hope of victory, and then he took off his general's stars and used his skills as a top imperial agent to simply slip away.

The future wasn't particularly bright, and he knew his road

would be anything but easy. Still, he'd find a way forward. And as long as he never had to set eyes on the cursed Far Stars again he would be just fine.

Blackhawk lay still, his eyes closed, savoring the warm feel of Astra next to him. She lay with her face on his chest, and his hand gently stroked the silky mass of her golden blond hair. He was as happy as he'd ever been in his extraordinary and tumultuous life—and as sad. This was all he wanted, not wealth, not power . . . just Astra, close to him. A life where the two of them could live simply, joyfully. But he knew it couldn't be.

For three years he'd fought to drive the last of the imperials from the Far Stars. In the end, the confederation forces he'd commanded had invaded the worlds of the imperial demesne, the five planets other than Galvanus Prime that had for so long been ruled by the empire. Never again, he had declared, would any world of the Far Stars be in thrall to Optimus Prime. And he had made it so, in a series of bloody and cataclysmic battles.

He'd struggled during the wars, strained to remain true to what he'd become, to hold back the darker impulses. His efforts had kept him back from the abyss, but they'd been far from completely successful. He'd led the confederation's forces ruthlessly. He'd ignored collateral damage, and he'd pushed his troops brutally, right to the edge of their abilities. He'd often refused to take imperial prisoners, ordering many of those who surrendered to be summarily executed. It was often his love for his troops that led him astray, and his rage at heavy losses loosened his hold on the Umbra side of his mind.

His friends had made excuses for him, and his subordinates declared that war was a savage endeavor, that the commands of a strong leader were easily misconstrued for brutality. But Blackhawk knew the truth. He was losing his control over Frigus Umbra. He had completed Lucerne's work, seen his confederation become a reality. But he knew he could go further, that he could reach out his arm and make himself a king, an emperor in his own right. None could oppose him, not after the victories he'd won. Few of his generals would even try, he suspected. If he declared himself king, most of the senior officers would rally to him, follow him willingly into the totalitarian future he offered.

There was only one option, one way to save the Far Stars from himself.

He had to get away.

Away from the army, away from the centers of power. And he knew that meant away from Astra.

"You awake?" he heard her ask, her voice soft, groggy.

"I'm awake." He felt her hand moving slowly across his chest. Her touch relaxed him like nothing else he'd ever experienced. She'd been at his side through three years of war, of struggle, and he'd come to love her even more, if that was possible. He didn't know how he would live without her. But he knew he had to find a way.

"Ark? We need to talk, my love."

Blackhawk sighed softly, almost silently. He'd known this was coming. They'd allowed their passions to rule them, and they'd said hasty words, made promises they both knew were reckless. He loved her with all his heart, and he knew she felt the same. That should have been enough. The songs and poems promised it was enough. But it wasn't. Not for them.

"I know, my love. You don't need to say it. You can't come with me. And I cannot stay." Blackhawk wanted to save her the anguish, spare her from saying anything that would cause her even more pain.

She had promised to come with him, to leave the confederation behind, to resign her offices and join him, wherever his travels led. But that had been months before, when war was still raging, when defeating the imperials seemed like the end of duty rather than just the beginning. Her words had been from her heart and not her head, and they both knew it.

"I'm sorry, Ark. I love you with all my heart, and I always will. Always." Her words came slowly, and he could feel the wet warmth of tears on his chest.

"I know you can't come. I knew it then, back on Antilles when you said you would. I might have allowed myself an instant of self-delusion, let myself believe for just a brief moment, but I've always known. We have love, Astra, strong and unconditional, but duty comes first, at least when the lives of billions are at stake."

He suspected it was the Umbra side of him providing some of his strength now, and for once he was grateful. He couldn't imagine anything more difficult than letting Astra go, and he knew he had to get through it any way he could.

He knew if he pushed her, if he asked her to leave everything behind, she'd probably say yes. *Perhaps on some level, that's what she wants. I know that's what I want. But then she will always carry the guilt of abandoning her duty. And the Far Stars will suffer terribly without her. I can't do that to her, I won't.*

There was no one else everyone would follow, no one leader who could step into her father's shoes, save her. She had DeMark's unrestrained support, and with that she could hold the confederation together and put it on course for a strong and prosperous future. Without her, it would all crumble. The Primes would jockey for power and influence—even as they did now, with only her resolve and Blackhawk's fierceness keeping them in check. And while DeMark was another option, he could only rule by force, and that was doomed to failure. His Celtiborian veterans were a fearsome force, but they were far too few in number to subjugate the sector—and even if they could somehow manage it, how much better than the empire would that be?

Astra, however, could lead with words and ideas—and she would have all of DeMark's force and military strength behind her. She would be the silk glove around his iron fist.

She buried her face in Blackhawk's chest, throwing her arms around his neck. The tears were coming freely now, and he reached out and held her. It was all he could do.

"I'd stay with you," he said sadly. "I'd stand by your side from now until the day I die . . . if I could. But you know I cannot. You saw me during the war. You made excuses for me, covered up the atrocities that accompanied my victories. But I am barely hanging on to myself, to the man you love. If I continue to hold the power I have for the last three years, I *will* destroy myself. What they did to me is still there, waiting for the chance to take control again. If I stay, I will become something you cannot even imagine. And I would leave you forever before I would let you see me like that. Before I would become something you hated instead of loved."

"Never, Ark. I could never hate you. No matter what you did. Who you became. That is my own weakness, perhaps." She pulled back and looked into his eyes, putting her hand gently on his face. "But I understand what you have to deal with. I can't imagine how hard it is to face what they did to you. I know you would stay with me if you could." Her face was covered with tears. "But we still have some time, a few days at least. So let's pretend; let's lie to ourselves a bit longer and squeeze a lifetime of happiness into the hours we have left."

She leaned in and put her lips on his. He put his arms around her and returned the kiss, but inside he felt only pain and sadness. She was the only thing he truly wanted, and of course she was the one he couldn't have. He thought for a passing moment of staying, of letting himself become a tyrant. But even if he was willing to sacrifice the freedom of billions for his own happiness, it wasn't an option. Whatever she said, he knew she couldn't love what he would become. She didn't understand Umbra the way he did. She couldn't realize how cold that part of him was. And how *integral*.

He tightened his arms, pulling her closer. His hands started exploring her body, and slowly he let the pain and sadness recede, just for a few moments. He wanted her, wanted to share in her warmth just a while longer, hoping to banish the frozen part of him, if only for a short while.

If a few days was all they had, he would make the most of them.

Blackhawk walked across the hard floor, his boots rapping loudly with each step, the sounds echoing in the otherwise quiet landing bay. He could see *Wolf's Claw,* once again fully repaired and upgraded, the damage and wear and tear from her service in the war banished to nothing but a fading memory. Danellan Lancaster had once again seen to the care of Blackhawk's beloved ship, bearing all the costs as he had before.

It's just you and me now, old girl, Blackhawk thought. It had been a long time since he'd been truly on his own. But it was a new era in the Far Stars, and for all the misery and detritus of war, few doubted that better times were coming. His crew—his friends—had their own lives now, and he wished them nothing but success and happiness. Despite the crushing loneliness he felt, he was genuinely happy for them. Bouncing around the Far Stars, always without a true home, without roots of any kind . . . it was a difficult life. They'd all been broken when he'd found them, talented men and women who'd struggled with their situations and surroundings. But now they were fixed, their demons gone, their problems solved—at least, as much as anybody could claim those things. Now it was time for them to live normal lives. Happy lives.

Lucas had made his peace with his family. His future now was to run the Lancasters' massive company, to live out his years as the wealthiest man in the Far Stars, not to fly the *Claw* from one fringe world to the next, as often as not with an enemy close on its tail.

Shira had found herself running a clandestine operation during the war, one that had ruthlessly hunted down every vestige of imperial influence, on the worlds of the sector, in the shipping guilds, in the hundreds of tentacles of the Far Stars Bank. She had done a magnificent job, and at Blackhawk's urging, Astra had offered her the top job at the new Confederation Intelligence Agency.

Tarnan was dead, lost in battle. The giant had never gotten over the death of his brother. He'd tried to adapt, but in the end it just wasn't in him. He'd found a glorious end in the fighting on Kalishar, a heroic stand that saved the lives of a hundred Celtiborian soldiers. The Celtiborians had posthumously adopted him as one of their own, placing his name in an honored place on their rosters. Marshal DeMark posthumously awarded him the Star Cluster, Celtiboria's—and now the Far Stars Confederation's—highest military honor.

Blackhawk had given Sarge a commission in the confederation military early in the war. He'd handed the flabbergasted noncom a pair of colonel's eagles, and Sarge had not disappointed his old friend and captain. His regiment had accumulated more battlefield citations than any other unit, and he was a sure bet to wear a general's stars in DeMark's postwar confederation army.

Drake had died on Galvanus Prime, but Sarge's other men had served in his regiment, each of them wearing a captain's bars and commanding a company. Von had been killed on Nordlingen, in the final battle for that tormented world. But Buck and Ringo survived, and Blackhawk had seen that their own considerable savings from their days on the *Claw* were massively supplemented. The two were gentleman farmers now, running huge vineyards adjacent to each other on Antilles. They were wealthy men, and they had a level of respect neither had ever known. Blackhawk had seen to everything. They had served with him for years, and he felt they deserved to hang their swords above the hearth and enjoy life.

Blackhawk had seen to Doc's appointment as dean of the University of Antilles. The academic had been driven from his former life years before by a scandal largely invented by his political enemies. But no group of scheming professors had the courage to stand up to Arkarin Blackhawk.

Sam's engineering genius was no longer the *Claw*'s carefully kept secret, especially after she got the freighters ready for the invasion of Galvanus Prime. She had pitched in to the war effort in her own way, and she'd reconfigured half the vessels in the confederation navy, squeezing more speed and greater weapons output from all of them. DeMark had offered her the top engineering position in the confederation navy, an admiral's billet that seemed a bit overwhelming for a shy, reserved woman not yet thirty. But she had other offers too, including one from Danellan Lancaster to invest one hundred million crowns in her own shipbuilding company.

Ace had traveled perhaps the strangest road of any of his people. The most notorious player in the Far Stars had fallen in love—with a cold-blooded assassin who'd taken more than two years to acknowledge she was anything but a passenger on *Wolf's Claw* . . . much less capable of returning love herself. Katarina had been in the hospital over a year, and for that entire time Ace Graythorn had been there. At first he stood vigil over her unconscious form, watching her every breath as if it was her last. Later, he kept her company as she recovered, stood by her during the grueling physical therapy sessions, snuck her food more edible than the tasteless slop they served in the hospital. And the day she walked out, once she was healed and had her strength back, he told her he loved her . . . and she said the same to him. They had both gone on to aid in the war effort in various ways, but they'd been together ever since.

They'd have no difficulty living whatever peaceful life they chose, wherever their impulses led them. Blackhawk knew Katarina had funds and hidden treasures all over the Far Stars, and Ace was an extremely wealthy man as well, his profits from his years on the *Claw* safely socked away in numbered accounts in the restructured Far Stars Bank.

Blackhawk climbed the ladder leading to the *Claw's* side airlock. He reached over and punched the code, and the hatch slid open. He stepped inside. It had been nearly a year since he'd set foot in his ship. She'd been badly damaged in the fighting at Kalishar, and she'd been in the shipyard while he led the final campaigns of the war. Now he was finally back on board. It was a bittersweet reunion. He missed her. They'd been through a lot together, and it felt somehow right to be back. But it felt wrong too, and he knew the emptiness would be unsettling. The *Claw* was back, ready for action, but this time she would lift off without her family.

And that was how it had to be.

Because his penance wasn't over. *One day, perhaps, I will master what lives inside me, learn to truly control the beast.* If that day came, perhaps he could return. If it came soon enough, before she had time to move on and find someone else to share her life, he might even have hope of returning to Astra. He didn't know, and he didn't dare think about it too seriously. Not now.

Hope could be a dangerous thing.

He walked down the corridor and onto the lower deck. There were images in his mind, shadows of the past, his crew milling about as they had so many times before. He wondered how long it would take for them to fade, before he grew used to being alone.

"Welcome aboard, Captain. Or should I say General?"

Blackhawk spun around. Lucas was leaning against the wall, just in front of the corridor leading to the crew quarters.

"No, captain will do just fine. Or Ark. I've had quite my fill of generaling for the time being." A smile slipped onto his lips. "Come to bid farewell in person?"

"Farewell? You don't think I'm going to leave you to pilot all this sexy new equipment, do you? Besides, I tinkered with the specs when she was in the shipyard, and I'm dying to try out some of this new gear."

"But what about Lancaster Interests? I thought . . ."

"You thought I could share an office with my father? That I could spend all day crunching numbers without hanging myself? Bah! If the *Claw* is lifting off, I will be at the controls. Why change something that works so well?"

Blackhawk walked across the deck and wrapped his arms around his pilot. "I can't say anything about your judgment, Lucas, but I'm damned glad to see you."

"You'll have to let me know if you still feel that way after you see some of the engineering changes he made. I'll be a month down there just rewiring everything back the way I like."

Blackhawk turned and looked back in the direction of the new voice. Sam Sparks stood just at the edge of the open deck, next to the door to engineering. She smiled and said, "Don't I get a hug too?"

"Sam!" Blackhawk turned and headed toward his engineer. She lurched forward and met him halfway.

"Who wants to sit around a big office all day designing spaceships anyway?" she said as she plunged into Blackhawk's bear hug.

"Or nursemaid a bunch of spies. Seriously, can you imagine a worse group of head cases?" Shira walked into the room, flashing a mischievous smile at Blackhawk. "What can I say? Home is home, and this shiny old tub is it."

"Damn right," a gruff voice declared as Sarge walked onto the deck. He was clad not in his colonel's uniform with its cluster of medals and decorations, but in his old fatigues, with the three fabric stripes on the sleeves. "To the seven hells of Sistus with all that saluting back and forth. I'm no officer, at least not when I don't have to be."

"And I forgot how boring academia was. If I had to listen to one more pompous fool trying to sound smarter than he is . . ." Doc stepped slowly into the room. "Besides, who's going to patch all of you up? You people are magnets for trouble, after all."

Blackhawk stood in the middle of the deck, speechless. He wasn't easily surprised, but now he wore an expression of outright shock. "I can't believe you all came back." He turned around, pausing for an instant as he looked at each of them. He felt the emotion welling up inside him. His family was back together. They had empty places, certainly, but it was beginning to feel like old times. He'd been ready to blast off by himself, but he knew the people surrounding him now would support him as he did them. And he knew he needed them now more than ever. Walking away, leaving Astra behind, was the hardest thing he'd ever done.

"I don't know what to say. What is there to say, except my family is back?"

"You're damned right it is!" It was another voice, from down the hallway.

Blackhawk spun around. He would recognize that self-assured tone anywhere. "Ace! What are you doing here?"

"My job is here, isn't it?" Ace said, as cocky as Blackhawk had ever heard him. "It's not as easy as I thought to get a first officer's spot on a normal ship." He flashed a glance at Lucas. "Besides, I couldn't miss the chance to see how comfortable a chair Danellan Lancaster managed to find for *Wolf's Claw* rehab number . . ." He smiled at Blackhawk. "What number are we on anyway?"

Blackhawk returned the smile. "I lost count, but I'm sure he found something plush enough for you." His eyes moved to the side, focusing on the woman standing next to Ace, holding his hand.

"And to what do I owe the pleasure of the best the Sebastiani guild has to offer?" He smiled at Katarina.

"Not Sebastiani, Arkarin, not anymore. I returned my talisman to the guildmasters." She paused then said, "But I have to warn you, Ark . . ." She smiled at Blackhawk. "I'm here to be a part of this crew, not a passenger. I'm not paying for my passage anymore."

Everyone erupted into laughter, and they all rushed to the center of the deck and a big group hug. They were all home again.

Astra stood in the observation deck of the half-reconstructed space station. Celtiboria was forty thousand kilometers below. Down there were offices and subordinates, armies and factories, decisions to make and work to do. Endless work, it seemed. But that wasn't what she cared about. Not now.

She stared out of the heavy polycarbonate at the beauty of space, a rich carpet of black decorated by the pinprick lights that spread across her field of view. Some of those stars were incalculably distant, in the empire and beyond. But she could pick out a few that were closer, suns that warmed worlds now part of the Far Stars Confederation she ruled. She held more power than any man or woman in Far Stars history, yet all she wanted was to shed it, to run away and leave it to someone else to take her father's place. But she knew that wasn't possible.

I am here, Father. I will not let your dream die. I will serve the Far Stars as you would have, prepare for the day the empire comes again to take our freedom.

Did you know what this would do to me? What the cost would be? Perhaps there was never any choice. Perhaps you would have spared me this if you could have. We like to believe we control our destinies, but that is an imperfect understanding to say the least.

Your daughter stands in your shoes, ready to move forward in your place. We are so alike, Father. So tragically alike. You loved my mother with all your heart. I know you did. Yet she died heartbroken and alone. And I love Blackhawk, so much it feels as if it will tear me apart. Yet I let him go. I sent him away, and I did not go with him, not because I didn't want to, but because I couldn't. Loneliness is the price we pay. Is it such a terrible bargain to keep billions of people safe, to see the Far Stars become strong and independent? In a century, or two . . . or ten . . . perhaps children will grow and play in the sunlight of a hundred safe and prosperous worlds. They will never know that cost, the price we paid to secure that future for them.

I love you, Father, despite all your legacy has done to me, to my own happiness. And I know Mother loved you too, always. Rest now, and I will stand this watch. I will stay focused as you were, steadfast, diligent. For I have nothing else but duty, nor shall I ever. My soul is dead, as yours was, and I have lost my chance at happiness, sold to destiny to buy a future for the Far Stars.

Astra was alone now. She'd ordered her guards to wait outside. They'd protested, insisting she needed an escort at all times. She sympathized with their position, but then she'd told them all to go to hell. She needed to be alone. This was for her and no one else, one last favor she'd asked of Lucas before he'd left for the *Claw*.

She looked out at the blackness, and there it was. *Wolf's Claw* floated across her view, far closer than normal to the station. But Lucas Lancaster was a pilot without any peers, and he managed to bring the ship within five hundred meters of where she stood. She knew he could only hold there for a few seconds, but she would stand and savor each one.

"Good-bye, my love," she said softly, sadly. Then she saw a flash as the *Claw*'s engines engaged, and an instant later it was gone.

She stood a long while, unmoving, staring out at the emptiness where *Wolf's Claw* had been. Then she turned slowly and wiped the tears from her eyes.

Blackhawk took a deep breath . . . and a last look at Celtiboria as it quickly faded to nothingness in the distance. He spoke softly, only for himself . . . and to a friend now gone.

"Rest now, Augustin. We stood in the breech and we kept your dream alive. Your confederation is a reality. Your sacrifices were not in vain.

"I had to leave Astra behind, Augustin. I love her with all my heart, but I cannot be with her. Not while I am still half monster. Not while the evil still lives inside me.

"But I promised you once, and I will promise you again: I will watch over her, my old friend. I will patrol the marches, seek out the danger in the shadows. I will be her protector, her guardian, unseen but ever vigilant. I will let no one harm her, whatever I must do. Her enemies will be my enemies, and I will destroy them utterly.

"And, most of all, I will love her forever . . ."

ABOUT THE AUTHOR

Jay Allan currently lives in New York City and has been reading science fiction and fantasy for just about as long as he's been reading. His tastes are fairly varied and eclectic, but favorites include military and dystopian science fiction, space opera, and epic fantasy—all usually a little bit gritty.

He writes a lot of science fiction with military themes, but also other SF and some fantasy as well. He likes complex characters and lots of backstory and action, but in the end believes world-building is the heart of science fiction and fantasy.

Before becoming a professional writer, Jay has been an investor and real estate developer. When not writing, he enjoys traveling, running, hiking, and—of course—reading.

He also loves hearing from readers and always answer e-mails. You can reach him at jay@jayallanbooks.com, and join his mailing list at http://www.crimsonworlds.com for updates on new releases.

Among other things, he is the author of the bestselling Crimson Worlds series.